Please feel free to send me an e
publisher filters these emails. G

Kimber Lee – <u>kimber-lee.aweso</u>

Sign up for my blog for updates and freebies!
<u>kimber-lee.awesomeauthors.org</u>

About the Publisher

BLVNP Incorporated, A Nevada Corporation, 340 S. Lemon #6200, Walnut CA 91789, info@blvnp.com / legal@blvnp.com

DISCLAIMER

Praise for How to Kill an Incubus

This book is simply amazing. It kept me enthralled from start to end, full of plot twists and cliffhangers that only left you wanting more. Rae is a strong character and you'll want to be her when you're two pages deep. How To Kill an Incubus is sexy, mysterious and everything everyone's ever hopes for in a book.
-**Cliente Amazon**, Amazon

Cannot wait for the next book!!!! I can reread this book so many times because of my love for all the characters. This is a book you cannot put down. And would patiently wait for the next book.
-**Alexis Barry**, Amazon

I'm so glad I finally purchased this book. I am now going to spend the rest of my afternoon reading this amazing book. I am so happy for you Kimber and I know this book will be a success.
-**Miechelle Monangai**, Amazon

This book is for readers who love a good story line with a bit of spice in between. I am a fan of this author and I found it hard to put this book down.
-**Abigail Mckenzie**, Amazon

I've read all her books on wattpad, but never got the opportunity to read this one until now. Absolutely amazing as always. Can't wait for the sequel!
-**Madison**, Amazon

How to Kill an Incubus

By: Kimber Lee

BLVNP

ISBN: 978-1-68030-845-7

Table of contents

For Jay and Kay…

FREE DOWNLOAD

Get these freebies and MORE when you
sign up for the author's mailing list!

kimber-lee.awesomeauthors.org

Chapter 1

Waking up to an incubus attempting to—violently, might I add—pull off my Baby Phat sweatpants at three in the morning wasn't a great way to start my twenty-seventh birthday. Granted, it was going to be pretty shitty anyway, but that was beside the point.

The fact of the matter was that I was being attacked by something that wanted to have sex with me and preferred me comatose, and I sure as hell wasn't going to stand for that.

My kick to his face definitely caught him by surprise, judging from the way he jolted back and uttered a low grunt, nearly stumbling. I didn't know if sex demons had pain receptors but I did know that years of kickboxing made my kicks a little more potent than the average five-foot-six woman. Alert and more than a little annoyed, I rolled out of bed and onto my feet, cursing when I stubbed my toe against the nightstand. Intense pain sizzled through my big toe. I felt a little warmth down there and figured the damn thing had drawn blood from under my toenail.

Now, I was pissed!

1

Damn you, Dad, I thought, dodging the incubus' repeated feeble attempts to molest me. He was staggering around the king-sized bed. I paused, regarding him in the pale moonlight of my hotel room.

He was drunk. And that was weird because alcohol didn't, wasn't supposed to, affect demons. So either this particular creature was so caught up in pretending to be human that he'd subconsciously induced the ill-effects of alcohol, or he was too weak and needed to recharge by sucking out most of my energy through what would probably be mind-blowing animal sex.

As much as I wanted—hell, craved!—mind-blowing animal sex, I wasn't desperate enough to willingly sleep with a creature of darkness. I wasn't my mother.

"You can sense me," he said suddenly, his voice low and weirdly singsong.

"No, shit," I told him, because what else was I supposed to say?

"No, at the club… earlier," he went on, slurring his R's. He resumed his catlike prowling toward me and I jumped onto the bed, well aware that this was a ridiculous position. "You could sense me. I could feel you sense me." He regarded me quizzically now, his eyes meeting mine.

The club. I mentally groaned, remembering what had gone down hours earlier.

Nicolette was a well-known rave club in The Left Bank of Paris that I'd been staking out for the past two weeks. The real reason I was there was because Derek Karr was there and I was tailing him. It sounded glamorous whenever I thought about it but the reality was far from it. Derek was supposed to be on a business trip (something to do with a software he was developing for some fancy French hi-tech company) not on a

2

grinding session with multiple redheads and blondes. And he did this in very obnoxious silk shirts and khaki slacks, too. Meanwhile, his wife was back in Florida.

Anna Karr had paid me a huge lump of cash to trail her husband of fifteen years to Paris.

At first, Karr had been all right—going to meetings, business lunches, ordering room service. All well and good for a man who was unwittingly making millions doing what he did. But come weekend? Karr decided to let loose, pretend he was Chris Brown, and hit Nicolette as if he wasn't a forty-eight-year-old man with a wife and a teenager at home. In fact, I had enough evidence of Karr playing around to send to Anna, which was why tonight was my last night at the Ange Noir— and in Paris.

This incubus, apparently, had checked me out at the club and followed me here. Of course, I'd sensed something at Nicolette. But an incubus would have been last on my list of suspects, which was utterly stupid of me. Clubs were their playground. Lots of fresh meat.

"I'm warning you," I said clearly. "You take one step toward me and I'm slashing off your demon dick. Got that?!" *With what?* my inner self asked me. *Your fingernails?*

He looked at me, his eyes so dark they were practically onyx. But everything else about him was light—the thick waves of blonde hair on his head, the full red apple slices for lips, and the paleness of his skin. If he were human, I'd probably find him good-looking—but he wasn't.

Once again, I cursed the supposed "gift" my father had passed down to me: The gift of knowing who was human and who wasn't. Ignorance was freaking bliss.

"Demon dick?"

3

He surprised me by bursting into a fit of ear-splitting, uncontrollable laughter. Doubling over, he fell to his knees, rocking back and forth with laughter. I was momentarily confused. My dad had never mentioned supernatural creatures possessing funny bones. Then again, I hadn't exactly been keen on listening to anything he'd told me about what he did in his spare time, which was hunting demons—specifically incubi and succubi, especially since my mother had run off with one and he'd sort of taken it personally.

"I'm going to count to ten and you're going to get the hell out." My voice was surprisingly calm, in light of this new situation.

"What are you?" the incubus asked, slowly getting to his feet. "A hunter? A witch? A medium?"

"None of your business," I snapped, in the same way I would have snapped at one of Dad's old hunter buddies. They weren't my people and I didn't care to help them "fight the good fight", as they put it. I preferred my low-key PI work because it paid a hell of a lot better than killing those freaks did.

"At least tell me your name," the incubus implored soothingly, almost like he was trying to seduce me.

I didn't want to admit to myself that I was a little freaked out. Actually, I was a lot freaked out.

I had never dealt one-on-one with any demons before and had spent the last few years after my father's untimely demise trying to pretend that they simply didn't exist. Aside from the occasional, creepy "sixth sense" warnings I got whenever I was in the vicinity of one, I was doing a pretty good job burying my head in the sand and ignoring the other things.

"Get the hell out," I fumed.

He shook his head, chuckling. He seemed so... human, and that was the scariest part. How many women fell for his charms and cheerfully opened their legs to him? How many women woke up the next day feeling physically drained with no explanation whatsoever? How many of them just put it down to the demon's mad sexual prowess?

He wasn't human. He was pure evil.

"Andrei would like you. You're just his type," he said, grinning, and it occurred to me then that he didn't sound or look intoxicated anymore.

"Go feed somewhere else," I spat, disgusted, and at the same time, afraid. Andrei was probably one of his billion-year-old incubus friends, and as evil and perverse as he was. The small part of me that clung to that stab of fear was praying for a miracle. I looked down at the demon and I didn't like that small part of me at all.

He was probably—no, definitely—stronger than me, and could probably take me down and have his way with me. Then, he could summon his buddy Andrei, who'd suck out the remainder of my life force, and I'd be dead as a doornail by the time the sun came up, with a smile of ecstasy on my inanimate face, no doubt. Mind-blowing animal sex tended to do that to a person.

"Will do," the demon said pleasantly. His eyes licentiously raked over my body and I instantly felt unclean, as if he'd actually touched me. "Nice Baby Phat." And he disappeared into thin air.

I sank to my knees, breathing heavily, and fell onto my back.

I survived that. I survived that and it felt... good. Really good.

But something nagged at the back of my mind.

Did he mean Baby Phat? I thought hazily, drifting to sleep again. *Or baby fat?*

"Renée, don't sweat it," I said, putting my BlackBerry in the crook of my shoulder as I simultaneously opened my front door and dragged my suitcase in. "I'm fine."

"Don't sweat it?!" she roared into my ear, making me wince. "Honey, the man attacked you!"

I rolled my eyes at Renée Marino's melodrama. I should've known she'd blow things out of proportion. Drama was embedded in her DNA.

"We were in a crowded place," I told her calmly. "Namely, an airplane."

"Yeah, but he could've strangled you, babe. He did."

I sighed, unconsciously fingering my neck. "Yeah, but by then, he got pulled off me. Come on, Ren. It's actually quite funny."

At the time, not so much.

It was just my luck that the guy sitting beside me on my return flight to Heathrow from Charles de Gaulle just happened to be Gavin Turner—and I hadn't recognized him. I hadn't recognized him because I was still recovering from last night's—well, this morning's—incubus attack. And also because Gavin Turner had gone from being an Abercrombie model to Zach Galifianakis' older, chubbier brother.

"I hate flying," he'd said conversationally, while I'd tried to find a comfortable way to sit that didn't involve my hip being crushed by his.

"Me, too," I'd said, when I actually didn't mind it.

6

"I'm Gav."

"Rae," I'd told him, absentmindedly giving him my working name as I flipped open a copy of *People* magazine. Sandra Bullock was on the cover and I loved her.

"Rae?" His voice had turned furtive, quiet. "Are you 'the' Rae? The private investigator?"

I set the magazine on my lap and twisted at the waist to look at him. "This isn't the way I operate."

And that was when Gav snapped.

It all happened so fast. One minute, he was blinking at me benignly with deep-set baby blues, and the next, his big hands were around my neck, throttling me and making his intent to crush my windpipe crystal clear. His hands were like a vise and I couldn't breathe, couldn't even smell. People started screaming and Gav started talking, his voice chillingly fanatical.

"You broke me and Zoe up, you meddlesome little bitch! I was with Mel once! Just once! You had no right! No right at all!"

And that was when I remembered where I'd seen Gavin before. Gavin, who had cheated on his gorgeous wife of three months with his sister's best friend and blamed me for the inevitable divorce.

Two men jumped into action and attempted to pry Gavin off me and, once his viselike grip loosened, I reached out and punched him in the throat, gasping for air when he finally released me. He spluttered, choking for air, and flopped back in his seat. Unbuckling my belt, I'd shakily gotten to my feet and swapped seats with a guy on the opposite aisle for the remainder of the flight.

"You're crazy, girl," Ren was saying in my ear. "You're crazy because this job you're doing? Yeah, it's gonna get you killed. You know what Lorenzo was saying?"

I kicked my suede ankle boots off and flopped back onto my couch. "What did the great Lorenzo say?" I snidely asked, although I did like Ren's firefighter husband. I just didn't enjoy the fact that he thought of himself as some kind of sage.

"He said you're doing this whole PI thing because of what happened with your parents."

"Is Lorenzo taking a psychology class now?" I asked sarcastically, examining my broken toenail from the previous night. It had turned a deep crimson and looked worse than I'd thought. My boots didn't help either.

"Think about it, babe," Ren went on. "This is a vendetta." She paused, letting her words sink in. "Your mom was cheating on your dad. She left you guys. Now you feel like all cheaters gotta pay. It doesn't matter that most of them are really powerful, ergo dangerous, they still gotta pay for... for, I dunno, defiling the sanctity of marriage."

Yeah, she was cheating, all right—with a sex demon, I thought, wondering what Ren would say if I told her. She'd probably put me in a straitjacket pronto.

"Wouldn't I be after cheating housewives, if that were the case?"

"Babe, screw that. Go back to powerful and dangerous."

"I can handle myself," I said sharply.

She had hit too close to home.

"Like today? When Gavin Turner nearly wrung your neck like wet laundry?"

I let out an exasperated sigh. "I never should've told you about what I do for a living."

"We tell each other everything," she said, and I could picture her pouting.

Everything? Ren didn't know that I was almost defiled by a demon last night. Ren didn't know that my father had been out banishing demons when one of them killed him and I found his mangled body. Ren didn't know everything. She didn't know anything.

"When're you coming to the Bay?" she wanted to know. "It's been two months. I feel like all we do is have phone sex. Fly on over so I can give you your birthday present, baby."

I laughed at the sound of her husky voice. She was ridiculous. "Soon," I told her. "Real soon. I just have to take care of some things here." I would never tell her, but each time I returned to my birthplace—Sallow Bay, Florida (*pop.* 21, 905)—a piece of me withered away, never to grow back again. Too many fucking memories.

"You know Jared's been asking about you," my best friend went on, instantly reminding me of the childhood friend I wanted to leave buried in the past.

"Great," I said monotonously, unsure of what she wanted me to say to that.

"Pick up a British boy," she instructed, "or any boy. Didn't you say your neighbor's got a sexy ass?"

I bit my bottom lip, looking out the window at the late afternoon fog that's typical of the English countryside weather. "Considering the fact that I only live here five days at the most out of the entire year, it doesn't matter if I find him hot. Nothing will happen."

"Well, fuck him on one of those five days and be done with it."

9

"Ren, you are so crass," I admonished. "Daniel Lawless doesn't fuck. He makes love." At least, that was what I assumed just from looking at him.

"Seriously? With a name like that, he should be a total badass."

"Nah," I said, lying on my back on the couch and staring up at the ceiling. "He should've been called Law-ful. He's the type who'd pay a parking ticket on time and add a thank-you note for being rightfully punished." I paused. "Actually, he wouldn't have gotten a ticket in the first place."

Ren giggled in my ear. "Yeah?"

"Yeah."

"Sounds boring."

"Well, he is attractive. I mean, really attractive," I explained, because he was.

I was twenty-seven now, therefore way too old to be infatuated with a man. But that was the only way I could describe what I felt whenever I was around Lawless, which was—as I'd mentioned—five days out of a year. Just knowing that Daniel Lawless was getting naked to shower next door made my heart palpitate and moonwalk across my ribcage. I got tongue-tied around the guy. It felt like I was sixteen again, and it was humiliating.

And that voice of his! God, he made a simple "hello" sound like something filthy. That wasn't good, because while Lawless might be a good guy, I was a bad girl and we were like water and oil—we just didn't mix. It didn't matter how much I wanted to get into his pants. It would never happen because he would want a Mary Sue. And truth be told, I was more of an Amber Rose than a Mary Sue.

"And you're attractive. So what's the big deal?"

10

I laughed again. "You're biased and I need to shower. Hanging up now, Renée."

"I'm not finished yet!" she protested, like she always did.

"Give Lorenzo a French kiss for me. Make it wet," I told her, like I always did, and cut the call. I loved Renée Marino to death, but she could talk the hind legs off a donkey.

As soon as I put my phone down, it pinged to notify me that I had an e-mail. I thought about ignoring it… for about a second. Sighing, I clicked it open.

Great! I thought morosely, quickly scanning through a message from a woman named Cassie Winer. *Don't I get to relax?*

Cassie was positive that her husband was screwing around on her with prostitutes. *Ick!* She wanted me to follow him to Las Vegas, where he had a casino opening that weekend, and report back to her immediately.

Money first, I sent back. *Then you give me all his details. – R*

Anyone who e-mailed me knew to wire my money into my offshore account. I had only given out the account details once before. Word of mouth ensured that I never had to give it out again.

I put my phone on silent, set it on my glass coffee table and went upstairs to take a long, steaming, and well-deserved bath. It felt good to be home (well, at one of my homes) and in a place I considered safe.

Out of all the rooms in this particular house, my favorite was the bathroom, simply because of the ivory claw-foot bathtub. It was spacious and old-fashioned, and I could spend hours lounging in it. I had more modern tubs in my homes in France, Italy, Greece and the States. But this one? This one was old-fashioned perfection.

I was still pretty shaken up by the incubus and wondered if I should call my dad's old friend, Teddy Bunting, who had been a hunter just like him. But I shook the crazy thought out of my head as I reached for my loofah. If I phoned him and let him in, I'd be letting them all in. I didn't want that. I was cool with following unfaithful husbands—and, on rare occasions, wives—around and getting paid handsomely for it. I, however, didn't want to end up as crazy as my father had been during his final years, hopped up on some fanatical quest to destroy the demon that had stolen the love of his life.

After my bath, I put on my silk robe and, glancing at the bedside clock that informed me it was almost six p.m., decided that I deserved an early night—sans dinner. So I went to draw the curtains... and froze.

Daniel Lawless was giving me my very own striptease.

His bedroom window was right across mine, separated by a measly picket fence, so I had a front-row view to a very private show. I didn't have anything to be ashamed of because, quite frankly, he was asking to be looked at, leaving his windows wide open like that.

His pea green T-shirt went over his head, ruffling his dark brown hair and making it stick out at odd angles. Then it went to the floor and I got a good look at his well-defined back. From what little I knew, Daniel worked in construction, hence the great physique. And now, I was getting turned on by his back. Was I pathetic or what?

My inner voice was about to answer with an affirmative, when a tall, lithe butt-naked blonde launched herself into Daniel's waiting arms and drew him into a very passionate, very sexy kiss. Mortified, I quickly drew my curtains. Like a voyeur, I just watched him undress for another woman and almost gotten off on it.

Yeah, pretty pathetic, Rainelle Erickson. But what's new? Yes, my inner voice was very vocal, all of a sudden.

Scowling, I went downstairs and checked my phone. Cassie Winer had sent me everything she knew about her husband, coupled with plenty of photos (he was a handsome, redheaded forty-something), and proof of payment. I pulled my laptop out and got online to book a ticket to Vegas for that weekend.

Today, Paris. This weekend, Vegas.

Maybe I'd get laid.

After all, my inner voice said conspiratorially, *what happens in Vegas stays in Vegas.*

Chapter 2

You can do this, Rae. You can do this.

I took a deep breath, steeling myself when Tad—I think that's his name—ran a hand down the side of my hip suggestively, his focus still on the roulette table. Being on his lap meant that I had the misfortune of feeling Little Tad hard and desperate beneath me. No matter how much I tried to inconspicuously shift away, Big Tad made sure Little Tad was always in contact and, to my horror, shifting around only made Little Tad happier.

Damn! I thought, my eyes casually flicking to Darryl Winer's table. Talk about a rock and a hard place.

As soon as I got to Vegas late that afternoon and had time to think, I decided that being alone in a casino would only draw attention to myself. Looking around, I noticed that almost every woman—many of whom were donning the unnofficial uniform of skintight, thigh-length dresses—was attached to at least one man. So I had to follow suit, and latched onto a guy and wore a skintight, thigh-length dress—despite the cool Nevada evening. I'd tamed my mass of inky curls into a

14

chignon, which accentuated my cheekbones, and squeezed myself into an indecent little black dress, which put everything on show.

Tad, or whatever he was called, approached me as soon as I stepped into the elevator of the Kamenev Hotel above the casino. Short, stout, and wearing a ridiculously large cowboy hat, he had proudly informed me that he was a wealthy stockbroker having a "chill-out weekend". Then he proceeded to boldly grab my hand and led me to the roulette table where he was on a winning streak. I didn't complain because from that vantage point, I had a great view of Darryl Winer sitting comfortably in a makeshift VIP section that consisted of some expensive-looking leather couches, glass tables, and some cronies I could only guess were his business associates of some sort.

Tad jumped, squeezing my hip with glee. "You're my lucky charm, babe," he murmured cheerfully, after winning on yet another substantial bet.

I looked at the dealer, who gave us a strange look, like he thought Tad was pulling a fast one on him somehow. Annoyed, I looked away. Just how much of this was I supposed to take?

I glanced over at Darryl, willing him to get up and go—so I could get up and go. But he was in the middle of what looked like an important discussion, and didn't look like he'd be leaving anytime soon.

Suddenly, one of the guys with him looked up and met my eye. I knew I was supposed to look away that very instant, to avoid being remembered, but for whatever reason, I found that I couldn't. Unlike the rest of his posse, he wasn't in a suit, favoring jeans and a faded grey T-shirt that did wonders for his torso, even from my vantage point. His eyes were, if I wasn't mistaken, an intense, pale blue and they were unwaveringly focused on me. His expression was blank but his gaze was so powerful, I could almost physically feel it sifting through my very soul.

I tore my eyes away, biting my bottom lip with worry. Just what was I doing making eye contact with one of Winer's buddies?

Don't you understand the word inconspicuous? I scolded myself.

It didn't matter anyway. Five minutes later, Winer was done. Ten minutes later, I extracted myself from Tad, faking a headache, and went up to Suite 304. Then I remembered Cassie Winer had informed me that Darryl was one floor below me. So I decided against the elevator and took the crimson-carpeted stairs up, intending to scope out the second floor. If I got lucky, I'd probably bump into Darryl bringing a skank to his room, and get to go home early.

However, the second floor was eerily quiet, so I shuffled up to my room, swiped the card in the slot, and pushed the door open.

I rarely drank, but tonight, I needed to make an exception. The bar fridge was well-stocked with the kinds of things I liked—good wine, good beer, and very good Mountain Dew. And I grabbed a can of the soda, forgoing my plan of getting shitfaced on the job.

Bed, I thought, crushing the empty can in my hand and flinging it into the dustbin.

I then went into the bathroom, admiring its nice black-and-white theme, and used the facilities. Once all my make-up had been cleaned off and I could look into the mirror without being repulsed, I went back into the room and wrote up my notes for that day. There was nothing to report.

16

After that, I peeled the godforsaken dress off, and pulled on cotton boxers and a peach camisole. I took out the bobby pins in my hair, pulled everything into a messy ponytail, and dove under the covers. Hotel beds were always a blessing. No matter which country or continent, I could never find fault with one. In fact, sleep was beginning to hit me as soon as my head touched the pillow—until I felt someone in the room.

I couldn't see in the dark, of course. But that didn't mean someone wasn't standing in my hotel room, watching me sleep, and freaking me the hell out. Experiencing a jolt of déjà vu, I took a deep breath, rolled out of bed, and flicked the bedside lamp on.

"I have a gun," I lied, and finally, the shadow in one corner came to life and walked into the hazy light.

"You don't have a gun."

I suddenly found it extremely hard to breathe.

Winer's denim-and-T-shirt buddy was standing there.

On closer inspection, I could see that his eyes were indeed blue, the blue of a clear morning sky. His hair was even blacker than mine, which I didn't think was possible, and contrasted severely with those pale eyes of his. Long and thick, it hung in a pulled-back mane that fell just past his shoulders, a waterfall of tar.

I took a step back and bumped into the nightstand, grimacing. "How did you get in?"

"Master card," he replied coolly, holding it up in the light. "I'm part-owner of the hotel." As if that gave him the right to waltz into his clients' suites at eleven in the evening.

Looking at him, I didn't want to ponder the fact that I would've at least heard the door being opened if that were true. And I didn't want to ponder the question of how he even knew which room I was in. Quite frankly, I didn't want to ponder

17

anything—except for how to get him out of my room as fast as possible and with minimal ruckus.

He was tall. Disturbingly tall. A Shaquille O'Neal to my Eva Longoria. I placed him at six foot six or so. I wasn't good at estimating but I was pretty sure I was close. I was also positive that this did not bode well for me. Tall guys generally meant trouble for someone like me.

Shit, what if he recognized me from somewhere?

Renée's words came back to haunt me. It doesn't matter that most of them are powerful, ergo dangerous... I really wasn't ready for another lesson in the joys of strangulation.

The Kamenev was a world-class hotel owned by a group of mysterious Russians. Just looking at this guy and knowing he was part-owner added up to "powerful and dangerous Russian"—even without the accent.

And he was standing in my hotel room!

I swallowed. "Is there a problem?" I mentally gave myself kudos for managing to keep my voice steady despite how jumpy I was inside.

"Rainelle," he said quietly, "you were eye-fucking me in the casino."

I didn't know what to be mad about first—that he knew my name when I didn't know his, or that he'd used the term "eye-fucking" to describe my looking at him for a few innocent seconds.

Folding my arms across my chest, I scowled at him. "Excuse me?"

His eyes pierced mine. "So here I am," he went on as if he didn't hear me. "Fuck me."

My face burned with humiliation. Oh, God! I thought, speechless. This is a dream.

18

I immediately pinched my left arm. Nope. Not a dream. He was still there, still sexy as sin.

Deciding to change tack, I spat, "That's right. Fuck you! How dare you break into my room and speak to me like this?"

There were no steps left to take backward when "Scary Russian Guy" approached me. The nightstand was behind me, digging into the exposed skin on the back of my legs.

Lampshade!

I instantly felt for it behind me and wrapped my hand around the wooden stand, yanking hard enough to rip it out of its socket and fling it into the air. The man, however, caught my wrist before I could whack him, and held that arm above my head until I was forced to drop my weapon of choice on the ground.

My vocal cords stopped functioning when his right hand shot out and cupped my chin, tilting it up to him. The instant he did that, every traitorous nerve and muscle in my body jumped to attention.

"So feisty," he said in a low voice, the pad of his thumb running across my bottom lip.

I involuntarily shivered.

"And I can see how much you want me."

"You can't see shit." My head snapped back and I slapped his hand away. "Arrogant jerk. Get out!" I was still irked by the "eye-fucking" comment. I'd never been accused of eye-fucking before. Stalking, yes, because that's what I technically did for a living. Eye-fucking? Never!

A slow smile spread across his face and it made him look twice as good, which wasn't good.

I was still admiring how perfectly shaped his lips were when, without warning, he pulled me to him, his big hands

19

cupping my ass. At this point, I was positive that my heart would thump its way out of my chest and splatter against his T-shirt. Then my hands came up of their own accord and my palms rested flat against his broad chest. But for some strange reason, they wouldn't push him away.

He considered me in the light, his eyes scrutinizing my face. And then he brought his mouth down on mine, one hand cupping the back of my neck and the other firmly on one butt cheek. His kiss started surprisingly tentative, like he was afraid to break me. I hadn't done any kissing in a long time so it wasn't a wonder that I instantly parted my lips and allowed his tongue entry. A surge of immense pleasure swirled in the pit of my belly when his tongue touched mine, as he deepened the kiss and gently sucked my tongue. It was powerful, pleasurable.

He then scooped me up, his strong forearms now firmly beneath my ass. This was when I was supposed to resolutely put him in his place and get some sleep. But no! His mouth was still locked on mine and I allowed him to scoop me up and set me back onto the bed. He wasn't wearing cologne and he didn't need to. The smell of his body musk was more than enough to titillate my senses. The scent made me want to taste every inch of his skin… and start all over again when I was done.

Once on top of me, he artfully scrunched my top up beneath my neck, exposing my breasts for scrutiny. My nipples yearned for attention. His fingers gave it. He tweaked them, slowly taking his lips away from mine and lowering them instead to one aching bud. He then took it into his mouth and rolled it with his tongue, pulling it, relieving it. My hands sank into his cascade of hair, tugging it less than gently. His long locks were soft and thick, and for whatever reason, that was a turn-on as well. With his mouth on one nipple and his fingers teasing the other, "Scary Russian Guy" was way too close to making me come. Just like that. Scary!

His mouth suddenly trailed soft kisses down my taut belly, threatening to undo me. My boxers came off before I could so much as blink, and at the back of my mind, I was thankful that I'd gotten a Brazilian before this Vegas trip.

He seemed to be grateful as well when he spread my legs apart and immediately placed his mouth on my opening. I gasped, quivering as he ran his tongue up my slit. Then he drew my pulsing clit into his mouth, sucking on it and sending intense shivers throughout my entire body. Heat built up where his mouth was and I arched my back, giving in to the burn. I released his hair and frantically clawed at the sheets, squeezing my eyes shut as his tongue plunged deep into me. I was right—powerful and pleasurable, a dangerous combination.

Over and over, his tongue lashed into me, tasting me, bringing me so close to the edge of orgasm, I could almost touch it. Then he placed the pad of his thumb on my clit and rubbed it to bring me there. Deeper, his tongue went, and I quickly came in a series of spasms, trying to keep myself from screaming. His mouth didn't falter as he coaxed yet another orgasm out of me. And I couldn't keep from screaming when I came the second time.

Wow, I thought, breathing heavily. No one had ever made me come during oral, let alone twice. No one.

Dazed, I watched through heavy-lidded eyes as he raised his head and regarded me, his hands cinched around my thighs.

"You ready?" he asked, his voice a low growl.

"For… for what?" I stammered, shivering where he touched me. I was lost in post-orgasm bliss.

"For me," he said, and he gracefully rose to his feet. He pulled his shirt over his head, and I got a good eyeful of flawless tan skin and faint wisps of dark chest hair. His eyes were on mine as he unbuckled his jeans, the denim skimming down his narrow hips.

He had gone commando.

That thing, I thought, now fully alert as I eyed his long, veined, and erect cock, is supposed to go inside me?

He grabbed the backs of my legs, pulled me toward the foot of the bed and brought my legs up and over his shoulders, so I was wide open. With my ass on the edge of the bed, I gasped when his fingers sought my opening once more. He pushed two inside me, stretching me. I bit my bottom lip hard enough to draw blood.

"So wet," he whispered, moving around inside me with his digits, "for me."

I was panting heavily, my hands gripping the sheets. This was wrong, wrong on so many levels. He was a scary Russian guy and I was supposed to be afraid of him, not gasping for air as he stood over me and finger-fucked me— after giving me two orgasms in a row with his amazing tongue.

Dammit! Why do the wrong things feel so damn right?

"You ready?" he repeated, retracting his fingers.

I felt devastatingly empty without them.

I looked him in the eye and decided to use his words. "Fuck me."

A smile tugged at the corner of his lips and he leaned over me, tilting my ass in the air in the process, and reached under the pillows to pull something out.

A condom.

There were condoms under my pillow.

Don't! Don't analyze this.

SRG had the foil packet open and the latex on in less than ten seconds. I only had one of those seconds to think about backing out before he was slowly guiding himself inside me and then I forgot every word synonymous to "no". I felt him at my entrance and our eyes briefly met—his a smoldering navy blue, mine probably an eager green—before he sank into my flesh.

I felt it then, the rush of euphoria that dampened the brief moment of pain that I felt. It coursed through my entire being like electricity, awakening my dormant senses. I didn't close my eyes. I wanted to watch. I wanted to see everything that he was going to do to me. Everything.

With his hands firmly on my ankles, which were looped over his shoulders, he plunged even deeper. This position meant that every sensation was out of this world. He was deeper than anyone had ever been and it felt like I could feel him everywhere.

I moaned loudly when he began to move inside me. Pulling back, he thrust into me again, turning my world upside down. He thrust again to the root, and I could feel a liquid warmth wash over me when I heard him give out a low, animalistic groan.

"You're so tight," he breathed out, and I could now hear a hint of an accent on his tongue. He punctuated his sentence by pushing inside me again, grunting loudly. "So fucking tight but you're not a virgin. How is that possible, Rainelle?"

I cried out, my toes curling and my heart pounding.

"Are you going to come for me again?" he demanded, his thrusts becoming faster and even deeper. "Are you going to show me how much you like this?"

"Oh hell, yes!" I hissed, because I could already feel another climax building up inside me, like a volcano waiting to erupt. I could feel it in every nerve, every muscle, every heartbeat.

Still inside me, he removed my legs from his shoulders and blessed me with his weight as he positioned himself over me. He leaned on his forearms on either side of me, regarding me through navy eyes. I wrapped my legs around his lean waist, clenching my sex around his cock as he continued to furiously thrust into me. His mouth placed gentle kisses on my neck, nipping the skin with his teeth. His breathing became labored, as did mine. And my hands flew to his now unruly dark hair and held on for dear life as I arched my back under him and climaxed. Hard. The spasms continued even as his body tensed and he joined me, coming even harder and longer than I did.

He gripped the pillows on either side of my head as he jerked violently in orgasm. Each time he'd shudder, I'd give out a moan because it felt like he was pounding into me all over again. I came once more, quick and short. My fourth orgasm in one evening.

He pulled out, rolled off me, and onto his back. I squeezed my eyes shut for a while, collecting myself. And when I opened them, he was sitting, removing the condom, tying it, and hurling it into the wicker bin at my bedside.

I sat up, astonishingly fine. My limbs didn't hurt, my pussy felt a bit overworked, but okay. And I was completely fine with this impromptu one-night stand. More than fine.

Damn. That is one sexy back, I thought to myself, eyeballing the hard planes of muscle there.

He must have felt my eyes on him because he twisted at the waist to look at me. "You okay, Rainelle?" His eyes searched mine.

"It's Rae," I corrected, amazed by how calm I was. "Um," I faltered, "I don't know your name."

"That's because I never told you," he countered, stating the obvious. His hand reached out and cupped my left breast, running his thumb across the nipple. "What beautiful tits you have, Rainelle."

I reddened, my erect nipple betraying my response to him.

He smiled, like he knew what I was thinking. Then his hand slid under the pillows behind me again and he produced another condom packet.

"Nuh-uh," I protested, snatching a pillow and flinging it over my shoulder to sate my curiosity. About a dozen unopened foil packets innocently lay there.

"They're in every room," SRG informed me, as if he really could read my thoughts. He tore the second one open. "And you want me again just as much as I want you."

"Very presumptuous of you. I'm saying no. Are you going to take me against my will?"

His eyes darkened as he stared at me. "No. Because…" He stroked the inside of my thigh and his fingers came back slick with my cum. "…you already miss the feel of me inside you." He brought his index finger to his mouth and sucked. Damn!

I swallowed, turned on beyond belief. He had a point. The aftereffects of him inside me were practically magical. I felt… revitalized. And yes, I wanted him inside me again.

"Get on your knees," he commanded, sensing his victory. "On the bed," he added.

After only a moment's hesitation, I did as he asked, facing the wall behind the bed. I felt him get off the bed and then I felt pressure on the mattress behind me as he settled on his knees there. His hands were smooth yet hard and they effortlessly glided across the globes of my rear, sending tingles of delight up my spine.

"Kneel forward, Rae."

One syllable, but he made my name sound like a poem. I knelt forward. My breasts were pressed into the coolness of the sheets and I squeezed my eyes shut because it felt safer.

"Beautiful ass," he commented, because it was suspended in the air and probably looked much better from that angle. I had never been prouder of my intense workout regime than when he'd said that. "Do you want me to fuck it?" he went on, his voice husky.

"I'm not…"

I didn't get to finish my sentence, whatever garbage it was I was going to spew, because he drove into my pussy then. And from that angle, I wasn't sure I'd ever be able to speak again, the pleasure was so intense. I cried out, my hands scrabbling to grab hold of something, anything. SRG's hands were on my hips, holding me steady as he continued his perfect assault. I screamed, so overtaken by the bliss of him plunging his cock into me, I thought I would break apart like glass.

I was vaguely aware of a loud smacking sound behind me and it took me a minute to realize that it was the slap of his balls, so heavy with suspended release, smacking against my clit. The faster he went, the louder the noise got. Every thrust made me see stars. Every thrust threatened to rip me to shreds.

And all the while he was talking.

"Say… no… again," he growled between thrusts, his big hands moving higher and resting under my ribs as he pulled me to him. "Tell me… no… again."

"Uhhh," I groaned, lurching forward with a particularly deep, beautiful thrust.

"No?"

"Yes," I murmured as I came, choking on a sob. The satisfaction was just too much. What did he want from me? "Oh damn, damn, damn! Yes!"

I couldn't take anymore, especially when he picked up the pace once more to find his own release. Thankfully, he quickly found it, his grip tightening and his breathing ragged, driving his cock into me until he came in a series of spasms.

Still inside me, he leaned over my back, pushed my hair aside—it had long ago escaped my elastic band—and kissed my nape.

"Greedy," he remarked into my skin. Then he withdrew from me and I rolled over, unable to believe that this had just happened. Again!

I was equally unable to believe that I just had the best sex of my life and didn't feel guilty about the dodgy circumstances. I didn't know my "partner's" name and I only met him that evening. Could eye-fucking even be considered a meeting?

I couldn't help watching him repeat the process of removing the condom. He made it seem like art. It was then that I knew that if he wanted to take me again, I'd be more than willing to oblige, even though my limbs would protest. I was greedy, after all.

God, listen to yourself, Rae! You need serious help.

Oh, go away. You're just mad because I got some.

"Go to sleep, Rae."

I didn't really think I was tired after all that—thoroughly worked out, yes. But at his words, I felt drowsiness wash over me. SRG pulled the covers over my naked body, and before I could object, slipped into bed beside me. He flipped the light off and the room was blanketed in darkness. Well, as dark as a third-floor hotel room in Sin City could get.

"I don't even know your name," I murmured, more to myself than to him. I had to repress a sigh of contentment when he spooned me from behind.

He rested one arm over my stomach and pulled me into the warm, male hardness of his body. He felt delicious. I never shared a bed with anyone before. I instantly decided that it was something worth looking into.

"Sleep, Rae," he repeated, his warm breath caressing the shell of my ear.

I slept.

Chapter 3

Not even a dirty martini could quell my rage and I freaking loved that drink. The guy at the bar already knew this. He'd made me three already—very dry, with three olives in each glass. And it wasn't even happy hour yet.

"What's eating you up?" a guy's smooth voice asked from beside me.

I jerked my head in his direction and was met with sea-green eyes, fiery red hair, and what was obviously a genuine Armani.

Great.

Darryl Winer was sitting in a bar stool beside me, wanting to know what was "eating me up."

Could this day get any worse?

First, I woke up to an empty bed that morning. Scary Russian Guy had, apparently, taken off sometime in the early hours and didn't even leave me a note or a goddamn card. I only had one one-night stand before him and that guy even told me his favorite color after sleeping with me. SRG only casually mentioned owning a hotel. I had no other info about him.

Of course, I didn't expect cuddling and breakfast in bed with him. I was under no illusions that what happened the night before would be more than just a one-off. But the whole mystery was eating at me. I liked knowing the facts, and the fact that I knew next to nothing about SRG pissed the crap out of me.

The simmering anger I felt, mostly at myself, continued in the shower as I thoroughly scrubbed the memory of him off my body. It continued as I pulled on yet another stupid skintight dress—ruby red this time, to highlight my jezebel status—and went downstairs for a big breakfast.

And it almost came to the fore when I bumped into SRG himself on my way out the large, lavish dining room after an incredibly delicious, hearty breakfast of bacon, toast, and bacon.

He was with an older silver-haired man who was clad in a smart charcoal black suit, and was at least a foot shorter than SRG, which made him roughly my height. SRG's hair was pulled back from his face in a low ponytail and I was horrified to discover that I itched to run my hands through it. He was in a sky blue V-necked T-shirt that matched his eyes, black low rise jeans and incredibly scruffy black motorcycle boots. Divine was the first word that came to my mind, despite the fact that I found it difficult to believe that he could possibly have any shares in a hotel of this exquisite standard, looking the way he did.

He'd glared at me—yes, glared at me!—and said nothing before leading his companion into the dining room without so much as a backward glance. No "Morning, Rae", or even a small nod of recognition. Those blue eyes of his just turned arctic and he ignored me as if he didn't break into my hotel room last night and fucked my brains out.

I felt like a prostitute. I certainly looked like one.

Darryl Winer sitting next to me at the bar ten hours later, asking me what was "eating me up", was not helping matters. He wasn't supposed to know I existed, let alone talk to me. I was being sloppy.

"Meeting someone?" I asked him, tipping back my glass and downing my vodka. I'd consumed olive after olive as well and was beginning to feel a little ill.

"Are you?" Darryl countered, and I looked at him. He really was attractive with those green eyes of his. Cassie Winer was right to be jealous of anyone that so much as blinked at him.

"Flying solo tonight, I'm afraid," I casually replied, motioning to the bartender, Dan, to get me another drink.

"Tad Thornberry not with you tonight?"

"Who?"

"Tad?" Winer gauged my blank look. "The guy you were wrapped around yesterday?"

Shit. Winer really did get a good look at me last night and I thought I was being inconspicuous.

Sloppy, Rae. Real sloppy.

"What's it to you?"

"Tad's an old friend of mine," Winer informed me, accepting the bartender's silent proffer of a scotch on the rocks. "He has a wife and two teenage kids. He does not need to have a beautiful woman like you wrapped around him like a snake."

This was rich. The guy I was following because his wife thought he was cheating on her was lecturing me for being a home-wrecker.

Dan was blatantly ignoring me. Probably because he thought I'd had enough. Idiot.

"What about you? You got a wife? Kids?" I asked Darryl, although I already knew the answer.

His eyes immediately glazed over—with genuine love, I saw. "Her name's Cassandra and we're expecting a baby." He paused. "That's why I need to wrap my business up here and get back to her tomorrow."

Cassie's pregnant? I thought, startled. *Huh! Guess I don't know everything.*

"That's, um, great. You do that," I told Winer, meaning it. His wife was dumb as a brick if she ever thought he'd cheat on her, especially when she was pregnant with what was obviously their first kid.

"And you'll stay away from Tad?" Winer downed his drink and set the glass on the counter.

"Absolutely," I told him truthfully. I prayed to God I'd never relive my "arm candy" humiliation and bump into Tad again.

Winer nodded. "Nice talking to you." Then, he got to his feet.

I realized then that he really was a good guy. He was looking out for his friend, and his friend's family by default, when he nicely told a perceived, slutty threat to back the hell off. And he wanted to get back to his wife and unborn baby ASAP, when he practically had carte blanche in Vegas with whomever he wanted.

"Wait," I said to him, and he turned to me, arching a brow.

"Yes?"

"Tall guy. Long, dark hair and really blue eyes. Owns the hotel?" I sucked in a deep breath. "You were sitting with him last night. What's his name?"

A smile that tugged at Winer's lips told me he knew exactly who I was talking about. "Last name Anghelescu. All you need to know."

Ang-hel-ess-coo. That didn't sound Russian to me. But before I could press it, Winer stalked off, leaving me alone at the bar with questions—and an anger that was still a long way from dissipating. I grabbed my handbag, hopped off the stool, and shakily got to my feet. Drinking had definitely been a poor decision. I was making a lot of those lately.

Like last night.

"Get a grip, Rae," I chided myself, because this was getting ridiculous. *Why was I so mad?* It wasn't as if this guy gave me any promises. It wasn't as if he committed himself to me. For all I knew, Angel-whatever-the-fuck made it a habit of randomly accusing women of giving him come-hither looks so he could have an excuse to break into their hotel rooms and fuck them senseless.

I felt myself get wet just remembering—remembering the feel of him inside me, giving me orgasm after orgasm while his big, hot body left a palpable imprint on mine. Just the thought of it was enough to undo me.

I'm not going to think about this.

Gambling. Gambling would take my mind off everything. Did being slightly tipsy mean I'd be more careless or more intuitive? I didn't know. I didn't care. All I knew was that my work in Vegas was done and I could go home, maybe even visit Renée, earlier than expected. Darryl Winer wasn't a cheating dog. Cassie could sleep easy. And so could I.

I was thinking that it felt good to be able to give someone some good news for a change, when I walked smack-dab into a tall, willowy figure that reached out and steadied me with his (I could see that they belonged to a guy) arms.

I muttered an irrational, "Watch where you're going!" and immediately pulled back.

"Baby Phat Girl?" the man queried, his voice laced with disbelief.

No, I thought in a wild panic, those three words giving me a jolt of recognition.

I practically sobered up in that instant, narrowing my eyes. Sure enough, the incubus from Paris was standing in the doorway of the bar, looking incredibly... good. I hadn't gotten that good of a look at him the first time we met (and who could blame me?), but it was safe to say that he wasn't even my type.

He was far too lean and boyishly fresh-faced. Icy blonde hair curled behind his pierced ears, furthering his cherubic image. His eyes were long-lashed, chocolate brown, and were set in an extraordinarily alabaster skin that if I didn't know any better, I would've thought he was a *Twilight* reject. But I did know better and I knew that I had to get away from him. If I hadn't gotten drunk, I would've felt him coming a mile away and this confrontation would've been easily avoided.

"You following me or something?" he asked, snapping me out of my trance.

My eyes focused on his chest. Incubus was splashed across his black T-shirt in blood red font. An incubus that wore Incubus band tees. It was not lost on me how apropos that was, which may be due to my intoxication. I didn't want to laugh but I was close to doing so, which is why I steadfastly bit my bottom lip.

"Baby Phat?" he repeated, arching a brow.

"It's Rae," I snapped, only because I kept thinking he meant the dreaded f-word.

"Ray," he said, now blatantly checking me out. He did it in an extremely offensive, leering way. "Like Ray Charles?"

I couldn't help it. The drunken laughter I'd been suppressing escaped my lips. In fact, I pretty much doubled over in laughter and would've fallen over in my stupid heels if the demon didn't reach out and wrap his arm around my waist. I knew I was supposed to recoil. Getting manhandled by a demon? Not cool. Getting manhandled by a sex demon? Well, I'd probably have to bathe in holy water... every day... for the rest of my life.

"Rae with an 'e', not a 'y'," I explained between laughs. I stopped, glancing down at his arm and looking up at him. "And you? What's your name?"

He cocked his head, his eyes dancing with humor. "You don't wanna know."

"I don't?"

"No. It's the stuff of nightmares."

I didn't even know if demons had names. Well, normal names. I knew about the biblical ones. Like Legion. My father had imparted that knowledge to me before he died. But never in a million years would I have thought I'd be standing in a bar asking a demon, who had once tried to force himself on me, what his name was.

"Well," I began, interested despite myself, "what is it?"

"Templeton," he intoned, putting me out of my misery.

"What?!"

He sighed heavily. "My mother's a big fan of The A-Team. The original A-Team. So she..."

"You have a mother?"

He smirked at me. "Yes, Baby Phat. I have a mother. How do you think I got here?"

"I..." I couldn't finish my sentence. Demons had mothers. How had my father not told me this?

"I'm a halfling. That means I have a human parent."

"I know what a halfling is," I mumbled, although I hadn't really thought about them. Looking at this... this demon, you'd never be able to tell that he could send you to eternal damnation with one crook of his manicured finger.

"You can call me Temp. Everyone does."

"Your mother clearly hated you," I whispered.

"I hate to agree with you, Baby Phat." His arm tightened around my waist and he leaned down, his lips brushing my ear. "So what are you?"

I sucked in a deep breath. "Get away from me. Now."

"You're drunk," he said softly. "Let me take you to your room."

I tried to push him away. "So you can... attack me?" The fear was there, the fear of dying at the hands of this creature. I thought of myself as spunky, brave even, but dealing with something like him was enough to make my backbone crumble into dust.

He rolled his eyes at me—actually rolled his damn eyes at me as if it were irrational to be terrified of him. "Relax, Baby Phat. I've fed already, on a more-than-willing subject," he said slowly, as if he were talking to a little child. "Even though you look," he sighed, "impeccable, I won't touch you." He demonstrated this by taking an exaggerated step away from me. "Better?"

"I don't trust you," I snapped at him, all the while wondering if that "subject" was still breathing, or if the poor woman was now a grinning corpse in a hotel room. "I don't want anything to do with... with your kind. Being around you makes me sick." *But that could just be the vodka.*

Temp did another eye-roll. "A little melodramatic, don't you think?" He reached out and gently pulled me out of the way as a couple strode past me, effectively closing the distance between us. "This place is crawling with my kind," he cheerfully enlightened me. "They don't call Vegas 'Sin City' for nothing, babe. So you might want to think about that before you strut around looking like this, especially when you're drunk and the next guy you meet won't be as nice as me."

I gulped. *Crawling*, he'd said. *Crawling with them.*

Oh God, I need to get out of here. I need to get out of here!

"I'll take myself upstairs, thank you very much," I whispered, and made a move to march past him.

His hands shot out and he pushed me up against the wall, positioning his body before me, and gently but firmly pressing his lower body against mine. To anybody watching, it looked like a frisky interlude, but to me, it felt like I was dying a thousand deaths. Temp's eyes weren't creepy in any way. In fact, they looked a bit familiar, but they were narrowed as he stared down at me.

"OK, Baby Phat," he said in a low voice. "I've humored you enough. Spit it out. What are you?"

Even if kneeing him in the groin was possible—which wasn't, considering how restricted my movement currently was—I was just simply frozen to the spot in fear.

Temp impatiently repeated himself.

"I-I'm a p-p-private investigator," I stammered, humiliated by how petrified I sounded. Enraged men caught with their pants down baying for my blood? No problem. Curious incubi who were touching me? Turned me into a pathetic, stuttering mess.

"A private investigator," he repeated, quirking a brow as if he didn't believe me.

I took a deep breath before saying, "I specialize in tailing unfaithful husbands. Huge market, if you must know.

37

Men can't seem to keep their dicks in their pants. I would've given you a business card but I don't believe in self-advertising."

Temp gave me a strange look. "Look, Baby Phat, I've been turning on the charm full force since we started talking—and nothing," he told me, now looking affronted. "You're supposed to be putty in my hands right now. Putty! You're supposed to want me. So I'll ask again, What are you?"

I felt anger swirl around inside me and I clung to it, releasing my hold on panic. "I'm a woman who's becoming extremely pissed off, so I'm giving you one last chance to get the fuck away from me before I beat the horse crap out of you," I said through clenched teeth. "I never asked to be able to know when your kind is around me. My father passed that gift on to me. No matter how hard I try to forget about it, I can't ignore it. Happy?"

Temp immediately let me go. "That still doesn't explain why you're immune to me." He paused, looking thoughtful. "Would you object if I kissed you?"

I couldn't mask my horror even if I wanted to. Revulsion and abject fear made me give out an odd squawk of shock.

"I guess that's a no," a cheerful Temp said for me. His face became sober. "I only wanted to know what you tasted like, Baby Phat. That's all. Every creature tastes differently. No need to look so dismayed." He let out a short laugh, grabbing my hand. "Come on. I'm taking you upstairs. What floor are you?"

"Three."

I allowed him to lead me out the doorway of the bar. I allowed him to lead me past the high-energy casino entrance. I even allowed him to steer me to the elevator. His hand felt surprisingly nice around mine. Comforting, even. I didn't want to think too much about that. Temp was nice-looking, but he was a demon and he wasn't my type.

I tended to lean toward tall, dark, and devilishly handsome.

This was my train of thought when the elevator pinged open—and Tall, Dark, and Devilishly Handsome stood inside the car, on his way out.

He was still in the same clothes I saw him in that morning, except that he'd untied his hair from its ponytail and it flowed in a thick curtain around his face. God, I yearned to run my hands through that hair again. I had to physically restrain myself from leaping inside and doing it.

Anghelescu, or whatever he was called, paused and threw me a look that could have frozen the entire percentage of water inside me. Temp either ignored it or wasn't aware. He dragged me into the car with him and the elevator doors came to a close.

"Evening," said Temp, pressing the third floor button. His tone was strange. Moderately reverent.

"Disappear," growled Scary (Possibly) Russian Guy, and I stared at him in puzzled disbelief.

"She needs to get to her room," Temp told him, further confusing me.

"Disappear," SRG repeated, his voice an octave lower.

Temp squeezed my hand before releasing me. "As you wish, Andrei." And he instantly disappeared into thin air.

All that air seemed to disappear with him.

Andrei, he said. *Andrei*.

It all came back to me in a rush of drunken adrenaline—Paris, Nicolette, Hotel Ange Noir…

"Andrei would like you. You're his type."

Temp's words replayed in my head like a scratched CD. Just how many Andrei's could Temp possibly know? And now he just left me in an elevator—a confined space—with Andrei, someone who was obviously one of his kind.

And all the while I was processing this, Andrei Anghelescu was watching me, taking up more space than was humanly possible—because he wasn't human.

I've fucked him, I thought, my face contorting with the horrible realization. *I've fucked a demon.*

"No," I croaked, my head pounding, praying that this was some sick, twisted joke. I pressed myself against one of the silver panels on one side, squeezing my eyes shut and opening them again. "No!"

It didn't make sense. Even in my vodka-addled state, I could tell that something wasn't right. If he were a demon, why didn't I sense him last night when he was inside me?! The fact that my brain was all fuzzy from martinis explained why I couldn't feel his energy surrounding me now. But last night? Last night, I'd been as sober as a judge.

Andrei extended a long arm and pressed the emergency stop button. "I take it you know what I am now?" he said quietly, narrowing his eyes at me as the car rocked to a stop. "The question is: What are you?"

I inwardly grimaced. I was getting sick and damn tired of that exact same question.

"I had sex with you!" I said breathily, still in a state of total shock.

"I know," he said impatiently. "I was there."

"I can't... I think... Oh God, I'm going to be sick!"

Andrei moved, now standing so close to me that I could see the minute hairs of a five o'clock shadow dotting his painfully masculine jaw. I pressed myself as far back as I could possibly go, breathing heavily but trying not to succumb to the mad hysteria inside me.

"I fucked you," he muttered, threading his hands in my hair. I was disgusted by the way I was still aching for his touch despite knowing what he was. "Fucked you hard. Consumed a shitload of your energy. By rights, you should be in bed recovering." He paused, considering this. "No, you should be half-comatose, maybe even dead. Yet here you are, wearing close to nothing and looking... the way you look."

I swallowed, my breathing ragged. Hearing him talk about what he'd done to me in such a crass way was enough to make my panties wet. I certainly was my mother's child, running around having sex with creatures of the underworld.

Maybe Temp was wrong, I thought hopefully. *Maybe I'm just as susceptible to incubi as the next person. Maybe this is just an involuntary reaction.*

But even as I thought those words, I knew they weren't true. I had hunter's blood in my veins and we were immune. No, this was attraction on a primal level.

"Don't lie to me," Andrei pressed. "Are you an angel?"

I couldn't help it, I laughed. I laughed louder then than when I'd laughed at Temp. I laughed louder than I'd ever laughed in my entire twenty-seven years. This was beyond ridiculous. An angel. *He thought I was an angel. An angel, for Pete's sake!*

He scowled at me, clearly not used to being ridiculed, and grabbed my chin, tipping it toward him. "Don't fuck around with me because you have no idea who I am. Now talk."

I had no clue what came over me, except that in the last twenty-four hours, I'd seen enough demons to last a lifetime, been manhandled by two of them, had the best sex of my life

41

with one, and was currently fighting to control the scream dying to get out of me. So I slapped his hand away and glowered at him.

"Don't try to intimidate me, buddy! I'm so not in the mood," I fumed, ignoring the intimidating look on his face. "I'm human and I enjoy a very mundane, very human existence, so if you don't mind," I spat as I pressed the emergency stop button and the elevator started up again, "I'd like to get some sleep and get the hell out of this hellhole, literally, first thing tomorrow morning so I can continue with it. You with me?!"

He stared at me. I stared back.

The elevator doors opened and a laughing couple patiently waited for us to exit. I slid past Andrei and tottered out, praying that he wouldn't follow.

But he did.

"What do you want from me?" I snarled, whirling around once we were at the door to my suite. Anger seemed the best thing to hold on to rather than absolute terror—and lust. Yup, despite my knowledge of what he was, I was still attracted to him—it.

Those eyes of his were several shades darker and I instantly knew what that meant. Before I could say something scathing, he seized me, angling his head, and smashed his lips against mine. The fact that I knew what he was didn't stop my body from reacting to the feel of his soft lips against mine. I melted against him, my hands grabbing the folds of his shirt, and I moaned when his tongue slipped into my mouth.

Heat immediately pooled in my belly and, without using my card, Andrei pushed the door open and picked me up, kicking it shut behind us and switching on the overhead lights.

My legs were wrapped around his waist as he led me to the newly made bed and set me down, leaning above me. Dammit, I wanted him. I wanted him so badly I wouldn't have cared if he suddenly revealed that he was really a goblin-turtle hybrid… or something.

My dress came off and my underwear followed, leaving me naked for his consumption. I wanted his mouth to soothe the heat overwhelming my entire body. I wanted his mouth everywhere.

He pulled back, his eyes gazing over my body with naked desire. I squirmed and he stilled me with strong hands.

"Stop," he growled. "You are completely and totally fuckable. Don't hide from me." He lowered his mouth to one breast. "I'm having you checked out, Rainelle Erickson," he murmured into my skin, pulling a nipple into his mouth and suckling it. "You know why?"

I whimpered with pleasure, unable to grab his hair like I wanted to because his hands were holding me down.

He raised his head. "Because I don't like complications," he said softly.

"I'm… not," I gasped.

One of his hands had released me to stimulate me.

"You are," he said huskily, teasing my swollen clit between his fingers, "because you are different."

I bucked under him as he slipped a finger into me at the same time.

"So wet for me," he murmured, that accent of his coming to the fore again. "Such a good girl."

He withdrew his fingers, and rolled off the bed and onto his feet. My eyes were closed and the only thing I heard was the sound of the drawers being opened. I'd thrown every condom in there that morning, disgusted with myself.

43

"Get up," Andrei barked, and my eyes flew open.

I was panting for air as I crawled off the bed. He'd shed every bit of clothing and stood before me, his encased erection massive and beautiful. He grabbed me to him and his mouth sent electric charges throughout my body once more before he pulled away and spun me around so that my back was to him.

"I'm going to fuck you hard and you're going to beg me for more," he snarled into my ear, kneading my swollen breasts with his hands. "You are not going to be sick. You are not going to want to get out of here. You are going to come until my cock is tattooed inside this sexy ass of yours." He squeezed my ass and I sucked in air. "You with me?"

I nodded, already close to orgasm at his delicious words.

"Words. Say it."

"Yes," I panted.

"Bend over," he commanded.

I did as he asked, bending at the waist and placing my hands on the soft, downy carpet. Andrei's fingers instantly sought my wetness, sinking into me and sending ripples of pleasure through me and brought my mind havoc. His knuckles nudged my clit, and I cried out, the sweet sensation almost painful.

Languid minutes passed as he held onto my waist and pleasured me at the same time. His fingers spread me apart and I held my breath, heart thumping in anticipation.

I felt him at my entrance. Felt him circle me, torturing me. Biting my lip, I prepared myself for what was to come— and come, it did. He thrust into me about halfway, stretching me to the limit. I cried out again, shutting my eyes. He pulled out, then plunged deep into me, to the hilt this time,

44

incomparably filling me up. Delicious pain morphed into intense, unbearable pleasure as he increased the pace, his thrusts becoming faster and deeper.

He grunted each time he drove himself into me, his hold on my waist tightening and my body was quaking with the force of each beautiful invasion.

I screamed through my orgasm, riding that wave until it evaporated. It was a powerful orgasm that didn't seem to have a beginning or ending. And I wasn't going to be able to support myself any longer and Andrei seemed to sense that. So he came, his big body racked with spasms as he groaned into the air, jerking inside of me.

Then he pulled himself out and I collapsed onto the ground, gasping for breath. He left me there, walking over to the bin and disposing of the used condom. I peered over the bed and watched him clean himself up.

"No more," I pleaded, my voice hoarse. I had no idea if he wanted more but if last night were any indication, I sure as hell knew that incubi had amazing stamina. I, unfortunately, did not.

"No more?" he repeated, tearing open another foil packet. His hungry gaze sent shivers down my spine. "You don't mean that, Rainelle. You're just as hungry for me as I am for you."

I gulped, watching him roll the latex on.

"How can you still be so hard?"

"You," he said simply, by way of explanation. "Get on the bed. I'll fuck you slowly."

That sounded delicious. My pussy seconded that thought by clenching in anticipation.

Jesus, Rae, my inner voice admonished. *What the hell's gotten into you? Have you forgotten that he—it—is a demon?*

No, I hadn't forgotten. How could I? It was right in front of me: the fact that he was a demon—an evil creature, and being with him was unnatural. But what exactly could I do? Tell him I didn't want him inside me when we both knew that was a bald-faced lie? I wanted him with an intensity I didn't know existed and I couldn't even blame it on his sex-demon magic because, apparently, I was immune to it. So I hopped onto the bed and lay flat on my back, my arousal coming back to me in a flood.

Andrei slid beside me, his sheer presence making me wet. Feeling bolder, I reached out and ran my hand down the planes of his hard chest. He made a low noise in his throat as I circled his navel and moved down his happy trail, pausing at the start of the short, dark curls of hair.

"What's it like?" I asked, my wandering hand stilling when he reached out and grabbed my wrist.

"What's what like?" he muttered, his darkened eyes on mine. "Being me?"

Well, that, too.

"No. Having sex with me."

His gaze never wavered. "You're different. Your energy, your life force, is more intoxicating than the average human's," he said quietly. "It's intoxicating and it's satisfying. I could probably go a few months without sex after being with you just once. I've never been with anyone like you," he added, looking like he was trying to figure me out.

This worried me. It sounded like I was incubus catnip, which would explain Temp's behavior. "Intoxicating? Like a drug or alcohol? You mean addictive?"

"Relax, Rae," Andrei said dryly. "I'm not going to enslave you as my personal fuck-toy."

The thought had never occurred to me until he said it out aloud. Images flashed through my mind of being locked in a dungeon for him to use for his pleasure whenever he was low on energy. I shuddered. Whether from fear or pleasure, I had no idea.

"There's nothing special about me," I said, more to myself than to him. I leaned toward him and kissed him on the mouth, pushing him back until he was propped up by the mounds of pillows behind him.

I needed to dominate him. I needed to show him that I wasn't afraid of being with him like this. I didn't know why but I just felt like I needed to.

So I hoisted myself onto his lap and impaled myself on his manhood, taking him in to the root. I released a moan of contentment, holding onto his shoulders as I slowly rode him. His hands came around my waist, steadying me and I ran a hand through his silky curtain of inky hair, clutching a hank of it and pulling.

He made a guttural sound in his throat and thrust upward, sending a wave of pleasure through me. It hurt to be fucked by someone as incredibly endowed as he was. It hurt and it didn't, because pleasure trumped pain any day. I couldn't decide if I was in control or if he was. But dammit, it felt good! And I felt guilty that it felt this good.

I leaned in to him, shoving my breasts in his face for attention. Having his mouth around one aching nipple was driving me crazy, as was the intense feeling of him still buried inside me.

"Ah," I gasped, when he nipped at my nipple with sharp teeth. The pain was surprisingly welcome and I decided that I liked it. Loved it, even.

What is happening to me?

"There, Rae," Andrei growled, holding me down on him as he thrust into me. "Right…" He drove into me again. "… there."

My inner walls clenched around him as I climaxed, crying out from such extreme pleasure. Andrei immediately turned me over, forcing me onto my back as he slammed into me, his thrusts faster, harder, angrier. A stab of fear shot through me when I saw his eyes briefly turn completely onyx— and then a shimmering, blazing crimson—when he came, the force of his ejaculation pinning me down into the mattress. I bucked under his weight, fear giving way to a second orgasm. And I dug my nails in his lower back, clawing my way up the hard planes of muscle.

Andrei barely flinched, even though I could feel that I'd drawn blood. Instead, he waited a beat before pulling out of me and sitting up, giving me his back. I watched in horror as the red welts I'd inflicted on the ridges of his back minutes ago healed. Unblemished tan skin was left in their place.

"Make me forget," I choked out, pulling the covers over myself and hiding my nakedness.

Andrei turned at the waist to look at me. "What?"

"Erase my memory. I know you can do that. Please!" I paused, biting my lower lip. "Make me forget you."

If I could pretend that this weekend had never happened, I would probably be able to look at myself in the mirror. Probably. The sight of him healing himself was enough to drag me back to the strange reality that I just had repeated sex with a supernatural creature.

Andrei was silent, his face chillingly impassive.

"Andrei, please!"

How could I live with myself after this? My father was rolling in his grave, I was willing to bet, disgusted and disappointed with me. I wouldn't blame him. I felt the same way.

Andrei rose to his feet, wordlessly putting his clothes back on. I sat there wishing I hadn't decided to choose tonight of all nights to get completely plastered. I had a massive headache to start with, and alcohol had been at least partly responsible for my weak will. Well, it was definitely responsible for my inability to sense Andrei Anghelescu's demon aura.

Right?

Much like Gavin Turner's assault on the plane, I didn't see Andrei's attack on me coming. One minute, he was standing beside the bed and the next, he was hovering over me with his hand firmly around the pulsing column of my neck.

I couldn't scream—déjà freaking vu. But I wouldn't have wanted to because, with his hand wound around my neck, Andrei had distracted me from what his real aim was: sticking two fingers up my sensitized sex and dragging out a gasp of surprise from my mouth. Deep inside me, he jerked his fingers toward himself and I whimpered, arching my back off the bed.

"Erase your memory?" he spat, his fingers furiously inflicting sweet agony to my insides.

His eyes were blazing, literally, and his face had become a picture of barely controlled rage—a rage that was unquestioningly directed at me. I couldn't speak, but I didn't have to answer his rhetoric, of course. The only thing I could really do was lay there and allow him to humiliate me by pleasuring me like this.

49

"Make you forget me?" The pad of his thumb was like hot coal on my swollen clit. "You can never forget me, Rainelle Erickson." His fingers were bringing me close—in and out, in and out, round and round, round and round. And I was going to come... again. "I feel how wet you are for me and I want to fuck you again," Andrei snarled, his eyes hungrily sweeping over me. "I am five seconds away from making you my personal fuck-toy. You have no idea how much you've just pissed me off."

I groaned, shamelessly and frantically rocking my hips and pushing myself towards him. I could feel my juices trickling down my thighs and onto the crumpled white bed sheets.

How humiliating.

"My answer to your request?" Andrei crushed his lips against mine, forcefully prying open my closed lips and taking what he wanted. He pulled away, leaving me panting. "Go fuck yourself."

And he rose, towering over the bed.

Before I could blink, he vanished, making me seriously consider finishing myself.

"Leaving without saying goodbye, Baby Phat?"

I whirled around, aware that Temp could hardly do anything to me in a hotel lobby full of people. I felt braver than I'd been the night before. Being sober, although a little hung-over, was a big plus.

50

I slipped my sunglasses to the crown of my head and narrowed my eyes at him. "You'd better get the hell away from me before I do something I won't regret."

Temp chuckled, flashing his extraordinarily pearly whites. "Charming, angel. Don't you want to hit the Strip or something?"

I wrinkled my nose. "No, I want to hit you."

"Come on, Baby Phat. I've got a pocket full of ones and I'm looking for some buns."

I stood in front of my suitcase, glaring up at him. "Andrei's your friend, huh?"

A strange look crossed his face. "Friend. Good one." He straightened the front of his peach polo shirt. "He fucked you?"

Despite myself, a blush crept up my neck from inside my V-neck T-shirt, and I knew Temp could see it.

"He did," he said, nodding. "I'm going to give you a word of advice, Rae," he said grimly, his increasingly familiar dark brown eyes on me. "Someone like you doesn't want Andrei in their pants. No matter how great the sex was, it's not worth it."

I let out a bitter laugh. "What about Paris? What about how you said he'd like me? Now, you're looking out for me?"

"That was before I knew you," he quietly replied.

"You don't know me! You know nothing about me!" I was almost crying from anger and frustration. My life was screwed up and it had only taken three days in Vegas for that to happen.

Temp reached out and placed his hands on my shoulders. "I know that demons are not your cup of tea, Baby Phat. I know that you're a good person because you're out here trying to put a suspicious woman's mind at ease." He tipped

51

my chin up. "I know that you've probably already figured out how dark and cruel Andrei is. Not all of us are like him."

I wasn't a sappy, spineless female who needed a man to rescue her every five seconds, but I liked how safe and secure I felt around Temp—Temp, a sex demon, the same sex demon that had tried to force himself on me on my birthday. It was ridiculous but true.

"Sweetheart!" a loud voice trilled from behind me, pulling me out of my trancelike state and forcing me to turn around because it was practically in my ear. "There you are."

It was a woman, and I recognized her as if I saw her in the mirror every day, which I sort of did. She hadn't changed over the years, which was impossible because I'd last seen her twenty-one years ago. Dressed in a white figure-hugging sleeveless dress with her strawberry blonde hair framing her heart-shaped face, she looked like the angel I'd always thought she was—until she took off with a demon.

My mother hadn't aged a day.

For a minute, I was shocked that she would recognize me after all these years—twenty-one years, and more so that she'd act so blasé, as if we'd only lost each other in the supermarket or something.

"Give Mommy a hug," she said in her vaguely familiar sultry voice... and then she threw her arms wide around Temp.

Chapter 4

"Dammit, Ma," Temp muttered, stepping out of her stifling embrace. "How'd you find me?"

"You think you can hide from me?" she grumbled good-naturedly. Her eyes swiveled in my direction as if she just noticed me. "Men," she said conspiratorially, giving me a wink. "Give them an inch, they take a mile. Well, in my son's case, several thousand miles, considering the last time I saw him was in Italy."

She hadn't noticed that I was completely dumbfounded and had barely heard what she just said. Temp hadn't noticed either. And I was too puzzled to even think straight.

Her son, I thought, shocked to the core.

Of course, my own mother didn't recognize me and I hadn't expected her to. The last time she'd seen me, I was still wetting the bed and wearing pigtails. She, on the other hand, looked the same, which could only mean one horrifying thing: she'd sold her soul to the devil for immortality. In order to be with the demon she loved, I was willing to bet.

53

I quickly did the math. She'd been thirty-five when she'd left and Temp looked to be in his early twenties. This meant that she'd been pregnant with him when she'd disappeared, which made him roughly twenty-one or so. But did demon halflings age like normal people? Or could they freeze time as they so pleased? My head was spinning with the possibilities that I could feel a migraine coming on.

"Mom," I breathed, and she looked at me strangely. The word tasted strange in my mouth, like sushi in peanut butter.

"Fed too hard on this one, huh?" she teased Temp, and he patted my back.

"This is Rainelle, Ma," he said politely, as if introducing his girlfriend to his mother. God, he didn't know and the idea of what he nearly did to me, wanted to do to me, made me taste bile. "She knows about us. She's immune."

"Rainelle?" Her voice became vague, as if she dimly recalled another Rainelle she'd met a long time ago but couldn't, for the life of her, remember where.

"Lauren Madeline Wilson," I snapped, anger surging through me. I hadn't said that name in years.

Lauren Madeline Wilson's eyebrows shot up to somewhere below her hairline. "Excuse me?"

"I'm Rainelle Erickson, not that you care or remember." My voice was cool, but inside, something shattered with the realization that what I'd just said was probably the truth.

My mother's eyes flashed with recognition and she took a step away from me, looking me over in disbelief. I could finally see the little things Temp had inherited from her— namely, her coffee-brown eyes and Phoenician nose. And then I felt nauseous, so nauseous it hurt. It was one thing to

54

willingly have sex with a demon, but to procreate in the process? Despicable.

"What the hell's going on here?" Temp asked, impatiently tapping my back with his fingertips.

But I was too focused on staring my mother to death. Immortal or not, she was just as susceptible to my death glares as the next person. The only reason I wasn't throwing myself at her was because the hotel lobby was incredibly crowded.

"Rainelle," Lauren murmured weakly, "Oh, my!"

"Ma?" Temp's voice was uncertain.

"How could you?" I snarled, all my pent-up bullshit swelling to the fore. "How could you hurt us like that? Did you even love Dad? Me? Or was great sex just too excellent an offer to pass up?"

A passing bellhop gave us a curious glance, no doubt catching the end of my sentence.

My mother's eyes widened and she had the grace to look embarrassed.

"You two know each other?" Temp asked, his tone impatient.

Lauren nodded, her eyes still locked with mine. "Temp, Rainelle's your half-sister."

"Well, this is about as awkward as it gets," Temp remarked, downing his second Budweiser that morning. He set the empty can back on the table, staring at me from beside Lauren.

I stirred my black coffee, unable to take my eyes off my mother. She, on the other hand, was looking everywhere but at me. I missed my flight for this crap and I was anything but happy about spending another second in The Kamenev.

It was a good thing the hotel's dining area was well-ventilated and filled with sunshine because I was afraid of what I'd do if I ever got these two people, demons, alone in a dark place. Decapitation was at the top of my list.

I turned my attention to Temp. "You were trying to get into my pants. You honestly had no idea that... well, that... this?" I gestured at all three of us.

His face contorted with unmasked disgust. "I might be a sex fiend but incest is not a turn-on," he said through gritted teeth. "In fact, I might just give up sex altogether and die of starvation to avoid sleeping with family members I have no inkling of!" He said the last part with his eyes narrowed at Lauren. "Explain yourself. Now, Ma!"

"Actually, I don't care. I need to get out of here," I muttered, getting to my feet. "You're lucky I don't have the means or opportunity to slash your throat."

"Sit," my mother commanded, her chocolate brown eyes finally meeting mine. "Please."

I sat.

Minutes of silence rolled by and I waited, my patience quickly waning.

Finally, Lauren began, "I loved Raymond. I really did." She was caressing her mug of hot chocolate. "But I'm in love with Vitaly. It wasn't fair to your dad but I couldn't help it. You can't help who you fall in love with."

"Do you hear yourself?" I instantly snapped at her. "In love with a demon? Don't you understand that you were seduced? Controlled?"

My mother shot me a dirty look. "That's what I am, too. A demon," she said, her voice brittle. "And FYI, Rainelle, I can smell Andrei's essence all over you like cheap perfume."

Heat enflamed my cheeks. *She could smell his "essence". Seriously? Could every other demon here smell his "essence"?! Could they smell that I just had sex with one of their kind?! Like animals in the wild, could they all smell who I had sex with?!* I averted my eyes from Lauren, mortified.

"If what Temp says is true, that you can't be seduced by one of us, then you had sex with Andrei willingly," she went on, "So forgive me if I refuse to be judged by you."

"That's too fucking bad, Mom," I choked out, "because you ruined my father's life so I have every right to judge you! You know how he spent his final years? Chasing demons! Looking for Vitaly! Chasing them like a madman because of you. And one of them killed him."

Lauren looked away. "That was his prerogative, Rainelle."

"Bitch!" I roared, leaning forward and gripping the white tablecloth in my hands. I directed all the rage I'd built up over the years at her. I felt it leave my body and get sucked up by hers. "You did that to him! You drove him mental with heartbreak and all you can say to that is that it was his choice? I'm going to fucking kill you!"

"Hey," Temp said gently, placing a hand on my arm. "Calm down."

I sucked in a deep breath, counting to five before glancing at him. It was perplexing but I felt safe with him. Safe and... calm. It was strange, since his and Lauren's combined aura was making me woozy and giving me a headache. I also realized that I probably couldn't kill my mother. Not in public. Probably not ever.

"Rainelle, you have to understand," Lauren was saying, dragging my attention from Temp.

"Understand what?"

"That I was a bored housewife. My life was going nowhere and I was getting old."

I couldn't believe how shallow and selfish she sounded. "You had me! I was six. Six, dammit! I needed you!"

She shook her head. "No. You didn't. Raymond doted on you." She paused, taking a delicate sip of her drink. "The first time Vitaly came to visit me, your father had gone to some seminar for a weekend. Vitaly had been in a fight with another demon and needed to heal. He… took me and I…"

"I really don't need to hear this," Temp grumbled, "and neither does Rae." Clearly the story of his parents getting together wasn't a favorite topic with him, as well.

"Fine. But I will say this, Rainelle. I fell in love with Vitaly the second I saw him." She bit her lower lip. "Your father had told me about his father and his father's father before him being hunters. But I'd pushed all that out of my mind until… until Vitaly. And then I knew that I wanted to be with him forever. So I… made a deal with Andrei. I sold my soul to Lilith."

"Andrei? Why him? Why does everything seem to come back to him?" *When I'm trying so hard to forget about him*, I silently added.

It was Temp who spoke up.

"Because, Rae," he said, "Andrei's a demon king. Our king."

Two days later, I was standing in the house I'd grown up in, feeling no nostalgia, only bitter "what ifs". Meanwhile, Renée Marino, my best friend in the whole world, was opening all the windows, allowing the earthy sea breeze inside.

I hated coming here.

"Babe, you OK?" she asked, standing in front of me with her hands firmly on her round hips. "Is it your last case? Did the guy make trouble?"

I gave Ren a weak smile. Shorter than me by a few inches, even in heels, she cut her long jet-black hair into a sleek bob that emphasized her high cheekbones and catlike green eyes. Today, she was in a high-waisted white pants and a turquoise vest, with bangles clanging together at her wrists—standard Renée-wear.

She was so clueless. How could I possibly tell her that, after twenty-one years, I found my mother was alive and kicking, and hadn't aged a day? How could I tell her that I had a sex demon for a baby brother and that I happened to have, repeatedly, fucked some kind of demonic royalty over the weekend?

What happens in Vegas, stays in Vegas, I bitterly reflected. I was never going to see any of them again anyway (at least that was what I'd told Temp and my mother to their faces) and I was never going to speak about them.

Lauren had accepted that graciously, probably because she couldn't care less if she ever saw me again or not. She probably preferred it that way. After sitting through a weird Q&A about what had happened to her (in which she informed me that she did indeed have to feed on humans to survive, and that she and Vitaly often enjoyed ménages à trois and orgies as a couple), I'd decided that no amount of chitchat was going to make up for what she'd done to my family. She wasn't there when I had my first period, when my breasts started developing, when I had my first boyfriend, when I went to my prom, when I graduated from college—nothing. As far as I was concerned, I was an orphan and an only child.

"You seriously don't want to hang out sometime?" Temp had asked me when I finally gathered up my luggage and tried to hail a cab outside the hotel. I'd been emotionally jostled left, right, and center for staying in one place too long.

"This is all too much for me, OK?" I replied, not meeting his eyes. "I need normalcy. You're not normal."

"Sure," he said, his voice forcibly neutral. "Have a nice life."

For one second, I did consider the possiblity that I might be hurting Temp's feelings, but then rationality kicked in and I told myself demons didn't have feelings, even halflings.

"I'm good, Ren," I told my best friend, living in the now. "Just starving."

"Why didn't you say so, hon?"

So she drove me over to her house where her husband, Lorenzo, was making his famous lasagna and playing Tupac, at low volume, of course, on the CD player in the kitchen.

"I'm seeing a ghost," he declared when I stepped into their small but cute kitchen, "because Rae Erickson cannot possibly be standing here in my kitchen, here in little old Sallow Bay."

"Very funny," I muttered, going over to him and throwing my arms around him.

He reeked of cheese, spices, and herbs, and looked pretty much the same—the same cropped black hair, same dancing emerald eyes and the same tall, athlete's build—as the last time I'd seen him, which was a while ago. Barefoot and in a red-and-white flannel shirt and faded blue jeans, he looked relaxed and at home in the kitchen, which was good because Renée couldn't cook for shit.

"Hey, sweetness," he said when he pulled back, holding me at arm's length so he could examine me with critical sea green eyes. "I need to find you a husband. You've lost weight."

I rolled my eyes at him and Renée laughed. "You're just not wearing your glasses, handsome."

"I got contacts now, so shut up. I have a cousin that I think you'd…"

"Hell, no!" I cut in, holding a hand up.

I loved Lorenzo but his entire family was batshit crazy. They were a handsome Italian bunch, originally from Naples, and all of the men were blessed with sexy olive skin, curly black hair, and bodies chiseled from stone. Half of them were cops and the other half lawyers. Lorenzo was the only firefighter. I'd been to a few Marino family reunions at the Bay and I'd witnessed firsthand their batshit craziness at its finest. Lorenzo's mom, admittedly, always did good Adam Sandler and Chris Rock impersonations, and his grandfather, Papa Marino, was dating Ukrainian twins only just over half his grandson's age, which meant we had fun making bets on when he was eventually going to get slapped with a child molestation lawsuit.

"Come on, Rae. He's a cop. You'll like him," Lorenzo promised, turning away from me and fixing his attention on the delicious smell coming from the oven. "His name's Paul."

"Yeah, babe," Ren seconded, handing me a glass of chilled red wine. "You'll like him. In fact, if I wasn't married to his mediocre cousin, I'd tap that ass."

"You want a spanking, Renée?" Lorenzo threatened without looking at her. He was busy taking the lasagna out.

"With your hands or a belt?" Renée teased.

"My hands."

"Bring it, baby. I love it when you punish me."

"Oh, Lord," I mumbled, sitting myself down at the tiny four-piece kitchen table. "Can't you wait until I leave?"

"Seriously, though," Renée murmured, plunking down opposite me as her husband moved around the kitchen behind her. "Something's wrong and I think a relationship, or one-night stand, would help. Paul would be safe."

I swallowed the remainder of my wine. "I think I'm done with men."

"Thinking of getting with females, huh?" Lorenzo shot me an adorable grin. "I wouldn't mind that."

"Pig," Ren shot at him.

"You love it."

My best friend sighed, giving me her full attention. "I'm worried about you, hon."

"Don't be," I said flippantly. "I'm good."

"I know you too well," she said sorrowfully, shaking her raven-haired head, "So I know you're lying."

Guilt pricked at me, but before I could say anything stupid, Lorenzo proudly announced, "Lunch is served, ladies." And hunger took precedence over everything else.

I was finally getting my first good night's sleep, when I felt the left side of the mattress beside me dip. Holding my breath, I mentally counted to five.

Deep breaths… Deep breaths… Deep…

Lips touched the bare skin of my shoulder and, even half-comatose, I knew they were Andrei's. Trembling, I squeezed my eyes shut, feeling his hands travel the length of my back. Now, I was wide awake.

"Get the fuck away from me."

His hand stilled. I took that opportunity to kick the covers off and slip out of bed, aware that I wasn't helping my case by being completely naked.

Andrei slowly and gracefully got off my bed and stood, his staggering height intimidating me for a millisecond. His hair was tamed into a low ponytail, his chest was strained in a tight black tee, and black denims hung low on his hips. In short, he looked like something on the menu of good sex—a menu I wasn't allowed to look at.

"I'm not your toy," I spat, grabbing the nightgown that was thrown over the armchair beside my bed. I furiously shrugged it on. "So you can get out. Now!"

His eyes were navy, a navy I was already all too familiar with. "You think you can order me around?"

"I think I know that you don't need to have sex. I think you're running on full tank. You don't need me."

He inclined his head to one side and I still felt naked. "You're right. I don't need it."

A thought suddenly occurred to me. "How'd you find me anyway?"

He held up one of my ankle bracelets, the one I'd had in my toilet bag in Vegas and hadn't gotten around to wearing. "I had this," he said, stepping around the bed and making his way to me. He shoved it into his pockets. "There's no place you can run to where I won't find you. It's like a compass."

I swallowed, more terrified than I was willing to admit. "Should I bow to you? I mean, you are a king. Is that what you do? Get a sex slave every twenty years? Am I the chosen one?"

His brow furrowed. "Who told you?"

I assumed he meant the first part, since I was being sarcastic about the last. "I wasn't supposed to know?"

"I don't particularly like mortals knowing my business."

"Oh, now you believe I'm human?" I snorted, and he grabbed my wrists and pulled me to him.

"Yes, because I discovered who your mother is," he replied glibly, his gaze undressing me and his touch scalding. "I also know that your father was a very unsuccessful hunter and I know that you spend your time making thousands of dollars off of jealous housewives."

"Let me go." I strained to get away and only ended up pressed against his hard, unyielding body. "I'll scream."

His erection strained against my abdomen. I felt myself get wet in response.

"The things I want to do to you," he murmured in my ear, his hot breath tickling me. "Despite how much you fight it, you want to fuck me." He gently sucked on my earlobe, eliciting a low moan from me. "You hate wanting me but you can't help it."

Crap! I thought, my knees turning to jelly.

"What do you want, Andrei?" I gasped. I knew my lust, my desire, how I was so damn hot for him, was what he fed off on. I knew it and yet I couldn't stop myself. "Tell me and get out."

"I want my cock inside you."

"Go to hell. That is not going to happen!" I screeched.

He released a low growl and scooped me up, throwing me over his shoulder. I writhed like a snake, screaming loudly, although there was no one anywhere near my house to hear me. It was isolated, just how my dad had wanted it.

Andrei ferried me to my bathroom, pushed aside the shower curtain of the old bathtub, and unceremoniously deposited me into it. I hadn't had the heart to demolish the house's original tub, and as a result, it was sitting tap to tap with the new, modern one.

"I'm going to kill you," I snarled, standing and trying to launch myself at Andrei.

He held me back, simultaneously ripping my shower curtain off the rail. "Quiet."

"Go to hell!" I spat, and he easily wrenched my gown off, flinging it over his shoulder. "Devil spawn!"

He got into the tub with me and, smoothly overpowering me, grabbed my arms, raising them over my head and binding my wrists to the rail with the shower curtain.

I bit back another scream, shooting him a death glare instead. Straining at the wrists was doing nothing, save for making the curtain dig into my skin. It felt like industrial rope.

Andrei was leaning against the tiled wall, his eyes drinking my naked body in. I was quite aware that my nipples were erect and that my breasts were aching to be caressed and kneaded to satisfaction. Furthermore, much as I tried to ignore the throbbing below my waist, my clit was so swollen it hurt.

I lowered my head, seething. Most of my anger was directed at myself. This kind of lust wasn't healthy. Lusting after a demon wasn't healthy. I looked up, scowling at him with my mouth firmly shut.

"You're going to beg me for it," Andrei said quietly, straightening up and tugging his T-shirt over his head.

My breath caught. He was playing dirty. Just the sight of his chest was enough to send me into a tailspin of unadulterated desire. I pulled at my restraints, but not to escape this time.

Andrei stood before me and cupped my breasts in his hands. The pads of his thumbs swept across the dusky tips of my nipples. I groaned, meeting Andrei's darkened eyes.

He lowered his head, capturing an aching nub with his mouth. He suckled on it, his hands sweeping down my sides and meeting at my pulsing apex.

I released a moan, spreading my legs slightly. It was shameless and it was wanton, but at that moment, I didn't give a damn. Andrei's finger teased my entrance and nudged against my already sensitized clit. It felt like he'd knocked over my insides. I moaned, unable to say the words I knew he wanted to hear.

"She says no, but she..." He thrust a long finger deep inside me. "... says yes."

I threw my head back and cried out, rocking against his hand as he slid another finger into me, feverishly thrusting and retreating, finger-fucking me until I couldn't see straight. Another finger slipped in and I swayed on my feet, dangerously close to coming. But Andrei chose that exact moment to withdraw from me.

I made a whimper of frustration, my entire body throbbing with the intense need to get off.

"I..." My voice trailed off. I couldn't say it. I just couldn't say it.

"You what?" Andrei growled, cupping my face.

I jerked my head away. "No." Begging just wasn't my style.

"Very well," he said in a low voice, and sank to his knees before me.

The sight of such a huge man kneeling before me—in a bath tub, no less—was such a turn-on, I thought I'd explode then and there. But he grabbed my thighs, angled his head and replaced his fingers with his tongue. He tortured my clit, the engorged bud of sensitive tissue weak in the face of such assault. I thrashed like a fish out of water, the shower curtain biting into my wrists, and screamed from the agonizing pleasure.

Andrei held me steady, his tongue flickering in and out of me, igniting a match somewhere inside my body. He licked his way up and down my slit and I pressed my opening into his face, wishing he could shove his whole face inside me and make me come just... like... that.

My orgasm was surging forward, building up inside me and threatening to liquefy me. But then, like before, Andrei pulled away.

I made an unintelligible protest, my knees practically giving way.

"Beg for it," he ordered, looking up at me. My juices were glistening on his lips and I groaned in frustration at the hot image he presented.

Beg. He was probably used to people begging him. He was a king, after all.

Well, I had pride. I had never been bullied into doing anything in my entire life and I wasn't about to start now with him.

"My arms hurt," I said, my voice hoarse. Not to mention the fact that the iron rail was pressing uncomfortably against my wrist bones.

Andrei rose, his brows knitting together. "You're stubborn."

"I thought I pissed you off," I said through clenched teeth, looking up at him defiantly. "Why do you still want me? You said you wouldn't...."

Then his lips assaulted my mouth and the rest of my sentence was cut off. His tongue dueled with mine, ever forceful. I moaned, vaguely horrified that just his searching tongue was enough to make me come. I shuddered, eyes shut, and could feel my juices trickling down my inner thighs, yet I wasn't satisfied. Not even close.

My eyes opened in time to watch Andrei's jeans come off and, as usual, he came with protection. Now that I knew that demons could have offspring with humans, I was doubly grateful.

A minute later, he wrapped my legs around his waist and his big, hard cock was deliciously midway inside me, rubbing against my clit. One arm was below my ass and the other was around my lower back. He was completely supporting me, which was good because my legs were quickly becoming boneless.

He thrust into me to the root, bouncing me on the thick length of his cock, and I felt heat engulf my body as he filled me up so completely. With each new thrust, I was coming undone. I screamed his name, I begged him not to stop, I told him I loved what he did to me—I came.

Andrei thrust, withdrew, thrust, withdrew, and held onto me tightly when he finally exploded, his body tensing before he spilled his cum into the condom. I tightened myself around him, milking him dry and driving myself half-mental when he erupted inside me again.

He searched for my mouth and I willingly gave it to him, allowing his tongue entry. Still buried inside me, he raised a hand to undo my restraints and I gratefully looped my arms around his neck as he stepped out of the tub.

He walked me back to my bedroom and set me down on the bed, slowly moving out of me, his eyes fixed on the place where we were joined.

I felt a frisson of excitement shoot through me when he gently pushed my hair out of my face.

"I can be so good to you," he said quietly, his hands traveling lower, to my collar bone, "yet you make me take you as if it's against your will."

I mewled when his knuckles skimmed my breasts.

"Any time I want you, Rainelle, I will have you," he whispered, tweaking my nipples with deft fingers. "You with me?"

I shut my eyes, biting my lower lip.

"You with me?" he repeated, tugging the hard nubs with his fingers.

I gasped, my eyes flying opening. Heat pooled in my abdomen and I felt that I was ready for him again.

"No," I whispered, and I dragged my ass up on the bed and sat up, hugging myself. "I don't want this. I don't want you. And if you think for a second that I'm going to lie down and allow you to… to have me, you have another think coming, Your Majesty!" I was breathing heavily, both out of breath and scared shitless by the ominous look Andrei was currently giving me.

He stood up, closing his eyes. In the blink of an eye, he was dressed. I stifled a panicked breath. Would I ever get used to that? I mean, I had never been a fan of magicians.

"What you don't seem to understand," he began, "is that for the first time in a millennia, I'm not fucking because I have to. I'm fucking because I want to." He edged onto my bed, keeping his eyes on me. "Sex with mortals is infinitely better than sex with another demon. And you, Rainelle, have hunter's blood in you. There are no records of a hunter mating with a demon... until now. And goddammit, now that I know that hunter's pussy is the best kind, you're not getting away from me." He spread my legs apart and pulled me onto his lap so I was straddling him. "As long as you do what I say," he said, bringing my hand to the front of his jeans, "you don't have to be afraid of me."

"I'm not afraid of you."

"Good," he said, grabbing the back of my neck and pulling me into a kiss.

I kissed him back, automatically rubbing my clit against the impressive denim-covered bulge in his pants. My hands cupped the sides of his face as we became more frantic and my chafing against him quickened.

Andrei was the first to pull away. "Get some sleep."

"You're... going?"

He gave me a wry smile. "You want me to stay?"

"No," I said fervently. "Get out."

Andrei's lips curled. "Tomorrow night, you'll suck my cock."

I looked away, unable to hide how much the prospect aroused me. "You won't find me tomorrow."

"You are mine now, Rainelle. I will always find you."

Chapter 5

"Renée, you and your husband are dead to me," I hissed, massaging my temples with two fingers as I scowled into the vanity mirror in my best friend's bedroom. "Dead, you hear me?"

She giggled, blindsiding me from behind and spritzing her fruity perfume into my neck. "You'll thank me when you've gotten some nice Italian sex with a nice Italian," was her response to my serious threat. "Now, you smell like you're ready!"

I whirled away from my reflection, glaring at her. "You're impossible!"

When I'd called Ren up that morning and asked her if I could come over for dinner, I never would have expected her to phone Paul Marino, one of Lorenzo's eligible first cousins, and invite him over as well. It was underhanded, it was unwelcome, and it was just like Renée Colette Marino, née Russo.

Sure, Paul was my type—tall, dark and devilishly handsome, and smart to boot. But I didn't need to be hooked up right now. Even if I wanted to hook up with him, I felt so raw and beaten up after being with Andrei, I wouldn't be much of a lay. Besides, Paul was a cop, ergo, a good guy. Good guys generally didn't fall for women like me. Case in point, Daniel Lawless. Evil guys were the type that went for me. Case in point, a demon lord that went by the name of Andrei Anghelescu.

I tried to tell myself that my reluctance to get hooked up wasn't because I'd been "claimed" by a demon king. And that I was only over at the Marino house for sanctuary because said demon had promised to swing by that night for a blowjob. But I was only lying to myself.

"Get your cute little butt downstairs and make nice, Rae Erickson," Ren ordered, giving me a gentle push toward her bedroom door.

I'd been hiding out in there for a while now.

"Paul's a catch, and so are you. I'm going to help my baby with the dishes and you are going to get back to the living room and seduce the shit out of Paul, okay? OK."

"Has anyone ever told you how bossy you are?" I muttered, marching out of her room. Renée was the only person—okay, the only living person—on this planet that had the power to push me around. Older than me by a year, she'd always acted like she had a decade over me, and often assumed an annoying big-sister role.

"I'm a regular dominatrix," she replied from behind me, and I smiled, approaching the stairs.

Back in the living room, Paul was kicking back on Lorenzo's beat-up leather recliner, watching some classic football game his cousin had recorded. His big Converse-covered feet were on the cluttered coffee table, and a bottle of Heineken was in his hand.

"Hey," I said, forcing some cheer into my voice and sitting on the couch nearest to him. I realized it wasn't his fault I wasn't in the mood to be pushed into his lap.

"You okay?" he asked, taking his feet off the table and sitting up. "You look flushed."

"Just the heat," I replied, fanning myself for good measure. It was hot. "So how's work?"

I felt guilty for not asking him earlier. Dinner had been a forced affair because, like a sullen teen, I'd wordlessly poked at my plate of Lorenzo's scrumptious spaghetti and meatballs, refusing to make Renée's matchmaking any easier. Conversation had passed over my head while Renée shot daggers at me, which I could feel even though I barely glanced at her.

"Oh, you know, the usual," Paul told me, guzzling down the rest of his beer before slamming the empty can on the table. "I'm practically on desk duty." Sallow Bay isn't exactly crime free but cops here didn't get a lot of real action.

"Sucks," I remarked sincerely, and he gave me a curious look.

"What about you? How's the book going?"

I almost asked him what the hell he was on about when I, thankfully, remembered that everyone I knew in Sallow Bay thought I was an eccentric nomadic writer. It was better than telling them I stalked married men in exchange for four figures or so in my bank account. No one would understand why little old Rae Erickson, who'd gone to business school before her poor father mysteriously passed away, was now a private investigator specializing in suspected infidelity cases. They wouldn't get what Renée got, that it was personal for me.

"Slow," was my response to Paul's question.

"Yeah?" he went, his green eyes boring into me. "What's it about this time?"

"Angels and… demons." I reddened, averting my eyes. Now why had I said that? *Because that's what's on your mind*, my inner voice helpfully pointed out. *Not to mention in your pants!*

"Interesting. I think I read about half of Dan Brown's book before I got bored." Paul leaned back in his seat, brushing aside a few errant dark curls out of his face. "But your book'll probably be as fascinating as you are."

Paul Marino was sweet—too sweet for me.

"Did Lorenzo and Ren tell you I was desperate for a good lay?" I asked, sighing heavily.

He choked on something imaginary and straightened up. "What?"

"Because I'm not. You seem really nice, Paul, and any other time, I would've wanted to sleep with you. You're sexy. Totally fuckable." I paused as he choked again. "It's just that I'm going through something personal and I don't need any more complications in my life and you would definitely be a complication."

"Rae," he said, after he'd collected himself, "I, uh, think there's been a… misunderstanding."

"What did they say about me?"

"That you've been having a tough time recently. I'm just here as a friend." His eyes, so identical to his cousin's, were sincere. "At least, I'd like to be a friend. I mean, I've only met you a couple of times before and those few times, we didn't even speak. But you seemed real cool."

Why can't I have a good guy? I thought, breaking into a rueful smile.

I was going to say that I'd really, really like that, when Ren ambled into the room, her eyebrows doing that thing they did when she was ready to burst with excitement. I was going to have to let her down easy if she was keyed up about Paul and me.

"Rae, you didn't tell me you had a visitor," she said breathlessly, looking down at me with animated eyes. She gave Paul an apologetic look. "Sorry, hon. This one's a real competition."

"What are you on about?" I asked, getting to my feet.

It was at that precise moment that I saw Andrei casually standing by the entrance to the living room like he belonged there, a bottle of beer in his hand and the darkened look of unmistakable lust on his face.

"If you hurt my friends, I will find someone that can kill you," I hissed at Andrei as menacingly as I possibly could in the privacy of Renée and Lorenzo's matchbox-sized downstairs toilet. We were practically pressed up against each other, something that was doing dangerous things to my nervous system.

From the unruffled look on Andrei's face, he didn't find me the least bit menacing. "Now why would I hurt your friends? They gave me beer."

Well, he didn't look like he was here to kill people. In a royal purple cashmere sweater and black jeans with his long hair hanging loose, he looked... normal. Like he'd genuinely come over to hang out on a Saturday evening.

But looks could be so damn deceiving.

"Why else would you be here?" I snapped, folding my arms across my chest and glaring at him.

"I believe I scheduled your mouth around my cock for tonight." He reached out and carelessly flicked a strand of my hair out of my face. "Hiding out at your friend's house was a big waste of time."

I couldn't believe he'd said the first part. I squeezed my eyes shut, breathing in deeply. When I opened them, he was standing right in front of me, his intense blue eyes boring into mine.

"I enjoy defiling you, Rainelle. You have to have realized that by now."

Oh, my God, I thought, heat engulfing my cheeks and other places on my body. *I would never get used to how blunt he was about what he did to me.*

"Don't you have anything better to do? Like, I don't know, rule a dark and evil underworld kingdom?"

His eyes flickered with annoyance. "You ask too many questions." And he silenced me with his mouth against mine.

His lips weren't the only things on me. His hands were slipping up the hem of my dress, dancing up my belly and quickly finding the lace cups of my bra.

"Mm," I murmured into his mouth, clutching the front of his sweater. Even if incubus seduction didn't work on me, Andrei seduction was proving to be a force to be reckoned with. "I want you so bad." It sounded like a cheesy line from a teenage porno flick and I was instantly mortified that it had come out of my mouth.

"You already have me," Andrei groaned, hoisting me up onto the porcelain rim of the sink behind me. "Here. Now. Open up for me."

"Yes," I hissed, hardly able to believe that I was about to have sex in my best friend's downstairs toilet while she, her husband, and his cousin unwittingly sat in the living room watching TV.

The only thing I could say was that I was glad East Coast weather had made me wear this stupidly short dress. All Andrei had to do was hike the skirt up, move my panties aside and fuck me senseless... which he did.

He had the condom on in seconds—no doubt one of the perks of being a demon—and was balls-deep inside me in a flash, drawing out a suprised cry from my mouth. My legs were coiled around his waist and then our lips were locked, his tongue slowly fucking my mouth in sync to the quick, sharp thrusts of his cock.

In, out, in, out, in, out... Andrei felt so... right inside me, so deliciously perfect. I clenched around his length, dragging a muffled curse from his mouth as his grasp around me tightened in answer.

I couldn't deny it any longer. Being with him was the first time I'd ever felt so fully sexually awakened. I'd had lots of sex before Andrei. But looking back, it was as if all I'd been doing was rolling around with Ken dolls. It wasn't even because Andrei was a demon, although that probably factored into it, but it was because of the sheer animalistic power he exerted. When he was inside me, he owned me.

That's so sexist, my inner voice chided. She was a die-hard feminist.

"Come for me," he murmured in the low, slightly-accented and sexy voice he used when he was close to orgasm himself. He was moving around inside me, his cock hitting every sensitive inch of my inner walls and I was seconds away from doing what he just told me to.

I moaned, arching my back as white-hot liquid heat bathed me and I came in a series of spurts.

But Andrei wasn't done.

"Milk me dry," he ordered, grunting when I squeezed him inside me. He sucked on my bottom lip. "That's it. Take my cock. Make me come."

"I'm... going... to... come," I gasped, still not used to climaxing so soon after the first time.

"Do it."

I did it. My second orgasm was only made better by the fact that Andrei was playing with my clit, teasing that little swollen, hardened knob and sending jolts of electricity throughout my body.

When it was over and I made a weak attempt at looking like I hadn't just gotten some under my best friend's roof. Then Andrei said, "We're leaving now."

I narrowed my eyes at his reflection in the minuscule mirror, my strength returning to me in full force. "Are we now?" I snorted. "You need to take a heavy dose of go-fuck-yourself before you even so much as think of ordering me around again like some lackey."

"I am far from satisfied," Andrei said, pointedly ignoring my rebuff. He punctuated his sentence by pressing himself into me and I felt his growing erection dig into my lower back. He was far from satisfied, all right.

I spun around and it was now pressed into my front. Bad idea. It was hard to think in this position, hard to remember that I wasn't supposed to want this.

"You will not spend another minute with that man," he said, his voice low and menacing. It was obvious that he meant Paul, but that wasn't what had me so puzzled. No, it was the

78

fact that he almost—almost—sounded humanly jealous, like a possessive boyfriend.

"You have no claim on me," I told him, forcing myself to meet his eyes. "I just met you last weekend! Even you have to see how ridiculous this is."

He cupped my chin in one hand. "The fact that I've had you more than once means that I do, indeed, have a claim on you," he stated, running the pad of his thumb across my kiss-swollen lower lip. "Incubi do not sleep with the same person more than once. If they do, it means that they have staked a claim on that individual. You're a smart woman. I think you know what I'm getting at."

The hairs on the back of my neck stood up. "Why do you want me?"

"Because sex with you is not just for feeding," Andrei replied, his gaze sweeping over my body, "and you enjoy it. Not because I've beguiled you, but because you're genuinely attracted to me. Like I said, after existing for a billion years, that is… refreshing."

I blushed furiously. "I don't enjoy it. I don't know what's happening to me but I know that this…" I gestured between him and me. "… is wrong."

"Is that so?"

"Yes," I said, bothered by the wild accusation that I enjoyed sex with a demon. "And by the way, you don't have to beguile anyone into sleeping with you. You have to know how hot you are as a human."

His lips quirked into a half-smile, which only made him look infinitely more handsome. "You think I'm hot?"

I rolled my eyes at him.

"Granted, but that's not what I meant," he said seriously. "Even if I don't have to outright seduce a woman, they're usually comatose when I'm through with them."

Something clenched in my belly. "And I suppose you don't kill."

"That would be sloppy of me."

"Then how would you explain...?"

"Enough." His face became an impassive mask as he stepped back from me. "We'll talk later," he ground out, and vanished into thin air.

I had no idea how I was going to explain his vanishing act to my friends. The living room was practically adjacent to this toilet.

There were already flowers at my father's grave and they'd obviously been put there recently. Kneeling before his tombstone, I picked the bouquet up (they were dahlias and I got the distinct impression that they were more expensive than my roses) and sniffed them before putting them back and arranging them beside my bunch.

"Looks like you still have a few admirers, Daddy," I murmured, slowly tracing my fingertips over the *Christoph Raymond Erickson* engraved on the marble stone.

I knew most of the townspeople had loved my father, we were sort of a close-knit community. But he'd never been the same after Lauren's disappearance and, as a result, had pushed most of his friends away. They had, of course, stubbornly continued to reach out, especially for his little daughter's sake. But the only people my father had truly communicated with then were fellow hunters.

Like Teddy Bunting.

I hadn't seen Teddy in years but my earliest memory of him was one evening shortly after Lauren's disappearance, when he'd come over toting old books with weird symbols on it, spouting interesting things about witches, wards, and banishings. Teddy's wife was a witch and, if I'd heard correctly from my hideout under my father's desk in his study, she knew how to put up wards to keep supernatural creatures away from our house—if that was what my father wanted.

"No," he'd told Teddy, "I want them to come here. Or I'll go to them. I won't hide behind magic like a coward."

"Think about Rainelle," Teddy had said, his raspy voice grim.

"I am. She'll grow up knowing how to go after demons. All of them."

That was what he'd thought. Instead, I grew up to sleep with the king of them all.

Sighing heavily, I plopped onto the grass on his grave, plucking a tuft of it and scattering it over the flowers.

"I know you must be disappointed in me," I whispered, "and I don't blame you. I couldn't even kill Lauren for you." I paused, considering this. "Is that what you would've wanted? Were you trying to kill her all that time? I wish I'd listened to you about this shit, instead of burying my head in the sand like a damn idiot." I let out a bitter laugh. "She had a son with that creature. Can you believe that?!" The tang of salt was suddenly in my mouth and I violently wiped at my eyes, refusing to break down completely. "I don't want to believe that you died still loving her. I want to believe that you'd buried her before I buried you."

Someone cleared their throat behind me.

"You don't have to do that, Ren," I said, my voice calm, and she sat beside me in a cloud of black chiffon and Chanel No. 5.

"I looked for you at Mass," she said softly, placing a lone red rose on top of the flowers before her.

"I should've told you I wouldn't be coming."

I was scared to death of being struck down by a lightning bolt for being a demon lover and trying to set foot on holy ground. It was irrational but I was equally afraid that Father Brady would point one wizened finger at me and cry "Unclean!" in front of everyone. I had an active imagination.

"Everything okay?" Renée asked, and I could feel her eyes fixed on me.

"I'm fine, Ren. I just… hate coming back here."

She sighed. "Oh, Rae. I know you do. I understand."

No, I thought bitterly. *You don't.*

"Is your friend still here? Andrei, right?"

"No. He's gone," I replied.

"Weird guy. Weird but hot. I mean, what was up with that thing about doors?"

I'd spun a story about Andrei's phobia of doors and how he had to abruptly leave through the toilet window last night. It seemed more believable than telling them that he'd teleported out of the house. The fact that he'd come in through the front door didn't seem to register with them. Heineken probably had something to do with that.

I gave Renée a sideways glance. "You're married."

"Yeah, but that doesn't mean I'm blind," she quipped, her voice high-pitched. "Jesus, Rae, and we were trying to hook you up with Paul. I feel stupid. Why didn't you tell me you had some hot guy hanging all over you?"

"Paul said he wanted friendship," I muttered, "and I don't have Andrei. He's just an acquaintance."

"Sure. An acquaintance you did the nasty with in my toilet."

I jumped. I couldn't help it. "What?!"

Renée laughed into the cool morning air. "I'm not stupid, hon. Lorenzo and I have enough sex for me to know what it smells like!"

I blushed, finally looking at her. "I'm so sorry, Ren. I swear, I hadn't meant for that to happen and he really is just a person I vaguely know so...."

"Babe," she interjected, holding a hand up, "I love you, okay? I'm just mad that it looks like you're keeping secrets from me and I'm supposed to be your best friend."

Now I felt guilty. But I looked away and said, "I wish I could tell you everything."

"Then tell me," she gently prodded, taking my hands in hers. "Please, Rae. I want to be your friend. I want to be your sister."

How could I tell her my mother was still alive but hadn't aged a day? Or that I also had a half-brother who was a half-demon?

"You're my only family, Ren," I murmured, tears collecting at my eyes again. I squeezed her hands. "And I love you, too."

But I couldn't tell her everything. So I chose to tell her about the safest thing I knew and something I hadn't thought about in a little while: mooning over Daniel Lawless.

Chapter 6

This was against my usual protocol but I found that I was genuinely thrown by Ana Fontaine. I told myself that this was the only reason I'd agreed to meet her at a cute bistro on the Left Bank—in broad daylight, no less. But the truth was that I was human and therefore allowed to get a little star-struck by a famous fashion designer that rang me up out of the blue. Face-to-face meetings were usually saved for after I'd done the job. However, since this was the age of technology, most of the time, they weren't necessary at all.

"I am quite sorry that I have made you come here," she said apologetically, her voice thick with an accent.

Sitting opposite me in a chic paisley blouse and elegant black pants, she looked every bit the renowned fashion designer that she was. What she didn't look like was a woman scorned and out to get some proof of it.

"It's quite all right," I said sincerely, eyeing her phone sitting on the table. It had been vibrating incessantly since we sat down at a window-side table inside the bistro. Ana had

steadfastly ignored it. "I was… intrigued when you called me."
Not to mention excited.

And it didn't matter which city I "ran" to anyway. The sale had recently come through, so I was in my new Parisian penthouse this week. Andrei Anghelescu could teleport and find me in a heartbeat. In fact, when he started unceremoniously dropping in every few days, my body welcomed him with open legs. And I was afraid that I was starting to look forward to his impromptu visits. I mean, I'd even gone back on the pill. I couldn't even deny that I experience a certain high when, with every ejaculation, he'd fill me up with his hot semen. And since business had been relatively quiet, I usually had nothing to do, which meant that he always found me lounging around, virtually waiting for him. So I was over the moon when Ana Fontaine rang me up, told me she knew I was in Paris, and asked if I could meet her at Chocolat for coffee. Although, there was also the little-known fact that I had a few Ana Fontaine LBDs in my closet, so she was kind of a celebrity to me. I would never say that aloud though. Still, it was a bit unnerving to discover that she knew my phone number and location when I was supposedly flying under the radar.

"Yes, I suppose you would be… intrigued," Ana was saying, giving me a weak smile. "After all, I have no lover to speak of."

"Exactly," I told her.

"I don't enjoy beating around the bush," Ana said, her face suddenly grim. "I need you to follow my brother."

"Your brother?"

Incestuous, creepy little woman, was the first thought that flashed through my mind. *Is she sleeping with him? Is she jealous he might be cheating on her? How am I going to look at her now?*

She smiled, none the wiser about my mental conclusion of her. "You did not know, of course. Few do. He is the product of our late father's affair with an employee." She dug into the adorable blood-red leather tote on her lap, pulled out a photograph, and slid it across the varnished table. "Jean-Philippe. He goes by JP."

There was zero resemblance between Ana and her brother. In the photo, he had his arm wrapped around a bikini-clad redhead in front of a swimming pool. Where Ana was fair, JP was dark. Her eyes were a piercing blue while his looked grey. She was an elfin woman while JP was a giant. She was sporting a few wrinkles on her face while her brother looked to be about a decade younger.

"He's only thirty-two," Ana spoke up, as if reading my mind.

"Oh," I said, pushing the photo back to her. I looked up. "Why exactly do you want me to follow your brother?"

Please don't say you're sleeping with him... Please don't say you're sleeping with him...

Ana looked mildly embarrassed. "Because I believe he's involved in something illegal."

"What would that be?" I sputtered, blindsided yet relieved.

"I... don't know," she said softly, clasping her fingers on the table. "JP was a problem child. And after our respective parents passed away, I had to raise him for the better part of our adult lives. He dropped out of school and wanted to become a DJ, despite my telling him not to." She sucked in a deep breath, laughing bitterly. "Now, he works for a man called Damien Ivanov, a character I don't particularly like because it is

86

rumored that he has ties to the Russian mob. JP says all he's doing is DJ-ing at a nightclub Damien owns here in Paris but..." Her voice trailed off and her brow furrowed. "My brother is not a bad man but I think Damien is using him somehow. He hasn't been himself lately."

"Meaning?" I forced myself to ask.

"He's... different," Ana replied, her brow crinkling. "The last time I saw him, he was with these strange girls, women who seemed a little off. He was keeping them in his apartment for some reason, and yet... and yet he seemed afraid of them—or for them. I'm very sure that that Russian is involved."

"Ana," I said soothingly, "I don't know what you heard but I usually get intel on cheating husbands. I'm like *Cheaters* but way classier and more discreet. No violent confrontations, for a start. I don't follow drug users and prostitutes around."

"Miss Erickson, you come highly recommended. I would not have asked you if this was not so."

"Thanks, but you're talking about the *Russian mob*," I hissed in trepidation. "I'm not sure I..."

"I don't want you to follow Damien. Just my brother."

I bit my bottom lip. "You're hoping I find out about those girls, too? Why can't you just call the cops? Or the— what is it?—gendarmes? That's their job."

"JP will inevitably get into trouble if I do that," Ana said practically. "This way, I can find out what's what and strategize. I only want to know, Miss Erickson. I doubt you will be at risk."

I sighed. What Ana Fontaine was asking of me was ludicrous. I was hardly a secret spy and my technology amounted to a Nikon, BlackBerry, and laptop. The only weapon I had the balls to carry was a Rampuri knife and I'd

87

never even used it, save for scraping the occasional gum off the soles of my suede boots. This was crazy!

Ana seemed to sense my inner turmoil. "I will, of course, generously compensate you." Her gaze became fierce. "If my brother is involved in shady dealings, I must know so that I can help him get out of any mess."

I looked at the older woman, amazed. She called him her brother when they didn't share the same mother. She clearly adored him. I was instantly reminded of Temp. Would I ever feel this sort of affection for him?

No, because he's a demon spawn.

"Okay," I heard myself say. "I'll do it."

"Do you know a guy called Damien Ivanov?"

His head on one end and motorcycle boots hanging over the other, Andrei arched a brow from his comfy sprawl on my couch. "What do you want with him?"

"Yes, or no?" I countered, unfurling myself from the recliner beside him so I could stretch.

He sat up, his eyes darkening—with anger, not lust. "Don't fuck around with me, Rainelle. I ask a question, I get an answer."

I frowned. "I'm not one of your minions. I don't answer to you."

He gave me a final glare and stood up, stomping out of the living room and leaving me alone with *Shaun of the Dead* continuing in the background. I was innocently watching the movie when Andrei appeared out of nowhere. I was getting used to that. But instead of attacking me like he usually did, he lounged on my couch and watched the movie I silently put on.

It was surprisingly… nice… to just be with him.

Now, I'd ruined it. He was pissed off about the Ivanov thing. He obviously knew the guy and didn't want me anywhere near him. Well, Andrei might be a king, but I sure as hell had no allegiance to him.

Actually, I like fighting with him.

The thought came out of nowhere but it was true. I enjoyed coming to blows with Andrei because after—or sometimes, during—he'd pleasure me in ways that were wicked and inconceivable, and left me panting for air. I was becoming addicted to him, the same way he was addicted to me.

Maybe this is how Lauren started out with Vitaly, I thought, my brow creasing. No, I couldn't start comparing myself to my mother.

There was no way in hell I was going to be as stupid as she had been, and fall in love with the freaking lord of sex demons, and have permanently horny demon babies. *No way in hell!*

"I know Ivanov," Andrei's deep voice startled me from behind my recliner. I looked up at his imposing face looming over me. "Does he have a wife I don't know about? A wife who's contacted you?" he continued, his face impassive.

I got up and sighed, staring him down. "There's a woman who has a brother involved with him. She wants me to tail her brother. I just want to know what I'm getting myself into, so don't get your panties in a twist."

Andrei's eyes blazed a traffic-light red and I instinctively took a step back. "You're not getting into anything because you're not getting involved. Period."

"Oh, I wasn't aware you were my protective boyfriend, here to save me from myself," I quipped, warily watching him as he rounded the couch and shoved his face into mine.

"You'll only get yourself killed, you stupid bitch."

Furious, I reached up to whack him across the face, but he caught my wrist midway, spun me around and held me to him with an arm firmly coiled around my waist.

"Listen to me, Rainelle, and listen pretty fucking good," he snarled into my ear, shaking me. "This guy is a common breed of... human that makes my kind look like the direct descendants of Mother Teresa. He's already got a one-way ticket to hell, fully paid for." His hand fanned out across my belly. "You with me? If you so much as breathe in his direction, you'll interest him, and you do not want to interest Ivanov."

My breathing grew rapid and I was trembling with suppressed rage. Oh, how I longed to beat the horse crap out of this guy, demon or not. I was even considering joining ranks with the hunters just to get a chance to do it. But I stood there passively, my heart pounding at an insane rate against my chest from adrenaline.

"Does every Russian on the planet know each other?" I asked through clenched teeth.

"Who said I'm Russian?"

I wasn't about to admit my initial nickname for him. It was too embarrassingly juvenile.

"If you want me to kill him, all you have to do is say the word," Andrei whispered when I didn't answer his very valid question.

"I don't want you to kill him!" I snapped in annoyance. "I don't know the guy!"

"Then promise me you won't go anywhere near him."

90

"I won't," I muttered, squirming in his mock-embrace. "I won't go near him." *I'll be at a safe distance with my camera, of course.*

"Good girl," Andrei murmured, his hand dipping low and tracing the waistband of my sweatpants.

"Don't. I already want to hit you," I mumbled churlishly.

He surprised me by laughing, a strange, deep sound that rang out so near my ear. "Do you think that would make you feel better?"

"Absolutely."

Andrei released me, turning me to face him. "Then go for it."

I had never tied anyone up but I'd watched a hell of a lot of movies and—considering the fact that I wouldn't let Andrei use his demon magic to tie himself up—I guessed I had been watching pretty closely.

The single high-backed wooden chair I had in my bedroom was dwarfed by Andrei's sheer size. I'd bought it at an antique store while roaming the lesser known *rues* of Paris. It was ancient, stately-looking despite having no armrests, and completely out of place in my modernized bedroom.

I stood back from Andrei, admiring my handiwork. Thick, industrial rope bound his denim-clad legs to the chunky wooden legs of the chair, as well as his hands behind the back of it. He was naked from the waist up, his upper chest had a smattering of dark hair that peppered down his stomach and into the waist of his jeans.

"Why are you letting me do this?" I questioned—when really, I was wondering why I wanted to hurt him, and why the prospect made me wet in my innermost nook.

Andrei looked up at me, his gaze dark. "Because I want you to."

He didn't have to explain. The jut of his erection in his pants said more than enough.

"But you'll heal, right?"

"Do you want me to?"

"No."

"Then I won't."

I ran my tongue across my upper lip. "If you want to, you can get out of the rope?"

He gave me a wry smile. "In the blink of an eye."

I considered this. "Well, don't. This will be so therapeutic for me." Taking a deep breath, I slipped on the knuckle duster Andrei had so graciously provided for me. It felt soothing, iron on skin, and I folded my hand into a fist, testing the weight out first.

"What are you waiting for?" Andrei goaded, his eyes flashing a dark red.

Exactly. *What was I waiting for?* I knew I was going to enjoy this, knew I was going to be hitting my mother, Temp, Vitaly, and every other demon I'd come across and done shit to—when I hit him. This was going to be more than healing. It was going to save my sanity.

"This is for breaking into my hotel room," I said to myself, and I delivered the first blow to his cheek, the sound of metal hitting bone filling my ears.

Andrei's head jerked to the side but he made no noise. Blood instantly ran, red and brilliant, from his flesh and made contact with my fist. I winced, although I knew that I probably didn't hurt him at all. And true to his word, he didn't allow himself to heal.

"Feel better?" he coolly inquired, the masculine perfection of his face marred by the bleeding gash.

"Not yet." And I struck him again, the sickening crunch of his nose sending goosebumps of intense pleasure up my spine. "That... Well, that's for giving it to me so good."

Blood was spurting from his nose in a steady, brilliant flow, splotches of it spattering onto his bare chest, bright red on russet. I sucked in a deep breath, squeezing my eyes shut. It was so twisted how... aroused I was from hitting him, from drawing blood—his blood. It made him seem so human to me, vulnerable. And it made me feel a delicious power that was so strong, I sensed it in my throbbing clit.

I was a sick and depraved human being. My conscience told me to stop but the anger I felt at myself for being so attracted to him, among other things, propelled me to land another venom-filled punch to his face—his jaw this time.

"And that's for calling me a bitch," I spat, and his face crinkled into a weird, pained half-smile. "A stupid bitch. No one calls me a stupid bitch, asshole. What the hell are you grinning about?"

Andrei tilted his head and spat blood out onto my carpet. "I am going to... fuck your brains out." His voice sounded husky, probably on account of his possibly broken nose and equally busted chin.

I hit him again, splitting his lower lip. "That's for tying me up in my own home that one time. I don't get treated like that. I'm a woman."

"You're only making me hard."

I socked him in the gut and he tensed in surprise, barely doubling over. "That's for ruining my life. My life is

93

ruined, Andrei." I flexed my hand, throwing him a death stare. "If my father were still alive, he'd disown me. You're a demon. You're evil." I reached out and lightly pressed a finger to the wound on the side of his face. "You're a demon," I repeated, wanting this to sink into my thick skull.

More than anything, I was scared. Scared that something this unnatural could feel so good, especially this fast. Scared that his grip on me was more than sexual attraction but something deeper, something I could never hope to understand. I was scared shitless of becoming Lauren.

I unbuckled his belt and unzipped him, letting his cock spring free. Sinking to my knees between the V of his long legs, I looked up into his blood-spattered face. "Under no circumstances do you get loose." And I curled my fingers around his rigid shaft, moving my hand up and down the swollen flesh, entranced by its thickness, and stiffness. "I hate owing people."

The tip of his cock was glistening and I rubbed the pad of my finger over it, lowering my tongue to catch the tiny, transparent bead of moisture that had already seeped out of the tiny hole on the head. As always, he tasted of hot, animal masculinity. I licked the throbbing veins of his shaft and I sucked on him, wanting to draw out more of his seed. This was the first time I'd ever put him in my mouth and the salty taste of him was indescribable.

Andrei made a low groan in his throat, his breathing becoming ragged. My fingers moved to weigh the heavy sac of his balls, feeling them tighten in my hand as I gently stroked them. The product of his arousal was in there, just waiting to spatter into my mouth and finally, inside my cunt.

"Fuck, Rae," Andrei breathed out, jerking his hips. "Suck me dry... with that little mouth... of yours."

I took as much of his curved length into said little mouth as I could, my own desire swirling in the pit of my belly and making it difficult to focus. Andrei jerked into me, ravaging my mouth and growling when my teeth lightly grazed his girth. My cheeks hollowed and my strokes quickened in determination to make him explode in my mouth.

When he finally did, roaring in a language that was foreign to me, I swallowed it, raising my head to look at him when I was done. His face was astonishingly blood-and-gash free and I figured he couldn't help healing if he was in the throes of passion. I stood up and pulled my T-shirt off—the motion was torture for my painful, pebbled nipples—and tugged my pants down, stepping out of them completely naked.

I moved to sit astride Andrei, my hands on his shoulders, and slowly lowered myself onto his manhood. A sharp moan left my lips as my aroused opening welcomed the entrance of his slick hardness. Holding onto him, I lifted myself off his cock and lowered myself again, purring contentedly as he filled me. He thrust upward and my nails dug into his bare skin as I bucked against him, wanting him deeper.

Somewhere along the line, the rope came undone—or disappeared, and his hands greedily tormented my skin as he held onto me. Our mouths connected—mine greedy, his tantalizingly domineering—and we came in unison, my cries of pleasure filling the night and drowning out his animal-like, guttural moans.

For a long while after, we sat like that and then he picked me up and lay me on the carpet, semi-hard inside me.

"Feel better?" he asked, slanting his mouth to capture the hard tip of my breast.

I mewled, spearing my fingers into his now unruly hair. He was twisting my other nipple between his thumb and forefinger and an oh-so-sweet pain ricocheted through my breast when he pulled, elongating the hardened nub.

"No," I gasped, feeling him move inside me.

His cock was coming to life again and I wasn't sure I'd be able to take it another time.

"Fucking listen to... me," he growled.

Even as my mouth protested, my body gave silent acquiescence, wet and throbbing and oh-so-ready for him. I allowed him to kiss me again, our lips brushing briefly before his tongue flickered inside, mimicking the slow, lazy strokes of his cock.

My hands were in the silk of his long, unruly hair, gathering it to me, and my hips bucked, meeting his every searching thrust as desire overwhelmed me. He took my hand in his, lowering it to the jigsaw puzzle of our joining.

"Feel us," he groaned into my neck, and my hand came between us to the place where we met... felt the moistened length of his cock as he gradually retreated... felt the dripping heat of my opening as it gratefully received him again.

I whimpered, arching my back, completely surrendering to Andrei's dominance over my body this time. His strokes quickened, became more frantic as he drove even deeper inside me, nudging my womb. He bit down into my neck as a long, violent orgasm overtook him and the feel of him emptying himself in hot, thick spurts pushed me to yet another earth-shattering climax. Tightening my core around him, I came, blinded by the almost painful ecstasy and quivering in the aftershocks.

Andrei rolled me over so that I was on top and our hot, sweaty bodies remained conjoined. I heard his heart beat beneath my ear—so normal, so human. Yet why did that make me hate what he was doing to me even more?

"Tell me about yourself," I asked, secure in his embrace not for the first time.

"Rae…" he started, ready to shut me down.

I raised my head, looking down into his cerulean eyes. "Every time I want to know more about you, about your kind, you disappear, bite my head off, or distract me with sex."

He was doing it right now, his hands slowly kneading the curve of my rear.

"I have the right to ask."

He swept a long wisp of hair out of his face with annoyance. "Your father was a demon hunter, wasn't he? A very unsuccessful one, of course. But didn't he tell you these things?"

"He tried to," I replied candidly, my hands threading his hair, "but I wasn't interested. I like my life supernatural-free."

"I noticed," Andrei remarked dryly. His fingers bit into the globes of my ass and he thrust upward. I gave a sharp intake of breath. "You want to know about incubi?"

"First, I want to know about you." I bit my bottom lip as the sensation of him moving his cock inside me sent a surge of need through my core. "Where are you from?"

"In this realm,…" He let out a low groan when I clenched my sex around him. "Romania. In the realms of the Underworld, I am lord of the incubi, demons of moral depravation. My personal Hell has no name."

"Anghelescu is Romanian, then?"

"Yes. It means son of Anghel, angel." His lips curved into a devious smile. "I have a dry sense of humor."

"I… don't know what to say. Is this your… real form?"

He gave me a pointed look that told me all I needed to know. "This is my mortal form. My true form... Well, let's just say I'd fit right into a Stephen King horror novel."

I swallowed, unconsciously tensing around Andrei's cock.

"You want to make me come again?" he said gruffly, his eyes clouding over.

"Andrei, why are you here?" I asked. "I don't mean here with me. I mean here... on Earth."

"To feed," was his immediate response. "To harvest more individuals like your mother. To take souls." He grimaced when he saw the expression on my face. "Eventually, that's what it all boils down to, Rae. What did you think we were here for, to host the Oscars?"

My father had said something about his type of demon, how they'd brought the destruction of many races—the Mayans, the Incas, and the Sodomites of Sodom and Gomorrah—with their intense hunger for sexual energy. Immoral acts, especially between married men or women and incubi, had often driven many to suicide. But then, if one's soul wasn't all that pure, it really didn't take much to be seduced by a demon.

"Am I morally depraved?" I asked, my voice barely a whisper. "Is that what you see when you look at me? Is that why you like fucking me?"

Andrei's eyes briefly turned red. "Nobody's perfect." He flipped me over, keeping his upper body off mine. "Your essence, Rae, is filled with pent-up rage. You give off a heat, a passionate heat, that burns me when I'm inside you. There's sadness, there's guilt, and there's a flicker of vulnerability, too." He brushed his hair out his face. "That anger, it rivals mine. And it feels so fucking good when I consume it."

I gulped, embarrassed to feel tears prickling my eyes. So much of what he'd said was true. I was angry about the way my life had turned out. I spoke from experience when I said that money couldn't buy happiness. Why couldn't my father have been a regular nine-to-five guy? Why couldn't I have lived in blissful ignorance, unaware that supernatural creatures walked this earth? Why couldn't my mother have stuck around to raise me? To teach me what heartbreak really was? Why couldn't I have two very alive parents, instead of a dead one and a dubiously living one?

And I was angry at Andrei, for tempting me to the dark side, for awakening a primal hunger inside me for something more carnal, more dangerous than sex with a human. There were still so many things I wanted to know, like why I couldn't be seduced by an incubus when the average human could be. But I was tired and I was quickly coming down from my high.

Andrei placed a tender kiss on my forehead before withdrawing from me. I felt his exit painfully and a gaping void where he used to be. I allowed him to effortlessly scoop me up into his arms and carry me to my bed.

He pulled the covers down and arranged me under them. I resisted the urge to ask him to stay, he never did, and shut my eyes instead. Then his lips brushed against mine.

When I opened my eyes again, he was gone and my bedroom had been plunged into total darkness.

JP Fontaine was angry. This was obvious because he'd just punched a guy in the face and, from my vantage point in my rental car across the street, I could see that his intent had been to squash the guy's eye into its socket.

JP had an anger problem.

Over the past four days, I watched him slap, punch, kick, and throw things like a spoilt child. I was never close enough to hear much of anything but I was sure he punctuated these attacks by shouting French obscenities. These disagreements mostly occurred outside Club Nicolette—which, coincidentally, turned out to be Ivanov's club, and happened in broad daylight. Yet no one so much as batted an eyelid at a guy hurling a liquor bottle at another guy.

"The perks of being a tool," I said aloud, taking a big bite out of my club sandwich before I snapped a shot of the dark-haired man with my camera.

Looking in from the outside wasn't going to help. If I wanted to find out what JP was involved in, I needed to get into the club. Andrei's livid voice reverberated in my head, telling me not to have anything to do with Ivanov. I shook it away. Even if I didn't want to do this, Ana Fontaine had wired me a ridiculous sum of money—so ridiculous I almost rang her up to ask if she'd meant to add the two zeros, which made me irreversibly bound to this assignment.

Clubbing time, I thought resignedly, starting the car up again and pressing the button that rolled the window down.

Andrei wasn't going to be pleased. But then again, he could go right back to hell, for all I cared.

Chapter 7

I sensed him before I saw him, except that "him" turned out to be a "her".

This radar thing should come with a gender-identification thingy, I thought, annoyed.

"You've been fucking Andrei," her heavily-accented husky voice rang from behind me.

Despite the loud dance music the Nicolette's resident DJ seemed to favor, I heard the succubus loud and clear. Since she was so close, I also felt the strong pull of sexual energy she radiated and it was all directed at me. I could feel it around me, like a helicopter hovering above my head, but it wasn't tugging at me.

So I guess this immunity thing has its perks.

Refusing to relinquish the barstool I'd fought tooth and nail for, I turned at the waist, still holding my half-empty glass of Coke. "Who are you and what do you want?"

She licked her lips, her voice loud and clear as she replied, "Selene. And all I want to know is how you… came to belong to my lord."

Selene was a tall, curvy knockout dressed in a ridiculously tiny strapless red dress. Her honey-colored hair fell in a stylish bob that framed her heart-shaped face. Her blue eyes were rimmed with kohl and her full lips painted blood-red. And those lips curved into a sly smile as she returned my once-over with one of her own.

"Belong to him?" I spluttered, despite my previous stance of not communicating with supernatural creatures. "What the hell are you talking about?"

"You shouldn't be here, *ma petite*. I sniffed you out the second you walked in. I'm sure I wasn't the only one."

I hopped off the barstool, annoyed to see that she dwarfed me by a few inches, even in my pumps. "I can handle myself."

She cocked her head, the crafty smile still pasted on her face. "I can see why he'd like you. You are... feisty. However, there are some out here who would love nothing more than to challenge Andrei and what better way than to take away his... plaything?"

I glared at her, ignoring the spike of fear in my gut. "I'm not his plaything. He has no claim on me, nor I on him. This conversation is over." I tried to move past her but she reached out and grabbed my arm, her inhuman strength keeping me there.

"Get your sticky hands off me, you little bitch!"

"Because you are his, I will watch over you," Selene murmured into my ear, her lips slightly brushing my lobe. "And you are very wrong. You are his now and, as such, are bonded to him because you have exchanged more than essence. Be careful tonight, *chérie*."

"Fuck off," I retorted, and she released me, allowing me to dive right into the sea of bodies, sweat beginning to

102

trickle down my back. "Bonded" to Andrei. "Belonging" to him. How ludicrous was that?! I had never heard anything more stupid or more insulting.

It was painfully obvious that dousing myself in Jennifer Lopez's Blue Glow did zilch to disguise the fact that I'd been having repeated sex with the king of the incubi. Just how long would his... "smell" last on me? Days? Weeks? Months? Years?!

"Deep breaths, Rae," I told myself, bumping into a grinding twosome and receiving heavy-lidded glares in return.

I had to find JP quickly. The fact that I'd scoped the club out the last time I'd been here following Karr was of little help. There were far too many people in my way, making it extremely difficult to locate my left hand, let alone the one person I was looking for.

After being bumped, grabbed and shoved, I finally gave up and returned to the bar to order a Pellegrino. My throat was dry and I was revoltingly sweaty. There was nothing worse than being sober and icky at the same time.

"Baby Phat! Fancy seeing you here."

I groaned, rethinking my decision to remain teetotal. "Don't talk to me," I muttered, positive he could hear me over the thumping sound of Sia trying to compete with a she-wolf. "Don't even fucking look at me."

"Come on, Baby Phat," Temp said loudly, sounding miffed. "We're kin!"

I turned to glare at him and did a double-take. Dressed in a teal golf shirt and dark jeans, he looked ridiculously good-looking. If I hadn't recognized his annoyingly sarcastic voice, I wouldn't have known he was the same guy I met two months ago.

"What did you do to your hair?" I choked out as I saw, from my peripheral vision, the bartender set a bottle of sparkling water in front of me.

"You like?" Temp grinned, running a hand through his thick jet-black curls.

It was completely ridiculous to think that someone's hair color could make you see that person in a totally different light, but I was completely taken aback by how it transformed him into someone who looked... well, related to me. We both inherited Lauren's high cheekbones, her ever-so-slightly pointed ears that I'd always despised, and the curves of her pouty lips. I could see it all now. It was made clear by the shade of his hair, which was as inky as mine. Seeing him in this new light made it too real for me.

"You dyed your hair?"

"I don't have to dye anything," he stated mildly. "I visualized it, it happened."

"Visualized it?" I was having trouble visualizing *that*. I was still stuck on our stark resemblance to each other.

Temp's chocolate brown eyes danced. "Don't tell me? You had no idea I could do that, did you?"

"I... Well, yes, I did. It's just... you look... like me."

"Hey, Vince! We look alike?" Temp called to the bartender.

Vince raised a puzzled eyebrow before his attention was captured by a woman raising an empty glass in his direction. Temp returned his gaze to me.

I glared at him. "Very mature of you." I jabbed a finger in his chest, hitting a wall of muscle. "So are you following me? Did she send you here? Does she want us to... to bond?"

104

He grabbed my hand. "If by 'she', you mean our mother, no. She did not send me to Paris to fuck, get shitfaced, and fuck some more. What is your problem?"

Good question. I was probably PMS-ing or some bullshit because even to my own ears, I sounded like an irrational nutjob.

I wrenched my hand away from his and threaded my fingers in my hair, which was getting messier by the second anyway. "My problem is that I thought I was rid of you both!"

"Rae..." His voice trailed off and he was giving me a look that clearly said he wished he were anywhere but here.

"What?"

"You're... sort of crying." And he looked away, embarrassed.

"What?" I repeated, angrily scraping the pads of my fingers across one cheek. Sure enough, they came back black with running mascara. "Shit. What is wrong with me?! I can't be drunk, can I?"

"I swear, Rae, this..." he said as he gestured around him, "... is purely coincidental. I've been coming here for years. Got a friend who moonlights as a DJ, so... I'm not stalking you."

"I know. Forget about it. This is stupid. I have allergies. It's probably all the noxious fumes in the air that pass for perfume."

Temp gave out a weak laugh. "You probably want to, you know, fix your make-up. Know where the restroom is?"

"Oh, wow! Are you going to take me? Maybe change our tampons in one cubicle?"

Temp arched a brow. "You know, they say sarcasm is the lowest form of wit."

I wiped at my cheeks, irritated. "Thank you for that. Now, buzz off."

"What a bitch," he said, a reluctant smile tugging at his lips as he shook his head. He grabbed Vince's proffered bottle of beer and turned on his heel to leave, weaving his way straight to a guy I immediately recognized as JP Fontaine. He was standing against one wall on the slightly empty side of the club and looked like he'd been there for a while.

He'd been a hair's breadth away from me the whole time! I felt like an idiot. Plus, judging by the way he and Temp were already laughing about something, it was obvious that they were good buds. It was time to befriend Temp.

But I needed something stronger than bottled water.

"Vince," I called, keeping my eye on the two chatting men. "A dirty martini, *s'il vous plaît.*"

"You're coming home with me," I said, dragging Temp away from the aroused-looking redhead whose mouth he was getting pretty familiar with only a second ago outside the club.

He made a low sound in his throat. "What the fuck, Baby Phat?"

"We need to talk about something," I told him, willing Red to disappear. Really, I was doing her a favor—maybe even saving her life—by tugging Temp away from her, yet she was looking at me like I'd pissed on her suede pumps.

"What now, Rae?" Temp snapped at me, his eyes blazing. "You want to tell me to stop listening to Incubus because you have all their albums, too?"

106

I sighed. "Maybe I was... illogical about your little... makeover."

"Gee," was Temp's sarcastic retort, "you think?"

"It's just that... Well, this whole 'being related' thing? I can't wrap my head around it. I'm sorry. Seeing you makes me want to rip you apart and feed your carcass to a pack of coyotes."

"You think this is easy for me?" Temp muttered. "I practically tried to rape you the first time we met because my... *our* mother didn't tell me about you! There's no support group for sick shit like that."

"She's not my mother."

It was getting cold, people were trickling out of the club, and I felt a little too "cheerful" with several martinis in me. So arguing with a sarcastic half-demon was the last thing I wanted to do.

"This is actually really important, Temp," I said earnestly, giving him my best puppy-dog eyes. "I know I've been... a 'female canine' but I wouldn't ask for your help if it wasn't important."

Temp's eyes glared at me for a long time before his head jerked in Red's direction.

"Go home, Nicole," he muttered, and she gave him a panicked look.

"Temp?" Her voice was barely a whimper.

"Tomorrow," Temp said gruffly, not even looking at her. "Do what I say and go home, babe."

"You've got to be kidding me," I groaned, staring at the girl. Now that I looked at her properly, she couldn't have been no more than seventeen, with her face caked with make-up and her stick-thin, girly body squeezed into an obscenely revealing LBD. "You want to give it up to him? Do you know

107

what he is? Do you know what havoc he'll wreak in your life?" I asked her in an annoyingly high-pitched voice.

"Shut up, Baby Phat," Temp said sharply, giving me a stern look. "She knows what she's doing. Besides, her English is basic. So keep up with the 'wreaking' and 'havoc'. See how far they get you."

But Nicole surprised even him. "Fuck off! My soul is a small price to pay for my first time to be incredible," she said fiercely, her green eyes narrowing at me. "Mind your own business, American slut."

"Now, now, Nicole," Temp said mockingly soothing. "The last part was uncalled for." He glanced at me, grinning. "She called you a…"

"I heard what she called me," I snapped, "and if you give me two seconds, I'll slap the 'Joker' off her face."

Temp caught me before I pounced on her, putting himself in between the teenager and the unreasonable typhoon that was me. "I take it you've been drinking?" he asked.

"Pfft. So what? No child calls me names and gets away with it!"

"Behave, Baby Phat." Temp shook me, his eyes imploring me not to cause a scene in front of innocent bystanders. "Okay? Behave. I'll deal with her."

But when he turned around, he found that she was gone.

"I never pegged you for boho chic," Temp remarked, flopping onto my floral print couch and grabbing the remote off one armrest. He then surveyed my living room from his vantage point. "I could totally see myself kicking it here."

"Don't get too comfy," I muttered, kicking my pumps off and wincing as the TV came on. My head was already pounding. "You just have some information I need."

"So, in essence, you're using me?" His voice was casual but I sensed something there, controlled resentment.

I folded my arms across the chest, weirdly feeling like a visitor in my own home. "Is this about my not wanting to hang out with you? For Pete's sake, Temp, how do you expect me to when you're a…"

"You don't have to keep reminding me, Rae," he said in a snarky manner, flicking the TV off and getting up. "This might come as a shock to you but I know exactly *what* I am. And obviously, you do, too. It's just a pity you don't know *who* I am."

"You steal people's souls. That's who you are."

He let out a loud, cheerful laugh. "I give women the best sexual experiences they've ever had in their miserable lives. I give girls the opportunity to pop their cherry with a guy who knows his dick from his middle finger. But that's not who I am, Miss I-Hate-the-Supernatural." He flicked at an imaginary piece of lint on the front of his shirt. "I guess sleeping with one hasn't made you any less discriminating."

I opened my mouth to say something but he surged forward, his eyes fixed on me.

"I warned you about being with Andrei, Rae." Temp's voice sounded terribly big-brotherly. "You have no idea what kind of Pandora's Box you've opened."

I flushed. "Right. Am I supposed to be wary of him? You don't seem to show him the same level of respect the succubus I met tonight did."

109

He snorted. "I'm a cambion, a halfling. Not even fit to lick his big toe, let alone talk to him. I'm cool with that. My human side keeps me earthbound, so forgive me if I don't think of him as my king." He paused, brow creasing. "What succubus?"

"Selene. Next time I see her, she won't be so lucky."

Temp laughed. "Selene's about a billion years old. What the hell are you gonna do, mace her?"

I laughed, despite myself. "You don't think I could take her?"

"Unless you have a death wish. That woman will rip you apart before you can say 'catfight'."

"Your faith in me is overwhelming. Want something to drink?" I was already shuffling to my kitchen, running my hands through my hair to push it back out of my face.

"I thought I wasn't supposed to get too comfy." Temp's laughing voice came from right behind me as he followed me to the kitchen.

I turned to look at him. "Yeah, well, I'm offering you a drink, not making you a bed in the spare room."

His eyes lit up. "Is that deal on the table? I'm tired of hotels. They lose their appeal after a while."

I rolled my eyes, pulling the refrigerator door open. "Coke, Sprite, OJ, or water? Those are your choices."

"Coke would be cool."

When I handed him the can, he was already perched on a stool at the island, surveying the room with sparkling eyes. "Nice kitchen."

I didn't say anything because it was true. It had actually been what had pushed me to buy the damn townhouse in the first place. Cherry cupboards, granite countertops, and the same wooden flooring that ran throughout the entire

110

house—all of those made it easy for me to vividly imagine cooking for a husband and a few kids on lazy Sunday afternoons after trips to the Eiffel Tower. Not that I was looking to settle down any time soon. Not that I was that corny.

"You okay?" Temp waved a hand in my face.

I nodded, pushing that image out of my head and settling onto the stool opposite him. "So tell me about JP Fontaine."

To his credit, he didn't look one bit surprised. "I saw you staring at the club," he stated matter-of-factly, taking a tiny sip of the cola. "You wanna hit that? You do realize that Andrei is not into sharing his spoils, right?"

A wave of heat washed over me as I glared at Temp. "Why the hell does everyone keep making out like I have an 'I Belong to King Andrei' sticker on my forehead?"

Temp chuckled, eyes dancing. "That's priceless. You should do that."

I flipped him the bird. "For the record, I don't want to… hit JP. This is business." I leaned forward. "And let's get one thing straight: If I did want to sleep with him, I could. Because I'm a grown-ass woman and Andrei does not own the gold between my legs."

"Gold between your legs?" he repeated, grinning. "Is that a Maya Angelou line or something?"

I rolled my eyes. If I kept doing that, my eyeballs would probably get stuck that way. "Can we get serious for one moment?"

He downed the rest of his drink, setting the empty can on the counter. "Okay, okay," he muttered, regarding me. "What do you want to know? I'm not his confidant, by the way, so I can't tell you how long it is."

111

At the mention of JP's manhood, I had to physically resist the urge to maim Temp with a kitchen knife. "What does he do? I mean, is he really a DJ?" I asked through clenched teeth.

Temp shrugged. "Yeah, I guess."

"You guess?"

"He does a lot of things, Baby Phat. But I don't have his résumé."

"What does he do for Damien Ivanov?"

He arched a brow. "Now I'm curious."

So I had to tell him what Ana Fontaine had told me, and at the end, he looked thoughtful.

"Damien's a bad guy but JP's cool. He has a temper, fine. But he wouldn't prostitute girls. Maybe Ana walked in on an orgy."

I wrinkled my nose. "You're disgusting."

He laughed. "Come on, Baby Phat. Don't act coy with me. Think about three guys pounding into you, ripping you inside out and giving you multiple orgasms. Disgusting?"

I swallowed, the mental image coming in clear and HD. "Not my thing. And not JP's thing either, I'm sure. So no, Ana did not walk in on an orgy. What does her brother do for Ivanov?"

"He DJs sometimes. Handles liquor orders whenever Ralf isn't around. Makes sure the VIPs are happy. That's about it."

I sighed. "Ana gave me a lot of money for me to tell her that her brother plays music and orders booze."

"That's all I know."

"Well, you're a fountain of knowledge," I commented dryly, tapping my fingertips on the countertop. "Thanks. Guess I'll just have to follow him."

112

"You really want to get mixed up with Damien?"

"You really want to act all brotherly here?"

He raised his palms in mock-surrender. "Relax, Rae. Just a question." He paused, giving me a sly wink. "Hello, Andrei," he said serenely, not even bothering to turn around. Show-off.

I glanced at the doorway, mentally cursing at the sight of Andrei leaning in the doorjamb, as imposing as ever. "Hey, you!" I said brightly, still feeling the effects of the alcohol. "I was beginning to think you wouldn't show up." I hopped off the stool, teetering slightly. "Martinis. Powerful things."

"Am I interrupting?" Andrei asked, his voice quiet.

"I'm sure you know that I recently found my long-lost, half-demon baby brother, right?" I stopped in front of him, drinking in the sight of his brick wall of a body, now that I was so close. As usual, he wore jeans and a T-shirt that fit him like a second skin. "Well, we're bonding," I said with a smile.

"You went to Ivanov's club when I specifically told you to stay away from him," Andrei growled. It wasn't a question.

"I'll be in the spare room," Temp said brightly, suddenly appearing at my side.

Andrei's head jerked in his direction, eyes glacial. "No. You'll be leaving."

Palms up, Temp stepped back. "Of course. She totally deserves a spanking."

"Hey," I protested, scowling at him before turning back to Andrei. "What am I, five?"

"No, you're stubborn!" Andrei snarled, now that Temp had evaporated. He grabbed my upper arm in a vise grip and dragged me behind him, leading me to my bedroom. "So fucking stubborn, Rae. Did he see you? Did Ivanov see you?"

"I went out for a few drinks! And no, I didn't have the pleasure of making his acquaintance!" I tried to free myself from Andrei's grip. "Andrei, I swear I'll beat the crap out of you if you don't let me go!"

He did, shoving me onto my bed. Anger swelled up inside me, threatening to turn me inside out as I sat up, attempting to crawl off the bed—which was hard work considering how I had been one drink away from getting totally plastered.

"Who the hell do you think you are?"

The cold look he sent me kept me from continuing. "Maybe I've been too indulgent," he said, his voice soft. "Perhaps you feel that I'm a feeble mortal you can fuck around with. Was it so wrong of me to treat you as my equal? Probably."

The gentle resonance of his voice chilled me more than the usual roar he'd have made if he just outright scolded me. I refused to show my fear as I got off the bed and stood. Then I folded my arms across my chest, silently daring him to continue.

"When you promised me you wouldn't go near that man, I believed you."

I didn't get why he had such a stick up his ass about this. "I'm not the type of woman that gets bossed around. Go find someone else if you want a doormat."

He stayed silent for a long time. The only sound I heard was the frantic tattoo of my heart against my chest.

Until... "Rae, come here."

"No."

His eyes flashed a brilliant red. "I don't repeat myself. Ever."

"Kill me, then. In fact,..." I said, "... rip me apart, Andrei. Because if you think for one second that I'm your bitch, someone you can order around on a whim, just kill me already. You don't own me." I paused, meeting his glare with one of my own. "I'm not afraid of you," I lied. "Kindly go back to hell. I'm tired."

He stared at me for a long time before he shook his head. "I don't understand. You are scared, yet you're mouthing off at me." He folded his arms across his broad chest, muscles bunching with the movement. "Such a mystery. Such a turn-on."

I yawned, sleep suddenly pushing at my eyelids. "I'd be a fool not to be scared of a demon but could I get some sleep, please? I had a lot of fun not seeing Damien Ivanov tonight and it would be great to recuperate." I was already slipping out of my dress, ignoring the look of naked yearning Andrei was sending my way—although, I preferred his wrath to his desire any day. Pausing in front of my closet to grab a long, faded blue tee, I asked, "Out of curiosity, am I the only woman you're sleeping with right now?"

I hadn't expected an answer, but his clipped response readily came from right behind me. "Yes."

"Huh," I said, tugging the T-shirt on after unhooking my bra. "An incubus that believes in monogamy. Who'da thunk it?"

He spun me around until my breasts were mashed against his hard, unyielding chest. "There's no reason for me to seek anyone else out, Rae."

"I think you should. Sorry, but I..."

His lips were suddenly crushed against mine, eliciting a sharp gasp from my parted lips when his tongue slid inside to brush against mine. My body was fully cooperative but my

115

mind was being logical that night. Palms flat against his chest, I pushed with all my might, jerking my head backward.

Andrei's brow creased as he stared down at me, hands still firmly on my waist.

"I told you to leave," I said, my hands on his in an attempt to extract them from around me. "Like I said, I'm not a doormat and when I say no, that is not an invitation for you to kiss me."

"You were being serious?"

I scowled. "I could kick your ass, Lord Andrei. Don't mistake my horniness for meekness."

He pulled my lower body to his, grinding his more than impressive denim-encased erection into my sensitive front. "What the hell am I supposed to do with this?"

"Jerk off like any normal mortal male."

He let out a mirthless laugh. "Jerk off?"

I cupped his bulge in one palm, meeting his eye. "Yeah. It's easy. You take your huge, throbbing cock out and you caress it with one huge, capable hand." I squeezed him, biting my lower lip when he flinched. "You close your gorgeous baby blues and you think about how it feels to be balls-deep inside me, fucking me hard. And how wet and tight I am for you. And how I scream your name when I come." I paused, the sound of a low, sexy growl escaped Andrei's throat, sending a jolt of electricity to my lower belly. "Imagine the feel of my sweet little cunt clenching around your thick cock, milking you dry as you spill yourself inside me." I released his erection before I could succumb, sidestepping him and calling over my shoulder, "'Night, Andrei. I have work to do tomorrow."

He swore loudly, spinning around to throw me an evil look. "You're playing with fire."

"Is that so?" I asked brightly, slipping into bed. "Good thing my best friend's husband's a fire-fighter, then."

In my dream, my father was slicing Lauren into bite-size pieces and Martin Solveig's *Ready 2 Go* was drowning out her ear-splitting cries while I stood by and watched. For some reason, I wore a wedding dress and black Uggs. Before I could ponder this weirdness, my eyes opened to blinding sunlight— and the unmistakable crash of Martin Solveig.

I sat up, rubbing sleep out of my eyes and kicking the covers off. I instantly regretted standing when the pounding in my head started up full force. Wincing, I quickly used the bathroom before snatching my Rampuri knife from the vanity table and padding to the source of the music—my kitchen.

What intruder plays dance music at full blast during a break-in, Rae?

But then, stranger things have happened.

Still, it was a shock for me to find Temp sitting on a stool in front of the island, casually flicking through the Sunday paper while Nicole—little, bitchy pubescent Nicole from outside the club—puttered around my kitchen like she belonged there. I was greeted by this strange sight, coupled with the tempting smell of breakfast.

"*Bonjour*, Baby Phat," Temp greeted without looking up from the paper.

Nicole turned away from the stove, beaming at me. "Good morning, Baby Phat," she said over the music.

"It's Rae," I muttered mechanically, squeezing my eyes shut and opening them again.

Nope, she was still standing in my kitchen and Temp was still relaxing in his seat. This wasn't a case of hangover-induced hallucinations.

"What the hell's going on?" I asked, marching to the radio perched on top of the refrigerator and turning it off. "To what do I owe this intrusion?"

Temp put the paper down. "Nicole wanted to apologize. Her mom's some kind of kickass chef, so she knows her way around a kitchen."

Nicole nodded, handing me a plate piled sky-high with bacon, pancakes and some sort of pastry. "I am so sorry for my behavior last night. Please accept this?"

I automatically took the plate, blinking at her. "Um, thanks?" Bacon was the surest way to my heart, as embarrassing as that was.

Nicole grinned, moved away from the stove, and went to stand beside a seated Temp. She placed a hand on his forearm, looking at him reverently. I felt a little sick right then.

"Temp?" I said, suddenly thirsty. "Did you... sleep with her?"

Temp arched a brow. "Prying into my sexual affairs, Rae?"

The dreamy look Nicole was giving him answered my question. I swallowed bile. *What was wrong with me? Wasn't I exactly like her, spreading my legs for orgasm after orgasm with a creature of Satan?*

"Honey," I said gently, setting my plate on the counter, "was that your first time?"

Nicole reluctantly dragged her gaze from the object of her affection. "It was... magical."

"And... and what did he want in return?"

Nicole shrugged. "A century of service after my death. No big deal." She paused, looking at Temp. "Is that the correct term?"

Temp nodded, pulling her to him at the waist. "Yeah, babe. No big deal."

"But you'll go to hell, Nicole," I sputtered, unable to contain my indignation. "Was being with him worth it?"

"Would you listen to yourself, Rae?" Temp gave me a grin. "Talk about the pot calling the kettle a demon-shagging ho."

I flushed, balling my hands into fists. "You'd better stop throwing that in my face before I throw a fist at yours."

"Word is he was raising hell in Vegas last night, probably after he left you." Temp winked at me, unfazed by my threat. "Got into unnecessary fights. Beat the shit outta people for looking at him wrong. I recognize a sexually frustrated man when I see one, Baby Phat."

I blew air out of my mouth. "You're telling me he beat people up because of his blue balls?"

"Honest to God," he replied, before laughing. "Right. Why would I be honest?"

"And how did word get out so fast?"

He shrugged. "Demons gossip just as much as humans do."

I poked at a rind of bacon before tentatively devouring it. Delicious, fatty goodness exploded in my mouth. "I need to find a gym," I mumbled to myself, munching on another sliver.

"Andrei isn't helping you work off those calories?"

I shot Temp a dirty look. "Hilarious. Why don't you let yourself out?" I directed that to Nicole, too.

It was obvious that she was a lost cause. *Besides, it was too late for me to do anything.* At least that's what I told myself. I didn't want to think about what "a century of service" entailed because fear constricted my throat whenever I glanced at Nicole's content, dreamy face.

Fear for myself.

Chapter 8

"Ana, I promise you, I'm still looking into this whole thing," I said into my earpiece, nimbly dodging a biker on steroids and turning to Parishville Park. "I'm only in London for the weekend. Back by Monday, I promise."

"It's just that I'm worried, Miss Erickson," she murmured.

I let out a heavy sigh into the cool, morning air. "I know, I know. I promise you, I'll get to the bottom of this mystery."

She went on for a little while before I cut her short with a gentle goodbye. Then, I paused beside an oak tree and clicked off, returning my phone to its place in the hip pocket of my running shorts. Lying to Ana Fontaine all the time was beginning to get to me. I was no closer to solving "the mystery" now, if there even was one, than I was a month ago when I started looking into it.

To be honest, I hadn't seen anything that warranted Ana's suspicion of foul play, except for JP's short temper and shallow taste in bottle blondes and fake tits. I was beginning to wonder if this was just a big waste of my time, and if I was just feeding the flames of an obsessed and overprotective big sister's ridiculous paranoia.

Bending over and touching the toes of my white Reeboks, I pondered if there was any way I could prolong my stay in town. Despite Parishville being archaic, boring, and woodsy at times, it did have one thing going for it: peace.

There were no out-of-control frat parties leaking out onto the streets, no huge smoke-emitting trucks, no random flash mobs in town, or grisly murders happening every day. The streets were cobbled, for Pete's sake! And everything was in walking distance. Sure, I loved the fast pace of cities like the Big Apple, Paris, Rome—the list was endless. But sometimes, I just want to close my eyes and shut down for a while. I was allowed that, was I not?

"You OK, Rainelle?"

It was then that I realized I'd been bent over for an odd period of time. Straightening, I wiped moisture off my brow before staring into a gorgeous pair of inquiring honey-colored eyes—Daniel's eyes. For a split second, all I could do was gawk because he'd obviously been running and his T-shirt was clinging to his chest like white on rice (appropriate, since it was a white T-shirt) and his navy running shorts were obviously being battered by the wind, which left little to the imagination when it came to Daniel Junior's size.

He was sweaty and he was hard.

God, help me!

"Ah."

"Stitch?" he asked, his voice thick with worry.

"Um," I muttered as I shook my head to indicate "no".

This was beginning to piss me the hell off. If I kept up my monosyllabic answers, I'd be reciting the freaking alphabet.

"Rainelle?" Now he just sounded annoyed.

"I'm... good," I practically choked, aware of his nearness when I noticed the day-old stubble peppering his very manly jaw. I cleared my throat and dragged my eyes away from him. "Just stretching. Don't mind me," I added breezily.

Excellent, Rae. You found your tongue. Guess it was in hiding with your dignity.

A slow smile spread across his face. "Sort of hard not to mind you when you're bending over like that."

Daniel Lawless was fucking flirting with me! What the hell was I supposed to do?

"Oh, I bend over a lot."

He arched a dark brow and I flushed. The stupidity of what I'd just uttered overwhelming me. *Could I sound like more of a whore? A whore that likes anal.*

"I–I don't mean like..."

"Does your job entail a lot of... bending?" he interjected in that deep, lilting voice of his, looking like he was five seconds away from bursting into a fit of laughter.

"I'm a writer," I mumbled miserably, the lie easily escaping my mouth. "I mostly just sit all day. Anyway, by bending, I meant stretching."

"Sure," he said, flashing me an unlawful grin. He brushed a sweat-soaked hank of hair off his forehead. "See you around, Rainelle." Then he started in the opposite direction.

"Um, yeah. Later, Daniel."

And then he called over his shoulder, "Don't bend over too long. Might hurt something. That would be a fucking pity."

"When I say freakin', you say weekend! Freakin'!"

"Weekend!"

"Freakin'!"

"Weekend!"

"Woo-hoo!" I called out. "George's, you've been great! I love you!" Someone, I couldn't see who, helped me hop off the bar with minimal drink spillage on my part.

Once I was on the ground, I finally realized just how many beers I'd consumed because the entire St. George's was spinning and I was seeing double of what looked like a tall, dark-haired man in a vivid orange T-shirt.

Orange, I thought, wrinkling my nose. *What grown man wears orange?*

"Freakin' weekend?" the man quipped, a laugh in his voice. He still hadn't relinquished his hold on my hand.

"They wer-r-re playin' R-r-rihanna," I murmured, slurring most of my letters. "App-r-r-ropriate."

"Christ, Rainelle. How much have you guzzled?"

I know that voice, I thought, simultaneously mewing and groaning internally.

"Daniel? Followin' me, love?" I put on an awful Cockney accent that suspiciously sounded like an Australian one to my ears. Being sober did nothing to my poor impressions.

Daniel led me to a quiet corner and made me sit down on a battered wooden chair. The world stopped spinning considerably and I was able to blink a few times to clear my vision. And I saw that yes, he was wearing an orange T-shirt with some sort of childlike lettering on the front and a pair of well-worn blue jeans that were ripped at the knees. Also, his hair was rumpled, like he'd been standing outside in the wind or something. I itched to touch his hair. Maybe I had a fetish.

124

"Imagine my shock when I walk into a pub for the first time in years and find my normally put-together neighbor standing on the bar giving her version of Rihanna's *Cheers* for the patrons," Daniel told me, cupping my chin and tilting my face upward. "Just how much have you had to drink?"

I jerked my head away, glaring at him—sort of. Inside, I was shivering because Daniel "fucking" Lawless just touched me and it felt so good. I prided myself on my sexual confidence. But with Daniel, I couldn't help these clumsy, teenage hormones.

"You're not my father," I murmured, standing.

A strange look crossed his face. "No," he said softly, "but if he were here, I'm sure he'd want me to take you home."

I snorted. "I can walk. It's close."

"You can barely nod your head, let alone walk home at one in the morning, Rainelle," he said sensibly.

And just for argument's sake, I nodded my head. "Then what the hell was that?" I nodded my head again to prove I could do it.

His eyes rolled skyward before he grabbed my upper arm and turned, dragging me along with him. I squealed, from the abrupt manhandling and from the shock of awareness at the feel of his cool fingers wrapping around my arm.

I definitely needed to get laid soon. I was in withdrawal after the incessant "Andrei attack."

"I thought you were nice," I muttered childishly once we were out the stuffy club and the cold night air assailed my skin. "But you're a bossy dick."

Daniel looked down at me, his eyes interested. "Ah, you thought I was nice?"

I nodded, the motion making me a little dizzy now. "Yeah. I mean, maybe Dream Daniel was just that, a dream, and Real Daniel's a controlling ass with… with poor taste in clothing. I mean, orange?"

"Dream Daniel," he said to himself, steering me out of the way of a staggering couple. This move brought me smack-dab into his side, sending a shiver of unabashed delight up my spine. "You dream about me, Rainelle?"

"I used to," was my reply, at the same time, the voice in my head hissed, *Shut the hell up!*

"I see," he said, his hand skating down my arm and gripping my hand. "Aren't you a bundle of surprises, Rainelle Erickson?"

Our fingers were lacing. *Shit! When was the last time I'd laced fingers with a guy? And why are you wondering what Andrei's fingers would feel like lacing with yours?*

"I think I'm gonna be sick."

"Drinking like a teenage lout will do that to you." Daniel's voice was scornful.

I almost expected a spanking. Then I started thinking about his hand on my ass and all my thoughts took a nosedive into the gutter.

I had the element of surprise on my side when I stopped abruptly and jerked Daniel to me in one swift motion. The sandalwood scent of his aftershave—cologne, or whatever it was—wafted into my nostrils as I pulled myself up onto my toes and pressed a kiss somewhere under his bristly chin. He froze and my lips migrated to higher territory—his lips.

I was kissing Daniel Lawless, the Adonis of my dreams. Where were the stars I was supposed to be seeing? The holy fanfare I should've been hearing? Instead, all I got was a big fat nothing.

At first, I gently snagged his lower lip between my teeth and suckled it, mashing my heavy, aching breasts against his chest. Drunk or not though, I was lucid enough to know that this was probably my only chance to do this. And so without further warning, I slid my tongue into his mouth, tangling it with his and tearing a low groan from his throat.

And then he was kissing me back!

With one hand around the back of my neck and the other still holding my hand, he tongue-fucked me until… until guilt wrapped an icy hand around me. I should have been a quivering, moaning mass of need out here, under the bright moonlight. My panties should have been damp and my poor, deprived sex should have been yearning to have him give her some attention, too.

But nothing. Nothing but a strong feeling of remorse… all because of Andrei.

When Daniel pulled back, a look of pure lust mixed with one of blazing anger was on his face. But I couldn't even bring myself to care.

"What the fuck?" he snarled, lips deliciously swollen from my assault.

Before I could say something to diffuse the situation, Daniel spun around, his tall frame visibly tensing in the moonlight.

"What's wrong?" I asked curiously, following his gaze. I finally realized that we were cutting through the park, which was, understandably, empty at this time of night.

"Shit," was Daniel's enlightening response. "Get away from me. Now!"

I narrowed my eyes at him. "Excuse me?"

He turned to look at me. "For fuck's sake! Run!"

And that was when someone lunged at him from out of the darkness.

I could have screamed. I could have whimpered. But I sure as hell did not run.

Daniel and whoever it was tumbled to the ground in a messy tangle of arms and legs, rolling about until Daniel got the upper hand and landed a punch in the other man's face. In that moment, I was able to see a set of glowing, scarlet eyes beneath Daniel's frame as he straddled the man. My breathing stopped and my head started spinning again.

A demon. That's a demon!

Panicked, I tried to voice those exact words, because Daniel was so going to get hurt. And it was going to be my fault. My fault for not knowing any banishing rituals. My fault for being useless when it came to this. My fault for getting this Adonis killed.

"Daniel," I managed, knowing that no amount of blows to the demon's face was going to kill it.

"Didn't I…" His fist connected with the demon's nose. "… say…" Then, he kneed the creature in the gut. "… get the hell away?!"

I squealed when the demon, who had the physique of a lanky eighteen-year-old and the resilience of a wrestler, maneuvered his way out of Daniel's clutches and rained blows on his face as Daniel struggled on his back. That kicked me into gear. Without thinking, I threw myself at the thing, knocking it off Daniel and unceremoniously landing on the absolutely unwelcoming ground with an "Oomph!"

So many places instantly hurt, some of which probably never hurt before.

"Andrei's," the demon rasped into my ear, its entire body keeping me down on the grass.

I squirmed, horrified by the close contact, as well as by the demon's insinuation that I was Andrei's. At least, that was

128

what I thought he meant. For all I knew, the demon could've been saying that it belonged to Andrei, and that it had been sent by him to teach me a lesson.

Thinking these worrying thoughts distracted me that I nearly didn't hear the creepy chanting starting up above me. It took me exactly three seconds to realize that it was Daniel's voice, uttering words that remarkably sounded like Latin.

His voice was deep and clear as he repeated, "*Vade retro satana… Vade retro satana… Vade retro satana…*"

I recognized the old Catholic exorcism chant. And for a second there, I couldn't understand why Daniel would even have the power to successfully get rid of a demon. Meanwhile, the demon writhed on top of me and I spotted a glint of silver in Daniel's hand, an amulet of some sort that looked all too familiar in my quickly sobering state.

"Just get the fuck off her!" Daniel snarled.

And slowly, I felt the heavy weight lifting.

"*Vade retro satana*, you piece of godforsaken shit!" Daniel said as he picked the demon up and threw him off to the side like yesterday's trash.

Squeezing my eyes shut, I felt hot tears spill down my cheeks as I quietly sobbed, every part of my body screeching with pain. I opened them again when Daniel's arms came around me, helping me sit up.

"You're… you're a hunter," I whispered, unable to muster any astonishment in my voice.

He cupped my face with his two hands, examining me with concerned eyes. "You okay?"

I reached out, gently pressing a fingertip to his split lip—the lip I'd sucked on just moments ago. "Are you okay?"

"I'll live," he replied gruffly, gracefully getting to his feet and extending a hand to not-so-gracefully haul my ass up. "Don't you understand English? Didn't I tell you to run?"

"I'm not good at following orders," I countered, refusing to react when he wordlessly pulled the hem of my dress down. It had bunched up around my waist during my scuffle with the demon.

Then, Daniel's fingers skimmed my thighs. But I stood my ground, his touch doing little to divert my attention from the discovery.

"You're a hunter, Daniel."

"I think we've established that, Rainelle," he muttered, taking my hand again. "Can you make it home? I can carry you if..."

"Carry me?" My most sensitive parts were screaming an affirmative but my brain shook its head no. "I'll live," I said, repeating the words he'd shoved at me moments ago. "Just... tell me how you're a hunter. This should be good."

He looked at me, his eyes inquisitive. But he just said, "You need to sleep. We'll talk later."

Yawning, I mentally agreed. Something told me that I would need my strength for whatever Daniel would tell me... later.

I was in my bedroom in the Parishville house... but something didn't seem right.

For starters, there were no walls, just an expanse of white that cocooned my bed and vanity table. Then there was the fact that, after glancing down at myself, I discovered I was wearing a baby doll I had lost in a hotel in Ibiza years ago. But that wasn't nearly as bizarre as the sight of this giant of a man sitting at my vanity table. His back was to me but there was no reflection in the mirror.

"So tell me." His voice quietly commanded my attention. "Why are you shutting me out?"

I swallowed, now knowing without a shadow of a doubt that this was a dream. "Hello, Andrei."

He rose from the stool, the muscles on his back straining under his black T-shirt with the movement. I had forgotten what his body did to me—what it did to my insides. I hadn't even seen his face yet. But when I finally did, my breath left me. Just like all the times before, I was entranced by the pale blueness of his eyes. It clashed so exquisitely with the inkiness of his long hair and the hardness of his face that it would have been impossible for me not to stare.

And stare, I did. Until he was standing right in front of me, his eyes burning holes in my skin.

"Why am I dreaming about you?" I whispered, tearing my eyes from his azure gaze.

"You were drinking tonight," he intoned, reaching out to touch my collarbone.

It was an odd place to cop a feel, but I still found myself trembling because it felt so damn real.

"Stop that," I told him, staying his hand with my own and shooting him a glare. A zing of electricity shot through my fingertips where we touched and I jumped, astonished. "What the hell?!"

"Kiss me, Rae," Andrei said, his voice thick with want. He pulled his hand out of mine and brought it to the curve of my waist, his other hand following suit. "Kiss me like you want to fuck me."

I made an odd noise in my throat and got on my tiptoes to do just that. Our bodies melded together when our lips met and my hands clutched at the cotton fabric of his shirt, pulling him even closer—lips parted, tongues dueled, and moisture pooled in my panties.

"Need... your... cock," I groaned, popping the button of his jeans and dragging the zipper down. "Now."

"Fuck, Rae," Andrei said in a gravelly voice. His hands ran along the curve of my ass and lifted me, pressing my overly sensitized clit against the hard tip of his erection through the fabric of my panties.

I moaned loudly, reaching between us to hold on to it. He jerked in my hand when my thumb ran over the first beads of semen at the head.

"You want me," I breathed into his mouth, nipping at his lower lip.

"You know I do," he growled, countering my bite with one of his own.

"Just fuck me, Andrei. I'm so ready."

"Yes?" Then his fingers sought my panties and I allowed them inside, parting my thighs so he'd have easier access to my swollen nub. "Ready for my cock?" He rubbed the tight bundle of nerves, sending heat to every inch of my body. "Ready to come?"

"Yes!" I whimpered, wanting to come so badly I was blinded by it. "Don't make me beg."

"But I like it when you beg," he said quietly, withdrawing his fingers and turning me around so that my back was against his front. "What did you tell me the last time I saw you? Jack off?"

This was all wrong. If I was controlling my dream, wasn't he supposed to be inside me by now? This level of sexual frustration was way too high. Why would I torture myself in my dreams? After all, I wasn't that masochistic.

"You deserved that," I whispered, biting my lower lip when his fingers traced the underside of one aching breast. "So… did you?"

"Did I what?" His fingers were dancing around my breasts, but nowhere near my nipples. It was agony.

"Touch yourself."

He let out a laugh, the sound vibrating against my back. "I don't engage in mundane activities like masturbation."

I whirled around and pulled away from him. "Well, since this is my dream, you're going to engage in a little mundane activity, Your Highness." I shrugged off the thin straps of my baby doll and let the sheer material skim down my hips and onto the floor.

Andrei let out an audible gasp, his eyes so dark they were like hot coals. "Rae," he bit out. "Dammit, come here."

"Touch yourself," I told him, my eyes sliding to the erection poking out of his jeans. "Look at me and touch yourself."

His brow creased. "A waste of my time when I could be inside you."

"What the hell is wrong with my subconscious mind?" I complained. "You're not supposed to argue."

A smile tugged at the corners of his lips. "I'm not?"

"No," I said, succumbing to my need and cupping my breasts in my hands.

They were a good pair, my C-cup girls. At this moment, they felt like heavy sacks of nerves. I put an index finger in my mouth. Then I took it out, brought it down, and experimentally rubbed it against one nipple, before pinching. Andrei let out a painful groan.

133

"Jack off for me, Andrei," I murmured, tweaking both nipples now. "I want to see the king of all the big, bad incubi jerking off for me. Coming for me."

"Fuck it," Andrei grunted, gripping the shaft of his cock in one hand. "Look at what you've done to me."

I looked.

Slowly, he moved his hand along his hard length, his grip so tight it looked like he was strangling it. I moaned, the sight so beautiful, so incredible I could've come right then and there. But where would the fun be in that?

Andrei's palm captured the juices at the crown of his cock and massaged them into his thick, veined flesh. His eyes made love to my naked body while his hand made love to his cock and, without any further thought, I dipped two fingers into the heat of my needy opening.

"Oh, Andrei," I exhaled, simultaneously rubbing my thumb against my pulsing clit. "You feel so... so good inside me."

His strokes became frantic, his large frame visibly shuddering as he continued to pleasure himself with increasing ferocity. His smoldering gaze never wavered from mine and his desire was so liquid that I was practically bathed in it.

"Can you feel how wet I am for you?" I murmured, adding another finger to the party inside my opening. "Can you feel how much I want you?"

"Witch." Andrei's voice was barely a croak. And before I knew it, he was right in front of me, lifting me up and settling me over his cock. My legs were tight around his waist as he walked us to my bed, leaning over me as he pushed himself even further into my tight channel.

"Yes," I gasped, the feel of him withdrawing and plunging in again was so delicious I could have died on the spot. "Just like that! Just... like that." I held onto his shoulder blades, my fingernails sinking into his skin through his shirt.

"Come for me, Rae," Andrei commanded, lowering his mouth to one side of my neck and sucking thoroughly before moving to one hardened nipple.

I cried out, my hands in his hair. "Almost," I choked out, meeting his every powerful, brutal thrust. "Almost... there..."

Andrei's thumb was on my clit in a flash, the sweet pressure bringing me to a climax before I could so much as blink. My insides clenched around Andrei's length, bringing him to an orgasm with me.

His body tensed. "Fuck," he barked, emptying himself inside me for longer than was humanly possible.

When it was over, his lips brushed against mine. "So perfect."

I looked into his eyes, wordlessly seconding that. It had felt so real, so real and so incredible.

"Rainelle! Rainelle, dammit!" Someone slapped me. Hard.

My eyes flew open and pain heated my right cheek. "What the hell?" Even to my own ears, my voice sounded hoarse from screaming.

I groggily sat up, rubbing my eyes with the heels of my hands.

Daniel cleared his throat. "You were having a nightmare. Or something."

I looked up, wincing. Daniel was hovering over my bed. In a white V-necked T-shirt and slate grey board shorts. He didn't look like he'd been attacked by a demon last night— save for the purpling bruise on his temple and a slightly swollen lower lip. I, on the other hand, was sore all over. Even my fingers hurt.

"A nightmare," I whispered, blushing. "Yeah. That's what it was." I paused, rubbing my cheek and scowling at him. "You didn't have to hit me."

Daniel looked sheepish. "Sorry about that. I, uh, made breakfast."

"You broke into my house?"

"No, I had a key made."

Now I was fully awake. "What?"

"This was a long time ago, Rainelle," Daniel said flippantly, not meeting my eye. "How else was I supposed to get Paisley in to put up the wards?"

"Paisley? Wards? What the hell are you talking about?" I kicked the covers off as I said this, getting to my feet and instantly regretting it. My entire body cried out in protest. "Well, I'm never drinking again."

"People like us should never drink. Shit, are you gonna put any clothes on?"

I looked down at myself, mortified. Sure enough, I was as naked as a newborn. Without faltering, I grabbed my nightgown and robe off the floor and shrugged them on, fastening the belt around my waist before turning to face Daniel.

"So who's Paisley?" I said coolly, a twisted part of me enjoying the sight of an obviously aroused Daniel Lawless in my bedroom. "Girlfriend of yours?"

Daniel scoffed. "Hardly. I'd never date a witch."

I groaned. "You really are a hunter."

"You say that like it's a bad thing."

"It is," I muttered, walking past him on my way to the bathroom. I closed the door behind me and quickly used the facilities. Well, as quickly as my throbbing body would allow me.

Jumping the demon couldn't have been the sole reason for my body aching the way it did. I tugged my gown open and examined my body, squinting into the mirror.

Dry cum was evident between my thighs—evidence that my wet dream had succeeded in satisfying me. This rankled me. Of course, it probably had something to do with the fact that I hadn't seen the guy in three weeks, since the night I'd kicked him out of my bedroom. My head was a conflicting mess. Half of me missed the sex like a missing limb, and the other half hoped that I'd never see him again. Both halves fought for total dominance in my head.

Clearly, the sex-crazed half had won last night.

"Dirty whore," I spat at my reflection, before doing a double take.

There, on the right side of my neck, was the unmistakable purple mark of a hickey—exactly where Dream Andrei had kissed my neck.

"Thanks for breakfast," I said politely, watching Daniel stack the dirty dishes in the sink. I was sitting at the center island, half a cup of lukewarm coffee the only remainder of the feast Daniel had made me that morning.

"Anything for a hungover damsel in distress," he retorted, chuckling.

"Very funny." There was no sting in my voice because I didn't have the energy for it. I was still chilled by my discovery in the bathroom and what it could possibly mean.

And being with Daniel like this only made me feel dirty and guilty.

For the first time ever, I noticed how empty my life was. All the beautiful, intricate details meant nothing if I was the only one that got to appreciate them. Seeing Daniel doing something as mundane and coupley as doing the dishes brought a lump to my throat.

"You okay?"

I hadn't noticed that he was standing opposite me, a concerned look on his face.

I nodded, forcing myself to smile.

"Last night," he began, "was a little overwhelming for you." He paused, cocking his head. "Have you ever considered that being the female counterpart to *Cheaters* isn't your calling?"

I gaped at him, nearly toppling the stool I was sitting on. "I... I thought you thought I was a writer." It hadn't been my most creative lie, but it was the most believable.

"Babe," Daniel said quietly, "I've been following you since Raymond died. I know everything about you."

I swallowed the ball in my throat, tears springing to my eyes. "You knew my dad?"

He smiled, and that made him infinitely more handsome. "He taught me almost everything I know, sweetheart. Good hunter, great guy."

I rubbed at my eyes. This was surreal. "Following... me?"

"I promised him," he said matter-of-factly, coming around the island. "Please don't cry, Rainelle."

Of course, whenever I thought of what had befallen my father, I did the opposite. Big, fat tears slid down my cheeks and into my open mouth. Daniel sighed heavily and wrapped

138

his arms around me, pressing my face into his chest. His scent, a sandalwood aftershave, calmed me down immediately and I found that my loud, choking sobs had quickly morphed to soft whimpers.

"There you go, pet," he murmured, gently stroking my hair and letting me cry it all out.

I sure as hell didn't want to raise my head and have him see me looking like a red-faced Cabbage Patch Kid. Pulling back and turning away from him, I used the sleeve of my gown to wipe my tears away.

"You up to talking?" Daniel asked, his deep voice filling the room.

I nodded, returning his gaze then. "Thanks."

"Don't mention it. Seriously, don't. My street cred will go down the toilet when it gets out that I don't flee from crying women."

I smiled, for real this time. "Wouldn't want that."

He flashed me a sexy smile in return. "Exactly."

"So," I forced myself to be serious. "Paisley and the wards?"

"You do know what a ward is, right?"

I thought about it. I had heard that term before. A long time ago... "Either a room, an area, or a charge? The Jane Eyre type of 'charge'."

Daniel cursed under his breath. "Bloody hell. I mean, I knew from Ray that you weren't interested in hunting, but come the fuck on!"

"Hey, don't raise your voice at me."

He took a deep breath. "Of course, of course. Sorry, babe. A ward is a spell that's put up to protect a place or a person. Now, basically, your house was a sitting duck. Any demon could've strolled in here and killed you." He paused, letting that sink in. It did. "I got Paisley to put a ward around your house. That means no demon can set foot on your land. It's like an invisible force field shutting them out."

"Thank you," was all I could say. If I'd known about wards, I would've put them up in all my homes.

"Don't mention it. It's what I had to do."

I sucked in air. "You said you… follow me?"

"To protect you. Although, it doesn't help that you jet off around the world all the time and I lose track of you."

Fat lot of good you've done me, I thought witheringly. If he had been protecting me, how come I was always surrounded by incubi?

Instead, I muttered, "It's my job," and folded my arms across my chest.

"Scorned women aren't that important, Rainelle. Raymond wanted you to…"

"Shut up, Daniel," I interjected, hopping off the stool. "I don't need to hear this. I can't believe my father made you my babysitter!"

His hazel eyes flickered with anger. "Your father knew that you were too stupid to want to know how to protect yourself."

My hand had a mind of its own when it lashed out and thwacked Daniel across the cheek. I stared at it for a moment, stunned. Then Daniel pounced on me, shoving me up against the refrigerator. A second passed before his mouth was on mine—warm, soft, and delicious. I groaned, looping my arms around his neck as he deepened the kiss, his tongue slithering into my mouth and dancing with mine.

"You taste so good," he rumbled into my mouth before sucking on my bottom lip. His hands ran up my sides, leaving a scorching heat in their wake. I was positive I'd have third-degree burns there afterward. "So, so bloody good."

"Mmm," I murmured, because despite everything, the swell of his erection against my lower belly was so welcome.

But he dragged his lips from mine, scowling.

"Not again," he fumed, pulling out of my embrace. "Dammit, Rainelle. Why are you doing this?"

"You jumped me," I protested.

"You provoked me!"

"Awesome excuse." I licked my bottom lip, shivering under his stare. "You need to go."

"God, yes," he said, his eyes so full of need that it was hard to believe it was all for me.

"Like right now, Daniel."

"Yeah. We need to talk about this though."

"The kissing?" *Yes, let's talk about how inexplicably guilty I feel whenever we kiss. Note the sarcasm.*

He rolled his eyes. "No, babe. The things you need to know, the questions you have to ask."

"Oh, right." I eyed him. "Actually, I have a question right now."

"Ask away," Daniel invited, now standing at a safe distance from me.

"Can… can incubi have sex with people in their dreams?" *Wow, you don't sound crazy!*

He regarded me for a long time before answering with, "Yeah, but the kicker is that even though it just feels like a dream, in reality, the sex happened."

I thought of the love bite on my neck and inwardly cursed.

Chapter 9

In the next few days after my unforgettable weekend in London, Google became my best friend. If someone went through the browser history on both my laptop and BlackBerry, I'd be forever labeled a kinky weirdo for search terms like "sexual encounters with incubi" and "are orgasms with demons supposed to be so awesome?"

From contemplating my existence on this earth (Was I really just meant to be demon catnip?) and ignoring Daniel's sudden frequent phone calls (I didn't want to know how he'd obtained my number when we'd barely said five words in person to each other in the past. The man was my own personal sexy stalker.) to following JP Fontaine around (something that had become as exciting as watching Oprah clip her toenails)—I didn't have any time to really delve into deeper issues.

There was something that niggled at my conscience, something that kept me awake in a cold sweat late at night—every night, as a matter of fact. It constantly pushed itself to the fore of my thoughts as soon as my head hit the pillow, ominous and persistent. If the witch's magic was supposed to keep demons out, how did Andrei get in?

Maybe there was an exception for the lord of them all. Maybe there was nothing that could keep him away from me. Maybe his power was too great for a simple witch called Paisley, of all names.

Whatever helps you sleep at night, my inner voice snorted.

Except that I wasn't sleeping at night. I was afraid of being defiled in my dreams and liking it. It made no difference that Daniel had confessed to only getting the opportunity to make my house in Parishville, and certainly not my Parisian penthouse, demon-proof. If Andrei wanted in, he didn't have to wait for me to fall asleep. Because of this, sleep was hard to come by.

My late-night suspicion was the one thing I couldn't ask Daniel. And Google didn't help either. Instead, I spent late nights in front of my laptop laughing uncontrollably at ridiculous forums like Demonic Encounters. They were filled with pathetic-sounding women claiming to have experienced "sexual encounters with otherworldly beings and suffering the physical ramifications because of them." One woman went so far as to say that she didn't even mind the intrusion, that sex with the demon was infinitely better than with her "disappointing, Viagra-popping" husband.

These women were of no help to me and many of the "seers" that offered to get rid of said incubi sounded like money-grabbing quacks as well. There was little luck of finding a way to separate truth from fiction.

So I kept my questions to myself... until **myrna_lake67**.

It was one late Friday evening, after hitting Nicolette for two hours in the hopes of catching JP doing something, I returned to my penthouse and kicked my heels off before settling on the couch with my laptop. Out of habit, I logged in to Demonic Encounters as a guest user and scanned the recent posts. The usual horny crazies posted outlandishly graphic—and made up, I was sure—descriptions of sexual encounters with demons. Leaning back on the couch, I rolled my eyes at **d3moan3r's** story of what had allegedly gone down in her apartment last night. She claimed she was practically paralyzed from the waist down and had been comatose for the entire morning.

Then there was a post from someone called **scared_&_alone**. She wanted to know why the witch's ward wasn't working on a particular demon that had been visiting her since she'd turned eighteen. The demon had been coming weekly, no pun intended, for ten years now, alternating once in a while with a second creature. And she was beginning to think that the "mental and physical anguish" would never stop. The second demon had since ceased his visits, which was how **scared_&_alone** knew the witch she'd paid hadn't been a hack, but the first one had continued to make his regular stopovers—albeit only in her dreams.

myrna_lake67 was the only commenter.

myrna_lake67: Do you have feelings for this demon?

scared_&_alone: What? OF COURSE NOT. My body and mind can't take this! I'm being attacked in my own home! How could you ask such a thing?

myrna_lake67: Please don't be offended. Oftentimes, an incubus' allure clouds our normal judgment and we end up with misguided feelings. We know having any kind of affection for this creature is wrong, but perhaps his magic sucks you into feeling things for him. It's quite common. The large part of a witch's magic is in keeping unwanted creatures out. But if you subconsciously want this demon, then that magic cannot fully work. Don't be alarmed. It is not love that you are feeling, merely the end result of years of abuse at the hands of an evil being.

scared_&_alone: can I PM you??? Please! I need to talk to someone that understands.

myrna_lake67: Even better – e-mail me here: houseofmystique@hotmail.com

Well, fuck me sideways and call me Bob!

I read and reread what **myrna_lake67** had sent the other woman and bit my lower lip until I drew blood. Feelings. Fucking feelings?! No! I slammed my laptop closed and placed it on the coffee table before getting to my feet.

scared_&_alone could've been me—except I wouldn't just lie down and take what she'd taken for ten goddamn years! And I wasn't scared, nor was I alone, because apparently, I had a freaking hot babysitter doing quite a shitty job of watching my back. Still, the fact that Andrei had made me come in my sleep was testament to the fact that, much like **scared_&_alone**'s witch, Paisley's magic hadn't worked.

Why are you shutting me out?

That was what Andrei had asked me in my pseudo-dream, wasn't it? I hadn't known what the hell he meant. But

145

now, after finding out about the ward, it clicked—except that he hadn't really been shut out because I most probably had feelings for him. *No, "it."*

I stood in my bedroom, peeling off my halterneck dress in front of the mirror. Naked, I pondered all this. Yes, I missed sex with him. I missed it so much that I thought about calling him. The fact that I didn't have Andrei's number was the only thing that had kept me from doing just that. And sure, I kind of gotten into the habit of faithfully taking birth control, even when I went without sex. But it wasn't because I wanted to be prepared when Andrei finally came around to inevitably fuck me.

Right?

Shit!

"What are we looking at?" a lazy voice came from the doorway.

Jumping, I spun around.

Shit!

"You can't come around anymore, Andrei," I said quickly, snatching my nightgown from the same chair I'd tied him to (that felt like it had been years ago). I put the gown on and pulled my hair into a ponytail.

"I prefer you naked," he growled, his words trickling down my body and entering my sex like warm liquid.

Dammit! What the hell am I wet for?

"I don't care. What do you want?" I folded my arms across my chest, giving him the once-over. As usual, he looked like a walking orgasm. His hair was pulled back from his face and hung in a low ponytail. A forest green T-shirt strained across the planes of his hard chest and a pair of dark jeans clung to his powerful thighs. And lastly, a pair of black motorcycle boots completed his I'd-Be-Sexy-in-Dog-Shit look.

146

This was the man that supposedly ruled an army of demons in the Underworld.

"You," he ground out, slowly striding to me. "But you already knew that."

I stood my ground, refusing to be a replica of the pathetic **scared_&_alone**—and running. "Aren't you going to ask about the ward?" I asked.

He paused before me, a wry smile on his face. "I should be hurt. You want to keep me out now?"

"Daniel, he's my hunter friend, wanted to protect me from your kind. He's such a great guy. Strange but great," I said in one breath, suppressing a groan when I noticed that Andrei was sporting a hard-on that could've impaled concrete. To say it was distracting was an understatement.

He arched a brow. "Trying to make me jealous?"

"Trying?" I spluttered, a thought occurring to me. "What about that flunky you sent after us last week? The one who attacked Daniel and me in Parishville? Was he a result of my trying to make you jealous?"

"What are you talking about?"

"Don't play dumb with me! He said your name. Before Daniel banished him, of course."

"You were attacked," Andrei said to himself, his gaze flitting to the wall. His piercing eyes finally swiveled to mine—and the look on his face then could have melted the skin off my bones. "Did he say anything else?"

I swallowed. Jumping to conclusions seemed to be my M.O. at the moment. "He just went, 'Andrei's' and that was it. I think he was insinuating that I... that I belong to you."

Andrei nodded, considering this.

"But I don't. I'm my own person and I don't appreciate the notion that..."

"And that's all he said?" he asked, interrupting my attempt at being assertive.

"Well, yes. He looked like a kid, if that's any help."

Andrei gave out a short bark of laughter. "No, it's not. Rae, I could temporarily transform myself into an eighty-year-old right this second, if the fancy struck me. So getting an APB out for a demon isn't a picnic. He probably picked a skin at random."

"That's comforting."

"Hey," he said, his voice suddenly gentle. "I'll look into it. No one touches you. No one."

I averted my eyes. There was no way I was going to feel all warm and fuzzy inside because he just told me he'd look out for me. I wasn't one of those women who stood idly by while a man fought her battles and opened her car door.

"You're getting sappy," I mumbled, gliding past him. "Is there ever a point to your visits besides wanting to fuck me?"

"Actually, there's one thing I could use your opinion on."

Before I could shoot him a curious look, Andrei had me pinned down on the bed, his front pressed against mine and his hands holding down my wrists above my head.

"What?" I breathed, alarm bells ringing in my head.

"Rough or gentle?"

Oh, hell!

How could I resist that? It was acutely impossible for me to think about anything beyond the thrill of his erection nudging my opening. In that position, my mind was in fuck-me-now mode.

"Rough," I gasped, because Andrei being gentle made me think about feelings, butterflies and... kittens licking chubby babies—all that nasty shit.

"I knew you'd say that."

He flipped me onto my stomach and yanked my gown off. "Are you fucking the hunter?"

"What?" I murmured into my pillow, shivering under Andrei's stare. "No."

I felt his hands stroke my ass and I whimpered when he pulled me to my knees. I loved my ass and I loved him in my ass.

"Why not?"

Holy crap, was that his finger?! Sure enough, his wet digit was closing in on the puckered hole between my butt cheeks. I automatically tensed.

"We're not like that," I replied hoarsely. "But I've thought about it."

I knew what I was doing, goading Andrei into a fit of jealousy, but nothing could have prepared me for the exquisite sensation of his index finger thrusting into me. He didn't even wait for me to become accustomed to the intrusion, and that undisguised malice was exciting.

"Fuck my finger," he grunted.

My hands tangled in the bedsheets beneath me as I automatically did as he instructed. The tight ring of muscles down there clenched around Andrei's finger, slowly sucking him in. Sweet, delicious pleasure washed over me by the bucketload when his other hand slid between my thighs, zoning in on my sopping sex.

Andrei leaned over me, his mouth inches away from my ear. "Did you tell the hunter how much you like my demon cock inside you?" he snarled before he flicked his tongue into the shell of my ear.

I wailed, wanting him to undress, wanting to feel his hot skin against mine. "No."

"What would he think of you if you told him?" His other hand was working on me now, his long, cruel fingers recklessly tweaking my clit. "Rae Erickson, the demon hunter's daughter who can't get enough of my demon cock inside her tight little pussy."

I shamelessly rocked against him, strange little noises leaving my lips. Everything he was doing threatened to bring me to a climax—even his freaking smell turned me on.

"Why the fuck aren't you speaking?" Andrei parted the drenched folds of my opening and dipped a finger deep within me. Every thrust sent me spiraling out of control.

I cried out, wanting my release.

"What do you want, Rae? My cock? My mouth? You want me to fuck you hard enough to kill you?"

Yes, yes, yes, yes!

"Cock," I panted, the word effortlessly rolling out of my mouth. "I want your cock."

"Too fucking bad," he spat, withdrawing his fingers from both my openings.

I collapsed onto my stomach, gasping for breath as hot anger enveloped me. I hadn't come yet. The letdown brought tears of frustration to my eyes. I felt Andrei's pressure on the mattress disappear and I bit back a scream. I needed to climax.

His husky voice came from somewhere above me. "Get yourself off."

I rolled onto my back, expecting to find him fully clothed. Instead, the sight of his powerful, hulking body was the one that greeted me. My throat went dry and everything else became wet.

"Okay," I whispered, knowing that with the visual stimulation his body was providing, I only had to flick my clit and it would be over.

Andrei's eyes were dark, almost onyx, with desire. His huge erection jutted proudly from the slab of his abdomen, translucent moisture glistening on its large crown. And veins strained along his thick, flush shaft while his testicles hung tight with unreleased liquid pleasure.

I spread my legs, opening myself to him. Glancing down, I examined myself. My sex pulsed with need and my clit stood erect from within its damp folds. I rubbed the swollen bud and moaned, shuddering. My eyes were trained on Andrei, not because he was "visual stimulation", but because there was no other place I wanted to look. He remained impassive, save for his darkening stare and ever-hardening manhood. When I slipped two fingers into my opening, I imagined it was him, fucking me harder than ever. I imagined the large, bulbous head pressing against my entrance and the throbbing shaft brushing against my inner walls.

"Ah, shit," I cried out, lifting my ass off the bed as I went deeper. "Ah, yes…"

And with that, I came apart in my own hand. Through heavy-lidded eyes, I watched Andrei sit on the edge of the bed, his legs dangling over.

"Get on the floor." His voice was little more than a murmur.

I wasn't in the mood to argue and, quite frankly, I wanted him inside me too much to do so. I slowly rolled off the bed and knelt before him, his cock in my face. I needed it inside me.

"Suck me off."

Aye. Da. Hai. Ja. Na'am. Oui. Sí. Sim. Fuck, yes!

I wrapped my hand around the thick base, sliding my palm along it. His cock was honestly the biggest I'd ever had and caressing him was like receiving an early Christmas present. Looking up and meeting his sharp eyes, I knew that it felt the same way for him, too.

I licked my lips. "It's always a surprise when you manage to fit this big, monstrous dick inside my tiny pussy," I remarked before I swiped my thumb across its glossy head. Desperate need tugged at my lower belly. "Does it surprise you, Andrei? Does it surprise you when my greedy pussy swallows it whole?"

Andrei's hands were firmly planted on either side of his thighs. "Yes," he hissed, his eyes momentarily turning crimson.

I stroked him lazily, every single one of his veins imprinting on my slick palm. "I'm going to deep throat you so good, you'll be fucking my esophagus," I said huskily, my tongue slipping out to taste the musky tang of his pre-cum.

He groaned, his hands immediately flying to my hair. "Rae." My name on his tongue sounded like both a curse and a prayer. "Such a fucking dirty mouth."

I licked my way down his shaft, his musky taste driving me batshit crazy. I could feel my own juices trickling down my thighs before I lowered my tongue to his crown and sucked him in. He drew in a sharp breath, his fingertips digging into my scalp.

"Cock-sucking Jezebel," he growled, tugging cruelly at my hair.

My ponytail had long come undone and so my hair fell into my face in wild, inky curls. Pain shot through my scalp but

152

I didn't give a damn. The only thing that mattered was Andrei's arousal in my mouth, hard and pulsing. I took in more of him, my hands circling him, holding him steady. And his filthy talk was only making me wetter.

Andrei jerked into me, and I scraped my teeth against his heated flesh, tugging a curse from his mouth. My cheeks hollowed and I felt him hit the sensitive tissue at the back of my throat. Suppressing my gag reflex, I hummed a tune, the vibrations turning him to a shuddering hulk of need.

"Oh, fuck," he hissed, "get off me. Rae, get off!" He pulled at my hair, lifting my mouth off his manhood.

I scowled. "You were just about to come."

"Inside you," he countered sharply, standing and pulling me up with him. "I need to come inside you."

He shoved me onto my bed and I drew myself up on my elbows, regarding him through hazy eyes. The anticipation was practically killing me. If I died right then, they'd put "Death from the female equivalent of blue balls" on my death certificate.

Andrei drawled, "But first, a lesson is in order, don't you think?"

"You're not going to spank me, are you?" I snorted.

Reaching out, he massaged my heavy breasts in slow, steady movements... before yanking my nipples toward him. I yelped at the sudden, sharp pain, moisture pooling between my legs.

"What the fuck?" I hissed, the pain dissipating when he gently rubbed my abused nipples with the pads of his thumbs. Contradicting sensations flowed through my responsive body.

"I'm understandably irritated that you sought a witch out," Andrei said in low, menacing tones. Before I could explain, his hand came down on my entrance, the thwack of his palm against my slippery flesh resonating in the room.

I arched my back, trying to close my legs. He held them apart.

"You like my cock only when it's in you, on your terms," Andrei snarled, his big hand connecting with my cunt once again. His middle finger entered me partially, the sensation turning me inside out with ecstasy.

I was so tightly wound I could've come right then. "Please," I begged, shedding my dignity along with my pain threshold. "Damn you, demon! Fuck me!"

He slapped my pussy again, harder than ever, his fingers taunting my clit in the process.

"Why should I? Why don't you get your hunter to fuck you?"

My breathing came out in short pants. "No one... no one can make me come like you do," I confessed, the throbbing in my crotch so intense it brought tears to my eyes. "Only you," I murmured deliriously. "Only you."

Andrei's mouth was suddenly on my opening, his tongue licking along my slit. His fingers parted the tender lips and his tongue plunged into me, furious and intense. I raised my hips to offer myself to him, screaming blue murder when he drew my clitoris into his mouth. He sucked on the swollen nerves until I could feel my orgasm surging up from within me like a bubbling pot of broth.

"I'm gonna... Oh, fuck, I'm gonna come!" I cried before coming onto his face. My climax went on for what felt like days, and all the while Andrei languidly lapped my release up.

When my breathing returned to normal, his mouth left me and his body came up over me.

A strange look crossed his face before he guided his cock into my soaked entrance. I didn't have time to analyze his expression when he abruptly plunged into me, to the hilt, before withdrawing and repeating the process.

My legs wound around his waist as he continued to pummel into me so ferociously that I knew I wasn't going to be able to stand for long periods tomorrow. His teeth nipped at my painful nipples and his hands clasped my sides while he drove himself into me.

"Harder," I demanded, sinking my nails into the powerful muscles of his back. "Oh, God. Yes!"

He didn't need any urging because that was exactly what he was doing. Every feral thrust brought me a renewed stab of pain because he was that big. He didn't care and I didn't mind. I didn't mind that he didn't care.

"Fuck you, Rainelle Erickson," he bit out, sinking his teeth into the plump flesh of one breast.

I wailed.

"Fuck you for being so obstinate," he continued as he rotated his hips, his manhood wonderfully hitting the most sensitive spots deep inside me. "Fuck you... for... being so addictive."

"Ah," I gasped, meeting his thrusts with the jerks of my hips. "You're so... so good, Andrei. So good."

His lips came crashing down against mine and I automatically wrapped my arms around his neck. I could taste myself on his tongue.

"Mm," I moaned, sucking on his tongue.

He groaned, a low and needy sound, before I released him, allowing him to explore my mouth more thoroughly.

I couldn't live without this sex. I couldn't live without him.

Feelings, my inner voice smugly articulated.

"I'm... coming!" I shrieked, clenching around Andrei's length buried inside me as an orgasm overtook me.

"Do it for me," he grunted loudly, his whole body tensing before he spilled his seed into my grasping channel.

My breathing was ragged and my heart beat as if I were running the Olympics. Andrei kissed my nose before easing himself out of me and gracefully flopping down beside me. I felt the emptiness immediately but his arms around me tempered that. He pulled me to him, until my head was on his chest and one leg rested over his. But I stiffened, unsure about this. The last time we'd done anything remotely close to cuddling was back in Vegas when I'd been blissfully ignorant of his name, let alone his species.

Nevertheless, as he stroked my hair, I found myself beginning to relax... and I exhaled.

"*Eşti frumoasă*, Rainelle," he intoned, in what I assumed was his mother tongue.

I drew circles on his flat stomach. "What does that mean?"

"Simply that you are beautiful, the most beautiful creature I have ever laid eyes on..." His hand trailed down my back and then squeezed one butt cheek. "... in every realm, in every millennia."

My fingers stilled. "Stop this," I breathed, hating every minute of this sudden turn of events. I wrenched myself out of his embrace, sitting up and staring straight ahead. "For the record, I didn't call any witch. Daniel did. Of course, I didn't mind you beating the shit out of my pussy, but I don't appreciate the accusations. Even if I did get someone to help me, that's my prerogative and none of your concern." I sucked

156

in air. "What does it matter anyway? You can screw me in my dreams."

Out of my peripheral, I saw him sit up. "Only if you've been drinking and your inhibitions are low."

I laughed, and turned to look at him. *Why the hell did he have to be so sexy?* "So as long as I go cold turkey, you'll keep your hands off me when I sleep?"

His lips twitched. "Can't make any promises."

I laughed again, pecking him chastely on his shoulder. His hands came up to my hair and he jerked my head back before grazing his lips against mine. Kissing turned to something else and all thoughts of what **myrna_lake67** said flew out the window.

"Baby Phat, you here?"

Temp's voice came from my living room. Sighing, I finished up the remains of my breakfast before hollering, "In the kitchen!"

Seconds later, he was striding in, a ridiculous purple fedora perched on his head, which looked completely out of place with his casual white shirt and grey board shorts. And from the few strands peeking out from under the hat, I noticed that his hair was icy blonde again.

"Morning, sunshine," he said, grinning as he pulled open my refrigerator. He came out with a Coke and stood before the center island, regarding me. "You look nicely fucked. Met someone at the club? Oh, wait… Andrei was here last night."

"As a matter of fact, yes. He fucked me quite nicely, thank you. Now everything hurts—in a good way, of course." I flashed Temp a serene smile.

He groaned. "I didn't ask for details, whore of Satan."

I shrugged, hopping off the stool and taking my dishes to the sink. "I didn't ask for any visitors today either. How'd you get in anyway?"

"Oh, I borrowed your iPod."

With one of my belongings in his possession, Temp could teleport to wherever I was with no hassle. It was how Andrei got to me so easily. Clearly, I need to stop giving demons access to my personal items.

"I don't remember loaning it to you." I let out a sigh of defeat, leaned against the sink, and glared at him. "Anyway, why are you here?"

He popped the can open and took a swig before declaring, "Got some info you may or may not be interested in. JP-type of info."

"Temp, stop dicking around. What is it?"

"All right, all right," he said, holding one hand up. "Isn't sex supposed to relax people?"

"Temp!"

"Okay! You know those girls his sister mentioned?"

I nodded.

"Well, I casually asked him if he was into ménages à trois," he paused to wink at me, "Because a friend of mine knew he'd brought a group of chicks to his apartment and wanted in on the action." He chugged more Coke, winking again. "Guess I was wrong, Baby Phat. He says he's a one-woman pony."

"That's it?"

"Yeah, and that the girls are part of an exclusive virgins-only club at some university. Could be a sorority, I don't know. Do the French get into that Kappa-Alpha-Delta bull? JP wouldn't go into detail, but said there were six of them. All babes."

"Why would he be hanging out with a bunch of hot nuns?" I fretted.

Temp shrugged. "I don't know but if I ever got myself into that sorority house... Well, let's just say 'Hymen! Bye, men.'"

I wrinkled my nose in disgust. "Ugh. Have you no shame?"

"I don't, actually. Shame is for the unfulfilled." He arched a brow. "Still ashamed of sleeping with a demon? Or having a demon brother?"

I sucked in a deep breath, meeting his eye. "No, not really."

Temp's face broke into a smile. "There's hope for you yet, Baby Phat." He inclined his head toward the doorway. "Let's go. I think it's time you were acquainted with JP."

Chapter 10

"Honestly, I don't even know why I'm doing this anymore," I grumbled, followed Temp into the elevator of JP's high-rise complex, and sighed heavily.

Temp was eyeing me as the doors closed. "Because you love a mystery just as much as the next person. We're like Fred and Daphne. Minus the sexual tension, of course."

Then Temp pressed the button that would take us to the penthouse. I rolled my eyes.

"I doubt there's any mystery, aside from the fact that JP is clearly taking advantage of a choir of virgins. Besides, you're so not Fred. He looked classier with that little scarf of his."

"The only person that's being taken advantage of is yours truly. I could be out getting laid right now."

I shot him a glare. "I didn't ask you to play Tag-Along Timmy."

"No, what you asked for was info. But all you do is drool over the guy and hope you'll catch him in the act of murdering someone." He snorted. "Quite frankly, I think his sister's trying to hook you two up over some fake conspiracy."

"I don't drool over him. Plus he's not even my type."

At this, Temp sent me a dazzling grin. "True. We both know you prefer your men to be hung like a horse with egos to match."

I glared at him. "So what's our cover story? I can't exactly start with a *Hey, I just met you, and this is crazy, but what's up with all those virgins, baby*?"

Temp laughed obnoxiously. "One, don't ever sing that again. Ever! And two, just let me do all the talking. He'll spill."

I playfully slapped his arm just as the doors opened. And beyond them, who else but none other than JP himself was blinking at us expectantly, a glass of amber liquid in his hand. It was nearly midday and he was still in his boxers—silk, as expected, red silk. I had no idea why that was unsurprising to me. It just was.

"Temp," he greeted, "I thought you were alone." He didn't even bother to mask the interest in his voice as he gave me a look that was customary between lions and prey out in the wild.

"I know three's a crowd," Temp said genially, stepping into JP's sunlit apartment and dragging me behind him, "but this is my sister, Rae," he pronounced, introducing me to the man I'd been stalking from afar.

I wanted to punch Temp right then. *What happened to discretion?!*

"By sister, he means non-related. We're just tight like that," I put in quickly, aware of how lame I sounded.

JP didn't bat an eyelash as he came over, bent slightly, and air-kissed both my cheeks, the smell of whiskey on him

161

washing over me. "Gorgeous. Too bad I'm in a committed relationship, otherwise…"

"Otherwise what?" Temp prodded curiously, throwing a heavy arm around my shoulders.

JP looked me over again, his slate-grey eyes practically undressing me. "We would be fucking." His eyes swiveled back to Temp. "Is that why you brought her? To tempt me away from Ava?"

"I'm right here," I fumed. "And you're not my type." I didn't appreciate being discussed like a prostitute.

JP laughed and Temp joined him. "Come. We can talk about your type on the balcony." Without preamble, he took my hand in his and tugged me into step beside him. "Quite the spitfire, aren't you?"

"I find your tone both condescending and irritating, especially when we've just met," I retorted, trying to pry my fingers out of his iron grasp to no avail.

"Really? And I find it quite pleasing that the woman that has been following me around for over a month now is as beautiful up close as she is from afar." He stopped before the glass sliding door that led to the balcony, pausing to slide it open before dragging me out with him.

Choosing my words carefully, I said huskily, "Just because you're not my type, doesn't mean you're not fun to look at." *Ick!*

The tiled balcony was empty, save for a wicker chair and a small, round table cluttered with empty liquor bottles.

JP threw his head back and laughed, leaning against the granite balustrade lining the perimeter of the balcony. "*Mais oui*, that does make sense." He regarded me over the rim of his whiskey glass as he took a small sip. For someone who was clearly an early morning drinker, he was astonishingly lucid.

162

I noticed that Temp, despite his I'll-do-the-talking speech, was taking his sweet time to come outside and I suddenly felt a little uncomfortable under JP's probing gaze. And another thing was bothering me: His unmistakable hard-on. I was no prude, but his blatant sexuality was a little too much for me. His boxers were tented at the front, obviously unable to contain what was definitely an impressive serpent.

And now I'm using animals to describe cocks, I thought self-deprecatingly.

"So, to what do I owe this visit, *chérie?*"

"I, uh, wanted to meet all of Temp's friends." *Real smooth.*

JP raised a questioning brow. "So you thought following me around was the best way to do that?"

I turned beet red, unable to answer that without sounding like a total idiot. I really needed pointers from Daniel. I was clearly getting rusty. But on the flip side, this wasn't what I usually do. Taking a bunch of pictures of husbands with their pants down was way easier than playing Sherlock in clubs.

"Okay, this has gone on long enough." Temp's bored voice came from inside. He sauntered onto the balcony and positioned himself between JP and me, his back to me. Running a hand through his already unkempt hair, he muttered, "Jean-Philippe? Come here."

"What are you doing?" I asked, puzzled.

"Rae, shut up for a second. I mean it. Don't say a single word," he hissed.

"Huh," I huffed, watching as JP approached Temp, towering over him by at least a foot.

"You want to please me, don't you... baby?" Temp said huskily, reaching up to stroke JP's cheek.

"I do," JP replied, sounding like an eager bitch.

"What the...?" I murmured under my breath, stepping aside so I could get a good look at the unbelievable scene before me.

"That's good, baby," Temp said gently, running a finger across JP's lips. "Tell me why you're recruiting virgins."

To my astonishment, JP was stroking himself through the thin fabric of his boxers, his erection curved and straining to escape. "Recruiting virgins?"

"Yeah. You told me there were six of them. Remember."

"Yes," he groaned in response, still gripping himself, a small patch of wetness the evidence of his pre-ejaculation. "Damien. The girls are for Damien."

"What for? Sex?"

JP groaned, his fist clenching so tightly around his length that his knuckles whitened. "No, vessels."

"Drug mules?" I spoke up, and Temp turned to glare at me before returning his gaze to JP.

"Bodies," the Frenchman whispered, and sank to his knees, his hands flailing to the front of Temp's jeans. "Please," he begged, his voice cracking. "Let me please you."

"Fuck, no!" Temp snapped, leaping back as if JP had the plague. "Stay. Don't touch me."

JP stayed on his knees but stopped touching him.

Temp cleared his throat and asked, "Is that all you know?"

"Yes. Bodies for Damien's friends. All I know."

"Good boy." Temp cocked his head to one side. "Now JP, you're starting to feel the effects of all this Jack you've been drinking. It has caused a hallucination."

"Yes."

"Close your eyes and surrender to the fatigue, Jean-Philippe," Temp commanded, his voice soft yet authoritative.

JP lay down and curled up, his eyes shutting. It was quite pathetic to watch.

"You used your... your demon mojo on him!" I squeaked in incredulity, marveling at how JP was already breathing—the even breathing of someone in a deep sleep.

"What of it?" Temp snapped defensively, and I laughed.

"I had no idea you could, you know, use it on guys." But it made sense. Men and women, it didn't matter, as long as they were humans... as long as they had souls... and as long as they had libidos.

To my surprise, Temp reddened. "I swear, Rae, if you ever mention this to anyone..."

"Relax. I won't tell a soul. You were helping me." I led the way back inside JP's apartment. "I just don't understand what he meant. Bodies? Does that equal prostitution?"

"You really are ignorant," Temp muttered, his tone compelling me to look back at him. "Damien's 'friends' are demons, which means those virgins are now possessed."

This time, I was absolutely positive that it was a dream fashioned by my sexually depraved and masochistic brain.

Lying in bed with a mountain of pillows propped under my head, I could feel that I was completely naked beneath my "one thousand thread count Egyptian cotton" sheets. Oh, Andrei and Daniel were, too—naked, I mean. They stood side by side (completely ridiculous because I had no doubt that

Andrei would rip the slightly smaller man to shreds if they so much as breathed the same air), waiting to do my bidding like a pair of sexy, muscular blow-up dolls. There was no doubt in my mind that this was going to be a sex dream because that was all my subconscious mind was into these days. Well, if this was what Inner Rae wanted, who was I to argue with her? This was her dream, after all.

"Hi," I said to the two men, my voice a few octaves lower than my regular one. Dream Rainelle had the sultry voice of a siren, whereas Real Rainelle was an uncultured cursing hussy. And Dream Rae wanted a little guy-on-guy action to get the party started. "Why don't you, um, kiss each other?"

This would be the real test. Both men were straight as arrows and I couldn't even imagine either of them being with anyone of the same sex—especially Andrei, who made it no secret that swimming in my pussy was one of his favorite pastimes.

Argh! Now I was getting wet.

Andrei's hair was just how I liked it—wild and undone, cascading in long, thick rivulets. It fell past his broad shoulders, brushing just beneath his ribcage. From there, the only hair visible was the dark smattering of his happy trail beneath his navel that showed the way to the V of his pelvis and the jut of his spectacular hard-on nestled in wispy dark curls. Daniel was just the opposite, his dark chestnut hair perfectly coiffed and his pubic area absolutely bare. I had no idea why Dream Rae thought he'd be bare down there, she just did. She also assumed that he'd be circumcised.

"Oh, and make it a wet kiss, m'kay? I want to see some tongue action," I added as an afterthought, licking my lips in anticipation as they looked each other over. Typical males, contemplating who would be the submissive and the dominant.

166

Finally, Andrei snagged Daniel's smaller form to his bigger one and pressed his lips against Daniel's. It was, quite probably, one of the sexiest things I'd ever witnessed—right next to Andrei playing with himself, of course. Then, Daniel's hands came up around Andrei's waist as the kiss morphed into something wetter and more animalistic. Their cocks, as hard and curved as they were, ground against each other, the sight enough to make me want to wedge myself between them.

"Okay, enough," I panted when it became too much, and they instantly broke apart. I kicked the covers off, they were only in the way. "I want the both of you inside me. Now!"

"Sure you'll be able to handle that?" Andrei asked lazily, his hand caressing his erection.

I knew from experience that he loved it when I traced each and every pulsing vein along his shaft with the tip of my tongue. I ached to do that.

"Oh, she'll handle it, all right," Daniel put in, approaching the right side of the bed.

I crawled to the edge and hoisted myself up onto my knees, reaching out to pull him into a kiss. His breath was hot and minty, and all the hairs on my body instantly stood up when I felt his tongue trace the seam of my lips. I felt pressure on the mattress behind me, and suddenly, Andrei's hands were planted on my hips. Leaning back into him without releasing Daniel from our lip-lock, I rubbed my ass against Andrei's cock, reveling in the moisture I felt there.

"Mm, you feel so good," I breathed into Daniel's mouth, reaching out to palm his impressive erection. "Can't wait for you to be inside me."

Andrei's fingers ran along my slit before he tweaked my erect little clit and generously began to finger-fuck me with two long, thick fingers while his other hand was busy massaging my left breast. The sensation was insane and it brought me tiny, intense shockwaves of bliss.

"Ah, shit," I hissed, pulling back from Daniel. "I'm gonna suck you off now. And you, Andrei, you're gonna fuck me good, like you always do."

"Lie back down, Rae," Andrei instructed, and I did as I was told, although I was somewhat peeved that even in my dream he was so freaking bossy. "That's right. You're so fucking wet for me, for your little hunter." Then I was spread wide open, my legs stretching across the bed with impossible flexibility. Andrei gently ran a finger along my inner thigh, feeling the juices coating my skin. "You're a dirty, greedy cock-loving whore and this dream proves it."

"Uh-huh," I groaned, shivering inside when Daniel knelt beside my head and pushed my hair out of my face.

His cock was probably about seven inches long (Dream Me wanted to be generous but realistic) and his shaft was thicker toward the bottom. The head was a deep pink and slick with pre-cum and I was aching to lap it all up. Licking my lips, I mentally urged him to lower it to my waiting mouth.

Gripping his length in one hand, he brought it down and I let my tongue slide out to taste him. I flicked the tip of my tongue into the tiny slit on his cock head, slurping up his juice. Weirdly, he tasted citrusy.

Orange cum, I thought, smiling before he pushed himself into me as far as he could go. *At least I'm getting my vitamin C.*

Slowly, Daniel began to fuck my mouth. Despite my attention being focused on deep throating Daniel, I hadn't forgotten about Andrei. No one could forget about someone like him. I wanted him to watch me with another man's penis in my mouth, but he was completely focused on running his index finger along my dripping cleft and around my clit, making his presence known down there.

I trembled, mentally telling him not to be gentle, to fuck me hard because I was so ready for him I was practically spurting.

He must have read my thoughts.

With no warning, Andrei drove himself into me, balls deep. As usual, he stretched me to the limit. My labia gratefully gave way for him, and protested as he withdrew, his shaft brushing the little sensitive bundle of nerves that was my clit in the process, before he plunged back in again.

"Ah!" I cried out, momentarily releasing Daniel's cock from the embrace of my lips.

"Oh, shut up!" Daniel admonished, sticking himself back into the wet cavern of my mouth and effectively shutting me up.

Andrei's fast, forceful strokes drew out the white liquid of my arousal. The feel of his heavy balls slapping against my butt cheeks was like music to my ears, because it was proof that he was just aching for release like I was.

You're going to tear me apart, I thought in delight since I couldn't open my mouth without depriving myself of Daniel's cock.

And you fucking love it, was Andrei's unspoken response as he sank into me again, his navy eyes fixed on mine.

I totally did.

I writhed and thrashed with pleasure, careful not to accidentally bite Daniel's manhood off. Every withdrawal and thrust pushed me that much further into the arms of my orgasm. And that, coupled with Daniel's throbbing salty dick in my mouth, was going to be the death of me.

Don't come yet, I thought, mentally sending the command to both men. *Flip onto your back, Andrei, and take my pussy while Daniel takes my ass. That's what I want now.*

In the dream world, logistics doesn't matter. In less than a second, Andrei was flat on his back and I was leaning over him, offering my behind to Daniel. Warm and hard beneath me, Andrei held me up with his hands. My lips were inches away from his so I kissed him. From behind me, Daniel was spreading my butt cheeks and, because this was just a wet dream, I allowed him to enter me without lubrication.

And goddammit! It felt like heaven to have both ends stuffed with dicks. But Daniel was only incidental, a pawn I was using to heighten the pleasure I experienced with Andrei. This was all about Andrei.

"Ugh!" I groaned when Daniel withdrew until only his head was inside me. "Oh, fuck," I gasped when he sliced back into me. The pain felt so real, so divine that I was beginning to have a hard time believing that I was only conjuring this up.

Daniel's thrusts quickened and as he hammered into me, Andrei's up-thrusts did, too. It was surreal how I felt the swell of his cock distend my sex, heard the whoosh of air with every quick breath he took, and saw his gem-like pupils dilate.

Someone cleared their throat… and it wasn't either of my men.

I raised my head and nearly choked on my tongue because there were 'two' Andreis—one buried deep inside me and one hovering over my bed, fully dressed with a dark look on his face. Because of shock, the scene I'd created disappeared and I was left naked and alone. In a flash, I strived to visualize a peach baby doll on me and soon felt a semblance of dignity.

"How dare you interrupt my dream?" I asked Andrei, hopping off the opposite end of my bed and putting some much-needed space between us.

"Were you about to come?"

To my surprise, he sounded like he was on the verge of laughter.

"I... That's none of your business," I snapped in annoyance. It was absolutely mortifying to have him barge in unannounced while I was right in the middle of fucking him, and someone else, in la-la land.

"For the record, I might be wide but my chest is not that broad."

The motherfucker was out-and-out laughing at me now. What was worse was that I could feel heat staining my cheeks like an embarrassed little girl caught red-handed with her hands down her panties by her grandmother.

"Wake up, Rae," I begged myself, pinching my arms. "Wake up from this nightmare."

"I'm very flattered, Rae," Andrei went on, that same smug smile tugging at his lips—but the smile vanished quickly. "Of course, knowing that you want to fuck the hunter isn't exactly appealing to me." He paused, and before I could so much as blink, he was beside me. "As long as you understand that I don't share, I'm fine with you dreaming." His eyes regarded me with a steely gaze.

"Don't share?" *I couldn't believe this!* But then, he really didn't have to know that I couldn't have cared less about Daniel. So instead of giving assent, my reply was, "I'm not some toy that boys hoard in the playground! How dare you?"

"On any given day, your insolence would turn me on but that's not why I'm here," Andrei said, completely unruffled. "I need a favor."

171

"A favor," I repeated, quirking a brow. "From me?"

"There's a function I need to attend next week. I need a date."

Because this was a dream, I was more than able to actually swallow my tongue. Then I felt it travel down my throat, ease through my esophagus before miraculously coming back up and reattaching itself, so I was capable of saying an astonished "You're asking me out?"

Andrei's brow creased. "Semantics."

"You're asking me out?" I repeated, finally noticing the twitch in his jaw.

"Fine. Yes, I'm asking you, Rainelle Erickson, to accompany me to an event."

Oh boy! This was certainly a day of surprises. From Temp seducing JP and discovering that JP was tangling with demons, to an intense wet dream, and finally, the badass Lord Andrei Anghelescu asking me out—in my dream, no less. This was turning out to be the most warped day of my life.

"Why couldn't you ask me in person?" I asked, enjoying the look of controlled annoyance currently on his face.

"Because I'm in the middle of something. In Novosibirsk."

"Surely teleporting from Russia would only take a second?"

Andrei's eyebrows creased into a frown. "Are you deliberately being difficult?"

"I can't help it. It's what you do to me." I sighed. "What event is this?"

His hand came up to cup my chin. "A bonding ritual."

"Bonding ritual?"

Andrei sighed heavily. "I forget how ignorant you are," he murmured, rubbing my chin with the pad of his thumb, causing twinges of desire to splice with my irritation. "Roan is an incubus that wants to be bound eternally to his... woman. I want you to witness the ceremony."

I stepped away from him. "Is it against her will?"

"No," Andrei replied vehemently, pulling me back. "It can't work if one doesn't want the other."

If one doesn't want the other.

"You don't have to be afraid that I'll force you to come, Rae," Andrei added, and he crushed his lips against mine, his arms around my lower back.

I melted against him, a billion thoughts swirling in my head. I thought about telling him about JP and the virgins. Then I thought about asking him why he wanted me to be privy to a ceremony that was obviously as ancient as time, and as personal as things could get.

But dream or not, all of those thoughts evaporated the instant he pinned me down to the bed, his skillful hands zoning in on my sopping cunt.

Chapter 11

From: rae_of_light@gmail.com
To: alfontaine@laposte.net
Subject: (No Subject)

'He should stay away from Damien.'

I couldn't do up my jeans.

After fighting with the size nine DKNY skinnies for at least fifteen minutes, I changed tack and pleaded with them to work with me. I didn't buy them to give me problems; I bought them to make my ass look good, which they did.

"I don't want to rip you but you're making this an impossibility," I muttered, hopping up and down before giving up and collapsing on my unmade bed.

To be fair to myself, I recently had my contraceptive shot and, since I was so freaking lucky, was probably one of those rare cases that experienced weight gain as a side effect.

Not that Andrei's complaining, my inner voice snorted. If anything, the extra junk in my trunk turned him on.

Sunlight from the large, open French windows streamed into my bedroom, a contrast to my gloomy mood. But arguing with denim was the least of my problems. I mean, I had way more important things on my mind.

Sighing heavily, I peeled my jeans off and settled on a flimsy white cotton dress, thankful that I shaved my legs the previous day. Just as I was attempting to tame my wild hair by the bathroom mirror, I heard a noise in my bedroom. Glancing out the doorway, I caught Andrei sliding the door to the balcony open.

"Why don't I ever sense you before I see you?" I grumbled loudly (not for the first time today), finally gathering my hair up into a bun. Then, I padded out the bathroom and met his assessing gaze.

"Because I don't want you to," was his enlightening response. "I thought we'd do breakfast before I take you shopping."

I quickly looked him over, taking in the grey T-shirt molded to his broad chest, and the casual slacks hanging off his lean hips. His hair was loose, just the way I liked it, and a pair of Ray-Bans was perched on his head to keep it out of his face.

"Breakfast?" I blurted out incredulously. "Shopping?"

Andrei's lips twitched as though he wanted to smile, something that actually happened once in a blue moon. "I do eat, you know. It continues to be a worthy distraction."

I swallowed, trying to process his suggestion. "Yeah, but we've never really gone out... together."

"Believe me, Rae," he said in a low growl, stepping into my personal space and sucking in all my oxygen, "Going out with me can be just as fun as staying in." His arms snaked around my waist and his hands cupped a handful of my ass, pulling me to him, pulling me to his scent, his hardness. "You

175

feel so fucking good," he said into my ear, nibbling my ear lobe.

Hot damn!

Ignoring the sudden dampness in my panties, I mumbled quickly, "You, um, mentioned something about shopping? What for?"

"The bonding ritual," he murmured, grazing his teeth against my bare shoulder as he spoke.

I pulled back, looking up at his hooded eyes. "Why, is there some sort of dress code? Care to explain exactly what I…"

The lustful look in Andrei's eyes vanished, replaced by one of annoyance. "I already explained."

"No, you just gave some half-assed reason for wanting me there." I wrenched myself out of his embrace. "I'm not an idiot. If this is your creative way of tricking me into offering myself up as some gullible freaky cultish demon hunter sacrifice, I'll see right through you."

Andrei's head jerked back as though he'd been slapped. "Why the fuck would you say that?"

"Because you're being so secretive! For all I know, I'm the one being bonded… to you."

Andrei's eyes narrowed. "Let's get one thing straight, Rainelle. I have no wish to be bonded to a human as mulish, unpredictable, and frustrating as you," he bit out, his baby blues turning crimson. "The only reason I'm asking you is because we've been fucking and this ceremony calls for the king, me, to have a female standing by him, preferably someone he has a physical relationship with."

I scowled at him and snarkily replied. "Glad you cleared that up, Your Majesty. Because there's absolutely no misconception on my side. This…" I motioned between the two of us, "… is just good old-fashioned sex. You're a demon lord, for fuck's sake, older than me by millennia. So there is no way in hell that this can even be labeled a relationship, physical or otherwise."

We stared at each other and I was positive my green eyes were as hostile as Andrei's blue ones. Then, I looked away.

"I'm hungry," I muttered.

Andrei chose the famous Les Deux Magots Café on the corner of a cobbled street in Saint-Germain des Prés, which was filled with touristy types snapping away with Nikons. The cafe was busy but Andre managed to find an al fresco round table for two under a red and white checked parasol.

Wordlessly, he pulled out a chair for me and I sat, momentarily stunned. Andrei gauged my reaction and rolled his eyes.

"What? I'm not a complete rake."

"Could've fooled me," I said before thinking.

Andrei's eyes caught mine. "You're a woman and I am, for all intents and purposes, a man. From time to time, I will do things like pull out your chair. I didn't expect you to look at me as if I've strangled a baby in front of you." He grabbed a laminated menu off the table and quickly scanned it before putting it down.

I laughed. "You're so sexy when you pretend you're not an ass."

To my astonishment, he flashed me a grin. "Shut the fuck up."

"And there he is," I said, sighing dramatically. "The ass."

Andrei let out a low, husky laugh that went straight to my nether regions. I clenched my thighs together and, as perceptive as he was, he noticed my discomfort and smirked. Thankfully, a waitress appeared with a pen and pad in hand, and Andrei ordered for us in fluent French. Since my command of the language was more than passable, I shot him a dirty look.

"I could've ordered for myself. What if I'm not in the mood for a chocolate muffin?"

Andrei's leg brushed against mine and I jumped, annoyed with myself for reacting so obviously. "I think you are."

This is just breakfast, Rae. Don't act like a hormonal teenager. Be sane.

"Are you okay?" Andrei's perfect features were a picture of mock concern as his leg touched mine again.

"I'm fine," I said through clenched teeth. It had only been two days since I had him inside me. *Two!* Surely my need for his body wasn't that strong? "So," I said in forced aloofness. "How long is this shopping thing going to take? I'm a busy girl, after all."

"Busy chasing after possessed virgins?" His voice was so quiet I almost didn't hear him. But when I did, all the hairs on my body stood at attention.

"How did you..." My voice trailed off as I mentally answered my unfinished question—Temp.

"Your brother did right to come to me," Andrei said, reading my mind, "and I will take care of it. Not you. Me."

I sighed, accepting my fate. "You're not mad?"

His eyes gleamed wickedly, burning into mine. "Oh, rest assured, I will punish you for disobeying me."

I couldn't remember if this was the part where I told him that I didn't take orders from him. I couldn't remember because my vagina throbbed in anticipation of the promised punishment and all witty retorts died on my lips. Blood rushed to my clit and I squirmed in my chair, wanting to relieve the ache.

There was something seriously wrong with me!

The sweet scent of coffee crept into my nostrils. And I realized that, while I drowned in Andrei's bottomless eyes, the waitress had come and gone, setting our respective plates on the table. Right on cue, my stomach rumbled.

Without preamble, I bit into my muffin and closed my eyes, savoring the moist chocolate setting off fireworks on my taste buds. I haven't had anything this good in a long time and when I opened my eyes, I found Andrei staring at me.

"Can you hang around me for five seconds without thinking of having me naked?" I asked, my voice heavy with sarcasm. Inside, I was panting because I knew that look. It was a classic I-want-to-fuck-you-hard-and-make-you-speak-in-tongues look.

"That's not what I was thinking," said Andrei, chugging down his coffee as if it were a bottle of beer.

"Really?" I arched a brow, taking another bite of chocolate-y goodness.

He nodded, leering at me. "I was thinking that is one lucky cupcake, cupcake."

I couldn't help it, I laughed—laughed until tears were streaming down my cheeks and I thought I'd choke to death. Passersby curiously glanced my way. I just couldn't help it.

"Who are you and what have you done with the real Lord Andrei Anghelescu?" I gasped when I was done.

Andrei had patiently waited out my bout of laughter before saying, "I don't know what you mean."

It was then that I noticed that he'd ordered a full English breakfast for himself, and my mouth watered.

"You're in a pretty good mood," I elaborated, although he knew exactly what I meant. Then I picked up my fork and stabbed a piece of bacon, before bringing it to my lips. "What?" I asked when I caught Andrei looking at me.

"What are you doing to me, Rae?" he ground out, shifting in his seat. "We should go. Shopping," he added.

Curious, I asked, "Which store are we hitting first?" Hey, I wouldn't be a female if I said no to a shopping spree, regardless of the weird occasion. "Actually, I've been meaning to check out Lafayette sometime. It's what? Ten floors?"

Andrei shook his head ruefully. "We're not going upmarket, Rae. Not for this." He rose and slapped a couple of Euros on the table.

There was no way I was letting perfectly cooked bacon go to waste. So I shot Andrei a pointed look and picked up his plate. A girl just had to eat.

The alleyway was far too narrow for a car to pass through, so we went on foot, much to my relief. Being trapped in such a confined space with such a big, sexual man would have been torture... again. Still, I told myself that this detour wasn't as dodgy as it looked... or felt. For all I knew, Andrei was leading me into an ambush. As quickly as the thought came, I pushed it away. He had plenty of opportunities to kill me, most of them when I was totally shell-shocked after multiple orgasms. But then again, he had no real reason to kill me. He basically told me that I was his sustenance. I was more valuable to him alive.

God, this is so stupid. I'm following a guy I'm sleeping with and wondering if he wants to kill me.

Letting out a frustrated growl, Andrei snapped me from my mental scolding. And without warning, he pushed me up against a wall, his entire body covering mine.

"For the last time, Rae, I don't want to fucking kill you!" he snarled, pinning my arms at my sides. "Why would I want to do that? Why?"

"Are you a mind reader?" I muttered, trying in vain to get out of his grasp. The cold brick wall bit into my back and I was acutely aware of the pain that came with Andrei's viselike grip on me.

"I don't read minds. I read you."

"Well, that answers my question!" I snapped, glaring up at him.

"I'll explain later. Not now." Andrei seemed to realize that his body was pressed against mine... and that we were both breathing heavily. Slowly, his fingers rubbed circles in my wrists and the tiny hairs on my arms stood up. "You're so soft."

A different kind of awareness overwhelmed me. I wanted him. Here. Right now. In this freaking alleyway. If he could "read me", he would know that.

Slowly sweeping over me, Andrei's eyes glinted and I knew he knew.

His fingers danced along the hem of my dress before tracing a path up my thigh. My legs spread of their own volition, allowing the man before me to make his way to my wet center unhindered. Then his eyes widened.

"No underwear, Rae?" he questioned, his voice hoarse.

181

"Forgot." I let out a gasp of raw need when his thumb found my engorged clit. Squeezing my eyes shut, I hissed, "Oh, God. Please!" I wanted more, needed more, and I wouldn't be able to live if he didn't give me more. The sense of danger that anyone strolling down the alley would catch us only heightened my need for gratification, only made my vagina weep for him.

Pushing myself up on my toes, I brushed my lips against Andrei's jaw, kissing my way to his mouth. Before he could draw away, I captured his lower lip with my teeth, shaking when he released a low, guttural groan.

"Want to fuck you," he rasped, already sinking two fingers into my vulva. He pushed in to the knuckles, practically turning me inside out when he began to finger-fuck me so sweetly. "Always wet," he murmured into my mouth, and I blindly fumbled with the fly of his pants, sighing when I could finally feel his throbbing erection against the clammy skin of my palm.

"Always hard," I retorted, squeezing him in appreciation.

"Fuck!" he cursed, bending slightly to lift me up effortlessly with one arm beneath my ass.

Looping my arms around his neck and twining my legs around his waist, I moaned when I felt the swollen head of his shaft at my weeping entrance. "Please," I whispered, tilting my hips into him, wanting him in all the way—not caring if I sounded way too needy, too desperate.

With one perfect upward thrust, Andrei drove into me to the hilt, holding me steady above him as I began to buck wildly against his body, whimpering loudly because he was so beautifully...

"Say it," Andrei said harshly, stroking into me again, his pelvis hitting my clit.

"Big," I panted, throwing my head back against the wall. "You're so big!"

He groaned, sounding like a wounded grizzly. At the back of my mind, I worried that someone would stumble into the alleyway and catch us going at it like a pair of rabbits. I bit my lip in a bid to stifle my cries but quickly gave up on that when Andrei increased the pace, punctuating each deep thrust with a grunt of pleasure.

"Harder," I begged, digging my nails into his shoulders. "Fuck... me... harder!"

Everything else that came out my mouth after that was unintelligible, especially when I felt him hit that spot... that sweet, sweet spot that made me scream from pleasure and pain as sweat trickled down my back, sticking my cotton dress to my skin.

"Come for me, little one," Andrei growled, his voice tinged with an accent. Reaching between us, he began to work the tight bundle of nerves he teased earlier. "Let me feel... your cunt... strangle me."

It might have been the way he rubbed my clit with such precise vigor, or the way he commanded me to climax for him, but when my orgasm hit and I clenched myself around him, nothing else existed but his cock swelling up inside me and bringing me such intense joy. Blinded and bathed in the white-hot ecstasy, I wailed his name, tears prickling my eyes when it felt like my climax would never end. Seconds later, Andrei exploded inside me, cursing at the skies. He held me during the aftershocks before pulling out and gently setting me on the ground.

Slightly disoriented, I clutched a handful of his T-shirt for balance, trying to catch my breath.

"We should go," drawled Andrei, looking none the worse for wear. I, on the other hand, was a sweaty, rumpled mess.

Quickly rearranging myself in a bid to look like I hadn't just been thoroughly taken in an alley, I allowed Andrei's hand to swallow mine as he led me down the street once more. His hand was warm around mine and, for some reason, it made me feel... cherished.

As we were walking down the alley, I was frowning at my blood-red toenails peeking out my gladiator sandals when I suddenly found myself walking smack-dab into the brick wall that was Andrei's back. He stopped in front of a door, which didn't really look like one because it was made of brick and was practically camouflaged with the rest of the wall.

Without warning, it was pushed open and a wild-haired, bespectacled redhead stood at the entrance, hands on her hips. She was so small though that her stance looked comical.

"I expected you an hour ago, Lord Andrei," she lectured, stepping aside to let us in. "I have far more important things to do than wait around for you to grace me with your presence."

To my surprise, Andrei let out a bark of laughter. "It's been a while, old friend."

"Has it?" she asked, closing the door behind us. "Was it during the Abraham Lincoln administration or the Woodrow Wilson one?"

"Different centuries, Myrna," said Andrei.

"My point exactly," she sniffed, pushing past us.

Okay, what is going on here? I thought, taking a deep breath and shutting my eyes, trying to get a feel for the redhead's aura.

She wasn't a succubus. But then again, Andrei was and I couldn't sense him—never had, come to think of it.

"Rae." Myrna's cheerful voice made my eyes fly open. I detected a hint of a Southern accent. "Come. Sit with me." She extended bony arms covered in jangling bangles, all ten of her fingers bearing gaudy rings.

Only then did I notice the room we were in. Small and intricately decorated, it had a high ceiling with one tiered chandelier hanging in the center. A myriad of Persian rugs carpeted the floor from wall to wall, even right up to the front of the fireplace. Rows and rows of shelves that held various books and weird artifacts took up most of the space on one wall and a red beaded curtain hung across a doorway on the opposite side of the room, which looked odd yet beautiful. There were no couches, only throw pillows placed in front of a rectangular coffee table.

I reluctantly took Myrna's hands and allowed her to lead me there.

"You a gypsy or something?" I asked, wincing at how condescending I sounded.

Myrna threw her head back and laughed, gesturing for me to sit as she did the same. "A gypsy. Seriously?"

I felt Andrei looming behind me and I glanced over my shoulder. Hovering, he had his arms folded across his chest.

"I'm a witch, dear," Myrna divulged, capturing my attention.

I looked at her, really looked at her. She couldn't have been a day over forty. And although her moss green eyes told of youthful mirth, it also showed years and years of experience. Also, if she'd been around in Abraham Lincoln's time…

185

"Don't look so shocked, sweetheart," she chided, patting my arm. "After all, you are sleeping with him." She inclined her head in Andrei's direction and I instantly flushed.

"Why am I here?" I said with more bite than I'd intended.

"To prepare you for some of the things you're going to see."

I turned to look at Andrei but his attention was steadfastly elsewhere.

"What things?" I asked, my voice suspicious.

Myrna gave me a smile and surprised me by taking out a battered Lenovo laptop and placing it on the table. Since it was on standby, I was able to see that her username was her full name: Myrna Lake.

Myrna Lake... Myrna Lake...

I knew that name. It wasn't one you forgot so easily.

"Demonic Encounters," I mumbled to myself, remembering the stupid forum I'd been haunting out of fear. I stared at Myrna, amazed that the world was incredibly small. "You're **myrna_lake69**?"

"Sixty-seven," she corrected. Her smile widened as she turned to me. "Welcome to House of Mystique, Miss Erickson."

Chapter 12

"You're a traitor," I hissed at Myrna when Andrei was out of earshot—in other words, he was taking a phone call outside.

Myrna arched a quizzical brow. "I don't know what you mean, darling."

"No?" I wrinkled my nose at her, racking my brain to remember what advice she'd dispensed online. "You told that girl that she was being abused by demons. Yet here you are, practically BFFs with their king! You made it seem like you were helping!"

"Calm down, Rainelle," she said softly, as if I were a crazy person she had to pacify. "I think you're letting your jealousy override your common sense."

"Jealousy?" I spluttered, my head reeling.

Myrna returned her attention to the laptop screen, opening a House of Mystique bookmark. "I know you're wondering about the strong feelings you have for him. You're alarmed... concerned. Every fiber of your being cries out for his body, his touch, and you don't understand why."

I sucked in a breath and sputtered, "Don't you dare tell me what I'm feeling."

Myrna stayed silent, tapping away at the keyboard.

"You don't know me. We've just met. So don't analyze me," I went on, balling my hands into fists.

At this, she turned to look at me, her green eyes narrowed. "Have you ever wondered what people who've been visited by incubi feel?" She tucked a tuft of wiry brilliant copper hair behind a jewelry studded ear. "There's not much difference between stolen moments in dreamland and real life-sucking sex. But you, Miss Erickson? You don't really have to worry about that sort of blissful death. You don't have to worry about your life slipping away as you reach orgasm after mind-blowing orgasm, do you?"

I shivered, and it wasn't even cold. "Tell me why."

"Tell you what, Rainelle Erickson?"

"You know what," I said through clenched teeth, feeling like I'm five seconds away from smacking the copper out of her hair.

It was more than the hunter's blood flowing in my veins, I was sure of it.

"You felt it the instant you saw him, didn't you?" Myrna drawled, her eyes fixed on the laptop once again. "That pull, that attraction, those had nothing to do with what he is and everything to do with who." She pointed at the screen. "There. This screams you."

I peered at what she was pointing at, a House of Mystique catalogue of some sort. "The ring?" Made up of three thin strips of silver and a glittering ruby in the center, the ring was cheap-looking and did not scream "me." I was a Tiffany's and Cartier girl through and through.

188

"Yes, this is the one," Myrna proclaimed as she clapped her hands. And like an agile cat, she gracefully rose to her feet and stalked away.

I stared at the ring in confusion. This whole day was confusing me, but I suddenly wanted to know the answers to questions I had been too scared to ask before, let alone think. Myrna Lake might be as crazy as a bat but she was the one person who seemed to know what was what.

"Here."

It took me a few seconds to realize that she'd returned to her seat beside me, her hand was outstretched and in her palm was a ring.

"Why?" I asked.

"You'll need it. Go on, take it," she urged, and I eventually did, albeit warily.

The minute I did, a searing heat tore through my skin and I dropped the stupid thing. I sent a furious glare Myrna's way as I exclaimed, "What the hell? That damn thing just burned me!"

"Yes," she murmured nonchalantly, picking it up and holding it out to me again. "Definitely yours."

"You okay, Rae?" Andrei's voice came from the doorway.

I didn't dare look at him.

"You felt that, Anghelescu?" asked Myrna. "Of course, he did," she added, addressing me this time. "Put it on now, darling. It's for your protection, a link to Andrei that..."

"I don't want to be linked to him. I don't want any of this."

"He is the only one who can protect you from people, and creatures, who would want to hurt you. The ring is your bond. Not a true bond," she clarified when she caught my anxious expression. "Simply one that heightens his senses where you're concerned."

"But he can read my mind now. It was so weird, how he was able to know." Glancing over my shoulder, I confirmed what I somehow already knew: Andrei was gone.

Myrna shook her head. "He can't really read your mind. He just senses your aura, and your emotions along with it. It's a bit like how you sense a demon's presence around you." Gently taking my left hand, she slipped the ring onto my index finger. It fit like a glove and, against my tanned skin, it actually looked quite beautiful.

Flexing my fingers, I admired the way the ruby sparkled with what little light it caught from the one window in the room. I was instantly attached to it, which was irrational.

"Now, come. We must choose an outfit for you. The lord's lover shouldn't appear in jeans and a wife beater." She let out a tinkling laugh. "And you look like you own several wife beaters."

"You didn't answer my question," I said softly, unable to keep the tiny note of dread in my voice. It was because, all of a sudden, I felt that it was important to know the biggest thing that had been bothering me since the night I found out what Andrei Anghelescu was.

As astute as Myrna was, she looked like she was about to ask me what I meant before changing her mind and exhaling heavily. "Give me your hands."

Without hesitation, I did exactly that, allowing her hands to wrap around mine.

Then she fixed her eyes on me. "The life your mother chose didn't entail a price that just involved her. A demon doesn't do simple favors like that. Offering her only child, a daughter, to Lord Andrei… that was part of her bargain. You were his before you knew him."

Her eyelids fluttered closed. "In addition to that, some say that when the world was young and gods roamed the earth, they felt pity for the mortals subjected to demons. And so they gave the demons *paries*, the untouchables, to defile. Basically, *paries* were men and women impervious to a demon's life-sucking enchantment." Those green eyes of hers that were a shade lighter than my own flew open. "You're an untouchable. But then, perhaps I just fed you a pile of bullshit."

"Whatever you do, Rae, do not let go of me," Andrei intoned, pulling me even closer into the all-encompassing heat of his embrace. "You got that?"

I nodded imperceptibly, aware of his chin resting on the top of my head, aware of every inch of his body that was pressed against mine. "Yeah, sure. Whatever."

"If everything goes according to plan, we'll end up in your apartment," he said, in what he probably thought was a soothing voice, but ended up sounding nerve-jangling instead. "If it doesn't, parts of your luscious body will be scattered throughout Paris."

"You really know how to show a girl a good time," I mumbled into his shirt, momentarily thrown by the laughter vibrating on his chest.

"After all, not every girl can say they've experienced the wonders of teleportation," he bluntly stated.

Not every girl can say she was offered up as a kid to a demon lord like a freaking sacrifice by her own mother.

"Hey." Andrei's voice was achingly soft. Before I could blink, he was tilting my head up with one hand. I hated it when he seemed so... normal. "Did Myrna make you uncomfortable?"

I blinked back the tears that were threatening to pour out. *Not here, please! Not now, with Myrna in the next room. Not with Andrei.* "No. I just... Let's get this over with, Lord Andrei."

His brow furrowed. "You're lying to me."

I jolted my head back. "Just take me home."

He didn't object, cupping my head to his chest with one hand. "Don't move. And close your eyes."

I shut them, squeezing them so tight that they started to tingle. Gripping the taut material stretched across Andrei's back, I concentrated on my breathing. As terrified as I was, a part of me just couldn't wrap my head around this whole day and wanted more. More revelations, more excitement, just... more.

But that was when I felt it—that more.

Bubbles of something fizzled inside me and every part of my body itched. It felt like my skin had been turned inside out and someone was feverishly stirring my insides à la Gordon Ramsay. The urge to move, to scratch became something I physically had to fight until... nothing.

"Open your eyes, Rae," Andrei commanded, his voice husky.

I did... and saw that we were in my bedroom.

Culebra, Puerto Rico, was an incinerator even at nighttime and the huge bonfire that had been lit didn't help any. It took all of my willpower not to tear off the sheer violet Grecian dress Myrna picked out for me to wear on this "wondrous" occasion. It was probably thousands of years old. But after soaking myself in a lavender scented bath, I couldn't smell the moth balls that, I was positive, had kept this dress intact.

Standing beside Andrei for what felt like decades, I was distinctly conscious of how little I knew about anything. From the ancient tongue he spoke so glibly to the way the other witnesses bowed before him, I realized that I was completely out of my element here... and that I was surrounded by demons. It didn't matter that they treated me like Andrei's queen or something (*mea domina*, I heard them say) or that they seemed to be quite harmless in his presence. My Spidey senses, where their kind was concerned, were tingling in overdrive and I had to fight back wave after wave of nausea the longer I remained in their presence.

Still, what little I understood of the ceremony seemed rather tame and actually pretty cute. All I basically had to do was stand on a gorgeous beach beside a gorgeous shirtless man as a glorified escort... until Roan, the incubus, and his female, a cute Puerto Rican minx called Nina, started stripping.

Judging from the poker faces of the other five witnesses surrounding the bonded couple, I was the only person taken aback by this—probably because, aside from Nina, I was the only actual person there.

"They consummate their bond before us," Andrei growled in a stage whisper, obviously sensing my discomfort. "Tonight, he will put a baby in her."

"A baby?" I blurted out, not too quietly. A few pairs of eyes swiveled in my direction. Lowering my voice considerably, I told Andrei, "That's disgusting. Is that necessary?"

He gave me a fleeting look. "It is… because once she sells her soul and makes the transition, she will no longer be able to conceive."

I nearly choked on my tongue. Nina was a stunning, strawberry blonde twenty-five-year-old, with her entire life still ahead of her. Was she honestly going to throw it all away for one rugged, sexy Irish demon?

That appears to be the case, I thought, unreasonably mad at the redhead.

I could accept the enchanted rings the couple had exchanged. I could accept the heavy making out. I could even accept the mutual bloodletting. But a baby? Hell, no! It would be an abomination and Nina should've known that.

Now completely naked, Nina knelt before an equally nude Roan. Submitting to him. Giving herself to him.

"Stand," Roan ordered, and Nina slowly did his bidding.

She was an elfin little thing and he was a tower of hard, muscular flesh. Blushing, I noticed his impressive hard-on. Nestled in a forest of blonde curls, it bobbed against his belly as he took one step closer to his woman.

I swallowed. Usually, I wasn't so prudish. But seriously? Watching another couple get it on right in front of me? Well, voyeurism had never been my thing.

At least until…

"Getting excited?" Andrei's voice was low and thick in my ear. The heat of his breath shot straight to my center.

I shook my head as if I could shake the sensation away. "Nope."

Roan and Nina were kissing now, really kissing. The sounds they made were loud and wet, and their touches, their caresses were fast and frantic. Slowly, they sank to the russet-colored sand and Roan kissed his way down Nina's neck, to her collarbone, and down the heaving valley between her dusky tipped breasts.

Fight it, Rae. Fight the feeling...

Too fucking late. Of their own accord, my nipples hardened and protruded against the filmy fabric of my dress and Andrei reached out and pinched my left nipple, which drew a stifled gasp from me. That alone was enough to make me wet.

"She's going to get sand inside her," I murmured, unable to tear my eyes away from Roan going down on Nina. "That's highly uncomfortable. Trust me, I know."

How could the others just stand there unaffected? Wasn't it turning them on in the slightest?

"I can smell you," Andrei causally remarked, ignoring my small talk. "Your arousal. The dripping heat of your sex."

Oh, damn!

"There are about a dozen other smells here, salty air included. You're just confused."

"Oh? I think I know what you smell like when you're wet for me."

I made some kind of whimpering sound that was, thankfully, drowned out by Nina's pants, wails, and screams of "Roan! Close! I'm so close, *dios*! So, so close!" as her demon tongued her into oblivion. She was spread for all to see, the glistening velvety folds of her soaked sex stark and bare. And although I never once considered being with another woman, I had to admit that the sight was quite hot.

"Like what you see, *mea domina*?"

I was now aware that Andrei had moved to stand behind me, and that he just tightly wound his strong arms around me.

That's Latin, isn't it? Yes, it's Latin. Such an old language. I bet he knows hundreds of other languages. Let's see... Greek, Italian, Romanian, Russian, French, Japanese...

Andrei's palm on my vagina made for a different sort of distraction. The skirt's wispy material was no match for the force of his palm cupping my heat. Myrna had informed me that underwear wasn't necessary and I took her advice to heart. Now I was paying the price for her so-called instruction.

"Sweet little one, you are so very wet," Andrei whispered in my ear, nipping my earlobe. The tip of his middle finger ducked inside me, dragging a sliver of cloth with it. "So very, very wet." He moved the probing digit around, the pad of his thumb slowly and painfully rubbing my aching clit.

I held onto his forearm, leaning against him. "No," I moaned, at the same time that Nina screamed "Yes! Yes, yes, yes, yes!" and arched her back in the sand, riding out her orgasm.

Through hooded eyes I watched Roan position himself between her splayed legs, and guide his thick shaft into her. Andrei's breath hitched in my ear, his hand slipping under my dress through the high slit at my thigh. I automatically parted my legs, allowing him to cup me again, skin to skin this time.

"Yes," I amended when he began to properly pleasure me. Grinding against his hardness, I whimpered, "Oh, God, yes, Andrei!"

"Look at them," he gruffly directed, but I already was. Roan was riding the woman in earnest, the back of her knees hooked over his very broad shoulders. "Look at the way they

196

look at each other. Their carnal desire. Their unquenchable need. Their unconditional love."

I dug my fingernails into Andrei's skin, riding the three fingers that were bringing me to a fast-approaching climax. At the small of my back, Andrei's erection made its presence known. Just feeling that and witnessing the scene unfolding before me, pushed me over the edge. Wave after wave, my sweet climax came, my cries mingling with Nina's screams of pleasure.

"Good girl," Andrei praised softly, holding me to him through the rolling aftershocks.

Once I came down from that high, I realized that the voyeuristic incubi had their eyes on me and had, in all probability, watched me come apart in their lord's arms. But I couldn't bring myself to care.

"You're mine. You know that?"

Without pulling out of his arms, I calmly responded. "And just how many years have I been yours?"

"What are you talking about?" He spun me around so abruptly, my head jerked back.

If only his beautiful, beautiful blue eyes held some truth.

"Lauren... gave me to you so you'd help her," I retorted bitterly, all the pent-up anger and disbelief coming to the surface in that statement. It was one thing to be bartered like a commodity. But for the barterer to be my own flesh and blood? Well, it hurt. "The fact that I don't die after screwing you only sweetens the deal, doesn't it?"

"She didn't give you to me," was Andrei's unruffled response. "She mentioned you but you were a child, the daughter of a hunter. There was nothing I could do with you. As a courtesy, I helped her contact Lilith." His hand cupped my chin. "I had no idea who you were until I had someone do some digging." His pupils had dilated and his grip on my chin became almost painful. "But now? You... are... mine. We both know this."

I shut my eyes, processing what he just said. He'd rejected my mother's selfish offer and I'd strutted into Vegas years later like a lamb to the slaughter, giving him exactly what she'd proposed to him—only twenty-one years later. If I hadn't taken the Darryl Winer case, would I have met Andrei? Would I be standing here, on a tiny island called Culebra, which I'd never heard of, surrounded by a group of demons who just watched me come for their king?

No. You'd be in bed with Daniel Lawless, your babysitter.

I let out a soft laugh and opened my eyes. Fat chance. That ship had sailed long ago. He thought of me as nothing more than his dim-witted, clueless charge.

"Did I say something funny?" Andrei snarled, his brows furrowed.

I gave him a coy smile and touched him. "Let's teleport back to my place so I can show you how hot this little show got me."

His lips twitched. "Oh?"

"I'm wet, remember?"

He brought his long, skillful fingers to his lips and drew them in, sucking on them hard before releasing them with a soft pop. "I remember."

Chapter 13

The knocking at the door was definitely not some kind of masochistic dream my subconscious had created to punish me for the sinful things I'd done last night, most of which happened on the floor. Ignoring the incessant banging on my front door was going to be impossible, however. Plus there was something heavy across my waist. Uncomfortably heavy.

I forced my eyes open and chewed on my bottom lip to keep from flipping out.

"Andrei?" I said, before clearing my throat so that my, "What the hell are you still doing here?" didn't sound like it was from a frog.

"Trying to sleep," he murmured drowsily, and I heaved his arm off me and sat up, surveying just how much space he really took up, which was all of it. "Who the hell's at the door?" he asked, eyes still shut.

"I, um, have no idea," I replied, mystified by how freaking normal he was behaving. "You spent the night?" My voice was filled with unadulterated awe.

"You should go get that," he said, a wry smile tugging at his lips.

But I was already up and shrugging my robe on. Feeling miffed, I asked in a tone heavy with sarcasm, "Can I get you anything while I'm gone? Tea? Coffee? The morning paper?"

Stretched out on his back, he growled, "Just your pussy... in my mouth. But that can wait."

At that, I stumbled over a lone Jimmy Choo on my way out. "You're insatiable," I called over my shoulder, shivering in anticipation, because seriously, the man gave pretty unreal head.

His throaty laugh followed me to the door. Ignoring security and common sense, I unlocked the door without peeking through the peephole—and was rewarded with opening it to none other than Daniel Lawless, the last person I would ever want to catch me reeking of illicit sex... with a demon who was still in my bed.

I stood there, gaping at him like a guppy until he tried to push past me. I hated it when people think they could walk all over me.

"What's your problem?" I snapped.

"Jeez, Rainelle, I took a bloody early flight to get here. So the least you can do is let me in," he grumbled, glaring down at me.

His hair had grown longer and fell over his forehead, and the Chelsea football shirt and black jeans he was wearing fit him like a glove. In short, he looked fit, virile, and totally capable of taking on a demon as powerful as Andrei.

I didn't know how I felt about that. Worried? Relieved? Indifferent?

"Why didn't you call?" I spluttered, not budging an inch.

"Because your mobile's off. Besides, this is sort of important, sweetheart." And he swaggered past me, heading into the living room like he knew the layout of the place. "Much too important for a phone call."

"Daniel, I..." I began, at the same time Andrei asked loudly, "We got company, babe?"

This is going to be ugly.

Andrei strolled in wearing nothing but the skin on his back and impressive morning wood. Daniel's brow furrowed as he took him in. I waited... waited for Daniel to get a feel on him and realize that I'd been vigorously going at it with a demon a few hours ago. I waited for him to repel Andrei to the pits of hell, or whatever dimension he'd crawled out from, and condemn me as a disgrace to my father and the entire human race. With that thought, it was strangely comforting to remember how strong Andrei was and that he would probably rip Daniel's head off before he could so much as take a breath to say the banishing words.

But all Lawless said was, "I had no idea you have company. Maybe I should've called."

Wait... what?

"He's, um, we're..." Clearly, I was quite disconcerted by the fact that in Daniel's eyes Andrei was apparently a normal guy who merely rolled out of my bed and was comfortable enough about his body to strut about in his birthday suit.

"I'm her boyfriend." Andrei folded his arms across his chest, biceps bunching together and reminding me that he really could do some damage to Daniel... if he didn't leave now.

Then it hit me like a blow to the solar plexus: Boyfriend.

I gaped at Andrei, stunned. Was this his way of marking his territory or was he simply having fun toying with Daniel? Did he know about my ancient crush on the hunter? Did he even know Daniel was a hunter?

Probably. He knew everything.

"Well, if you don't mind, I need to speak with Rainelle. Alone," Daniel added, as if that was unclear.

Andrei's eyes narrowed at me. "Rae?"

To be honest, I was completely shell-shocked. This wasn't the way I'd have ever imagined their first meeting. For starters, Daniel wasn't chanting in Latin, or Italian. And Andrei was... naked.

"It's fine," I murmured. "And for Pete's sake, put some clothes on, babe."

An awkward silence descended upon us. Andrei's face clouded over but he surprised me by leaving without a fight. And I didn't realize I had spaced out with my eyes on his retreating ass until Daniel cleared his throat.

"So he's your boyfriend?" His voice was faux casual. "What's his name?"

"That's none of your business, Daniel," I muttered, gesturing for him to take a seat. Once he was in an armchair, I followed suit. "So what's so important you had to be here at..." I glanced at the clock above the TV. "... nine a.m.?"

Daniel didn't beat around the bush. "I know where your mother is. And her mate."

"So you know she's a demon?"

He cocked his head. "I could ask you the same thing." A slow smile spread across his face. "You said you had no interest in the supernatural. Yet I'm assuming you met up with Lauren somewhere, and discovered what she is now."

"It doesn't matter. What matters is killing her, right? Isn't that why you're here? To let me know that you're going to do that?"

"We," he amended, golden eyes gleaming. "*We* are going to kill her."

"My boyfriend, huh?"

Andrei was out on the balcony of my bedroom, probably giving a hundred pedestrians a private show. He turned, giving me one of his rare smiles, the kind that usually disintegrated my panties.

"It has a nice ring to it, doesn't it?"

"No, it's just weird. I haven't had a boyfriend since high school. And you..."

"I've never had a girlfriend," he said it more to himself, as if he was in awe of the concept.

"I think we need to have a talk," I muttered. "Put some goddamn clothes on. I can't think when you're saluting me like that." I stalked back into my room and waited for him to follow.

When he appeared seconds later, he was in a pair of boxers, which still made him a health code violation.

"Why are you looking at me like that?" He quirked a brow.

"Like what?"

"Like you want to fuck me and rip me apart at the same time."

"I wasn't aware irritation could be so wrongfully interpreted." I rolled my eyes. "Sit down, Andrei. There's no point in my attempt at being intimidating if you're hulking over me like a mountain."

"You're right." He was humoring me but he sat on the edge of my bed, rolling his shoulders back. "Intimidate away."

"You know that that was Daniel, right?"

The playfulness left his face. "The big, bad English hunter? He's a lot smaller in person. But then again, they usually are."

"Are you seriously being this... petty?"

He gave me a strange look. "Petty?" he said, sounding the word out. "Of course."

"Why can't hunters sense you?"

His face hardened. "You almost sound disappointed. Is that what you wanted? Your hunter to make a move against me? To prove his worth?"

Sarcastic Andrei was proving to be ten times worse than Enraged Andrei or even Scary Andrei.

"You know exactly what I mean and he isn't my hunter." I folded my arms across my chest and gave him a dark look. "Myrna and I have been texting and..."

"You what?" Thunder clouded his eyes.

"And...," I stressed. "Don't interrupt me." I paused, mentally daring him to berate me. He didn't. "Myrna and I have been texting and she said nothing about your ability to... to, I don't know, pull a Harry Potter and cloak what you really are. So you tell me...right now."

He rose, instantly towering over me. "If you had any idea how powerful I really am, we wouldn't be having this conversation. For fuck's sake, Rae, I'm a king. If I don't want anyone to know what I am, no one will know what I am." He

204

shrugged. "It takes a hell of a lot of energy to shroud myself but sometimes I'm just not in the mood to kill a bunch of crucifix-obsessed hunters."

I blinked up at him. "Are you the only demon that can do that?"

"Only the extremely strong ones. Lords, queens, and other rulers like me. Rae, calm down."

Calm down? Only when he put his arms around me did I realize that I was shivering, which was the beginnings of a massive panic attack. What if I'd gone to school with demons? What if they lived in my neighborhood? What if my damn friends were demons?! What if...

Breathe, a voice in my head commanded, and I clung to Andrei like he was the only normal thing I knew. My fingernails dug into his back, piercing his skin.

"You don't have to be scared, little one," he murmured into the top of my head. "How many times have I said that you are mine? Nothing will ever happen to you."

"I'm supposed to be in Greece now... or Italy. Someone somewhere is cheating on his wife and I'm supposed to be there," I babbled, inhaling the scent of sweaty sex on Andrei's chest. "I have my Nikon and everything. Don't you think I should've been a photographer? Candid snaps, that's what I'd do. And maybe even family photos. As long as the parents are, you know, really nice to their kids and it shows."

He was stroking my back with one hand and toying with my hair in the other. I raised my head and he swooped in to claim my lips. I let him. I let him because I needed it.

It took me a few seconds to realize that he'd lifted me up, carried me inside, and set me down on the bed. A hyperventilating female certainly brought out the gentleman in the guy. And I was ashamed to admit it, but sometimes a little part of me yearned to yell, "Screw equality!" and let a man take care of me.

But just a little part.

"Breathe," Andrei gently commanded, sitting awkwardly in front of my feet. He had one leg hanging over the edge of the bed and the other folded at the knee.

"I am breathing," I hissed, shivering when he took my feet in his hands. They were awfully big and warm, those hands of his, and his fingers were incredibly gentle as they tickled the arch of each foot. "What are you doing?" I asked as my foot tingled where he touched.

"Just relax."

"Said the demon to the woman," I muttered, punctuating my wisecrack with an involuntary little moan. My eyes widened. "What was that? It felt so good."

Andrei was giving me a foot massage. Andrei, the freaking king of horny supernatural creatures, was sitting half-naked in my bed rubbing my feet. And he was good.

"Tell me what's on your mind," he said gruffly, his fingers seemingly making the balls of my feet sing hymns.

"On my mind?" I echoed, rolling my head back onto the pillows against the headboard. Aside from "Oh, God!" and "Wow!" there was nothing else on my mind, nothing at all. "I thought you could... oh, that feels good... read my mind."

Andrei ran his hands up my legs, slowly and gently kneading my calf muscles. "You know I can't," he murmured. "But I wish I could." He brought my foot up and kissed all five toes before switching to my other foot and doing the same. "I can sense how you feel but I can't hear your thoughts. So you have to tell me, Rae."

Sanity, however, was slowly creeping back in. "It feels weird telling you that I want to kill another demon," I said honestly, wiggling my toes to make sure they were still there. I looked him in the eye. "Won't you try to stop me?"

He disregarded my question. "You're really going to follow that fucking hunter?" His grip on my ankles tightened. "Do you realize what a fool he is? You go after Lauren, you go after Vitaly. He's an old demon, and he won't just let you and your little hunter buddies waltz in, all holy-watered up, and kill his succubus."

"I knew you were listening to us!" I hissed. "You're protecting her." I wriggled, trying to get him to release me. I kicked with one foot, lashing out at him. No dice. Breathing heavily, I spat, "This is why we can't discuss these things. I'm Alien and you're Predator. We can't fucking join forces. Andrei, let me go."

"I'm not protecting her," he calmly replied, rubbing the pads of his thumbs along my skin. "I'm protecting you. You yourself said you know nothing about the supernatural. You'll only get yourself killed and I'll be damned if I just stand back and watch that happen."

"Then, kill her for me."

The idea was so simple, I felt like an idiot for not thinking about it before. Daniel thought he was doing me a solid by helping me kill the woman that had almost sold me to the devil, literally. But at the end of the day, did it matter who killed her as long as she was killed?

Andrei's fingers stilled. "I can't do that."

"You can't?"

His brow furrowed. "Fine. I can, but I won't."

"Get out."

His grip on one leg loosened and I was able to kick my foot free, hitting him right in the middle of his perfectly sculpted chest. He barely flinched, which was most probably due to the orgasm I'd given him last night.

"I said, get out!"

"Rae…"

"This is crazy! I'm crazy!" I rolled off the bed, shoving him down when he tried to get up. "Listen to me," I said as I sucked in air, surprised that he actually let me push him. "The sex is great, explosive even! But I feel guilty about plotting with hunters one moment and fucking you, a demon king, the next. Daniel… he's a good guy. And once upon a time, I tried to be good. Being with you, Andrei, is not just pretty fucking bad. It's a treachery."

Andrei eyed me for a long moment before squeezing his eyes shut, long lashes kissed his cheeks. And because of that stupid distraction, I didn't really notice that he was putting some clothes on until… well, until he was fully clothed.

"I'm not going to apologize for what I am." His voice was roughened by barely controlled rage as he rose to his full height. Cold blue eyes stared down at me, practically piercing through the flimsy satin of my robe. "Causing dissention in my ranks for nothing? That's what I'd be doing if I went after your mother. Have your little sulk." In one fluid motion he was breathing in my ear, "But if you go near that hunter again, I will slit his throat. I will not be made a fool of… by a human, no less."

"I'll do whatever the hell I please." I made a noise in my throat when he pecked my earlobe. "Get out. I mean it." I closed my eyes, mentally counting to ten.

"That's the thing, Rae," he said, almost regretfully. "You don't."

When I got to ten, Andrei was gone and a thought popped in my head.

Since Daniel was still in Paris, maybe he could help me out with Damien's demons. Maybe I could finally be a real Erickson. That being said, I now realized that thwarting my father's attempts at getting me into the family business was one of the dumbest things I'd ever done in my life.

But only second to falling for a demon king, of course.

Chapter 14

I needed him.

No, I mentally rephrased. *I don't need him. I just want him.*

There was a huge difference between the two words. But either way, as I kept telling myself every day for the past five freaking days, Andrei wasn't going to come back to me, no matter how much I needed and/or wanted him. I was well aware that I had pissed him off. And much to my surprise, it hurt.

It hurt like hell that I couldn't see him. It hurt like hell that I couldn't touch him. It hurt like hell that I couldn't hear his stupidly sexy and rare laughs, the ones that I distinctly felt were reserved for me. It hurt that I couldn't have him inside me, turning my whole world upside down. He told me to have my "little sulk," but I would never have anticipated that it could turn into a big one... and would result in me wanting him even more.

If this was what love felt like, I didn't need it in my life. No, what I needed was a tub of Ben and Jerry's, a dirty martini, and my favorite movie, *Kill Bill: Volume One*, playing on TV. That was the best way to get over... whatever the hell this was. How stupid did a person have to be to go and fall for a demon, one who was using her?

"Pretty stupid," I huffed at myself, looking down at my stained sweatpants and baggy T-shirt. I looked like shit and felt like it, too.

My phone rang, like it always did at this time. And as always, I rejected the call. Daniel could go to hell for all I cared. He'd been phoning me incessantly. And when that didn't work, he resorted to banging on my door. He was way too eager to be the Jackie Chan to my Jaden Smith, in my opinion, and that had my guard up.

I had plenty of time to mull over my anger at Lauren and had decided that she wasn't worth risking my life for. Now I just felt plain stupid knowing I was beating a dead horse. There really wasn't any need for me to mix with the supernatural world anyway. I had bigger things to worry about, things I'd put on the backburner to deal with my own crazy shit—things like Ana Fontaine's brother and a posse of demon-possessed virgins.

I am an idiot and I know it.

So, after sitting cross-legged for hours on the couch with a tub of Rocky Road in my lap, I decided to dial the one person that could probably help me fix my fucked-up mental state.

Myrna answered on the first ring.

"Rainelle? What a pleasant surprise, hon!" she chirped, sounding a billion times more positive than I did.

I decided not to beat around the bush. "Do you know where he is?"

Myrna didn't need to make five guesses to know which "he" I was referring to.

"You sound terrible," she remarked, her voice heavy with concern. "What's up?"

I had a strong suspicion that she knew "what was up". I was pretty sure that pissing off a demon king would become public knowledge in supernatural circles seconds after it happens.

"I don't know," I sniffled into my phone, trailing my fingers down my cheek and horrified to find them wet. "Do you think that maybe... maybe I'm not one of those untouchable beings? That maybe I'm... normal?"

A long, uncomfortable silence elapsed. I was about to end the call when Myrna spoke up, "Have you taken a pregnancy test?"

She had some fucking nerve!

"I'm not pregnant," I snapped, my grip on the phone tightening. "What would make you say that? Did Andrei say anything to you?"

She let out one of her annoyingly joyful, tinkling laughs. "No, honey. I haven't seen the man since you came in with him a week ago. I was just curious, is all."

"I'm not pregnant," I repeated. "I just feel like shit because he stormed off in a rage five days ago and I haven't seen him since. He's mad at me."

"What did you say to him?"

"I'd rather not," I said carefully, chewing on my lower lip thoughtfully. Then I took a deep breath. "I think I'm attached... to him."

Silence stretched once again before I heard an encouraging "Go on." from Myrna.

"We're not even technically in a relationship but the last time I saw him, he called himself my boyfriend," I babbled.

But Myrna didn't need to know the extent of that situation.

"Can demons date? Is that done? Can they honestly remember romantic stuff like anniversaries, Valentine's Day, and all that cliché shit? I've never really even had a boyfriend and it's just my luck that the first guy who claims that position is the lord of sex demons!"

Myrna made little noncommittal replies to get me to continue.

"Then again, he acts so freaking human sometimes and I get fooled into thinking he is human. Maybe I want him to be human, but then he wouldn't be Andrei if he was, you know? What am I saying? Of course you don't know." I sighed heavily. "I really am my mother's child, aren't I? Because, Myrna, I think I might be in…"

"In love with him?" she put in.

I let out another sigh, relieved that I didn't have to say the words myself. "It will never work. He'll be forever young while I'll age. And he'll watch me die. This is so screwed up." I was seriously starting to hyperventilate.

"I think you should know a few things, though," Myrna said quietly. She waited for me to calm down. "One, Andrei is not using you. Tell me, were there times when he didn't have sex with you? Just hung out and enjoyed your company?"

I thought back to the first time that had happened. He found me watching *Shaun of the Dead* and I'd pissed him off so much that he let me have bloody, gory sex with him. If we hadn't fought, he would've simply been content to finish the movie with me. There had been subsequent times when he just

213

hung around, watched me do my own thing... and just gave me a chaste kiss when I went to bed, much to my disappointment.

"Yeah," I reluctantly replied.

"Two, his kind craves sex on the most primal of levels—with whomever," Myrna went on, as if I didn't know. "Male or female, it doesn't matter to them. Sex is sex and the variety is just as exciting as the act. But for Andrei, there is only you. Haven't you wondered about that?" She didn't wait for my response. "I've known him for centuries and he's never been monogamous before. He's never been bonded to a human, too. And the fact that he's, well, faithful when it comes to you... without the ceremony. He cares about you and I never thought something like that would ever be possible in his case."

"I have to go, Myrna. I shouldn't have called you," I added, although speaking to her had weirdly been as reassuring as speaking to my best friend, Renée, who I missed way too much these days.

"Call me any time, *mea domina*," she said, and judging from her tone, I knew that she was smiling.

Resisting the urge to chastise her for using that cursed title, I ended the call and flung my phone to the coffee table along with the half-eaten tub of ice cream. My appetite had vanished. First, there was the persistent dull ache in my gut that had something to do with a certain six foot six giant's disappearance. And then there was the repulsive idea floating in my head about a baby growing inside me that was just too horrible to even contemplate.

I sure as hell wasn't ready to be a mother, and definitely not to a demon king's child. I couldn't bring a baby into a fucked-up world like the one I found myself in at the moment.

214

But then I started wondering if Andrei would want a baby, if he ever even had one. There was a strong possibility that someone as old as he was could've fathered millions of hybrid spawn across the world. That thought further dampened my mood.

After checking my cheeks for more moisture, I was just about ready to call it a night, maybe after a glass or two of well-deserved Zinfandel, when a group of demons materialized in the living room like it was the most normal thing in the world, which I supposed in this case it was. Demons came in and out of here like flies, which prompted me to reflect that asking Daniel to demon-proof this house was long overdue.

I curiously stared at all four men, wondering if this could possibly be a hallucination brought on by brain freeze and my pathetic misery. But the wave of awareness that washed over me told me that no, this was as real as Sofia Vergara's accent.

"Don't be afraid, *mea domina*," the biggest one, a fiery-haired meathead, said in what he probably thought was a soothing voice, but in reality sounded like how a psycho would most likely talk to his victim.

However, I couldn't even get up—that was how worn out I was from being useless. "Get the hell out," I muttered warily, and they all blinked at each other, stifling their laughter.

"Our king sent us." This came from a demon that looked like he'd just left high school. He even had a baby face and a black, grungy Ke$ha T-shirt on. "All you have to do is come quietly."

"And where, pray tell, am I supposed to come quietly to?" I asked, my voice dripping with sarcasm.

"You'll find out when you get there," another one declared, which was pretty much the response I expected.

"Okay," I said, slowly getting to my feet. "Let me just change."

They glanced at each other before the meathead said incredulously, "Really? He said you'd be difficult."

So he sent four demons to get me? I was flattered he thought I was Xena, the Warrior Princess.

"It's not my time of the month," I said with a shrug, when really, I wanted to say that the thought of going to him filled me with unbelievable joy. It was too humiliating to admit it to myself though, let alone say it aloud to a bunch of strangers.

I strode past the small group of demons and headed to my room, kicking the door closed and locking it behind me. Shedding my filthy clothes, I decided to wear a dress Andrei had casually admired on me a while back. Black and clingy, it fell just a little above my knees and it was during my make-up that I came to the dismal conclusion that I, Rae Erickson, was absolutely dick-whipped to the nth degree.

"*Mea domina?*" someone said politely while rapping loudly on my closed bedroom door.

I had to have a talk with them about calling me their queen, in Latin or otherwise. I certainly wasn't married, or bonded, to Andrei.

"Almost done," I assured the disembodied voice as I set my mascara down on the sink.

I admired the finished product in the mirror, satisfied that I didn't look like I'd been wallowing in my penthouse for close to a week because I was missing Andrei. I looked like a fully functional adult that just happened to look great in a black Versace.

When I finally unlocked my bedroom door—after slipping into my favorite pair of Louboutin pumps, of course—

I was met with the stare of the kid demon. I totally recognized that hungry look and it pissed me the hell off.

"You want me to tell Andrei you looked at me like that?" I snarled, the ferocity in my voice visibly startling the demon.

"Um, no," he said quickly, schooling his face into nonchalance. "I'm very, very sorry."

I nodded, mentally high-fiving myself for being unaffected by a demon that obviously wanted to jump my bones. "So... where are we going? Which restaurant is he meeting...?"

"Restaurant?" Meathead queried as he approached us. He gave me a strange look. "No, *mea domina*. Tonight, we go to the king's castle. You'll teleport with me."

Andrei's castle was located in a dense forest on the Romanian part of the Carpathian Mountains. However, I wasn't able to admire the scenery because Meathead, who'd cordially introduced himself as Trick, teleported us right into the castle, which, by the way, was an oven.

Trick wordlessly left me alone in the chambers, gently closing the large, creaking oak door behind him. It felt like I'd been transported back in time and goosebumps prickled my skin. There wasn't even any electricity, if the oil lamps flickering on the marble pedestals were anything to go by.

Something wasn't right.

Andrei had never even mentioned a castle, and if he had, I certainly wouldn't have thought it would be in this realm.

God, I was such an ignorant idiot. I knew nothing about anything.

I sat on the edge of the old-fashioned queen-sized bed in the center of the room, feeling stupid. What a waste of a perfectly good outfit. And for what? To be summoned to the king's castle like a subservient little...

"You're a little overdressed, *cherie*," a voice said from the shadows.

I leaped off the bed, nearly twisting my ankle in the process. Stupid, overpriced shoes.

I glared at the corner, my brow furrowing in recognition of the blonde-haired woman, I meant succubus, stalking out of the shadows. Dressed in a practically nonexistent red satin dress that just about covered her crotch, she definitely had every right to call me overdressed.

"Selene," she said by way of introduction. "We met at Nicolette, remember?"

I racked my brain trying to remember her. When I finally did, I folded my arms across my chest. "Oh, right. You wanted to know why Andrei was sleeping with me. Did he answer your question himself?"

Her blood-red lips quirked into a smile as she approached me. "Not sleeping with. Fucking. Call it what it is."

"What the hell do you want?" I snarled, standing my ground.

She held her hands up in surrender. "Relax. I'm just here to make sure that you are dressed appropriately."

"Appropriately?" I screeched in disbelief. "What the hell's wrong with what I'm wearing?"

She tilted her head, licking her lips lasciviously as she undressed me with her eyes. "Nothing," she said huskily. "In

218

fact, if you didn't already belong to someone, I would have you for myself. Such is your appeal, *ma petite*."

I felt heat creep up my neck. "You're definitely not my type." *Fucking whore.*

"You've never thought about trying a woman? Ever?" She let out a laugh at my horrified expression. "You know, I could make myself a man... just for you."

I tasted bile in my mouth. "Why am I here?"

"Here you go. You must wear this."

Of course, it was only then that I noticed the collar in her hand. It was black leather, probably smooth to the touch, and had a silver clasp on one part. Little diamond studs running around it glittered in the dim light. I instinctively recoiled.

"You want me to wear that?"

"No. My lord wants you to wear it. Take it, *chérie*."

"He wouldn't do that to me," I said unconvincingly. "Collar me like a dog?" I shook my head. "Andrei would never..."

"You are mistaken. Being collared is not demeaning. It's an achievement."

"Oh, really?" Sarcasm crept into my voice. "Where the hell is Andrei? If this is some kinky experience he wants to share with me, he can count me out. I'm requesting someone to take me home."

"Remove your clothes and put the collar on," Selene snapped. She gestured at a mirror in one corner. "You can use that to help you snap the clasp. I'll be back in five minutes and so help me, you had better be ready."

"You won't tell me what's going on and now you want me to undress and degrade myself? Are you out of your mind?"

Her icy blue eyes narrowed. "I don't know what you know about my kind but there are certain rules about respect, especially when it comes to lowly humans," she said in a low voice. "You have obviously insulted my lord in some way. And now, as a result, you have to suffer the consequences. I don't care what you said or did, but my instructions were to get you ready to see him. Do we understand each other so far?"

I bit my lower lip, fear inching up my spine. "He's seriously going to... to punish me for kicking him out of my bedroom."

Selene shrugged. "Just do as I say and you'll be fine." With that, she flounced out the room, leaving the ostentatious collar on the bed.

In a flash, I was at the door but, as I knew it would be, it was locked.

"Fuck me sideways," I muttered, leaning against the wood. "What the hell have you gotten yourself into, Rae?"

This just didn't make sense. When I thought back to the last time I'd seen Andrei, I didn't really say anything that warranted this, whatever this was. Seriously, this man was going to get it when I eventually saw him.

It was this thought that propelled me to the bed to snatch the collar up for a closer inspection. They were definitely real diamonds. The Tiffany's girl inside me squealed and dropped the whole thing.

"You want this?" I said aloud, violently tugging at the straps of my dress and all but ripping it off. The material pooled at my feet and I stepped out of it, placing one hand on the foot of the bed for balance and removing my pumps.

I kept my underwear on for self-preservation. Then, with shaking hands, I grabbed the collar and stood in front of the mirror. It was relatively easy to put on. And the fact that I'd tamed my difficult hair into a chignon helped.

"No underwear."

Selene's voice came from right behind me and her reflection appeared immediately after. I spun around.

"You really are crazy," I informed her on the off-chance that she didn't know.

She rolled her eyes. "This is the way it has to be. Is that Agent Provocateur, by any chance?"

I glanced down at my black lace strapless bra and matching panties before looking at her. "Yeah."

"Nice. But they have to go."

"Is he going to kill me?" I asked as nonchalantly as I possibly could, slowly unclasping the front of my bra. I could've thrown up when Selene's eyes followed the spill of my breasts.

"Hmm? Kill you? Why would he do that?"

I shrugged, tugging my panties down. "I just think this whole abduction thing is a little extreme. Honestly, Andrei could've come to me anytime."

Selene's eyes thoroughly swept over my body as if she were committing the image to memory. Snapping out of her brazen eyeballing, she extended a hand to me. "Come. He's waiting."

Despite my complete hatred of the woman, I took her hand and was surprised to find it cool to the touch. On the other hand, I was close to sweating buckets that could probably fill a lagoon. They had to have some kind of mega-furnace in the dungeons or something.

Selene was silent as we navigated the passageways. Lit torches were suspended on the walls on either side of the passages. Meanwhile, I just focused on my shadow dancing on the stone, blocking out the fact that I was walking butt-naked in a castle, which was probably overrun with all kinds of demons.

Shit! Shit! Shit! I thought in a panic when I heard voices getting louder as we approached a marble archway down one passage.

They were, no doubt, the voices of demons. What the hell was I doing walking into this situation? Naked, no less! And what was I doing holding hands with a succubus?

As if she were following my train of thought, Selene released me as soon as we entered the large room. The entire room fell silent and I got the vibe that told me I was literally surrounded by demons. But the only thing I really registered was the man sitting on a large iron throne on a raised platform. He was on the throne with a little naked redhead sitting on his lap.

My eyes narrowed at Andrei, and suddenly, my nudity didn't matter. No, what mattered was clawing that skeletal bitch's eyeballs out and shoving them down her throat. I didn't have my knife so my French tips would just have to do. I just prayed they wouldn't break.

"Stop growling," Selene said serenely. "Jealousy is not a good look on you."

"Go to hell," I hissed, meeting Andrei's cold cerulean stare.

I broke the gaze, giving the entire room a sweep. The ceiling was incredibly high, propped up by chalk white marble pillars that ran along the entire room. There was no décor, no niceties, just stone and marble. But there were thirty or so sex demons sitting by the long wooden table that spanned the length of the room, which stopped a long way away from the throne, giving Andrei the proverbial bird's eye view of everything.

I stifled a gasp when I noticed that the people with the glazed expressions on their faces were humans. They either straddled the demons in different positions or knelt before them like trained pets. The whole sight was sickening.

Seconds later, their dead eyes became curious stares directed at me, and I paused for a second, staring right back at them... until Selene prodded me in the back.

"Go and kneel before him," she instructed, and right then, I wanted to slap her.

"He's not my king."

Several ears perked up at that and I was quickly reminded of their extra sensitive hearing. Flushing, I slowly made my way past the table and paused before the throne. Now that I was closer, I was able to see that Andrei was shirtless and in black leather pants—leather freaking pants that, on any other day, would've made me cream my panties. However, being in the current confusing-as-fuck situation (on top of that, my lack of clothing and the fact that he had a bony skank on his lap) sort of made that impossible.

And then, there was the downright rude glare he was giving me.

It sort of took me back to the day after we'd first slept together. My uneasiness increased tenfold when he gestured for me to kneel. No words, just the casual twirl of his fingers. If I wasn't in a den full of his cronies, I probably would've told him to go fuck himself. Monogamous? What a fool I was.

Giving Andrei my most mutinous look, I sank to my knees at his feet. I'd expected my knees to be burned by the scorching, hard floor but I found that the heat, though uncomfortable, wasn't unbearable. It wasn't just the air that was hot, so it was a miracle that my bare feet didn't get burned during my long walk to what I assumed was the throne room.

Andrei jiggled his knee, wordlessly telling the girl to get off him. I resisted the urge to pounce on her as she sashayed down the set of steps that led up to the throne and strode past me.

Stop being so petty, Rae. You and Andrei are not an exclusive couple. You're not Jay and Bee, or Brangelina, or even O and freaking Stedman.

I sucked in a deep breath, my scowl vanishing as I calmed myself down and focused on the stone floor. However, my composure was immediately ruffled when a menacing shadow fell over me.

No, it's too soon, I thought in a flash of dread.

Andrei came down the stairs in two effortless steps, stopping before me. Compelled by his sheer magnetism, I looked up at him. Crouching at his feet, he seemed bigger than a giant that I couldn't help but look away.

Then he reached down and grabbed my hair, unraveling all my hard work. Then, tugging a handful of it, he forced me to look him in the eye. An intense pain burned through my scalp and heated my neck. I stifled the yelp that was threatening to escape my lips. I wasn't going to give him the satisfaction of seeing my pain.

"Get up." His voice was harsh, so harsh that it would've been foolish of me not to obey him.

His hand remained in my hair as I awkwardly got to my feet. As soon as I did, he jerked me to him and twisted me around, until my back was flush against his chest and I was staring back at the demons and their mortals.

"Do you see them?" Andrei growled in my ear, shaking me with one hand.

See them? What else was I supposed to look at? Two human girls were on their knees before demons, feverishly sucking them off. A man kneeling between an incubus' legs was doing the same. The rest were staring at me with hunger in their eyes. The redolent smell of sex and desire hung in the air like a heavy blanket.

"Answer me," Andrei demanded, shaking me again.

"Yeah. I mean, yes. I see them," I sputtered, knowing that there was going to be a nasty bruise on my upper arm tomorrow.

"These are my people. This is what I am," he snarled, his hot breath tickling my ear. Then he pinched my nipple and I jumped. "I fuck, I kill, I dominate. You don't mind the fucking part, do you?"

I kept my mouth shut.

"Answer my damn questions."

"No," I whispered, squeezing my eyes shut, "I don't mind the fucking part. As long as you're only fucking me." I honestly hadn't meant to say the last part aloud but my mouth was on autopilot.

Judging from the tension I felt behind me, I could tell that Andrei hadn't expected that either.

He quickly collected himself. "Do you love being dominated? Controlled? At my mercy?"

I thought about this. Did I? I was pretty independent. I didn't bow to any man, never had. I never just lay there during sex. I usually took control, or put myself on equal footing with my partner, and gave as good as I got. That was the way it had always been.

But with Andrei?

"Yes," I replied candidly. "I love it when you dominate me."

His hand wrapped around my throat, around the collar. His fingers fanned the narrow column and I knew that with one squeeze, he could choke the life right out of me. Instead of freaking me out, that thought sent an arrow of heat down to my groin. I was so twisted.

"Good," he rasped, rolling his hips, pressing himself to my back. "Good."

I held my breath, awareness racing through my entire body at the familiar feel of his erection. His skin was hot and damp against mine, but I didn't want to imagine why he was sweaty. The room was oven temperature, after all. *That was probably why,* I kept telling myself.

"Get on the table."

I nearly asked him to repeat himself because I couldn't have heard what I...

"I said, get on the fucking table!" he impatiently repeated, releasing me and urging me toward the wooden table with a hand on my back.

Despite myself, I was getting heavily turned on by his sharp commands, as stupid as that sounded. Lowering my ass onto the edge of the table with my back to our audience, I gave him a snarky questioning look, which most probably came off as rude. His beautiful eyes narrowed as he stood before me.

"Lie down," he instructed, folding his arms across his broad chest.

On the table? I thought, glancing over my shoulder at the plates of food.

The audience stopped all manner of fornication and their eyes were firmly trained on me. I shivered. I felt so uncomfortable it almost felt physically painful.

"Don't make me repeat myself."

Andrei's low menacing tone was what pushed me to finally obey him and lie flat on my back. Selene was sitting on a chair to my left and our eyes met. She wasn't even hiding how much she wanted to fuck me and I wondered, not for the first time, if I really was demon catnip.

Andrei's hands were on my thighs as he spread my legs, and a blast of air hit my throbbing center. I made my first involuntary response, a whimper, in his presence then and instantly regretted it.

His hand came down against my pussy, catching my swollen clit. Biting my lower lip, I smothered a cry.

"Quiet. You're not receiving any pleasure." He ran a finger up my center and I quashed the moan that desperately wanted to come out. "Hands above your head... on the table."

Without hesitation, I did as he asked. My hands hit a plate somewhere above my head and it was instantly removed.

"You can look but you cannot touch," Andrei was saying, but it wasn't directed at me. "She is mine. If any of you doubt that, try to lay a finger on her."

Chairs scraped along the floor as the demons stood. This was probably my cue to sit up and tell Andrei where the hell to get off. But my pathetic little mind zoned in on the "She is mine." and wouldn't let me move.

So I lay there like a body on an autopsy table, on display for a small crowd of incubi to... to goddamn inspect. Nothing about this scenario made any sense, except that I was positive that Andrei was trying to prove a point. To me, or to his followers? I had no idea.

But that didn't calm my wariness when a bunch of eyes strained to get a peek at me. Naked and throbbing from Andrei's pussy-lashing, I couldn't stop the heat staining my cheeks. My entire body felt like it was in flames from being in such close proximity to these supernatural creatures. I watched them walk around the ridiculously long table, examining every inch of my body at every angle. My hairs stood on end when I

227

felt eyes on my opening. My first instinct was to slam my thighs together. But a voice in my head told me that these creatures could look all they want, Andrei would rip apart any of them who would dare to touch me.

And that was what kept me from seriously hyperventilating.

"You can feel how much she likes sex," someone commented, as if I wasn't in the room. "How lucky the king was to have found a responsive mortal. What I wouldn't give to have one at my beck and call, to fuck for the hell of it and not for sustenance."

"Would you bond yourself to a human?" another voice asked.

"Never. What would be the point? They would only die in a few years."

"Then you take another. It would be like trading up for a newer model."

Selene's face came into view. Her stare was both longing and disdainful. God, if I ever got the opportunity, I wouldn't hesitate to kill her. She freaked me out by simply being in my vicinity.

Andrei barked out a command in a language I didn't know and all movement around me ceased. Chairs were pushed back in and I realized that he'd instructed everyone to sit back down. My sigh of relief morphed into a squeal, however, when he dragged me down the table until my ass was just on the edge.

"Shut the fuck up," he roared, his palm connecting with my aching vagina once again. My entire body jolted from the sting but my eyes were locked with Andrei's. "This is for my pleasure alone. You are not going to come," he said in a hoarse voice, simultaneously releasing his erection from his pants. "Got me? You... won't... come."

I was flat on my back so I couldn't really see his hard-on, but I knew that if I could, I'd disintegrate on the spot and disobey him. So I nodded imperceptibly, receiving another slap that further battered my poor distended clitoris.

"Say the words," he commanded, looming over me.

"I won't come." I probably wouldn't be able to, what with the thirty pairs of eyes on us.

Don't lie, Rae, the voice in my head scoffed. *You've wondered what it would be like to fuck in front of an audience. Like Roan and Nina.*

"Good."

He gripped my hips and I felt him at my entrance, just the slick touch of his cock's broad head. And then he was inside me in one merciless thrust. He hadn't bothered to check my readiness, but then he had probably seen it. I was wet, so wet for him that I was worried I was sick in the head—because what sane person could get turned on by this whole scenario?

I was clearly insane... particularly when I noticed the questioning look in Andrei's stormy eyes. As if he were asking me, "Do you want a taste of my darkness? Do you want me to show you what evil is in me, even when it comes to you? Do you want this, Rainelle?"

The look on my face must have given him an affirmative because Andrei's eyes instantly hardened and he proceeded. I let out a small gasp of pain, my body trying to remember what his thick shaft felt like inside me... and failing. He was too big, or I was too swollen, but he wasn't holding back at all.

229

"Don't close your fucking eyes," he growled, withdrawing and slamming back into me with a muffled shout. "Watch me fuck you."

I opened them, wincing from both the brutality of his every invasion and the friction I was feeling between my back and the table. I couldn't climax like this, couldn't even begin to feel any pleasure. This... onslaught was solely for his enjoyment.

I could only lie there and accept each violent plunge of his member. My vagina was contracting around his cock with each thrust, squeezing the slick, hot member with all the strength it possessed. He pulled back, drove in, pulled back, drove back in. The force of his thrusts shook the table, the scraping of wood against the floor reverberating in the now silent room.

"Who do you..." Another thrust. "... belong to?" Andrei panted, his brow damp with sweat. He held himself inside me, his turgid member beating away in my channel. "Answer me, damn it!" He withdrew and ruthlessly pushed back in.

I cried out, the pain becoming an intense pleasure I hadn't expected. "You!" I screamed, bathing in my own sweat. "I belong... to you!"

"Fucking right," he barked, resuming his repeated, thorough pounding. "You are mine. Say... it."

"I'm yours!" I screamed, feeling the rise of my explosion building up inside. "I'm yours."

"Tell me you will never fuck around on me." He slowly rotated his hips, his swollen shaft hitting me in all the right places that should have sent me over the edge. I was on the cusp of climax but, with great effort, I held on to it.

"I'll never fuck around on you," I wailed, the strength of keeping myself from coming taking too much from me.

"Are you sorry?" he demanded, his thrusts quickening again. Sweat glistened on his chest and strands of his loose long hair were clinging to his face and shoulders.

"Yes! Yes! I belong to you."

"Argh, fuck," he groaned, spilling himself inside me. I brought my legs up around his waist, keeping him there, as the heat of his seed poured into me.

Still buried inside, he slumped over me and the table groaned with the added weight. I held onto him, burying my nose in the damp crook of his neck. It was the only thing I had the strength to do.

Chapter 15

The room was modern, masculine, and intricately designed. It was like stepping out of the nineteenth century and back into modern civilization. Instead of the flagstone flooring, there was dark velvet carpeting. Instead of lanterns and torches, a tiered chandelier dangled from the plaster ceiling, spilling bright light in the room. And a gigantic king-sized bed sat in the middle of the room, covered in a sleek black comforter. Animal skin was strewn beneath the many pillows and a bar fridge sat on one side of the bed in lieu of a nightstand.

This was his bedroom.

"I hope you slept well, *chérie*," Selene said gently, gesturing at the massive bed. "You must be extremely sore."

Sore? Sore didn't even come close to it.

"Fuck off," I muttered in a voice hoarse from screaming.

As soon as the words left my mouth, she disappeared, and I was left alone in the vast room.

Every freaking part of my body ached. Then there was the fact that I hadn't come when my body had been so viciously assaulted by that damn demon. I held him for the last time, I had to repeatedly tell myself, and it was a bittersweet affair. My mind was completely frazzled but one thing was painfully clear: I was a sick little fuck that secretly enjoyed being so viciously abused—and publicly, no less. I was turned on, and being so out of my comfort zone hadn't even mattered in the end.

Andrei had made his point, though. I wasn't going to confuse him for a mortal man ever again. No, what I was going to do was remember my father's legacy and for what he'd given up his life.

I fuck, I kill, I dominate, I thought, remembering Andrei's words and eyeing the bed warily.

Well, he didn't have to tell me twice. Everything was crystal clear to me now. *Boyfriend? What a fucking laugh!* Boyfriends didn't fuck about with stick-figure redheads and flaunt them in front of their girlfriends. Boyfriends didn't treat their girlfriends like shit stains.

You can't tame the devil. Didn't someone somewhere say that?

The smartest thing to do for now would be to stay amiable and ensure that I got out of this place in one piece. No matter how much my blood boiled from the humiliation, acting out would only bring me another disciplinary sex, probably somewhere in the underworld the next time... or worse, permanent imprisonment in the castle's dungeons. Now that I knew how little I meant to the damn prick, how I was just a convenient trophy, I wasn't going to risk my life by attacking him and receiving the wrath of his minions.

I'm yours? I thought, snorting. *You must be out of your fucking mind.*

As soon as I got back to Paris, I was going to call Daniel. I had politely declined his invitation to hop on the Let's-Kill-Lauren bandwagon and asked that he just take me under his wing. Self-preservation, that was what life was all about. The weak got the scraps, plus their asses got kicked. Meanwhile, the strong left the scraps and dished out said ass-kicking.

And I wasn't a weakling.

But that state of mind was momentarily paused when a wave of familiar awareness washed over me and I sensed a demon in the room. My skin prickling gave way to downright queasiness and I honestly thought that I was turning inside out. My reaction had never been this bad before, even in the face of a demon horde.

"Why aren't you in bed?"

I wished I could say that I didn't find that voice familiar, but I did, and I hated myself even more for it. Taking quick, deep breaths, I turned around and saw him standing in a corner, still as sticky and disheveled as he'd been when Selene ushered me out the banqueting hall.

"Is that you?" I wheezed, slightly doubling over. "Are you doing this to me?"

The closer he got, the worse the pain became. I knew that it was all in my head, that I wasn't really itching everywhere, nor was I actually feeling the overwhelming need to puke my spleen out. But it was pretty damn close to reality.

"I'm not cloaking myself at the moment, so you're feeling my aura," he said matter-of-factly. "I'm stronger than whatever you've encountered before, so I affect you more." His eyes closed briefly and the pain dissipated.

I could've collapsed in relief. I nearly let myself, if I wasn't so wary of Andrei.

"Why aren't you in bed?" he repeated impatiently, apparently done with his show-and-tell. He advanced, his hands behind his back.

I stood my ground, mentally begging my heart to stop running the Olympics without my permission. "Are you going to drag me out and have your friends fuck me, perhaps? That should really get the crowd going."

His eyebrows creased into a deep frown. "What did you say?" He began to circle me.

He heard me. I knew he heard me, and he knew I knew.

"How do you feel?" He tugged at my loose hair. It wasn't hard enough to hurt me but it was enough to piss me off.

"I feel like bowing to you, my lord." Could I control the revulsion dripping from my voice? *No.* "I feel like you've enlightened me and I feel like thanking you profusely. I was blind, but now I see."

His hand was around my neck in a flash, pressing the collar in my throat. "Who the fuck do you think you're talking to?" he snarled in my ear, his chest pressed against my back.

"Either you kill me right now, or I find a way to kill you," I whispered harshly. "But just know that I'm not going down without mutilating your lying, filthy dick."

He let me go as if I burned him. "I can't do this with you," he murmured, and I just had to turn around.

He looked dejected and that baffled me. Gone was the antagonism on his face, and in its place was regret.

Then suddenly, Andrei's hand shot out to gently grasp my hand… and my entire body enflamed with a different kind of awareness. His eyes were fixed on my upper arm, drawn to the already purpling mark his hand had left from earlier.

"Fucking hell," he breathed, running the pads of his fingers down my bruised skin. "I did that to you. I hurt you."

235

I pulled my arm away from him. "Don't... touch... me!"

"Rae, please," he said, his voice gruff. He grabbed me to him again, his grip decidedly tighter. "Please."

His tone surprised me. He was beseeching me and it was confusing.

I did the one thing I shouldn't have done in that moment and looked up into his eyes. They were bluer, moodier. And they were pleading.

"You made your point, Andrei," I said slowly, my throat throbbing in pain with every syllable. "Now let me make mine." I leaned in and steeled my heart. "I'm not a fucking toy you can own, use, and put on display to fuck. You're full of shit, you know that? Fucking some skinny little thing and bringing me in to witness the aftermath? Fuck you!"

"You are not a toy," he said, his thumbs rubbing the insides of my wrists, "and I don't know what the hell you're talking about."

"You don't know what I'm talking about?" I tried in vain to wrench my arm away. "Do you think I'm stupid? That... that naked girl on your lap was a figment of my imagination?"

His eyes flashed a deep red. "Her?" He pulled me against him, our bare chests flush against each other. "There's only you. I don't need or want anyone else."

"You must think I'm a gullible idiot!"

He released me and I backed away, the incensed look on his face enough of a warning to me. "No, you know what I am? An insanely jealous fucking wimp!" he snarled, as he violently swiped his hair off his face. "You know what I've been doing these past four days? Moping around this fucking

236

place wondering if you'd act on your feelings for that little fucking hunter! Do you know what a pussy that makes me?"

It took me a long moment to even think straight. "What," I began, "are you talking about?"

His eyes narrowed. "Don't feign innocence," he snapped, his voice sarcastic. "The last time we were together and that fuck stopped by, you were wearing my ring and I felt it. I felt your attraction to him."

Of all the things I'd ever expected him to say, that was definitely last on my list. I automatically glanced at the empty finger that was supposed to have his ring. *Now, how am I supposed to remember that he's an incubus when he said things like that?*

"I know," he said quietly, as if reading my mind. "I sound like a human. You don't have to tell me how fucked-up that is. Believe me, I know."

"You didn't say anything," I murmured, my mind going back to our fight after my foot massage. "Why didn't you say anything? You were laughing, for Pete's sake!"

His eyes softened. "Because jealousy was just a word in the fucking Oxford Dictionary before I met you." He looked away. "This feeling… I've never felt it before."

I thought about Lorenzo's cousin, Paul, and Renée and Lorenzo's attempt at hooking him up with me. Andrei had mentioned jealousy then, too. I had to call it bullshit. He knew exactly what the hell it meant and we hadn't even known each other that long back then.

"But you weren't attracted to him," Andrei explained slowly, as if it were that obvious. He took an experimental step toward me, waiting to see if I'd back away. When I didn't, he said, "It's dangerous for someone like you to have so much power over someone like me."

"Someone like me?"

"You might not be a hunter but you are a hunter's daughter. And one day, you'll want to learn the family business."

"You're such a fucking contradiction, Andrei. I said the exact same thing to you and you stormed off in a huff."

"At that time, I took that to mean that you were eloping with the fucking hunter," he countered, his face impassive. Then he emphatically put a fist to his chest. "This isn't who I am. This...green-eyed mortal..." He wrinkled his face in disgust at the word. "... resorting to petty name-calling and senseless fucking retribution."

"Retribution," I parroted. "Who was that girl?"

His eyes landed on mine. "Were you jealous?"

Was he being serious?

"Insanely," I replied through clenched teeth, throwing his little word back at him. "Did you fuck her?"

He was standing in front of me now, his eyes connecting with mine. "No. Did you fuck the hunter?"

"No!" I replied in astonishment. I wasn't even attracted to the guy... not anymore. And he thought I was dating someone.

"Then the girl did her job."

I gaped at him, the wheels in my head whirring incessantly and pieces of the puzzle fell into place. He wanted to make me jealous. And he was smug because he'd succeeded.

It was petty. It was immature. It was so human.

I reached up and slapped him, the satisfying sound of my palm connecting with his cheek echoing in the room. Before he could react, I grabbed a handful of his matted hair and tugged, dragging a low growl from his mouth.

"Don't ever do that again," I threatened, grabbing his hair and pulling for a second time.

He could've demonstrated his incredible strength. He could've flown into a rage and punished me... again. But I watched as he fell to his knees before me, forcing me to release his hair. Then he hung his head.

"Don't ever make me do that again," he said in a hushed voice.

"Make you? I didn't make you do anything, Andrei. I didn't ask for any of this supernatural bull." *And I didn't ask to fall for you.* "Did you enjoy humiliating me like that in front of all your minions?"

His head snapped up. "Humiliating you?"

I restrained myself from clouting him again because I didn't think I'd stop there. I was bound to kick, punch and claw his eyes out—and that would only end badly for me, I was sure. I bet bipolar Andrei could make an appearance at any moment.

"Do you think I was excited about being summoned here like a little slave? You think I was clapping in delight when you put me on show like your shiny new toy?" My voice broke on the last word, at the memory of being in my worst nightmare. "And gosh, I bet you thought I'd be delighted at the prospect of being fucked like I was some kind of whore! You got your point across, thank you very much." I forced the pain out of my face and made way for the violent rage swirling in my chest. "I will never underestimate you again, Lord Andrei. I will never mistake you for a human. You are what you are."

"I was angry... with you... with myself."

"Andrei, get up," I whispered. Speaking to him when he was on his knees felt strange.

"Let me make you understand something," he said firmly, ignoring my command. His eyes were beckoning me to drown in them. "You are not a whore and fucking you like that... Fucking you like that was the only way I knew how to show you, and them, that you are mine. That I want you, only you." He gracefully rose to his feet, towering over me once more. "This is what I am, Rainelle, and you haven't even seen the worst of it."

That was true, wasn't it? Tonight had brought with it a major epiphany, one that I realized only now I'd wanted some confirmation about for so long.

He'd taken me out on a few dates after our initial breakfast, hung out with me with no expectation of sex, given me a foot massage once and even slept over. He'd seemed so human and maybe I'd wanted to take a walk on the dark side and see what exactly I was dealing with.

If you can't handle me at my worst, then you sure as hell don't deserve me at my best.

I couldn't remember the beginning of that quote but I read somewhere that Marilyn Monroe said it... I think. But whether she really said that or not, I believe it to be absolutely true.

"I'm not yours," I said.

"Come again?"

"You very well know that I didn't even come the last time."

He instantly looked remorseful, a look I wasn't used to seeing on his face. "I was angry. You needed to know and understand that."

"You said that. Now get back on your knees."

His gaze became thoughtful before he complied and fell to his knees. I was naked, I was battered, and my entire being was being pulled in two directions by Human Andrei and Demon Andrei. But I was sure about one thing: I was never going to be treated the way he treated me in front of his underlings again.

I snatched a mass of his hair, yanking his face even closer. He let out a soft hiss. "I'm not yours, Andrei."

"You already said…"

"What I said out there? It doesn't count. None of it counts. I was being fucked within an inch of my life in front of a demon audience." I mentally shivered at the memory. "You could've told me that I was Wiz Khalifa and I would've repeated it. So, you repeat after me: I am not yours."

His upper lip curled into a snarl. "Remember who you're talking to."

"I remember," I spat, leaning in until our faces were inches apart. "How could I forget when you reminded me oh-so-nicely?"

His eyes shut, long lashes brushing his cheeks. He looked like he was in physical agony. "You are not mine."

"But you are mine." I cupped his chin and his eyes snapped open. "You're a demon of pleasure. A demon of my pleasure. Only my pleasure."

"As your boyfriend, that would be my main focus."

My hand fell from his face and I froze. "What?"

"Tonight you came to a realization? Well, I had mine four days ago, when I discovered that you find another man desirable." He was still on his knees and it was highly disconcerting. So was the look of pure vehemence he was giving me. A vein in his forehead looked like it was throbbing. "I meant what I said about slitting his throat."

My hands cupped his face and I stooped slightly until we were eye to eye. "I can slit throats, too, so don't ever test me with another whore again, Andrei."

His pupils had dilated and his breathing became hitched. "There's only you," he rasped, and he closed the distance between our lips.

It took me only a second to decide that I didn't want to push him away. And desire sparked until it lit a fire between us. My hands held him to keep him in place and I kissed him harder, taking control of our movement. Teasing his lower lip between my teeth, I savored the pained groan he released into my mouth. Meanwhile, his hands were gripping the back of my legs, and before I could even fully taste him, he yanked me into him and hauled me over one broad shoulder.

"What the hell?" I shrieked, amazed by how high up I was.

"I ran you a bath."

As the enormous, stark white bathroom came into view, I realized that he was telling the God-honest truth. He set me down in front of the Jacuzzi-style tub. And because of the steam wafting up, I knew that he hadn't just run this bath a while ago. Magic was definitely responsible.

"Get in," he gently commanded, and the plea in his voice was unmistakable. He didn't want me to refuse, the bipolar shit.

I gingerly hopped in, expecting scalding boiling water and was mildly surprised when it felt instead like a warm blanket swathing my legs. I sank down until the water was waist-level, letting out a sigh of immense pleasure as I did so. My fatigued muscles practically wept with joy.

"Oh, God," I exhaled, shutting my eyes and splashing my face with water.

My moment of bliss was cut short when I felt Andrei descend behind me. I stilled, feeling his long, muscular legs next to mine. He'd obviously shucked his pants and the instantly recognizable hardness of his erection was digging into my lower back.

He pushed my hair out of the way and kissed the back of my neck, inhaling my scent. "I don't know how to apologize," he admitted, his voice gruff. "I've never apologized to anyone before... ever."

My head bent forward as he continued giving me soft butterfly kisses on my neck.

"I never knew what it felt like to be regretful," he murmured, "until tonight. Until I hurt you."

I didn't want to moan and make him aware of my response to his sweet attention but I couldn't stop the sound leaving my lips when he licked around the base of my neck.

"Say it already," I whispered, leaning forward and away from his mouth. I turned at the waist to look at him. "Say the fucking words."

He ran his tongue across his lower lip. "Rae, if I could go back, I would have gone to bring you here myself. I would have told you exactly why I was so fucked up in the head," he said in a low voice, "but I would have still fucked you hard on that table in front of my subjects because you needed it."

"If that's your apology, I should tell you never to touch me again."

His face clouded over. "Rae..."

"But I know what you're capable of. I know that I want this, that I want you." I looked away. "You said you would never apologize for being what you are." I looked back at him. "Apologize for messing with my head then."

He reached out and pulled me back to him, water swishing around us. "I'm sorry for hurting you." He kissed my upper arm, rolling his tongue against the bruise there. "So sorry, baby."

I twisted at the waist. "Did you mean what you said about dominating me?"

His mouth stopped moving and he raised his head. "Did you mean what you said about submitting to me?"

"You didn't give me any choice." I didn't want to dwell on how it had turned me on. Everything about what happened tonight was insane.

Andrei grimaced. "With any other human, there wouldn't be. But for you, Rae, there is always a choice," he said gently, brushing a mass of hair out of my face before he tugged me to him. "But don't you see, you did not submit. I took you. It had to be done but it shouldn't have been to feed my wrath. I… apologize."

I could feel his heart beating against my back, and I decided to fully turn and face him to make my point. "You know I'm not good with commands. You know I'm difficult. And you know I will never let you do that to me again."

He continued to regard me in silence, but I persevered.

"You're a demon. I know that. I don't give a fuck anymore," I pronounced, feeling absolutely absolved of any guilt I had about that. "What I do give a fuck about is how you treat me. You say I'm more than a whore, more than your… your sustenance. You have to prove that, Andrei. And sometimes, that just means that sex isn't always a means to an end."

"It's the only language I know," he rumbled, sliding a finger up my inner thigh.

I slapped it away, completely refusing to acknowledge my shuddering response. "Stop that. I can't right now. You hurt me."

A pained expression crossed his face. "I can't make it better. But let me see, Rae."

"You are not examining my pussy!" I exclaimed, horrified. Besides, I didn't have to look at it to know that it was bruised and viciously red.

"Lean against the side of the tub," he calmly demanded.

"Andrei…"

"I said, lean back."

I narrowed my eyes at him.

"Lean back, please," he amended.

And to prove how much progress he was making, I obeyed him and rested my head and upper back against the marble. Then, placing my hands firmly at my sides, I gave him a sassy quizzical look.

Andrei gripped my legs at the knees and slightly raised them, lifting my ass clean off the bottom of the tub and exposing my vagina to the open air. His face was only a hair's breadth away from my clit.

Before I could protest, his tongue was slowly, agonizingly licking its way up my gaping slit. The beginnings of a complaint died on my lips and was instead replaced by a sharp cry of intense pleasure. I squirmed as he blew cold air against my distended bud before covering it with his hot, wet mouth. The he started sucking.

"Ah, fuck, Andrei," I panted, already way too aroused for the sweet assault.

His tongue plunged inside me and the bridge of his nose was nuzzling against my sensitive flesh as he vigorously ate me out. The appreciative moans he was making sent tormenting vibrations deep within me and I arched my back, completely surrendering to the sensations.

"Don't stop," I wailed, bucking wildly and chanting his name like a prayer. "Don't you dare stop!"

Each firm stroke of his tongue jolted me against him, made my entire body boneless. His nose was rubbing my clitoris. I was going to come and I was going to come hard...

Then I exploded all over him as he gently nibbled at my flesh.

Andrei continued to lick his way through the little aftershocks of my climax, and then he scooted forward and brought me down on him. I cursed aloud, still so swollen from the night's events to take his tumescent rod again.

But the pain quickly frittered away when he didn't move inside me. He was just waiting. And when his hands came up to push the hair out of my eyes, I could see that he wanted to make sure I was fine.

"You're the only being that I bow to, Rainelle Erickson. I'm a fucking human in your hands."

I held his face and looked him in the eye. "You... won't... come."

The shock in his face almost made me laugh. But he quickly collected himself. "I see."

"That's it? You see?" I could feel his throbbing cock inside me and knew that he was harder than ever before.

He squeezed his eyes shut and leaned back against the side of the tub. "Fuck me, then. Use me. You're here and that's all that fucking matters."

I stared at his beautiful, hard face for a long time before I pinched one of his nipples and his eyes flew open in surprise.

"As cute as that was, I want an energetic, eager sex demon inside me." I leaned forward and kissed his neck. "You will fuck me and you won't come."

He gripped my waist and thrust upward, surprising a scream out of me. "Very well," he declared.

246

"Real smooth," I murmured, placing my hands on his shoulders.

Our eyes locked when I began to ride him. I went slow at first, until slow just wasn't enough. Meanwhile, his powerful thrusts drove his rigid shaft against my womb and I felt completely consumed by it. Water splashed onto the floor as his thrusts became faster and all kinds of sensations overtook me. I squeezed him inside me, as tight as a vise, and languished on his answering grunts of pleasure. The faster our movements became, the more contact I wanted with him. Sensing this, he kissed my neck, kissed my breasts. His tongue set my skin ablaze and his teeth grazed every erogenous spot on my upper body.

"Too much," I cried out, when he was rolling one of my nipples in his mouth. Sweat tasted salty in my mouth. "Oh, shit! I can't…"

"Baby, come," Andrei urged, his voice like sandpaper. "Come around me."

I threw my head back on one of his thrusts and let it go, climaxing again so soon after my first one. I grabbed his hair in both of my hands and yanked his mouth to mine.

"Baby, come," I whispered to him, biting his lip.

The familiar heat of his seed filling me up prompted yet another, although smaller, orgasm. I clenched around him, squeezing every drop of his release.

"Rae, Rae, Rae," he groaned into my mouth, sucking on my tongue. "Don't ever leave me."

Too exhausted to speak, I could only make a small grunt of acknowledgement. I would never leave because I was stuck with him for life… and I totally didn't mind.

And my boyfriend knew exactly what that grunt meant.

Chapter 16

The first thing I saw when I woke up was Temp's big head hovering over me. I experienced a moment of confusion—*Where the hell am I? What day is it? God, is that my breath, or did something die in here?*—that I instantly quashed.

I sat up and rubbed my bleary eyes with the heels of my hands. And only when I was fully awake did I take in the fact that I was in my own bed, in my own penthouse.

"You deaf? I've been yelling in your ear for the past five minutes," Temp groused, holding a cup of coffee in his outstretched hand. "Come on, Nancy Drew. We've got some work to do," he said in a singsong voice. Although, he actually looked less annoyed than he sounded.

I gratefully accepted the coffee, surprised to see that he knew how I liked it—black. "I love how you ended that little rhyme with lyrics from the *Scooby Doo* theme song," I muttered dryly. "What are you doing here at…" I glanced at the digital clock on my nightstand and winced. "… seven o'clock?"

The asshole even had the audacity to look chipper. He was in a bright green T-shirt that actually hurt my eyes and grey board shorts. And he completed his low-key surfer-dude look by letting his icy blond hair down, looking all shaggy and windswept. He still, however, managed to look sufficiently well-dressed. I, on the other hand, was stuffed into a ratty old nightshirt and in desperate need of a toothbrush and Colgate.

"Well, as your admittedly sexy sidekick, I feel the need to…"

"Whoa, whoa, whoa! Sidekick? What are we, eight?" I scoffed, raising an eyebrow at him. "Besides, I don't need one, Temp. I never have."

"You've never dealt with demon stuff, either." He flashed me a megawatt Temp grin. "Although I hear you have been busy, Baby Phat. You went to the Carpathians?"

"I didn't exactly go for the mountains," I said sarcastically as I set the now-empty mug on the nightstand. "But you already knew that. Word about things like that probably get around fast in your world and I bet you're the Perez Hilton of your kind."

Temp looked offended. "Did I or did I not warn you about Andrei? And oh, hell, Rae! What is that?" He pointed a finger at my left hand.

"What?" I looked down… and suppressed a curse when I saw Andrei's ring back on my forefinger. "Oh… that."

"Tell me it's not what I think it is."

"Depends on what you think it is." I was stalling and he knew it. We stared at each other. "Temp, one minute you're the happy mother of the bride, next minute you're the old man warning the kids not to go up the mountain. Pick one character and stick with it."

"I don't comprehend those analogies," he informed me with a poker face.

I rolled my eyes. "Sure, Temp. Let's pretend you don't." I flexed my left hand. "This is supposed to connect me to Andrei, but we're not really bonded. There was no ceremony. No freaky, gothic blood-letting, no creepy animal sacrifices, and no public sex." I flushed. "Well, all right, so there was some sex in front of some…"

"So I heard, Baby Phat." Temp's face softened and he sat on the edge of my bed. "You know how weird it is that we're, you know, related? It's weirder that even though you're older than me and we just met, I have this freaky, protective-older-brother vibe going on."

God, he was getting all sentimental and I… liked it. I never had anyone looking out for me before—well, except for Renée and Lorenzo. But they didn't know the truth about me so they didn't really count. And so it was quite ironic that the two people who were actually looking out for me now just happened to be demons.

"What are you saying, Temp?" I asked, looking him in the eye.

"I guess what I'm trying to say is… Bitch, don't kill my vibe," was his response. Then his lips tilted into a smile. "Let me be your brother and protect you."

"Do you want matching T-shirts now?" I was trying to be sarcastic, but my heart wasn't in it. Instead, I was mortified to realize that there was a ball wedged deep in my throat. "Fuck you for making me want to bawl like an Oscar-winner," I added.

He laughed and I threw my arms around him on impulse. He froze and it was my turn to snigger.

"Just go with it," I told him, as I tried to really remember why I'd once tried to shut out the only family I really had. It was an unconventional family, yes. But it was all I had.

"Did he hurt you?" Temp's voice was gentle as he stroked my back.

"Not physically," I answered candidly, drawing back and finding his brow pinched in confusion. I decided to put him out of his short-lived misery and explain.

A few minutes later...

"That sounds like an episode of *Days of Our Lives*," Temp remarked when I was done. "Making you jealous? Not very kingly."

At that, I finally got off the bed as I replied, "Yeah. We already covered that."

Temp was looking at me strangely.

"What?" I asked, looking down to see if all my private girl parts were perfectly covered. Since I wasn't flashing him, I was perplexed by the look on Temp's face.

"You know I'm not a conformist and Andrei isn't my king," he slowly began, "But in all the years I've known him, he hasn't talked about his feelings like a teenage girl and he's never been monogamous. What fucking sex demon even knows what monogamy means?"

"Your point is?" I snapped, feeling on the defensive.

"My point is that if anyone wants to overthrow him, or some such shit, you're the best way to get to him."

Oh! I haven't thought about that. But then again, I didn't think much when Andrei was near me. *Or over me, or under me, or in me...*

I shook my head. "But he's immortal. Surely nothing can happen to him."

He raised a brow. "Darling, you really need to do your homework. Sure, he can't be killed, but there are other more painful ways to skin a cat."

"Whatever. I need to take a shower before we go sleuthing. That cool with you?"

Temp didn't bother to continue a conversation that was threatening to make me want to do my homework. "Be my guest," he murmured, flopping onto his back on my bed. "I enjoyed this little heart-to-heart, Baby Phat. Maybe next time, we can include *The Notebook* and a mani-pedi."

The fact that the small group of girls were chattering outside Nicolette in the carefree we-don't-know-a-thing-about-taxes-and-real-life-bullcrap way college students normally did sort of made it hard for me to associate them with demons. They were all gorgeous, stick-thin model types—Megan-Fox clones from *Jennifer's Body*, which was ironic.

"Are you sure?" I asked Temp, who was sitting beside me, casually chugging down a can of Red Bull as if stalking six random possessed chicks was an everyday excursion. "I mean, they kind of look like prostitutes, which isn't exactly evil. But everyone has to eat, right? Well, not you, obviously."

He rolled his eyes at me over the can. "Sure, I don't have to eat, but I love food. And yeah, I'm sure, Rae."

Since we were sitting in my rental car across the street, I wasn't close enough to get a read on their auras, but Temp obviously was.

"I'm curious, Baby Phat," he said after a moment of me staring out the window. "What's the plan?"

"Well, I can always call Daniel," I mused to myself, although I knew that that would be like signing his death warrant. Andrei, after all, openly admitted that he was jealous enough of the guy to actually think of mindlessly killing him.

Still, if Daniel was the only hunter I knew, what else could I do?

Maybe get rid of the demons yourself? my conscience suggested.

Right. Easier said than done. I knew next to nothing about demon hunting because I'd run away from my so-called destiny and decided to be a private investigator. Putting me up against a gang of demons would be like sending an infant to war.

"Hey, don't freak out," Temp soothed, putting his hand on my shoulder. A wave of calmness instantly washed over me.

I closed my eyes, opening them again to ask, "How do you do that?"

"Do what?" He withdrew his hand, clearing his throat.

"You know, calm me down like that? It's... weird."

He shrugged. "Just happens. Listen, Rae. In my humble opinion, I think you should let Andrei handle this one." He shot me a sober look. "It was a bad idea for me to bring you here. Whatever these demons are doing, possessing innocent girls... Andrei will deal with it."

"Yeah, but they don't answer to him, do they? Besides, this is probably last on his list of priorities. I mean, he's hardly a good guy." And I was completely okay with that now. I was no angel, either.

"But he is higher up on the food chain than these body hoppers are."

253

"Body hoppers?" I arched a brow.

Temp sighed. "You really need to do your homework if you're gonna roll with demons. Body hoppers are scavengers, practically at the bottom of the food chain." He returned my blank expression with a look of frustration. "You know how you channel surf, trying to find something good on TV? Well, they body surf. Honestly, they're harmless but if they're being controlled by somebody, somebody with double their IQ? It can only mean trouble and I don't know what."

"And you couldn't tell me this sooner because...?" I said through clenched teeth, gripping the steering wheel a little tighter.

"Sorry, okay? I keep forgetting that you're a demon hunter that doesn't hunt demons," he replied, shrugging.

"I'm not a hunter!" I hissed emphatically, but I suddenly wished I was. It sucked being so clueless about something I shouldn't have been clueless about.

But then again, what kind of hunter would I be when I'm related to demons and dating another?

I was like an exterminator that lived in a house filled with roaches and rodents.

"Okay, okay. You're not a hunter. You're a gatherer," Temp quipped, grinning. His eyes twinkled with mischief. "A gatherer of information about hunting."

I laughed. "Okay, that one was kind of funny."

I despise homework... always have, always will.

It was for this very reason that I stopped googling demonology and ended up watching a whole bunch of must-see movie trailers on YouTube—an activity that actually lasted a few hours. Movie trailers always take the good parts of a movie though and make them seem so freaking appealing. But then when you go to the movies, you find out that the trailer is the five-percent of the movie that is not shit. Still, zoning out in front of my laptop watching a clip from *The Other Woman* certainly beat drowning myself in demon lore.

All the while, I was absentmindedly twirling Andrei's ring around my finger... only stopping myself when I realized what I was doing. I couldn't deny the truth, however. I wanted to see him. He was in Vegas today, I knew that. But it didn't mean that he couldn't be here in a second. He could, and I wanted him to.

Is this what being a girlfriend is all about? Pining for a guy... desperately missing him?

Yeah. This was exactly why I didn't date. Correction: why I hadn't dated.

"Rae, you're being ridiculous," I told myself out loud, getting to my feet and stretching. Then, I massaged the crick in my neck and yawned.

Friday night in Paris, I was in sweats and my hair was in pigtails. The only drink I had in my house was Coke and I barely had any food in my cupboards since I hadn't done any shopping in... a while.

But then I heard the knock at my door and excitement sizzled through me. I practically bounded to the door, unlocking and yanking it open without checking the peephole.

To my dismay, Andrei wasn't the one standing outside my door, which made total sense because Andrei never knocked, he simply appeared.

"Rainelle?" the man who was standing outside my door asked, looking me over.

He looked to be in his late forties, or early fifties, and had the shiniest, whitest head I'd ever laid eyes on. The thick black eyebrows above watery brown eyes were in contrast to his gleaming bald head, as was the carefully groomed moustache above his thin lips. Just slightly taller than me, he was swathed in a black trench coat and slacks.

He didn't look threatening, but then again, they never did.

"Yes, do I know you?" I demanded to know, sounding more confident than I actually felt, because let's face it, he could totally take me in a fight.

"Excuse my manners, Rainelle," he said apologetically, stretching out a gloved hand. "Uncle Teddy. You might not remember me but I was friends with your father, God rest his soul."

I stared at his hand, unable to register that it belonged to a man I didn't think I'd see again until... well, until never. Teddy Bunting was unable to make it to my father's funeral but he did offer to pay for it, something that I flatly refused. Now, the only thing I was able to remember about him went back to the night he showed up at our house after Lauren vanished. Oh, and also that his wife, Aunt Josephine, was apparently a witch that freaking attended mass on Sundays. The irony.

"Rainelle? May I come in?" Teddy asked, and I became conscious of the fact that, at this point, he already dropped his hand and was staring at me expectantly.

"How'd you find me?" I questioned, but I already knew the answer to that.

"Danny Lawless gave me your address. And since I had business to attend to in Paris..."

The rest was pretty much obvious. If Daniel knew my father, then he knew Teddy.

I stepped aside, allowing him entry into my living room and closing the door behind him. He stood and observed, nodding all the while as if he approved of what he saw.

"How have you been, girl?" He turned and appraised me once more.

"Um, good." I motioned for him to take a seat and he did. Hugging myself, I asked, "How's Aunt Jo?"

"Oh, she's dead. Happened two years ago. You look exactly like your father, Rainelle. It's uncanny."

His legs were stretched out before him, crossed at the ankles, and he commented about my appearance in the same breath as the casual announcement of his wife's death.

"What?" I sputtered, a familiar pang of loss hitting me in the chest. "What happened? Was she sick?"

"A demon got to her," he said in a quiet voice, and this time, there was some flicker of emotion in his eyes. It disappeared as quickly as it came though. "It was an occupational hazard, Rainelle. We all know the risks of our jobs."

I didn't even remember Aunt Jo that well but I still felt devastated. But her husband was brushing her death off as a freaking occupational hazard? I had to sit down right then. With nothing to do, I went to work undoing my braids. *Why did I do them, anyway? They only make my hair curlier and harder to manage and...*

"So you're a private investigator?" Teddy wanted to know.

I nodded and my hair fell into my face. "And you're still... hunting?" I pushed the stray strands behind my ears.

He smiled. "Yes, Rainelle. And I wanted to tell you about Lauren..."

257

"Stop right there," I broke in, holding a hand up. "I don't want anything to do with demons, Uncle Teddy. I just want to get on with my life." *However fucked-up it might be.*

"It's nonsense for you to go around pretending you're normal," he surprised me by grumbling. "Not to mention dumb. You're not normal, Rainelle. Not even close. The sooner you realize that, the safer you'll be."

I narrowed my eyes at him. "Thanks for the concern but I've been doing fine pretending thus far. I don't need you randomly appearing on my doorstep, telling me what to do."

He held his hands up in surrender. "I don't mean to come off too strong but I promised your father that…"

"Did everybody, and their mothers, make a promise to my dad?" I snarled, suddenly unable to stand this man. How was it that the two worlds I successfully managed to avoid in the past were coming together so instantaneously? Hunters and demons, they were everywhere now.

"Rainelle, please listen to me," Teddy implored, taking a deep breath. "The only thing I want is for you to at least know how to defend yourself. Just a simple banishing spell and maybe a little…"

"I've been perfectly fine with Danny getting witches to put up wards in my house behind my back."

"But this one isn't protected. Do you want me to…?"

"No," I said quickly. "I don't want you to get someone to put up a ward." *Because that would keep my boyfriend out and that would suck.*

He quirked a questioning brow. "Why not? Wouldn't you feel safer?"

"I just… Magic gives me the creeps, even if it's supposed to do good."

He nodded slowly. "So you won't let me help you?"

I regarded him for a long while. "Help me what? Turn into a cold, unfeeling person that doesn't bat an eyelash when relaying the news of a loved one's death? No, thanks."

His jaw twitched and his eyes hardened. A minute shiver of impending danger skated down my spine. I wasn't afraid of Teddy, not necessarily. But I was afraid that I'd gone too far and maybe nonchalance was just his way of coping with Josephine's passing.

Movement in the doorway that led to the passageway caught my attention... and I was both relieved and anxious that Andrei suddenly appeared. Teddy was sitting with his back to the doorway, which was why he didn't catch Andrei's magical appearance.

"Who's this?" Andrei asked curtly, his voice dripping with animosity.

God, is he seriously jealous of a man old enough to be my father?

Teddy rose to his feet, completely unruffled as he turned to look at Andrei, who strode right into the room. "I didn't know you have company, Rainelle. I'm Teddy, a family friend." He held his hand out and Andrei simply looked at it, as if it were diseased.

I stood. "Teddy was just leaving."

"Was I?" Teddy arched a brow. "And who might you be?" His critical eyes were trained on Andrei as he said that and I wanted to sock him. *Who the hell does he think he is, my father?*

Andrei's eyes flickered over to me and I knew he sensed my silent wrath. "Her boyfriend, not that it's any of your fucking business, friend of the family," he bit out, keeping his eyes on me.

Teddy let out a mirthless laugh. "Certainly." He approached me and placed a soft kiss on my forehead. I tried not to flinch.

Somewhere behind him, Andrei growled.

Ignoring him, Teddy reached into the pocket of his coat and pulled out a piece of laminated paper. "Here's my card. Call me anytime, girl. And take care of yourself." Then, he glanced over his shoulder, staring long and hard at Andrei before stalking out of my house.

I let out the breath I didn't even realize I'd been holding as Andrei closed the distance between us and pulled me into his arms.

"That was a hunter," I said breathlessly, "and one who's infinitely better than my father was."

"I know of him," Andrei commented, rubbing circles on my back. "You don't have to be worried on my behalf, baby." He pulled back, cupping my chin and appraising me. "I've missed you."

We were together the previous night but I absolutely felt the same. The whole day, I was wondering when I'd get to see him again... and be in his arms like this. It was probably the most annoying thing about being official.

"I've missed you, too," I mirrored, receiving a soft, teasing kiss on the column of my neck when he lowered his head. I moaned, low in my throat, when he sucked on my skin. "God, Andrei, you have no idea how much."

He raised his head, a slow smile spreading on his face. "I think I do," he said huskily, glancing down at the T-shirt I was wearing. My nipples were straining against the cotton, begging for attention.

"Then what are you going to do about it?" I pouted, pulling him back to me.

"Well…" He released a groan of longing when I played with my nipples through my shirt. "First, I'm going to feed you."

That made me pause. "Feed me?"

"How does Italian sound?"

At the mention of food, my mouth started watering. "It sounds like Adele to my ears."

"Great! Go get dressed, then." He turned me around and smacked my ass. "Don't take too long or I'll come and get you."

And what's so bad about that?

"I won't," I said softly, ignoring the moisture between my legs. "Are we driving or walking?"

"Neither," he replied, and I grinned up at him.

Oh, I was totally getting used to teleportation as a mode of transport. It meant I could wear my Jimmy Choos with minimal ankle-twisting. And yes, I always try to see the best in everything.

Andrei let me open my eyes the second we arrived at our destination, which was a little bistro just outside of Naples, he quickly explained. I never heard of it before, but judging from the lavish décor, it was obviously an expensive place. Andrei, though, was seriously underdressed in his usual T-shirt and jeans ensemble, which actually didn't matter since the place was completely empty.

"Where is everyone?" I had to ask.

"The restaurant is closed to the public tonight," Andrei replied. "And I've also charmed the entire staff to remain in the kitchen until we're done. You're all mine."

The chandeliers were lit, hanging high above the cloth-covered tables and high-back suede dining chairs. Only one table was set though. And once I spied the food on the table it instantly caused a very audible rumbling in my belly. Andrei heard it and chuckled.

"So... are you hungry?" he asked, taking my hand in his and leading me to the table.

"Well, yes. But why...?" I realized how ambiguous that question was so I quickly amended it. "What's the occasion?"

"No occasion," he replied simply, pulling out a chair for me. "Well, save for the fact that I enjoy watching you eat."

"Oh, like it's a sport or something," I remarked dryly as I gingerly sat down.

Andrei laughed, the sound making me crane my neck to watch the beautiful transition on his face. "No, baby." He crouched, until his face was level with my chest. "I imagine your zeal for eating food matches my enthusiasm for feasting on you," he stated matter-of-factly before placing a sensual kiss to my exposed kneecap.

My body instantly responded, heating up and trembling for him. I was in a skintight virgin white dress that fell mid-thigh with my favorite Jimmy Choo heels, but I might as well have been naked and ready for him.

"You will finish everything on the table," Andrei huskily commanded, rubbing my left calf. "No one else is here to help you."

I tore my eyes away from him to look at the steaming plate of lasagna, which I realized, was actually cooked in Italy by an authentic Italian chef. My mouth was watering just sniffing such a delectable aroma.

"Of course," I told Andrei, giving him an incredulous look. "Is there any other way?"

"Good girl," he said approvingly, rising to his full height. "But you will sit on my cock. Up, Rae."

Desire spiked high in my veins. "Excuse me?"

"Up."

I shakily got to my feet, gripping the edge of the table for support and allowing him to take my place on the chair. His palm connected with my ass and I jumped, releasing a childlike squeal.

"What was that for?"

"For twitching it in my face like that, temptress. Are you wet?"

I couldn't keep up. One minute he wanted to feed me, the next he wanted to know what was happening between my legs. I had no idea which to focus on, especially when his hand effortlessly parted my quivering thighs and snaked a path up to the heat between my legs. I was bare there and completely at his mercy.

"Andrei," I gasped when he dipped a searching finger inside me.

"Wet," he confirmed in a growl, hiking the hem of my dress up my thighs. "Off."

His monosyllabic words definitely made me wetter and I wordlessly obeyed his command and tugged my dress off. My bra followed. I heard the slow drag of the zipper of his pants and bit my lower lip in anticipation.

"Sit."

Warm air wrapped a hand around my lower body as I slowly lowered myself down. Andrei made me spread my legs slightly before wrapping two big hands around my waist, his fingers spanning my lower belly. I gasped at the first feel of his erection at my entrance.

"Oh, damn," I breathed, my grip on the table threatening to break my nails. "Oh, you feel so good."

He brought me down all the way, groaning softly when my body swallowed his entire length. I already felt full... of him.

"Eat," he commanded, raising me off him a little before bringing me back down on him with a grunt.

I moaned loudly, wanting so badly for him to fuck me. After the weird day I had, I needed to feel close to him. This was the only way we knew to do that.

"Eat?" I panted, raising myself off him and coming back down with a cry. "Are... you... out of your damn mind?"

"Rae," he growled at my back, "don't let good food go to waste."

And that just did it for me. I hated wastage.

With a trembling hand, I picked up a fork and dug it into the pasta. Andrei's hands skated down my stomach until he parted my swollen folds and unerringly found my pulsing clit. It took all my power to bring my fork to my mouth. When I did, the unbelievable taste of the piquant tomato, beef, basil and various vegetables sent a shock of pure delight through my body at the exact same time Andrei began to rub the nub with the pad of his large thumb.

"How is it?" he whispered in my ear, jerking inside me at the same time.

"Oh, fuck," I panted, unable to resist the urge to buck against him. "Good. It's so good!"

"Rae," Andrei groaned, "finish it."

He was tweaking my hypersensitive spot and thrusting upwards in earnest now as I was rocking back against him. Every thrust ripped a moan from my throat and every stroke of my sensitized bud sent me doubling over my plate.

"Please," I whimpered, because this was absolute torture. "Need... to... come! Let me!"

"Eat," was his grunting response to my breathless plea.

So I forced myself to attempt the said task.

The lasagna was incredible, out of this world, in fact. But Andrei taking me like this was a painful pleasure. I was caught between savoring the spiciness on my tongue and reveling in another kind of sensation altogether between my legs. It was a tough choice, and so I tried to accommodate both.

"I can't stop," Andrei murmured, weighing my breasts in his palms now. "I can't fucking stop."

"Don't," I exhaled, crying out when he tugged at the rock-hard tips of my breasts, which nearly sent me over the edge. "Oh, God. Andrei, don't stop."

"I need you," he snarled, as if he were angry about that and blamed me. He drove into me, harder than before, hard enough to bring me to a shattering climax. "I need you so fucking much, *mea domina*. My fucking queen. My fucking mistress," he groaned while I rode out my almost blinding orgasm.

It felt like I just exploded into a million pieces, and the painful pleasure was almost too much for me to bear. My entire body trembled with my climax, bucking and shuddering with it. Andrei continued to ram into me, not stopping his sweet assault, increasing his tempo until he was closer to his own release.

"My king," I said under my breath, knowing that he would hear me. I was so blinded by my ecstasy that I didn't know or care about what the hell I was saying. I didn't really give a damn. "Love..." My voice trailed off when I caught myself.

You're fucking nuts, Rae! I scolded myself.

Was I really about to admit to Andrei that I loved him? Yeah, I was a total nutjob.

"Baby," he growled, his mouth on my shoulder as he sank his teeth into the skin there. "Fucking hell." And then he jerked himself inside me, coming hard and coming long.

My vaginal muscles contracted, squeezing around him like a fist, knowing that it was sweet agony for him. He moaned louder, cursing into the air. And when he was finished, he soothed the tooth marks on my damp skin with his tongue.

He held me upright against his chest and I realized that sometime during our lovemaking, his clothes had vanished and he was just as naked as I was. It felt like being home in his arms, my back against his chest.

"I had a shitty day," he said suddenly, easily lifting me off him so that he could turn me around and set me back down on his lap. He looked into my eyes, a billion unnamable emotions in the blue pools, and slid his arms around my waist again. "I can't stay away from you anymore."

"Then don't," I told him, lazily sifting my fingers in his damp hair. "Tell me about your day."

His eyes momentarily widened before clouding over with confusion, as if he'd never heard that request before and was wondering how to answer it.

"My day?" he echoed, looking slightly uncomfortable.

"I want to hear about it."

He cleared his throat. "You sure?" When I nodded, he released a heavy sigh. "It was just a regular day at the office, where lesser demons try in vain to get rid of me, forcing me to rip them apart in front of mortals." He wrinkled his nose. "Which means I waste my time erasing memories. I fucking hate that part."

My hands froze in his hair. "Get rid of you?"

He took my right hand in his and placed a soft kiss on my palm. "You don't have to look so... terrified." His lips were twitching in that way they did when he wanted to smile but was fighting himself not to. "They figure I'm weaker in your world and try to take advantage of that. It's been like that for millennia and it's not about to change. We demons are opportunists, no matter the risk."

I swallowed. "And in your... realm? When you're in your true form, do they..."

"Attempt to kill me? No. Lesser beings cannot kill the strong in the same way a mouse can't conquer a lion."

I didn't bother to mention the fable of the lion and the mouse.

"But here? In this place? If someone stronger than you wants to... end you? Can you be...?"

"If I haven't fed for a while, I'll degenerate, I suppose. That would be the best time to strike. Weaken me so that I'm forced to be in limbo between two worlds until... Well, until it turns into an eternity of suffering." He tilted his head to one side. "I'm not giving you any ideas, am I?"

I slapped his arm, surprised at the anger that rocketed through me at his somewhat playful words. "Are you crazy? I'd never..."

Once again, he cut me off, but this time with his mouth. His hand came up behind my neck and his tongue slid between my lips, sparring with mine and swirling around my mouth. His kiss was hungry, desperate, and liquid heat seeped into my pores, bubbling in my abdomen.

Andrei swallowed my moans, his tongue confident in what it was doing to me. "Finish your damn food, temptress," he murmured between kisses.

"Later," I told him, reaching between us to grab him. He let out a soft hiss, his smoldering eyes clouding over with lust. "I need to feel you inside me again."

His breathing was ragged as he lifted me to my feet, whirled me around and pressed my belly down against the empty half of our table.

"Then I need to fuck you again," he announced in a low voice, and I felt his rigid tip slide up and down my wet, swollen labia.

"Yes!" I gasped, tilting my pelvis and pushing back against him, wanting to speed up the process. "Fuck me, Andrei."

He then pulled out and I felt his hands run along my back and rest on my butt, gathering up the firm globes in his palms and squeezing. "My ass," he whispered, the quiet sound sending shivers down my spine. He released my ass, reached around me, and cupped my boobs. "My tits. Fucking beautiful tits, don't you think?" He pinched my nipples and I yelped, glad that I was half-lying on the table because my legs were useless at this point. Andrei's deft fingers moved up my slit, delving into the wetness they found there. "My pussy, Rae. I fuck it, I own it."

He owned it. He knew he owned it. If my vagina were a piece of real estate, it would've had a "Sold to Andrei" picket sign on the lawn.

"Do I own this pussy, baby?" he asked, lazily tracing circles on my clit with a finger. It was swollen and pulsing for some attention… any attention.

"Yes!" I screamed, shuddering from his unbearable touch. "Andrei, please!" It was crazy how much I needed to feel him, to know that he was powerful beyond measure, and to assure myself that no one could take him away from me. I wanted him so badly even after my powerful release moments ago. It was never enough with him. Never.

"You own my cock," he murmured into my ear, and I could've come at those words. "Every time I'm inside you, I want you to think about that, about how the only pussy my cock wants is yours. And when I'm not inside you, I want you to imagine that I am, because that's exactly what I will be thinking."

"Baby," I whispered, "don't fucking make me beg."

Andrei grabbed my hips and effortlessly slammed into me with his first thrust. I cried out, my body remembering his size and protesting that it was way too soon for an encore. I accepted all of him, his entire thick shaft, and murmured for him to fuck me, hard.

He was moving inside me, grinding his hips, punishing the walls of my channel with his silk steel.

"Like this?" he barked, thrusting into me harder than I thought my body could possibly withstand.

"Oh, yeah," I wailed in response, each subsequent thrust dragging my painful nipples along the table. "Oh, hell." His balls were heavy as they slapped against the backs of my thighs and his skin was hot concrete against my back.

The table was shaking from the impact and at the back of my mind and through half-closed eyes, I worried that my half-eaten meal was going to meet an untimely demise on the carpet. But all thoughts of food and spices flew out my mind the minute he fingered my sensitized nub and simultaneously plunged into me.

"Come for me, *mea domina*," he rasped.

I was his queen and I was coming for him, convulsing so hard with my orgasm that he had to tighten his hold on my hips, lest I collapsed. Through my own climax, I felt the rush of his cum deep inside me, hot and thick. His strokes inside me became even until he stopped, holding himself still inside me and gathering me up into him. He held me upright, placing his hot mouth into the crook of my neck, still buried within me.

"Did I hurt you?" he murmured, lightly biting my skin.

I felt incredibly safe with his arms wrapped around my waist, although I was far from comfortable standing on my tiptoes. "Nah, I'm not made out of china, remember?" Although I was probably going to be sluggish tomorrow and sporting a couple of interesting bruises in interesting places.

"No, you're not," Andrei conceded, running his tongue along the side of my neck. "But you should know that you can't lie to me. Let me take you home."

"Okay," I moaned, stifling a yawn, "but I want you to spend the night."

I turned to one side until he was kissing my mouth.

"Anything you want," Andrei said to me, and I knew he meant it.

Chapter 17

"Oh, you're answering my calls now? Pigs must be flying GVs somewhere," Renée's wounded voice said into my ear.

I didn't have the heart to tell her that I accidentally pressed "Accept" when I was fumbling for my phone to put it on silent. That would've been bitchy of me and I couldn't be bitchy to Ren, of all people.

"I've been busy," I said softly, slapping my right leg, which was starting to fall asleep. I'd been lying in the same position for about an hour now, which was flat on my stomach like a kid reading a magazine.

"Busy? Do you know how worried Enzo and I have been, thinking you'd been killed or something?"

"Killed?" I absentmindedly flicked what I was praying was a piece of lint off my left forearm.

"Have you forgotten how you were attacked on a plane?" she asked, in full-blown Renée-the-Hysterical mode. "We care about you, Rae, but you're being so freaking thoughtless by not returning my calls. Busy!" She snorted, clearly skeptical.

I heard low voices outside the door, which meant that someone was coming in any minute now. My best friend might as well have been in the same room as me—that was how loud she was.

"Ren, can I call you back?" I mumbled. "Please?"

"Why are you whispering? Are you in church?"

I could've laughed. Yeah, because Damien Ivanov's office on the second floor of his club was holy ground.

"Talk later. Love you," I hissed quickly, before hanging up and putting my phone on silent. Thinking better of it, I turned it off altogether.

The door swung open just then and I instinctively froze, although I knew that it was impossible for anyone to see me from under the double bed in one corner, especially because the room was still dark. I didn't even want to brood over why the guy would have a double bed in his office.

The door was closed and the light was flicked on.

Snakeskin-clad feet (*Good God, are those Salvatore Ferragamo Python Loafers?*) strode past the foot of the bed, followed by booted feet. I heard a chair being pushed back, and then the steady stream of what definitely sounded like heated Russian. For some reason, I knew that that was Damien's voice, just like I knew he was the wearer of the ridiculously expensive dress shoes.

Well, shit, I thought, when Damien's Russian monologue seemed to be endless. *How the hell am I supposed to spy if he's going to be speaking in tongues the whole time?*

My James Bond operation didn't exactly come with a standard-issue Google Translate app.

It was while I was pondering this that I realized the monologue had come to an end and the second person was talking. I had to cover my mouth with one hand to stop a dirty word from escaping, because I fucking recognized that voice.

What the hell were the odds?

Andrei's voice was low, giving nothing away about what mood he was in. Then again, I wouldn't have been able to tell if he was threatening Damien since he was speaking in freaking Russian as well.

"You must be out of your fucking mind, Anghelescu," Damien astonished me by snarling, in English, no less. "Get the fuck out of my club before I call security."

"If you want bloodshed," Andrei casually informed him. "You're a complete and total clown fuck," he said after Damien mumbled something back. Andrei's voice was louder this time. "A fucking Bible college? How many times have I told you what kind of shitstorm that'll bring?"

"This is the hundredth time you've mentioned that little fact, and quite frankly, you're becoming a broken record," Damien snapped. I heard his chair being violently pushed back. "Don't you have some humans to seduce and fuck? Go get jiggy with it, incubus."

Andrei switched back to guttural Russian and I suddenly felt that extreme wave of nausea and unbelievable prickliness I had endured the night he uncloaked himself. Biting my lower lip, I held it in, fighting not to puke my guts out and give away my location.

"And you forget who I am, demon," Damien was saying, but it was getting harder to keep up with their pissing contest when I was so damn uncomfortable.

Dammit, Andrei. Stop it! I mentally implored him—and, wonder of wonders, he did.

I sucked in a grateful breath, shifting slightly to alleviate the pressure on my stomach. I had never been so

273

appreciative of God's clean air before. Sure, there was quite a bit of dust under this bed, as if it had never been vacuumed or something, and my incredibly minuscule strapless dress would definitely need dry cleaning. But nothing was worse than being hit with a heavy dose of Andrei Anghelescu.

My relief was short-lived, though, because the bed was lifted clean off of me and I was exposed, my hiding place hovering above me. Panic immediately knocked me in the solar plexus. Andrei was towering over me, holding the bed up with one hand as if it weighed as much as a marshmallow. And if looks could kill, I would be buried in the Erickson family plot back home in Sallow Bay in a few days. Despite the fact that he looked absolutely delectable in his usual all-black ensemble, I knew there was no way I was getting the opportunity to run my hands through his snug shirt or loose mane of dark hair… which I think sucked.

"Hi," I squeaked, awkwardly getting to my feet and ducking from under the bed and into the center of the room. Stretching to relieve the kinks in my muscles, I turned to get a look at the elusive Damien Ivanov. I finally had the opportunity to see him in the flesh, even though it was under the worst circumstances thinkable. *Although,* I was thinking, *seeing him is totally worth all the shit I find myself in.*

My arms fell to my sides and my jaw dropped when my eyes settled on him.

Damien was beautiful. No, Damien was… angelic!

He was standing behind his large mahogany table but I could tell that he was tall—not as tall as Andrei, but towering all the same—and lean, like an athletic teenager. I could see all these, even through his charcoal black suit. On top of that, he had platinum blond hair that curled around his face in tiny, glowing ringlets and long lashes that framed cornflower blue eyes. And at the moment, his lips were pursed and there wasn't a hint of hair on his face. The man had rosy cheeks, for Pete's sake! How the hell was Damien the evil Russian?

Maybe I had it wrong.

But God, I so wanted to touch him, to stare at him forever because his face was like...

An almighty crash resounded behind me and I whirled around, finding that Andrei had flung the bed across the room, mattress and all. I stared at him with an open mouth.

"Was that really necessary?" I spluttered.

"Was that look on your face necessary?" he countered, glaring at Damien over my head.

"Ah, so the rumors are true," Damien's singsong voice came from behind me. It physically compelled me to turn and look at him, look upon his face. "The great, almighty lord has found himself a mortal pet to play with. Green is not your color, incubus."

My face creased up with annoyance. "I'm not a pet, you asshole."

His eyes narrowed at me. "Maybe so, but you are a trespasser. What shall I do with you? What shall I do to you?"

"Nothing," Andrei growled, stepping before me and blocking my vision. "You touch her, I fuck you up. Simple."

"My, my, my, incubus." Damien let out a mirthless laugh. "Oh, how the mighty have fallen. What a pathetic demon you are."

"Why the hell are you letting him talk to you like that, Andrei?" I really wanted to know, and felt more than a little incensed on my behalf and his.

"Pathetic?" Andrei snarled, ignoring me. "If I'm so pathetic, why do you keep running away from me?"

275

"Take your little eavesdropping bitch with you and get the hell out of my club," Damien spat in response.

Andrei launched himself at the guy and I prepared myself to witness the death of a stupidly courageous human. But Damien ruined that by vanishing into thin air... literally.

"Okay, I get it. You're mad at me," I stated, watching Andrei stride past me and onto the balcony outside my bedroom, "but could you please explain what I just saw?"

The sky was dotted with stars tonight, and that—coupled with the nightlights on earth—would have made it so easy for me to think of just curling up on a deckchair outside, leisurely observing life around me.

Not tonight, though. Tonight, I felt like a teenager caught sneaking out by her father. It wasn't a great feeling. Andrei was standing outside now, his back obstinately turned to me. It had been torture teleporting back to my penthouse, since it meant that we had to be pressed really close and I could feel the anger radiating from his powerful frame. What probably took five seconds felt like an hour to me.

Sighing heavily, I peeled my dress and underwear off, throwing on a very unsexy old basketball shirt to sleep in. Although I knew I wouldn't be getting any sleep that night. First, I had to text Temp and let him know that I got busted by His Royal Sexiness. And then I had to piece together what little I found out that night. Sift through the little English that had been said, that is. And lastly, figure out what the hell Damien Ivanov was, since he sure as hell wasn't a demon. My brain was already aching thinking about it all.

Whipping out my phone and turning it on, I shot Temp a quick text letting him know that I was fine and didn't just ditch his ass at the club. When that was done, I flopped onto my bed, raising my left hand and staring at the ruby that was glimmering in the light. This little thing was the reason Andrei found me under the bed, that much was obvious. It was proving to be extraordinarily traitorous.

"How did you get into his office?" Andrei stood at the foot of my bed, staring down at me. "And don't lie to me. I'll know if you do."

I let out an exasperated sigh. "Temp might have worked his magic on a couple employees there."

"Temp might be dead tonight," Andrei said through clenched teeth.

I instantly sat up. "He's my brother." It felt weird saying it aloud. Nevertheless, it was true and I didn't care how warped it was. "He only wanted to help so don't even think of going after him. Damien's only human, right?" I snorted. "Well, maybe not so much."

Andrei's nostrils flared. Grabbing my ankles, he tugged me down the bed, until I was sprawled in an ungainly fashion.

"What did I tell you about Ivanov?" His voice was dangerously low, dangerously promising. "What did you promise me?"

I blew out a breath. "That I would stay away from him."

"And sneaking into his office is synonymous to that?"

"I didn't expect you, of all people, would be there," I muttered, trying to pull my legs free from his grip. "Andrei…"

He held fast, his eyes gleaming with a familiar menacing red. "If I hadn't been there, do you know what would have happened?" He didn't wait for my answer. "First, he

277

would have thrown you to his friends. They would've raped you, defiled you in all the ways my kind could not. By the time they were done with you, you'd be begging them to kill you." He paused, stroking my feet. "But they wouldn't. Because Damien would want that honor."

I swallowed, shaking off the mental image. "So if he isn't human and he isn't a demon, what is he?"

Andrei's lower lip curled in disgust. "He's worse."

"You have to tell me, Andrei," I told him. "Relationships need communication. You can't keep something important like this from me."

"If you'd just minded your fucking business…"

"Minded my business?" I freed my leg with a hard tug and pushed myself to my feet on the bed, so that I was looming over Andrei. "This is my business. Whatever Damien is doing, he's using innocent humans and it involves demons. Sure, this scares the bejesus out of me. But hey, what can you do? It's my job to investigate. And up to this point, I've been very good at it."

A long moment of silence passed, in which we glared at each other.

Andrei finally broke it with a muttered, "Fallen angel."

"Excuse me?"

"Damien… is… a… fallen angel," he bit out. "Is that communication enough for you?"

"An angel?" I tried out the word, found it to be ludicrous, and so collapsed on my bed in stitches.

"I'm dying to hear the joke," Andrei remarked sarcastically, his face hard as he glared down at me.

I held up an index finger as I attempted to rein in my laughter. This was just all too much, too soon.

278

My boyfriend was a demon lord; my long-lost brother just happened to be a demon, too; and the owner of the nightclub I sort of frequented in Paris, who spoke Russian and cursed like a truck driver, was an angel.

I guess that's why he fell, I mused, and laughed even harder at the thought. I just couldn't stop and Andrei's peeved expression only tickled me further.

"You done?" he asked in a warning tone.

"I just..." I choked out, rolling onto my belly and pressing my face into a pillow. "He owns a nightclub! But he looks like... like a choirboy!"

"Could you be serious for one second?" Andrei barked. "He knows you exist now, Rainelle. Since you obviously don't understand the implications of that, I'll spell it out for you. Any chance he gets, he'll kill you, even if it's just for the heck of it. He'll kill you just because it'll piss me off. So quit laughing because this is no joke!"

As I finally realized the gravity of the situation, my laughter instantly died.

Yeah, so that sobered me up, I thought to myself.

I zoned in on the one thing that really stood out from his mini rant. "My death would piss you off?" I sat up and shot him a glare. "Gee, thanks. I'm touched."

"What?" he said, completely nonplussed.

"I keep forgetting you're a cold, heartless demon." The minute the words left my mouth, I regretted them.

Andrei's brow furrowed.

"Sorry. Didn't mean that," I whispered.

He pulled my ankle again and I was once more brought to the edge of the bed. But this time, he let my legs go, so that my feet were dangling over the bed. Then he sank down to his knees until we were almost eye-level.

"Cold?" He took my hands in his, the heat of his fingers transferring to mine. "And heartless?" Then he brought them to his chest, where I felt the beat of his racing heart. "No. But I am a demon. Yours."

"Mine," I whispered, bringing his other hand over mine. "When you're like this, it's hard to believe I ever referred to you as Scary Russian Guy."

He arched a brow. "Scary Russian Guy? Seriously?"

"Only when I didn't know your name!" I said, laughing. "Can you blame me? You were scary as hell and I thought you were Russian."

His brow creased and he looked at me with questioning blue eyes. "Are you scared of me now?"

I shook my head, stroking his cheek. "Not anymore."

"But there will come a time when the smartest thing will be for you to be scared." He gently took my hand and kissed my palm. "No one defies me but you."

"And Damien, obviously," I mumbled.

His face changed. "Demons don't exactly get along with angels, even dark ones like Damien. He'll never listen to me."

"You were talking about the girls, right? They're from a Bible college?"

"Rae…"

"Either you tell me, or I find out myself."

He gave me a level stare. "Fine. Yes. And that college just happens to spit out the strongest exorcists in the world. Damien's twisted. He does things out of spite because of his expulsion." He pushed himself to his feet. "But who knows what his plans are. All I know is that he's on his way to attracting the attention of the Big Guns. And that means my kind are in for hell."

"Does he have to be so beautiful?"

Andrei glared at me. "He's an angel. Your response to his face is a reflex."

"He's not as gorgeous as you, though," I coyly remarked, leaning back and propping myself up on my elbows.

"No, Rae," Andrei said, although I could see the distinct bulge in his jeans. "We're communicating about something important."

"We can communicate and... play." *Honestly, I am done with discussing yet another anomaly in my once peaceful existence. Fallen angels?* I internally scoffed. I needed to sweep that under the carpet, ASAP. Maybe I could pretend I never heard of them.

"Sometimes I swear you're the sex demon," Andrei quipped, his lips twitching with amusement.

"Sometimes I'd swear you're a monk," I mumbled, peeved. "An incubus who refuses sex so that he can talk. I've created a monster."

"Probably because I've fed," he said huskily, his eyes turning into dark pools of lust. "I fed this morning." He lowered himself onto the bed, hovering over me. "I fed last night. Twice." He placed a kiss on my nose. "I fed the night before..."

Andrei's mouth found mine, and I slung my arms around his neck and wrapped my legs around his waist, as I parted my lips. His tongue stroked mine and I moaned, desperate for him to be inside me. My fingers slipped into his hair—the hair that I was borderline obsessed with—and yanked, drawing an appreciative groan from his mouth. I swallowed the sound, grinding against him.

"Shit, Rae," he gasped, bringing a hand up my shirt and finding me bare. Then he slid his other hand between my thighs. "Wet, wet, wet," he chanted, tearing his mouth from mine. He dipped into the crook of my neck, the feel of his tongue there so erotic. I could've come then and there.

His fingers were teasing me, slowly exploring me as if he had all the time in the world... like I had all the time in the world.

"Andrei," I pleaded, bucking against him. "Oh, crap."

His fingers began to work me and I couldn't stop the soft moans from leaving my lips, even if I wanted to. I rocked against his hand, unashamedly using it for my own pleasure... and then it was gone.

"I have to go," Andrei was saying, but in my pleasure-addled mind, it sounded like "I have to cruelly leave you hanging on the brink of climax like the dickhead that I am."

He disentangled himself from me and got off the bed. "Stay in the house, Rae. I mean it," he said firmly, but his eyes were pleading. "We'll continue our discussion later. You know how to reach me." He let out a heavy sigh. "Call Templeton."

I knew how big of a concession it was for him to say that last part. But it didn't matter because I was pissed off and sexually frustrated.

Andrei gave me a full-blown smile. "No fingers when I get back. Just you and my cock. Got that?"

I bit my lower lip, nodding, and he disappeared.

Closing my eyes, I counted to ten and took deep breaths, trying to calm my raging libido. I certainly wasn't going to relieve the aching down there, not when there was a better option later.

I crawled off my bed and grabbed my phone from the nightstand, dialing a number I was surprised to already know by heart.

"Wanna swing by and watch Uma Thurman hunt Bill and company?" I asked as soon as he answered.

"Just us, Baby Phat?" Temp was obviously surprised.

"Yup. Bring something fried and I'll tell you all about the elusive Damien Ivanov." I nearly smiled. Nearly... until I thought about him killing me. "You won't believe it."

"If you, he, and Andrei had a threesome, I don't wanna know. I just had sex with a girl who thought Led Zeppelin was a Dr. Seuss character. My night just can't get any more disturbing."

Chapter 18

When I got the call that JP Fontaine was dead, I still had one foot in dreamland. But Ana Fontaine's agitated voice quickly dragged me back to the waking world.

"Dead?" I echoed stupidly, sitting up in my rumpled bed. The scent of the man I'd spent the entire night with filled the air, as strong as if he were still there, naked and awake beside me.

"You said you would help me," Ana sputtered, promptly bursting into tears, followed by a stream of unintelligible words that I could only guess were French. "You promised! He was my baby brother… and now he is gone."

Guilt wrapped an icy hand around my neck. "What happened?" I forced myself to ask, knowing full well that if he was tangled with a deranged fallen angel and body-hopping demons, he was bound for an ugly end.

"I don't know!" she said, only it came out as a high-pitched '*Je ne sais pas!*' "I saw his ghost. I saw it and no one believes me. No one believes that my little brother is… is dead."

Ghost? She saw his ghost!

I was pulled out of a very satisfying dream because she'd seen a ghost?

"Ana," I said through clenched teeth, "have you tried his cell? Gone to his apartment?"

"He's dead!" she insisted, and I pinched the bridge of my nose, mumbling to myself.

This was an extremely talented, famous fashion designer whose work I admired… and she was mumbling about ghosts like a crazy person. But then again, I'd seen and heard stranger things.

"You should calm down. Wouldn't it put your mind at rest to actually go to his…"

The woman actually hung up on me.

"Brilliant way to start the morning," I mumbled, getting out of bed.

My foul mood came to the fore in the bathroom when I discovered that my period was early. There was no way in hell I was ever getting another shot, not when irregular period and weight gain were the side effects. It was back to the pill for me, that was for sure.

Can't make it. Stuck in a blonde. R U crazy? WWAD?: What Would Andrei Do? ~ T

I deleted Temp's text and switched my phone off, shoving it into the back pocket of my cut-offs and simultaneously nodding at the bouncer, who I was beginning to recognize as Club Nicolette's weekend muscle.

Once inside, I slid my aviators on, shielding my eyes from the psychedelic lights as well as from anyone who might recognize me. It felt strange being there in a T-shirt and shorts when every other female was in a flimsy dress. But tonight wasn't about blending in.

Tonight was about finding JP.

Even if his sister was a mental patient, I had to know for myself. JP was, as she'd said, an "okay" person. It wasn't his fault he'd gotten himself tangled with the supernatural.

WWAD, Temp mentioned in his message. *He'd probably slice my clit off and feed it to me for disobeying him... yet again.*

I winced at the image, feigning enthusiasm when Stromae's *Alors On Danse* came on and the dance floor suddenly became congested. Never in a million years was I going to find the guy in there. So I sidled up to the bar, elbowing my way to the front and capturing the gangly bartender's attention.

"Qu'est-ce que je vous sers?[1]" he asked in a hurried tone, leaning across the bar to hear me over the pulsing music.

"Do you know JP Fontaine?" I asked in English.

He leaned back, quirking a dark brow. "Who's asking?"

I rolled my eyes at him from behind my shades. See, this was where Temp's incubus charm would've come in handy. "Forget it."

That was the problem with shady guys. They always had someone paranoid to protect them.

---

[1] "What can I do for you?"

Deciding that my sleuthing would probably only get me killed, I shoved my way to the exit, all the while attempting to inhale air that wasn't 99.9% cologne.

"What's the rush?" a deep voice said, close enough for me to make out the words. "Is this club not to your liking?"

I turned around and a hand shot out to grab my forearm.

Fear prickled my skin, peppering it with tiny goosebumps.

Damien Ivanov was holding me, and his grip wasn't the least bit loose.

"You look like a vodka girl," he said, casually regarding me from his seat on the edge of his desk. "I have a private bar."

Sitting on the chair opposite his desk, I could've reached out and touched Damien, if I wanted to… which I most certainly didn't. Andrei was going to kill me, if Damien didn't beat him to it.

"So you want my last meal to be… Stolichnaya?" I sucked in air. "It's only fair that you give me actual food and not alcohol. Preferably Italian. I want to die smiling."

Damien surprised me by laughing. "That's actually my favorite brand of vodka. The Russians certainly know what they're doing with that one." He gave me an assessing gaze before reaching out and removing my sunglasses. "Feisty until the end. No wonder the lord of 'oversexed' demons is interested. But who said anything about killing you?"

I stared back at him in bewilderment. The last time I'd seen Damien, he'd been in a suit. Today, he wore a powder blue long-sleeved T-shirt that made his eyes look even bluer, and brighter. Dark jeans hugged his thighs and calves, and some of his flaxen hair fell across his forehead. No wonder I didn't exactly notice or recognize him standing by the exit. He looked way too Abercrombie & Fitch-like. Or Disney Channel-esque?

Fully understanding what he just said, I could've sobbed with relief. "So if you're not going to kill me..."

"I just want to talk," he said brightly, sitting up straight. He winked at me. "Get to know you. I presume you wanted to get to know me, which is why you were snooping around in my office last week. Correct?"

I glanced at the closed door, my only viable way out.

"Don't even bother," Damien said darkly, following my gaze. "By the time you stand, I could be in the process of snapping your neck in two."

"I kind of... need my neck."

"Yes, you most certainly do." He grinned at me. And if I thought he was beautiful before, he was positively Pre-Raphaelite just then.

His smile literally made him glow... made the whole room glow.

I shook my head, dispelling the warmth I felt inside my belly. "What's your game?" I snapped, balling my hands into fists beside me.

"My game?" He blinked at me. "I have no idea what you mean."

"I recall you calling me an eavesdropping bitch. And let's not forget a pet," I bit out, annoyed that he was grinning at me like we were tighter than Jay and Bee. "And today… today you're being nice."

"I was kicked out of heaven. I think that gives me the right to have a bit of a temper."

I snorted. "Right."

"If it means anything, I apologize."

It was my turn to blink at him in confusion. "You're… sorry?"

"Your demon and I have history. I fucking hate that creature," he told me, the smile permanently etched on his face even as he said the words so vehemently. "That was no excuse though to treat you, Miss Erickson, with such disdain. That being said, do you enjoy fucking him?"

I flew to my feet, my skin on fire. "What did you say?" I snarled, tilting my head back to look him in the eye.

"You're filthy. Tainted with the stench of the lord of fucking." Then, darkness marred his beautiful features, the smile dropping from his face. "Do you enjoy it?"

"Fuck you," I hissed, barely able to get the words out through my quivering lips. "Go to hell!"

He let out a joyless laugh. "I'll see you there." He sidestepped me, striding toward the bar. "You're an untouchable, aren't you? Which means you might or might not be a demon hunter." He grabbed a bottle of water and flung it at me. I automatically reached out and caught it. "A demon hunter… that fucks demons," Damien mused, shaking his head. "Did you get your job description confused with that of a whore?"

"I am not a hunter and I don't go around…"

"Oh, don't justify yourself to me, Miss Erickson," he cut in, holding a hand in the air. "Far be it for me to judge. I

289

was cast out for committing lustful, sordid acts. I'm no angel."
He let out a bark of laughter at his own joke.

I dropped the bottle of Evian onto the floor. "I'm leaving now," I firmly announced, sounding more confident than I felt. "Thanks for the heavy dose of creepiness, but I have a headache now."

In a flash, he was before me, blond hair everywhere. "You don't leave until I tell you to leave."

Sweat snaked down my back and my heart jogged a mile within my chest. Damien's breath tickled my face, cool and minty, and his eyes burned into mine, daring me to look away.

I couldn't.

"Now that we've established that," he began with a slow smile, "I think it's time for me to inspect the merchandise."

He'll rape you then kill you...

Niggling fear turned to blinding panic. It throttled me, choking the very breath out of me. I took a step back from Damien, the flesh beneath my ass hitting the edge of Damien's desk.

Frantic. Trapped. Weak.

Even if I attacked him, what good would it do? What good was a roundhouse kick to his sadistic head? What good was my knife, which wasn't even on me? I would only succeed in pissing him off.

Damien's tongue swiped across his pink bottom lip. "Relax," he growled. "I'm not going to touch you."

"You're... n-not?" I stammered, hating the sound of my own voice.

He shook his head, swiping a handful of golden curls out of his eyes. "You made it too easy for me," he said brightly, giving me another disarming smile. "It's no fun when the gazelle skips into the lion's den," he informed me. "No matter how badly the lion wants to fuck the gazelle senseless to teach its master a lesson."

I scowled at him, at his choice of degrading words. "If you so much as come near me…"

"Of course, knowing that creature, he's been inside you bareback," Damien mused, ignoring me. "You'll have to disinfect that pussy. Only when I've ripped you from the inside out will I return you to him. We'll see how much you mean to him then, won't we?"

He closed the distance between us as he spoke. I held my breath.

"I will enjoy shutting you up," he whispered into my ear, toying with loose tendrils of my hair. "Fucking every orifice, ignoring your desperate pleas for me to simply kill you. And Miss Erickson, you will beg. That, I can promise you."

A knock at the door became my respite. Damien turned slightly, barking a "Come in!"

I bit back a gasp when JP stood in the doorway, looking alive and well, if slightly worn-out.

"What is it, you dumb shit?" Damien asked, his voice impatient.

"Downstairs." JP slid his eyes in my direction. "Basement."

I squeaked out a protest when the angel threw an arm around my waist. "Seems like you're on a mission to find out all about me, demon's whore," he said, ruffling my hair in a demeaning fashion. "Well, you're in luck. I'm feeling very… forthcoming tonight."

"You said you'd let me leave!"

"You are a very gullible gazelle, Miss Erickson," said Damien, removing his arm from my waist and gripping my hand instead. "You're coming with me."

I struggled, dug my nails into his skin. No dice. Utterly futile.

My phone was off and something told me Damien wouldn't just allow me to whip it out.

JP was standing stock-still in the doorway. I cut him a pleading look and received nothing but a blank look.

And then his entire body shook, his eyes widening in horror, in fright. "Help me," he wailed, his body slamming into the doorjamb. "*Aidez-moi.* Please!"

Help him? How could I, when I was frozen to the spot in shock?

Damien reached out, grabbed a handful of JP's dark hair, and slammed the back of his head against the door. "Fucking demon can't even possess this idiot right," he muttered, shaking his head as JP's limp body slumped to the ground. "They're all useless."

I was five seconds away from a complete and total meltdown.

"I really don't know what possesses some mortals to willingly fall for these beasts," Damien was saying to himself, his iron grip still on my wrist. "They're stupid, irritating wildlings with no sense of ambition. What's your opinion, Miss Erickson?"

"Tell me where you're taking me," I demanded, my voice hoarse for some reason. Damien stopped in front of a set of elevators. The thought of being in such a confined space with someone who just threatened to rip my insides apart moments ago made my knees buckle.

"You must have a magical golden pussy if Andrei can put up with your whining." He shoved me inside the elevator once the doors opened and strode after me. "Don't be offended. Mortals, in general, are whiny pests."

I watched as his finger pushed a button that made the doors close, sealing me inside the metal coffin.

Where the hell are we going? And then I realized...

B... for Basement.

Chapter 19

I stared at my ring until the ruby became a blurry haze of crimson. But trying to convey every ounce of my fear and apprehension into the little piece of jewelry seemed to be futile. This was the one thing that was supposed to protect me when I couldn't protect myself—and it wasn't working.

Andrei isn't coming.

That was my sole thought as Damien half-dragged, half-carried me into the large, vast space beneath the club: the basement. Above it, the steady thumping of the bassline of a song made the chandeliers (damn chandeliers!) tinkle prettily. The place was packed, and it wasn't a normal crowd, that I knew.

Men and women sat on high-back chairs, which were arranged in a large circle. And beneath my shoes, I could vaguely feel cold hard concrete. But it was the figure inside the circle that made my heart race. It was a little inconspicuous at first, but as I got closer I could make out a young woman tied up in an uncomfortable-looking wooden chair. I instantly recognized her as one of the college students who had been standing outside the club a few days ago.

"What the fuck?" I twisted to get a look at Damien, who was just as comfortable hovering in the background as he probably was in the limelight.

"Welcome to the Russian Inquisition, Miss Erickson," he said, his voice eerily calm. "You have a front-row seat. You should be honored."

He shoved me into the waiting arms of his henchman—one of many, I'm sure—before sauntering into the ring (for that was what it was), and approaching the young woman. She had glassy red-rimmed eyes and a split bottom lip. I tasted bile.

"Do you claim to hear the voice of God, Miss Roche?" Damien asked her, digging a hand into her unruly brown curls and tugging hard so that she was forced to look up at him.

"Yes," she answered, her voice nothing more than a whisper.

"I can't hear you, Miss Roche. Perhaps you should speak louder."

"Yes!"

"You're a liar. Where is your God now? Why isn't He saving you?"

She remained silent, and that was answer enough.

"Let me go!" I hissed, sensing what was coming. I tried to yank my arm away from the man, but it was utterly useless.

In response, he rolled his eyes down at me and tugged me to him, his arm snaking around my waist.

"Maybe we should put you in the ring, hmm?" His hot breath fanned the shell of my right ear and I instantly recoiled.

"Maybe you should go fuck yourself," I spat. "That girl's barely a teenager!" I screamed the last part out, praying that someone would be decent enough to feel even a hint of fucking remorse.

But no.

The scene was disgusting. Damien didn't physically harm the girl, but it was clear that she was broken inside already. Then he repeated the question, "Where is your God now?" And her shoulders sagged.

"Why would You talk to this mortal and not to me?" Damien growled, looking up at the ceiling. "Save her now! Save her!"

"Lord, God of vengeance, God of vengeance, shine forth," the girl murmured. "Rise up, judge of the earth; repay to the proud what they deserve!"[2]

"Psalm 94. How quaint," Damien sneered, lowering his face to hers. "Say hello to Him for me, Miss Roche."

Meanwhile, Damien's henchman hissed, "You need a closer look," as he dragged me to the frontline.

People parted for him like the Red Sea, and before I knew it, I had a highly unwanted front-row seat to how long the brunette had endured emotional and physical torture. Eyes swollen shut and one lip torn, she was held up on the chair only by the rope around her upper body.

She's dying, I thought in horror.

And next thing I knew, I used all of my strength to whip around and punch the tall man in his long, almost elegant throat, so hard that he instantly released me, wheezing a flurry of curses that would make Satan blush. But I didn't hang around to listen.

In all the commotion and shouts of "Kill her!" and "Her god won't save her!" that were brought on by Damien's sudden grip on the girl's neck, nobody noticed that I'd clouted the demon holding me. I could've run, could've unassumingly crept away and sprinted upstairs to relative safety.

---

[2] Psalm 94:1-2, English Standard Version 2011 Edition

But that wasn't who I was.

Kickboxing was something I did to keep fit, flexible, and strong enough so I wouldn't be helpless in an alleyway. The funny thing about doing something you love is that even though you haven't done it in a long time, your muscles remember. Your brain remembers. It's like riding a bike.

So I made a frantic dash to the makeshift ring and lashed out at Damien, but he was faster. In one effortless move, he crushed the girl's windpipe with his bare hand. Then, with a finger to his lips, he vanished into thin air.

Cheering from the crowd was deafening, but funnily enough, no one lunged after me. I mean, I was more than prepared to die even if my attempt at saving someone else was a complete and total failure.

At least I tried.

"Oh, God," I breathed, pressing two fingers against the side of the girl's neck. There was no pulse there… nothing but broken bones and purpling marks. She was gone.

She was so young. I couldn't understand how someone could be this evil. Evil enough to hammer a baby-faced redhead, who was still wearing little black *Mary Janes*. Then I realized that the "why" didn't matter. Andrei had already said it: Damien did things for the hell of it.

"Did you think you could save her? Do you think you can save any of them?" Damien's smooth voice came from behind me.

It took me half a second to realize that the room was jarringly quiet. The mob's sudden shift from chaotic uproar to statue-like stillness was creepy as hell.

"Why are you doing this?" I asked, my voice surprisingly calm as I crumpled to the ground, unable to stand any longer.

"Can you imagine being denied entrance to the only home you've ever known, Miss Erickson?" Damien stared down at me, looking godlike and freaking innocent. "Unable to communicate with the One who should have loved you unconditionally? I suppose that His unconditional love only applies to you mortals."

I went from being a "demon's slut" to an esteemed "Miss Erickson." His "Dr. Jekyll and Mr. Hyde" shtick was getting old fast. I bit back a scathing response and just slowly undid the knots of the rope around the young woman. It was a blessing that I wasn't convulsing from being around so many supernatural creatures. That could only mean that the crowd was made up of humans—humans who were little more than vessels for Damien's demon cronies. They were probably trapped in their own bodies, watching the world from the inside out.

"No, I don't think you truly know what that is like," Damien surmised, crouching down low beside me. "Well, I do. And if these human girls can indeed commune with God, what better way to exact my revenge than to take them away from Him?" He was running his hand up and down the girl's pantyhose covered thigh. I yearned to chop that wandering hand off.

"You humans are so expendable. Kill one and a human female breeds more," Damien went on, chuckling to himself. "Do you know that every second, four of you inferior beings pop out? You're like rabbits, but less tasty." He continued his exploration of the girl's leg. "So I figured, if I'm stuck as a godforsaken being on this godforsaken planet, I might as well enjoy myself. Right, guys?" He gestured to his mob of merry demons and they cheered as if he were a talk show host.

"Enjoy yourself?" I snarled. "This girl…"

"This girl is barely eighteen and claims that angels speak to her," Damien spat at me, surprising me with his vehemence. But not a second later, his fury dissipated and it was as if he never lashed out. Then a sardonic smile spread across his face. "Pardon my tenses, Miss Erickson. I meant was, claimed, and spoke."

Beneath my fingers, however, the girl's pulse grew faster, contradicting what Damien just said. I kept silent, hoping he didn't notice anything.

"So you... put her on trial? Decided that she was guilty of being a Christian and killed her for sport?" I was shaking, anger so raw and tempting I couldn't resist it.

"I'm a fair man. She could have told the truth, said that she'd been lying, and I would have let her go with no memory of this."

"You're out of your fucking mind if you think..."

"Oh, but Sarah had faith, you see. She had a Higher Power speaking to her, supposedly protecting her." Damien threw his head back and laughed, pushing soft blond curls out of his eyes. "I asked. I gave her a chance to confess, instead of killing her outright like I should have. I give them all a chance."

He rose to his feet, eyes turning to slits. "Marco, Nicolas, hold this one down," he calmly instructed, and before I knew it, hands were yanking me away from the girl... from Sarah.

I struggled. I kicked. I dug my French tips into skin until I broke through it.

Nothing.

Marco and Nicolas turned out to be twice my size, plus they had supernatural beings going along for a ride inside them.

Nothing I did affected them. Nothing. They held me down on the cement and all I could do was sit there and let them.

"Now you will see what happens to girls who aren't as polite as Sarah Roche," Damien said darkly. And I could only watch as another girl was brought to him, dragged kicking and screaming across the floor.

"Damien, don't," I begged, despising myself for stooping to that level. *Barely eighteen*, he'd said.

The new girl was probably the same age, and she was about to be subjected to the same fate.

"You want me. You want to torture me!" I screamed. They were so close I could almost touch them. Almost.

He held the girl up against his front, and to my surprise, there was a determined look in her moss green eyes, which were brilliantly shiny with tears.

"Sometimes I can take away people's pain," Damien was saying, hands on her shoulders. "Most times, I just don't fucking feel like it."

If you're a normal person, there are probably two things that go through your mind when you know someone is about to kill another person. The first is if you know it's going to happen, shouldn't you stop it? And the second is that if, for some reason, you couldn't save them, you hope the innocent person's death is quick and painless.

Unfortunately, before I could even contemplate the first, it was all over.

For without any hesitation, Damien crushed the girl's skull and ripped her, this barely eighteen-year-old girl, into two almost equal halves… with his bare hands.

It was surreal. She didn't scream, didn't make any noise, but her lips were moving before it happened and I knew

300

she was murmuring a quick *Notre Père*. That, coupled with her shiny eyes on me, tore a fresh stream of pleas from my mouth.

But it was too late. Even before he crushed her skull in the palm of his hand like it was a peanut, it was too late. Even before he tore through her pale skin and found the muscle and bone, it was too late. It was too late because there was no one of use in that room... no one who could help her... not even me.

I felt hot in my sheer clothing. It was because of the girl's blood, which soaked through my clothes and warmed my skin. But only when I ran my tongue across my lips did I taste the blood and realized that I was baptized in it. Sprayed. Spattered. Showered.

"Please save her," I whispered, over and over again—thinking back to the first girl, the one called Sarah. To God? I didn't know. Perhaps I did want to ask Him to do this one thing for me, but I was too scared. Would He hear my plea? Does He listen to prayers that came even from the wicked? Was I still good enough of a person for Him to consider, regardless of who, or what, I loved?

"Marco, dispose of the bodies," Damien called, dropping each half of the headless girl onto the ground with a sickening thwack. He laughed over the renewed chatter. "I hope I have proven a point here tonight."

"You're a monster," I breathed.

"I don't claim to be anything else," he said, winking at me conspiratorially. "And I like to get creative... in everything I do," he finished suggestively. "Take Miss Erickson upstairs. Through the back exit. I don't want my patrons to call the cops...or think she's Carrie or something." He watched them tug me to my feet. "Oh, Miss Erickson, you keep sobbing like that and I might just have to shove my dick in your mouth to make you stop."

"Fuck you," I raged, launching myself at him. I barely got one step toward him before his Neanderthals yanked me back.

Damien merely laughed, wiping his bloodstained hands down the front of his jeans. "Rest assured, Miss Erickson, you will. The chase is what I most enjoy, so don't ruin it for me by sashaying in here again. Agreed?"

Damien's two henchmen was leading me past his open office to get to the back exit when suddenly, Temp leapt out the room, eyes wide as saucers.

"Temp?" I sputtered stupidly, blinking quickly to make sure he wasn't a figment of my imagination.

"What the fuck?" His face hardened as he took in the scene. "Rae, is this your blood? That's my sister you're manhandling, dickfaces!"

"Just get her out of here, then," the man, who I guessed was Nicolas, said, shoving me at Temp.

I threw my arms around him, sobbing gratefully. "Why are you here?"

"I knew you'd do the exact opposite of what I told you." He held me away from his body, looking me over. "This isn't your blood?"

"It isn't," I whispered, and cried all over again.

I even cried during the car ride to my penthouse. Temp didn't tease me at all, not even once.

I made Temp leave, even though he vehemently argued against it. As a result, we had a huge fight. But he understood in the end. And he didn't come right out and say it, but he knew that the only person I wanted to see was probably the one going to rip me to pieces... then put me back together again.

Once he'd slipped out of my apartment, after promising to call later, I shuffled to the shower and stripped. Then, I watched the water at my feet turn crimson. I could've pretended that it was menstrual blood—or even better, hair dye.

But it wasn't. I knew it wasn't. I knew it was Sarah's blood.

Guilt was a funny thing, wasn't it? It could consume you like a starving child but it could fill you up as well. Ate at your insides and replenished them... ate and replenished... ate and replenished...

Useless, useless woman, chanted the voice in my head. And she was so fucking right.

All I had been able to do was try to futilely punch Damien in the throat and get myself splattered with a girl's blood and guts. My existence was pointless. Aside from being a "demon's slut"—as Damien had so nicely put it, what use did I have? None. None at all.

"Fuck," I muttered in disgust, realizing that my eyes were misting over.

There was no point feeling sorry for myself like a pathetic loser.

That asshole will pay, I thought to myself, imagining Damien's twisted leer and cheerful malevolence as he forced me to watch two innocent girls get slaughtered.

It didn't matter that fallen angels were, in essence, powerful immortals compared to someone like me. It didn't matter that he had promised to violate my body to spite Andrei,

303

or even that he could crush me between his thumb and index finger.

One way or another, even if I had to get Father Brady to help me do it, Damien Ivanov was going to burn in the pits of hell with the scum he so despised. I was done being absolutely powerless. Teddy Bunting was right. Daniel Lawless was right. It was stupid of me to be so stubborn.

It felt like hours passed until the water turned arctic and I was forced to step out of the stall and grab a towel. Shivering, I wiped the steam off the mirror and stared hard at myself. Red, that was all I saw. Iron, that was all I could smell, all I could taste. It filled my nostrils and stayed there, a permanent ghost of a scent that was anything but pleasant.

I took Andrei's ring off and cried.

"The first time you see someone die isn't easy, Rae. To be a hunter, you have to block out the overwhelming feeling to feel. It's the only reason I've survived this long."

"So in essence, you have to turn yourself into a cold, unfeeling thing? A robot? I don't want that kind of life, Dad. I thought you understood that."

"You're the one who asked if an innocent has ever died on my watch." He sighed, rubbing the bridge of his nose as though frustrated. *"Why did you ask if you didn't really want to know, sweetheart?"*

"Because death scares me, Dad. It freaks the fuck out of me and that is the real reason I'm in business school, bored out of my damn mind. Massacres don't happen in boardrooms."

"Rae," a voice growled from my bedroom, ripping me from a very unwanted bout of reminiscing.

I wrapped the towel around me, tucked it, and warily stalked into my room, expecting Damien, or one of his minions, to be there with a sadistic grin on his face. In retrospect, that would have been better than the sight that met my eyes. I was already a bundle of nerves and this did nothing to control them.

He fell to his knees, blood spraying against my carpet with the movement. So much blood. So much blood and suddenly it was like I was back in the basement, retching at the sight of the girl being ripped in half right in front of me.

"Heal," I said, my voice shaky, barely a whisper. "Heal, dammit!" Begging. Yeah, I was pretty much begging.

He shook his head, reaching for me. I ran, crumpling in front of him. Even on his knees he still looked impressive, a fallen giant. I cupped his face.

"Andrei," I whispered, tasting salt in my mouth. "What happened? Why aren't you healing?"

"Fuck... you," he rumbled, half-heartedly pulling me to his bloodied frame.

I instantly recoiled, hurt. Then I considered the very real possibility that he was mad at me and had gone after Damien, and that this was the result. But that was impossible, wasn't it? Damien ran from Andrei... because Andrei was stronger.

"Need to... fuck you," he amended, pressing his mouth against my upturned one.

I tasted it, the copper, the thick emulsion that was his blood. This wasn't like that time he let me hit him. No, this was different because he needed to heal; he needed me.

I kissed him back, surprised that he was letting me lead. Or was he just too weak to direct me himself? It didn't matter, and I didn't care. The only thing that mattered was that I need to make him better.

305

Our tongues collided, teeth clashing. It was sloppy and it was messy. It was urgent. I reached between us and undid his belt buckle before undoing his fly, dragging his pants as far as they could go in our position. He needed this. He needed me to heal him.

My towel fell off and I gently pushed Andrei away. He moved to lie flat on his back, doing what was necessary. His T-shirt had once been white but the entire front was stained a startling burgundy shade, almost onyx. It was practically ripped to shreds and pieces of it hung off his body. It was disconcerting to straddle him and stare down at the hellish aftermath of whatever it was that he had gone through, and even worse to see angry red gashes on his body—gashes that would not heal until he was deep inside me.

"I'm sorry," I whispered, grasping his rigid shaft and guiding it to my astonishingly slippery folds. I was sorry for being way too headstrong, sorry for the pain he'd obviously gone through tonight. Sorry for being so damn useless.

Andrei's eyes fluttered shut as he let out a soft sigh when I lowered myself on him. I leaned forward, legs spread further, and placed my hands on the carpet, bracing myself on either side of him. He was rock-hard inside me yet he wasn't thrusting.

So instead, I rode him, murmuring stupid, meaningless things such as "It's going to be okay." and "I'll make it better." He was swelling inside me then and my inner muscles clenched around him—eager to massage, eager to work on him. The low groans in his throat sounded so pained, so agonized.

Then I put my hands on his face, tracing the cuts, bumps, and bruises, committing them to memory. I refused to think about what would have happened if I wasn't around.

Would he have fucked someone else to heal himself? Would I have blamed him if he did, perhaps hated him for it?

Furious with myself, I resumed riding him up and down and in quick succession, faster and harder... as if time was running out... as if my climax was within arm's reach—when in fact it was oh-so-far away. As I pinched my nipples with determination, I leaned down and traced Andrei's lips with my tongue.

As if electrocuted, his hands shot out to grip my waist. The ripped T-shirt vanished before my eyes, as did the feel of the denim beneath me. I fed him my surprised cry of pleasure when he maneuvered me onto my back, all the while, he remained inside me, throbbing.

"*Mea domina*," he said, his breathing ragged. The cuts had vanished, and I reached out and touched his unblemished skin. "Get ready to be fucked," he added as his lips claimed mine and his arousal claimed me.

Looping my legs around him, I allowed him to take over. He withdrew himself almost completely, before slowly pushing back into me. I bit my lower lip, moaning softly. Every satisfying inch of him was inside me then. And when he began to ram into me, earnestly so, the tears I shed were because it felt so damn good. With each deep thrust, he groaned out my name, pressing his mouth against my damp skin—licking, tasting, and biting. The hard planes of his chest were torture against the hard buds of my nipples, and his pelvis hit my sensitized spot whenever we collided. He bore me down on the carpet, so harshly I could feel the imprint of each individual thread on my bare ass.

"Shit, Andrei," I cried out, arching my back on a particularly incredible thrust.

And then the pad of his thumb sought what his pelvis was previously taunting, rubbing circles there before teasingly swirling around it and repeating the process. I was delirious from all the sensation and the feel of his weight on me.

"That's good, my little one," he ground out, tweaking my nub between two fingers. "You deserve to be fucked. You deserve to come."

"Yes," I agreed on an exhale, deciding to spread my legs to give him better access. "Oh, Andrei!" I cried out. His mouth came upon mine and he swallowed my gasps and wails and moans, feeding me his own cacophony of pleasure.

Biting my lower lip, he whispered, "Come with me, *mea domina*."

Thrashing my head from side to side, I squeezed my eyes shut. Images of Damien tearing Sarah in half rolled through my mind and I knew that I couldn't come... wouldn't come.

I felt Andrei's breath caressing the column of my neck and when he drew the sensitive skin there into his mouth, the decision was made for me. I let go. I convulsed around him, tightening my hold on him inside me as I came.

Andrei's entire body tensed and my eyes flew open. I didn't want to miss the beautiful image of him reaching ultimate bliss. This time, he raised his head and released as he said my name, dragging it out as if it were made up of the entire alphabet. Hot liquid jetted into me, so thick and copious that it set me off again. It was a mini orgasm, but an orgasm nevertheless... and I found that I didn't want it. I didn't want to feel this good when there were innocent people out there suffering simply because they were at the wrong place at the wrong time and I...

"Stop it," Andrei commanded, pulling out of me.

308

My body instantly bemoaned his absence. "Stop... what?"

"Worrying. Stop worrying." His mouth was nestled between my breasts. I shivered from the vibrations of his voice against my skin. "You think the coward, Ivanov, could do this to me?" He created a delicious path of liquid heat down my belly with kisses and traced my navel with his forefinger. I was never so grateful before to have an innie than I was at that moment. "That's my cum," he observed, his attention obviously fixated on me. The sudden change of topic from Damien possibly attacking him to Andrei's ejaculation glistening in my most intimate part made my head spin.

His warm liquid spilled from me and trickled down my ass. I was incredibly sticky and filthy but all thoughts of yet another shower flew out the window when Andrei slowly tongued his way up my wetness and swirled his tongue around my highly sensitive bud.

"Don't!" I yelped in disgust, but cancelled out the refusal when I involuntarily clamped his head between my thighs. "I'm... I think I'm still bleeding."

"We taste so fucking perfect, Rae," Andrei groaned, stroking me there with his expert tongue. "The only thing I see is your beautiful pink pussy. I can only taste you and me. Only you and me."

I moaned, dragging my nails across the carpet as I arched my back. "Oh, God, Andrei. I can't... Not again."

He ignored me, the loud noises of his ministrations filling the air. It was hard to describe what the slurping, swishing, and appreciative groans did to me. It wasn't just the feel of him tonguing my swollen labia, driving into me like a tiny but powerful shaft, or even his sucking on my sensitive nub like it was a mint. No, it was the fact that he wanted to please me. Just me. It pleased him to please me and that was what made me come so hard that I broke three fingernails desperately clutching the carpet... and probably almost suffocated Andrei between my thighs.

Breathing heavily, my eyes fluttered shut as Andrei extricated himself, giving me one final kiss there. Then he lay beside me and gathered me in his arms, burying his nose in my still damp hair.

It took a long stretch of silence for me to clear my head of all things sexual and ask him.

"What happened to you?"

"No."

"No?"

"No, you don't need to know."

"So it wasn't... Damien?"

"Don't insult me."

"And don't insult me by... Oh, fuck this, now you've made me cry." I wrenched myself away from him and sat up, wiping at my eyes. Andrei likewise sat up beside me, hoisting me on his lap so that I was facing him. "I thought you were hurt, Andrei," I mumbled, refusing to look at him. "I'm such a wimp because I was ready to fall apart in the blink of an eye. And now you won't even tell me what the hell happened?"

He cupped my chin, making me look at him. "Does it matter, Rae? Nothing I tell you will change what has happened today."

I stared at him for a minute. "You're such a dick."

His eyes burned with an intensity akin to anger, but not quite so. "Name-calling. Cute," he remarked in a low voice.

"If I hadn't been here, would you have screwed someone else?"

310

Andrei's eyes were dark pits of something I couldn't quite put my finger on. "No matter where you go, I will find you, remember?"

I resisted the urge to sigh like a lovesick teenager. "What if I were... in an accident and unable to... see to your needs? Would you go somewhere else?"

"What do you want me to say?" he growled, glaring at me.

"What if I were in a deep sleep, a coma, for instance? If you were injured like you were injured tonight, would you...?"

"No, I wouldn't fuck someone else," he snapped, his voice bouncing off the walls in my room. He pushed me onto my back, looming over me with murder in his eyes. "I would fuck your comatose body and you would be wet. Because even then, you'd still want me."

My breathing hitched and I forced myself to be afraid of him at that moment... but failed miserably.

"I was at Nicolette earlier tonight," I whispered.

Andrei heaved himself off me and rose to his feet, his naked body glistening with sweat. "I know."

Two words, two syllables and they filled me with a boatload of dread.

"You know?"

"Was the girl your first mortal death?" he asked quietly.

I stood up, slightly wobbly on my feet. I didn't bother asking him how he knew. The violent barrage of mental pictures that popped in my head was enough to make his gentle questioning a salve. "Yes," I answered.

"Come here."

So I went to him, releasing a sigh when he wrapped me in his arms. He felt hard and unyielding around me, but he also felt like the softest cashmere blanket I could ever imagine.

"I know why you went there," he said into my ear, his hands tangling my hair between his fingers. "You continue to defy me at every turn, Rainelle. Why?"

The cashmere blanket became barbed wire. I carefully disengaged myself from it.

"Are you going to chastise me like a child?"

"Are you going to continue to act like one?"

"And what do you know about children?" I let out a snort before regret seeped into my mind. "I mean, maybe you have some kids somewhere in the…"

"I don't have any children," he curtly interjected. "Stop changing the subject."

Well, at least now I know for sure.

"Ivanov would like nothing better than to kill you," he went on, hands on my shoulders to make me look at him. "I don't know how many times you want me to stress this fucking point, Rae."

The memory of what he did to Sarah was one that I was fighting to forget but needed to remember. "I know how stupid it was of me to go back there. I'm sorry."

He quirked an eyebrow. "Right. Anyway, what I'm saying is that you need a… minder."

"A babysitter?" I choked out, slapping his hands away. "Excuse me?"

Andrei only pulled me to him, his hands roaming down my sides. "Fine. A babysitter."

"You've got to be kidding me. And who is it? My brother?" That actually didn't sound all that bad. Temp and I could even…

312

"Selene," said Andrei, and he silenced my protest with a rough kiss.

Chapter 20

It took a few more weeks to arrange it, but I was finally able to leave Paris. There was nothing for me to do there anymore. And on top of that, for the very first time, I had failed a client. Did it matter that JP wasn't cheating on Ana? Wasn't dating her even, or married to her? No. What mattered was that I had failed her, and failed her brother. Never in my life would I have imagined that sleuthing would lead to demons, fallen angels, and a succubus hell-bent on getting into my Agent Provocateur thongs.

So after refunding Ana Fontaine every cent she paid me, I hurriedly got the hell out of dodge... with a little baggage, of course.

"It's quite small, don't you think?" Selene pouted, eyes scanning the only guest room in my house, the one I grew up in and the place I would never have guessed would become the temporary home to a billion-year-old succubus.

She appraised the queen-sized bed as if it were a matchbox, wrinkled her nose at the awesome antique vanity table I'd gotten just last year, and swiveled around to glance at the partially open door of the en suite bathroom.

"I think," I began, leveling her with a withering look, "you'd better be fucking grateful I'm not shoving you into the basement like fucking Sylvia Likens."

We glared at each other for what felt like hours, until Selene looked away and glided over to the window, barely wobbling in her mile-high stilettos. "So what is there to do in this one-horse town?"

I rubbed at my temples, feeling the onset of a colossal headache. The fact that I survived multiple plane rides with Selene to get back home (away from Daniel, away from Damien, and even away from Andrei) was almost hard to believe. The only light at the end of this dismal tunnel was the fact that I would see Renée again after months of distance. My best friend wasn't too happy about being ignored and I knew that I would probably have to do major groveling to get back into her good graces.

It just didn't feel right for Selene to be here with me when all I wanted to do was escape the supernatural and pretend that I was normal. Even for just one precious second, I would have liked to pretend that everything in my life was sane again. Then there was the fact that there were too many memories in this house—both the bad and the good. Memories that seemed tainted by Selene's presence. My father was probably rolling in his grave now.

"I'm sure Andrei told you that killing anyone while you're here is unacceptable," I muttered, digging the frayed toe of my pink Converse into the thick carpet. The thought of Selene hunting in my hometown filled me with dread. I knew almost everyone in Sallow Bay. Guilt would slay me if my neighbors disappeared one by one—death by climax.

She jerked around to look at me. "Since you can't be killed during feeding, are you offering me your body, *ma petite*?"

I felt heat crawl up my neck at the blatant come-on. "Yeah, you wish."

Laughing loudly, she waved a dismissive hand at me. "If I were to touch you, my lord would have my head on a platter. I am many things but *une idiote*[3] is not one of them."

"Just don't hurt anyone," I muttered, yawning. I turned on my heel to leave, intent on locking my bedroom door and crashing.

"Rainelle?"

I hated hearing my name on the succubus' tongue but there was nothing I could do.

"What?" I spat.

"Your derrière fills those jeans very nicely."

Renée stood on her doorstep, sniffing at the bottle of Chianti I brought her. Folding her arms across her chest, she narrowed her jade green eyes at me. It was ridiculous to feel three feet tall in front of someone shorter than you, but that was what Renée Marino's evil eye did to people.

"When'd you come in?" she demanded.

"Yesterday," I replied, holding the bottle up. "I come bearing alcohol."

"Yeah, I can see that, bitch."

---

[3] an idiot, French phrase

"Oh, come on, Ren. I'm sorry for hanging up on you," I griped, uncomfortably shifting from one foot to the other. "Could you at least let me in so I can pee?"

"It's not about the hanging up." She let out a heavy sigh, stepping aside to let me in and accepting my peace offering. She examined the bottle as I strode past her. "It's the fact that you don't seem to give a damn that my husband and I worry about you… a lot. The least you can do is email us so we know some billionaire hasn't murdered your snitching ass and thrown your body over the River Seine."

I let out a laugh on my way to the bathroom, ignoring the way my heart swelled at the thought of her obvious concern. "Is Lorenzo home?"

"There was a fire at Quincy's," Renée called out. "You know, the burger place on Brooke?"

Only once I was done in the bathroom did I respond.

"How could I forget?" I said incredulously, following her voice into the pristine kitchen. "Best Texan-style burgers ever. Was it burnt to the ground?" My stomach grumbled at the thought of sinking my teeth into the juicy beef patties and melted cheese. What I wouldn't do to get my hands on one at the moment?

Renée shook her head, sighing with relief. "Fortunately, no. Would've been a shame to have to stoop to Mickey D's."

It didn't take long for Renée and me to get back to normal. Well, as normal as it was possible to be, without telling her that I just snuck out of my house for the afternoon, successfully tiptoeing past my succubus babysitter, who just discovered my *True Blood* box-set.

Renée poured us each a glass of wine, reheated a plate of Lorenzo's spicy lamb cutlets, and brought everything to the living room. She set them on the coffee table before me.

"The best fucking wine on the planet," she remarked after taking a huge gulp from her glass and plopping down beside me. "Thanks, babe."

I decided to skip the liquor for now and dig into the food. One thing Lorenzo definitely knew how to do was cook. The man was a firefighter, knew his way around a kitchen, and spoke fluent Italian. Renée lucked the fuck out when she got him to put a ring on it.

"Jesus, you'd think you were starving in France," she said, watching me unabashedly lick the sauce off my fingers.

"Shut up," I said, letting out a moan. "So good. You know I'd steal your husband the second I get the chance, ungrateful wench."

She laughed. We both knew that Lorenzo Marino was madly, deeply in love with her and would only leave her if he went to the grave.

"I've missed you, Rae," she said, her voice somber.

"Uh-oh. What's up? You're getting sappy on me." I brought the glass of wine to my lips, inhaling the fruity scent of plums Ren and I both liked. I sipped... and was surprised to realize that I hated it! So much so that I heaved, spraying crimson liquid all over my white cargo pants. "Shit," I spat, standing.

"What the hell, Rae? You okay?"

"Too strong," I murmured, my stomach turning. I was beginning to regret stuffing my face like a greedy six-year-old at a friend's birthday party.

"Are you sick?" Renée was standing now, as well, gently patting my back.

318

I took a deep breath. "Nah. Don't think so. Guess I should take it easy, huh?"

Ren gave me a doubtful look. "You're positive it's the food?"

I gave the meat a wistful look as I sat back down. "Yeah. Loan me some pants?"

After we went upstairs to get me some pants, Ren and I continued talking about anything and nothing in particular. We were so engrossed that before I knew it the moon was out and I started wondering if Selene would call Andrei to let him know I disappeared for the entire day. The idea made me laugh out loud that Renée paused in the middle of a story about something that had happened at her office.

"Is there something hilarious about my colleague Frank getting fired when he has four kids to feed?" she asked, her voice dripping with sarcasm.

"What? Of course not," I said quickly, stifling a yawn. We were sitting on her bed and the mattress suddenly felt so comfy beneath me. In fact, so comfy that I could probably just close my...

"What's up with you?" snapped Ren. "For real now, Rainelle Erickson."

I rubbed the sleep out of my eyes. "Just tired. Might be jetlag."

She glared at me. "That's not what I mean and you know it. You're keeping something from me. What is it?"

There were a lot of things I was keeping from her that I didn't even know where to begin. The only thing I did know was that I didn't want to ruin her perfect life by unloading the supernatural on her.

"I'm dating someone," I finally blurted out.

Ren clapped her hands so hard her fingers turned bright crimson. "Are you kidding me? Who is he? Some French businessman? A sexy Parisian artist? Lord, how good is the sex?" she fired at me, eyes glistening with excitement.

I couldn't help but laugh. "Um, I know for a fact that your sex life's on point. You don't have to live vicariously through me."

She rolled her eyes at me. "I know that. Doesn't change the fact that I'm interested in hearing about yours."

"Pervert."

"Prude," she countered.

"If only you knew…"

She playfully slapped my arm. "I do want to know! I feel like we don't talk as much anymore." She gave me a pointed look. "First, who's the guy?"

I sighed heavily. "Andrei."

"Who?" she asked with a blank look.

I watched her rewind through the film of her memory before she let out a whoop of laughter when the name finally clicked.

"That fucking friendly giant? My God, Rae. He must be playing in the big-dick sandpit!" she screeched, bouncing excitedly in her cross-legged position. "You lucky beast."

Lucky? Was I? Lucky to be in love (because, God help me, that was the only way to describe this overwhelming feeling) with a demon king? Lucky to be caught in some crazy revenge plot on said demon king by a sadistic fallen angel? Yeah, I was rolling in four-leaf clovers, all right.

320

"Well?" Renée prodded my arm. "Is it serious? Because, honey, the look you just got on your face says a million words."

My face heated up. "It isn't serious. He's... not the type of guy to... settle down," I said vaguely. *That's certainly putting it mildly.* "Besides, you know me. I'm all about the orgasms." Twisting Andrei's ring on my finger, I thought about how the last part was a bald-faced lie.

Ren, however, cackled with laughter and went on about how lucky I was. But I was too distracted to make any kind of response beyond the occasional affirmative or negative. My best friend's line of questioning certainly brought up an unwelcome feeling: longing.

I had been quite content to be my own person, have my own homes, go wherever I wanted, do whatever I wanted, and fuck whomever I wanted.

But now, I thought, *I want more.*

And that was the pathetic part, wasn't it? I couldn't have more because the person I wanted to have it with couldn't give it to me. He wasn't even a person.

Selene caught me as I sauntered through the front door. Instead of her usual glamorous get-up, she was in a pair of navy-blue Baby Phat sweats that looked suspiciously like mine.

"Enjoy yourself at Renée's?" she asked, following me into the living room.

I turned to look at her. "How'd you...?"

"I have been around the block, *chérie*," she interjected wryly. "Both literally and figuratively. She lives quite close to you. Did you really think I would not hear you leave? You insult me."

"So you were watching me," I said in a defeated voice. I collapsed onto the couch, just wanting to curl up into a ball and sleep until the end of time.

"That is my job, *non*?"

"Did you tell Andrei I left you?" He was quite vehement that Selene was to be my shadow. Well, if he thought that he'd fucked me into compliance, he had another think coming.

"My lord is quite... attached to you," she replied candidly, perching daintily beside me. "He would not have appreciated that bit of information."

It was funny that her closeness didn't affect me that much. In fact, it barely made me tingle with awareness. After what had happened at Andrei's castle, I would never have suspected that I would ever be able to resist the urge to at least pull her freakishly perfect golden hair.

"Thank you," I said as I exhaled. I grudgingly met her eye. "He would've had my head and I'm not in the mood to be brutalized tonight."

She arched a perfectly sculpted brow. "You're thanking me? Are you ill?"

I let out a weak laugh. "I'm just not in the mood for a fight. Don't get me wrong though, I still hate your guts."

It was her turn to laugh. "You know what they say about hate..."

I shook my head, hardly able to believe that Selene and I were bantering. *What alternate universe have I crossed into?*

"So," I said slowly, "what season have you gotten up to?" I gestured at the TV screen and kicked my sneakers off, putting my feet up on the coffee table.

Selene's face instantly brightened. And not for the first time was I struck by her beauty. "The third one."

"Great," I told her, thinking that that was the end of the conversation. But I was way too achy to get off the couch and officially put an end to it.

"I have never considered bestiality but that big *loup*—I mean, wolf—makes it an intriguing possibility," she said breathlessly, pressing play on the remote and bringing Sookie's face into focus. "I would drop the bloodsucker and fuck the wolf-man in a New York minute."

I stared at her in blatant amazement and she finally dragged her eyes from the screen. "Why are you looking at me like that? Is it not acceptable to discuss the events of an episode with a fellow enthusiast?"

"Yeah," I began slowly, "but you're a…"

"Succubus?" She shrugged, the slight motion making her look decidedly more human. "I suppose I have always envied the human race its simplicity."

"Zoning out in front of the TV and shipping Alcide and Sookie? Yeah, I'd say that's a pretty simple existence."

Selene didn't respond.

"For the record, I think Bill's too wimpy in this season. And short," I offered. I thought about it. "But that's in every season. And by the way, he loses those ridiculous sideburns by Season Four."

Selene's painted lips twitched at the corners. I ended up finishing the episode with her before deciding to call it a night. It was weird to feel relaxed around her, but I did. I didn't even want to find out if she fed today. Probably because I didn't want to know. It still felt like I was aiding and abetting an extremely fashionable psychopath.

I was in the middle of brushing my teeth when I heard the noise in my bedroom. Déjà fucking vu. Marching out the bathroom, sluggish and annoyed, I found Andrei drawing the curtains closed—something I should've done the minute I stepped into my room.

"Oh. It's you," I murmured, barely able to sound surprised.

He whirled around and eyed me suspiciously. "Were you expecting someone else?"

Ignoring his question, I quickly scanned his body for blood and mentally breathed a sigh of relief when it was clear that he was fine.

More than fine, I thought lasciviously, parts of my body awakening at the sight of him in a white vest and board shorts with so much skin exposed it was surely a sin. *I'm such a horny deviant, my God!*

"Where did you come from?" My voice sounded breathless, lustful.

"Somewhere hot," he murmured cryptically, closing the small distance between us in a few strides. His eyes scanned me in the same way I just appraised him. "You weren't feeling well," he added.

"You could feel that all the way in 'somewhere hot'?"

I sighed when he cupped my cheeks in his big hands, his fingers caressing my skin.

"Yes," he replied, and I could see that he was resisting the urge to smile. He placed a palm on my forehead, the gesture so considerate I nearly lost the ability to breathe. "No fever," he calmly pronounced.

"Oh, but I do have one," I whispered, bringing his hand to my right breast where the nipple was perked up against the

T-shirt I usually slept in. "Here." Then I moved his hand to my other breast. "And here."

And before he could retract his hand, I brought it under my shirt and over my crotch. "And finally, right here. Make it go away."

Andrei's eyes flashed as his fingers lightly played across my slit. "Dripping already," he rumbled appreciatively, sinking a finger into me as he dipped his head and crashed his mouth against mine.

I latched onto him, pouring every ounce of passion I felt for this man into the curling and crashing of our tongues. Groaning, he led me to one wall, shoving my back up against it. Sleep was instantly forgotten as he relieved me of my shirt and whipped off his own clothing, returning his mouth to mine once those tasks were done.

"Fuck, you taste good," he growled, nipping my bottom lip with his teeth.

I moaned his name, arching my back and pressing my breasts into his chest. Between us, he reared forward, hot and hard against my lower belly. Moisture from the tip drizzled into the sparse curls between my thighs. Had I taken my pill? Did I care? I had to rack my brain.

'Yes' to both questions, my ever-present conscience put in.

I trailed my fingernails down his back, pausing before the slight dip at the base of his spine. "Oh, God," I gasped when he sank his teeth into the side of my neck. A flash of welcome pain zipped right through me and he soothed the area with his mouth, relieving the bite with his tongue.

"Is he the one who is doing this to you?" Andrei demanded, detaching himself and turning me around.

"No," I replied, completely mortified. "Andrei, fuck."

"Not yet," he whispered, kneeing my legs apart. "Brace yourself against the wall."

I put my hands on the wall for balance, knees buckling when I felt his hands playing with the lips of my opening, toying with my swollen, sensitive nub.

"Fuck me," I pleaded, trying to find purchase against his fingers, trying to get him to exert more pressure there. "Please. Please, fuck me."

Andrei's low groan produced another wave of moisture between my legs. I pressed my forehead against the soothing cool wall, panting heavily. The hairs on my back stood up. The quivering in my knees grew stronger. Then, he sank two fingers deep inside me.

My head rolled back. My speech grew unintelligible. His fingers were thick, blunt and oh-so-forceful as they stroked me to an impending climax. Faster and faster, they rammed into me, his knuckles nudging my already overly stimulated bud with every entry and withdrawal.

"Almost... there," I panted, moaning low in my throat when his mouth found mine again. His kiss was brutal, passionate. I brought one of my hands down between my legs and pinched my nub.

And then I was coming on a shudder. The sheer force of my orgasm propelled me backward, into the solid wall of Andrei's body. I bucked against his fingers, riding the blissful waves. I didn't care that Selene could probably hear me, and would definitely know what was going on. And when it was over, I didn't care that I was greedy for more of Andrei, that I wanted him to fill me, to burn me all the way to my womb.

"Beautiful," said Andrei, tracing my lower lip with the pad of his forefinger. My tongue flickered out and I tasted the salty tang of myself. Then he brought his hands to my hips and whispered, "Bend for me, baby."

On shaky legs, I tipped forward, putting my hands up against the wall once again. Without warning, Andrei slid into me, deep and hard, rearing back before immediately pushing in again. The force of his thrust took me by surprise and I cried out, balling my hands into fist against the wall.

"Oh, fuck," he ground out, pulling me back to him. "Sweet fuck."

"Yes," I cried out, clenching my muscles around his cock, keeping him buried deep inside me until he slid out again, the mushroomed tip hitting a spot he knew drove me crazy. "So good," I affirmed, the tightening in my belly attesting to that. The hypersensitive nub in my crotch pulsed. Sweat drizzled between my swaying breasts, and with one hand, Andrei gave my rock-hard nipples the attention they so desired.

"Oh God, yes!" I wailed, nudging my breasts into his hand, allowing him to pinch my nipples, knead my flesh. "Harder!"

Andrei sank into me again, my tightness swallowing his burgeoning shaft. "Coming," he groaned, increasing the pace of his strokes into me as he fought for release. "Come with me, Rae. Can't... fucking... stop."

I pushed back into him, shuddering when he began to rub my nub in furious circles, sending me over the edge to join him as he blasted his seed inside me. Heat filled me, the sensations drove me dizzy and all the while I was coming, milking the still-hard length of his member for all it was worth.

Breathless and covered in sweat, we languidly remained by the wall, until I reached behind me and pulled Andrei out. My body mourned his exit. I turned around and he gathered me in his arms, carrying me to my bed.

After two orgasms, I was more than ready to call it a night but to my complete and utter shock, Andrei was sporting wood again. Lying on the bed while he loomed over me, I shivered when he raised my legs in the air before spreading them apart.

"Again?" I croaked, my need for him growing anew despite how sore I was. "You're a monster."

He didn't respond, the look in his eyes was answer enough. Instead of sinking into me again, he lowered himself onto the bed and buried his face between my thighs. I jerked in response, arching my back off the bed when he dipped two fingers past my slippery, swollen folds and deep into my heat.

"Andrei," I moaned, unable to believe that I could need him so much, so soon. "Oh, hell." I felt his tongue at my entrance and then he was licking me while his fingers were steadily probing me.

I wrapped my thighs around his head, wanting to keep him there, wanting to prolong the assault. But he wasn't going anywhere. Slowly, agonizingly so, he plunged his tongue into me, his nose bumping painfully against my sensitized bud.

I cried out, bucking against him, rocking my hips. It hurt. It was too much. I needed to explode.

"Please, please, please," I chanted, and he only licked me faster, sucking me into his mouth.

"Let go," he murmured around my slippery flesh. He ran a finger along the rim of my anus and suddenly, that was all I could do—I let go.

"I love watching you come, *mea domina*," Andrei commented, lapping up my juices. The slurping sound his mouth made was one of the most erotic things I'd ever heard. "I love the way your cunt is so greedy, so hungry. So pink and wet and bruised from my cock."

The sound of my heavy breathing filled the air. My heart beat like a drum against my chest, and tears pooled at the corners of my eyes. *Too fucking much.*

"I don't know what I would do if something were to happen to you, Rae," Andrei continued, tracing a path up my leg. He raised his head and I forced myself to look into his eyes. "You were mad at me... for telling you to go. But you understand why this is best... for now."

I paused and breathed deeply, not answering until I cleared my head. "Yes."

He gently disengaged himself from my legs and raised himself over me. Nose to nose, we were closer than before.

"Selene will lay her life down to protect you. For me."

If I were a guy, my boner would have deflated at the sound of her name leaving Andrei's lips.

"And why Selene? You know I can't stand her," I said, feeling a little guilty about that. After all, *True Blood* had brought us closer. Strange, but true.

"Because I trust her and because she's powerful enough to protect you. She's ancient." Andrei swiped a clump of my damp hair away from my face. "Your brother is a hybrid. Weak. Young."

Damn. He knew my train of thought as if he were inside my head.

I huffed out a breath. "If you say so."

"I say so." He licked away the remaining moisture on his lips, his blue eyes darkening. "Delicious."

For the next few hours, sleep was definitely the last thing on my mind.

I woke up deliciously late the next morning. And with eyes squinting in the sunlight, I stretched a hand out to the other side of the bed. Cold and empty.

"He's gone," a cheerful voice proclaimed. An accented, husky voice.

"Selene?" I croaked, sitting up. "What the hell are you doing in my room?"

She was obviously the sadistic person who'd let the sunshine in. Now she was standing in my room, already dressed in a cornflower blue summer dress, which looked suspiciously like the one I bought in Italy.

"Is that mine?" I grumbled.

She smoothed the front down. "Yes, but I presumed you haven't worn it in… a few years. It is a bit small for you."

I narrowed my eyes at her. "You calling me fat?"

She appraised me, eyes zoning in on my chest.

Belatedly, I realized I was completely naked and my breasts were on show. I glared at her and pulled the bedsheet up, making myself decent.

"Curvy, *mon amie*."

"We're so not friends, Selene. I think you slightly misunderstood what happened last night."

She winked at me. "There is no misunderstanding the sound of a satisfied woman."

"I'm not talking about that," I mumbled, feeling my face heat up. There was no denying that the noises I made were pretty embarrassing. "I'm talking about us watching TV. We're not suddenly best friends."

"Well, fine then," she huffed, flipping her hair over her shoulder. "I am going out for breakfast. I do hope you will listen to me and stay here."

330

"Please don't kill him or her," I said through clenched teeth.

It was Selene's turn to glare at me. "I think, after many millennia, I know how to leave my victims alive, Rainelle."

"Good."

"I suppose you don't want any breakfast?" She nodded at my nightstand.

Only then did I notice the tray of food beside me. My mouth watered. Bacon, eggs, and coffee. Selene was a fucking psychic.

"Thank you," I offered sincerely, receiving a genuine smile from her before she teleported away.

The coffee went down quickly but I could barely stomach one rind of greasy bacon. God, it killed me to leave it there. Selene might be a total nuisance, but I had to give it to her, she knew how to fry pig's meat.

I threw my nightgown on and carried the plate downstairs, sticking it into the refrigerator for later. Then, once I got my second cup of coffee, I padded into the living room and flicked the TV on. One horrendous reality show later and I was ready to claw my eyes out from boredom.

The doorbell rang just when I was contemplating which eyeball to tear out first.

And like a bad penny that keeps coming back, Daniel Lawless was standing on my doorstep, hands shoved deep into the pockets of his jeans.

Chapter 21

I closed my eyes and opened them again, positive that a fitful sleep last night was making me see things.

Nope. Daniel was still on my doorstep, dark brown hair shaggier than ever. With his hands still in his pockets, he asked me to let him in. Standing my ground, I folded my arms across my chest.

"Just how many frequent flyer miles do you have?" I asked incredulously.

"Enough," he said dryly, brushing hair away from his face. "Hello, Rainelle. May I come in?"

"Absolutely not. I have company."

"Of the male variety?" His eyes did a slow sweep of my nightgown-swathed body as if he could see right through it. See the hot pink of my bruised pussy, the smattering of deep purple hickeys against shocking parts of my body...

I automatically tightened the band around my waist. "That's none of your business."

"It isn't?"

"Just tell me what the hell you want," I mumbled. I glanced over my shoulder, back into the empty house. I was freaking fortunate that Selene had disappeared. The fact that she could return at any moment was the only thing making me antsy.

"I thought we were friends," he said, holding his hands up in defeat. "Can't a friend visit another friend? Spur of the moment?"

"Not when the friend is on another continent. That's not the definition of 'spur of the moment.'"

He had the nerve to look chagrined. "Well, you won't pick up the bloody phone, so what else am I supposed to do?"

"Because you were harassing me!"

He looked taken aback. "Harassing you? What the fuck?"

"No means no, Daniel. Sending Teddy fucking Bunting over to my place in Paris to, I don't know what, bully me was the last straw," I fumed, grateful for the first time that my neighbors weren't close enough to the house to watch this show out on my doorstep. Pulling Daniel inside was out of the question, for his safety. "I want nothing to do with the man. And if push comes to shove, nothing to do with you."

"The man was a mate of your father's. He's a good guy! It's not like I gave a sociopath your address!"

I glared at him. "No, because you're the sociopath."

He glared back. "This is stupid. I actually came here to tell you something important."

"Yeah? What?"

"Paisley's in the car. I never got 'round to demon-proofing this house, did I?" He gestured at the silver Mercedes in my driveway, a car I didn't notice until he did that. "You remember Paisley, right? The witch?"

From the passenger window of the car, a blonde woman waved at me. My eyes swung back to Daniel.

"Oh, hell, no! No."

He quirked a curious brow. "Why not? Rae, the least you can…"

"How'd you know I was here, anyway? Were you following me?"

"No," he replied, bracing himself against the doorjamb. "You should hide your location every time you update your Facebook status if you really want to be incognito."

"Goddamn stalker," I said under my breath.

This time, he laughed, easily brushing off the half-hearted insult. "So you don't want any protection?"

"I'm supposed to believe you came all this way to do that? Put up a ward?"

Daniel leaned in, way too close for comfort; so close our noses almost brushed.

"Let me in, Rae," he said, his voice barely a whisper. Then he straightened up abruptly, eyes wide as he stared past me, into the narrow hallway.

Mildly unnerved, I whirled around and came face to face with Selene, who looked more refreshed and revitalized than she had hours ago—before she fed.

"We have company?" she asked in a husky voice as she squeezed herself beside me.

Momentarily mute, I could only stare.

"Introduce us, Rainelle," Selene demanded, sizing Daniel up with hungry baby blues. She made no attempt of masking her attraction to him. I was once like her, judging Lawless by his cover. What a fool I was.

For his part, Daniel did an equally poor job of hiding his instant reaction to the succubus. I was instantly forgotten—

334

practically shoved aside, actually—as he drank in the sight of Selene dolled up in her ironically indecent thigh-length plaid schoolgirl skirt and transparent button-up white shirt. Obviously she decided to dress up for whoever she was just fucking. I could only hope that he, or she, was still alive after their encounter.

"Daniel, this is Selene. Selene... Daniel," I muttered. As far as I was concerned, he could have her. It would serve him right if he found out, the hard way, that she was a succubus.

What has Daniel ever done to you? my annoyingly remorseful conscience wanted to know.

Nothing. He didn't do anything. And Selene didn't do anything, either. I was just grateful that she had the foresight to shield her aura from Daniel, which made things easier for me, too. Nausea was no joke.

"It's a pleasure to meet you," Selene cooed, holding her hand out for him to (*I swear to all that is holy!*) kiss.

Rolling my eyes, I watched him do just that.

"The pleasure's all mine," he smoothly replied.

"Ooh, an Englishman. *Délicieux!*"

"I thought the French couldn't stand the English. Or is it the other way around?" I mumbled, receiving a glare from the succubus. "I was just telling Daniel to leave, so if you don't mind, Selene..."

"Leave? But why?" she wanted to know.

I shot daggers at her. "I said, it would be awesome if you could get back inside."

Selene's glare definitely turned deadly. Without taking her eyes off me, she said through clenched teeth, "There is something I must do. If you would excuse me, *cher* Daniel."

"Who's that?" Daniel asked, watching Selene storm back inside.

Her skirt rode high on her thighs, exposing the tannest skin I'd ever seen.

"I can do the breaststroke in the drool you've just deposited on my doorstep," I told him, dodging the question.

Daniel flashed me a grin that made him look a decade younger.

"Jealous, love? Don't be. You know what I think about your body."

"I can't believe I ever thought you were a gentleman," I snorted. Then, I took a deep breath and added, "Look, I think we could be friends that..."

"We are friends."

"Sure. Whatever. Anyway, about your witch friend coming here... My answer's no." I continued before he could interrupt again. "My dad didn't want any magic here. I want to respect his wishes."

"Rainelle..."

"No, Daniel. Thank you for flying out here but it was a big waste of time. Magic creeps me out and the less I'm exposed to it, the better."

His lower lip curled in disgust. "Demons are everywhere, Rae. It's mental to think a bunch of kickboxing classes and an old Indian knife are enough protection!"

"I've survived all these years, haven't I?"

Daniel bit out a curse. "You're a stubborn little thing and I pity the man who gets to call you his woman."

I fought against the smile that threatened to appear on my lips. At least that was one point Andrei and Daniel were able to agree on: I was stubborn.

"Meow to you, too."

"Oh, shut up." He softened his words by lowering his head to place a chaste kiss on my forehead. "I'll go. See you soon, then."

"Yeah. Great," I said brightly, watching him leave.

Little did he know that I was planning to do no such thing.

When I was younger, my father would take me down to the beach as often as he could. The waves would be so blue, sometimes green, and the russet sand would be hot beneath my bare feet. Houses lined the beach and many of them were huge, which made our modest two-story look like a matchbox. And I envied the people who got to wake up to the view of the beautiful beach every single morning.

I made up stories about the residents of each house. Stupid stories. Almost all of them were gooey, about queens for mothers and princesses for daughters. The high balconies became turrets of a castle, and the intricately designed rooftops became steeples. Between that and pretending the sea was overrun with mermaids, I clearly had an active imagination. And every weekend Ray Erickson took his daughter to play in the sand at the beach, I became even more jealous of the families in the big houses. They had their own private beaches, each with their own paradise.

Meanwhile, I had a crazy father and an absent mother.

Little did I know that the only reason Ray even took me to the beach was so that he could meet Teddy Bunting's wife, the witch, in secret. Nothing sordid. That wasn't Dad's style. No, he just wanted a special spell from her, one that she

337

failed to successfully cast since the trips to the beach suddenly dwindled... until I barely even saw my father.

But I was over all that now, at least that was what I constantly told myself.

At the moment, though, what I was doing was trying to ignore the fact that Selene was unobtrusively sunbathing at a distance from me, giving me the opportunity to hang with Renée and Lorenzo. She was an undercover babysitter and I hated it.

"I know that look," Ren said from her towel beside me, slathering a huge dollop of sunscreen onto Lorenzo's back. He sat between her raised knees, leaning forward so that his wife could reach every inch of his olive skin. "What's up, honey?" Ren went on.

I rubbed sunscreen onto my arms, squinting at the fading mark on my left bicep. "Just thinking." Andrei's ring glinted in the sunlight. I flipped it around my finger, hiding the ruby.

"It's obviously something bad. Tell me."

"Leave it, Ren," Lorenzo said in warning, getting to his feet when he was sure that his wife was finished.

I smiled up at him, grateful. He always seemed to sense when I wasn't in the mood to deal with Renée's pushy behavior.

"I'm just being a friend," my best friend whined, pouting adorably.

"Come on, baby. Let's take a swim." Lorenzo pulled her up, looping his arms around her waist. His green eyes glittered with mischief. "Aren't I lucky? I'm going to get the two most gorgeous girls on the beach wet."

Ren and I snorted with laughter. Lorenzo and Renée were my favorite couple because they didn't make me feel like a third wheel. But I shook my head when he reached for my hand. I wasn't going to swim today.

After giving me matching looks of concern, Lorenzo and Renée reluctantly ran down to the waves, laughing like little kids as they chased each other. Today was one of Lorenzo's rare days off and the fact that he wanted to spend it entertaining me was endearing. I made a mental note to call my friends at least once a week from then on. They deserved at least that from me. After all, they were all I really had now.

"Fuck," I murmured, appalled to feel a slow trail of tears down my cheeks. I wiped them away, glancing at Lorenzo and Renée frolicking in the waves before I turned to lie flat on my belly.

Modesty had never really been a factor in my life, so I wasn't the least bit shy about being in the ivory micro bikini Ren had insisted I wear today. The top was a little too tight around my tits but the minuscule bottom ensured minimal tan lines.

Then, a shadow fell over me, and I peeked over my shoulder.

"I am going to feed," Selene announced, and my tears were instantly forgotten.

I could practically see up her ass crack. She could probably see up mine. I instantly wished I followed my instinct and worn a one-piece; I was having a "fat" day.

"Do you think you could be a good girl for a few hours?" she continued.

"But you fed yesterday," I pointed out, absolutely horrified. The beach was jam-packed with families: fathers, mothers, and little kids. And the idea of a succubus in a polka-dot bikini on the prowl for fresh meat was not a very good element to put into the mix.

339

"What is your point?"

"That you fed yesterday."

"I have a voracious appetite, *ma petite*," she coyly retorted, eyes roaming my body, "And today, I feel like doing the fucking."

I pushed myself to my feet, and in the process, got a glimpse of my friends locked in an embrace in thigh-high water. I turned back to Selene. "What do you mean 'do' the fucking?"

She smirked, leaning forward. "Today, I will be a man and fill another woman's hot, wet cunt with my cock," she said, her voice husky. She ran her tongue along her lower lip. "I will have her suck me and I will fuck her mouth. Only when I have come and come and come will I be satisfied... for today."

I swallowed, recognizing the arousal in her eyes. "Don't kill anyone."

"That remains to be seen, *chérie*. Tell me, has my lord ever been with you as a woman?" She tilted her head to one side, the bangs that completed her bob falling on her face. "By the look on your face, I would say he has not."

"You're disgusting."

Laughing, Selene sashayed off, in search of her next victim.

My first kickboxing instructor was in the gym when I got there, and my initial impulse was to avoid him. I was about to slip past him on all fours when he looked up from his post at the front desk, where he was clicking away on a computer. It was too late.

"Rainelle?" Jared's deep voice registered surprise. He stepped around the curved desk and approached me, arms outstretched.

Inside, I was groaning as he pulled me into a hug, my gym bag between us as a barrier. I'd expected him to smell of sweat and too much Axe but the sweet scent of soap filled my nostrils instead. He probably just finished up with a class and showered before coming out front.

"Jared," I said as I pulled away, "long time."

He hadn't changed much over the years, save for getting a bit beefier. He still had his dark hair close-cropped, still had the same tattoos spiraling up his arms and disappearing into a vest, and still wore contacts that ensured there was no masking his long-lashed grey eyes.

"Indeed," he said quietly, looking down at me. "I mean, I hear things about you coming back now and then, but I've never gotten the chance to..."

"I haven't been to the gym—heck, any gym—in a little while," I interjected. It was vital to cut off what would be a dangerous conversation. How could I have forgotten that Jared worked at the Witness Fitness?

It doesn't matter, I thought fiercely. *I have a membership here and I'll be damned if I let something that happened years ago get in the way of getting my ass firm.*

"You look great," Jared asserted, giving me a small smile. "Listen, Rae, I..."

"I'm on a tight schedule, Jared. Talk later?"

I didn't wait for his answer before I turned to slink away like the coward I was. Oh, how easy it was sometimes to just pretend that my life in Sallow Bay was limited only to my family home and best friend—that my whole past here was nonexistent.

Annoyed, I decided to punish myself with a three-mile run on the treadmill. I already stretched at home. So ignoring the few people on machines around mine, I popped the earbuds of my MP3 player to my ears. Once the sound of Sick Puppies was all I could hear, I hopped on.

Once upon a time, geeky, awkward Jared Holland had been like a big brother to me. That was back when a good time for him had consisted of video games and R.L. Stine books. And then he turned eighteen and joined the army, leaving me alone. Well, as alone as a person can be with someone like Renée Marino for a best friend.

The first time he returned home, I fucked him. He was my first. Later on, just before Lorenzo came into the picture and we were reminiscing, Ren had said that Jared was proof that geeks could grow up to be gods, so she was waiting for Zuckerberg to mature properly.

For me, it wasn't just about his looks, although he was fucking edible, it was about how he'd always been a constant. He felt... right. Yeah, I wasn't all about the orgasms when I was younger. Back then I was a completely delusional idiot.

It was in the backyard of the Holland house, after a very grueling one-on-one Muay Thai 101 with Jared, that I said something I instantly wished I hadn't. Things had been awkward after we slept together, and of course, we could never go back to the brother-sister thing we had. But I made everything worse by telling Jared I loved him. And as nicely as he possibly could, he apologized for taking my virginity and told me that he loved me, too... as a sister.

"I've realized that you feel more like a sister to me, so I'm awfully sorry for popping your cherry. Now can you show me that jab again?"

Okay, I'm paraphrasing.

342

Either way, it wasn't my finest moment and when I went away to college, I cut him out my life. He eventually left the army and I eventually came back for a little while. And I had no idea how it happened, but we ended up sleeping together... again. For me, it was just convenient. He was around and I could stand to look at him. For Jared... Well, I still have no clue why he wanted to have sex with me again. And again.

Then years later, I ended up leaving and forgetting him completely. I hadn't seen him in almost two years. Now that I had, I knew that I never truly loved him, or wanted him. Never ached for him. Never yearned to feel his hands trace every inch of my skin, with his fingers, with his tongue. Never felt his absence like a disease and his presence like a cure.

Not the way I do with Andrei, whom I loved.

I was done running, both literally and figuratively. I hopped off the treadmill and grabbed a towel. My vest and yoga pants clung to my body, soaking with sweat. Wrinkling my nose, I headed for the showers, quickly shedding my clothes in the locker room. None of the stalls were occupied and I heaved a sigh of relief as I claimed one. I needed to be alone with my thoughts.

But of course, nothing ever goes according to plan for me.

"So tell me," a smooth voice said from the other side of the curtain, "would you like me to kill Mr. Holland quickly, or slowly? Or should I finish him quickly, and save the slow and painful death for Mr. Lawless?"

"Andrei?" I sputtered, pulling the curtain aside and staring at him incredulously. Even though I was shocked, it didn't lessen my response to seeing him, especially when he was all in black. "You can't be in here! These aren't communal showers."

"Ask me if I give a fuck. Tell me why Selene felt the need to call me."

"I have... no idea," I said breathlessly, the slam of the hot water against my back paling next to the flood of heat between my thighs. Steam swirled around us, its grey fingers curling and flexing. "Wait a minute. Is Selene in the gym?"

"But of course," said another male voice.

I hissed out a curse when I recognized the blond lanky guy stepping beside Andrei. He had Selene's blue eyes and was wearing a simple white tee and black running shorts.

"It's only Selene," Andrei muttered when I cowered behind the curtain again.

"Steven, my lord," the guy corrected.

"Whatever."

God, this was weird. I poked my head around the curtain, staring at Selene, Steven, as if I'd never seen a blond guy before.

"Thank you, Selene. You may leave us," Andrei continued, and Selene instantly disappeared. It was a good thing, too. If any woman came in to shower, they'd think I was some kind of whore, entertaining two men in a public place. This was my gym.

"Well?" Andrei's voice could've cut through diamonds.

I let the curtain fall away. "Well, what?"

"Did I not tell you not to see that hunter?"

"He came to see me, Andrei," I said quickly. "And Selene actually knew who he was? What a fucking snitch. It was nothing. I chased him away and..."

"You're hoping I fuck you in this shower, aren't you?"

I was all screwed up in the head. One minute he was mad about Daniel and Jared, and the next, he was teasing me with filthy words. His hard, menacing tone was making my sensitive nub throb, my belly growing taut in anticipation. When he was mad, his eyes took on a stormy color. Or they flickered a strange red. They were dark and stormy right then.

"Won't they call you a slut?" He folded his arms across his broad chest, regarding my naked body with hunger in his eyes. "When you're pushed up against the wall with my cock fucking you, won't they call you a slut?"

"Probably," I whimpered, my breathing erratic.

"You're not getting my cock," he spat, stepping even closer to me. The ceramic floor of the shower stall was elevated from the ground but I was still nowhere near his height. Towering over me, he reached out and turned the water off. "I can smell your pussy. Why are you so wet when you're not getting my cock?"

Desire thrummed in my veins. My pulse raced. I desperately needed to be joined with him.

"Andrei," I whispered.

"Touch yourself."

"But…"

"Close your eyes," he said sharply, "and touch yourself. Or I will kill Mr. Holland. Decapitate him, perhaps." The hardness in his eyes said that he was serious. "Or turn him into a eunuch."

Instead of fighting him, I shut my eyes and cupped my breasts. They ached. The tips felt like hard pebbles and I pulled them, pulling them with trembling fingers.

I heard Andrei's heavy breathing and knew that I wasn't the only one turned on. The sound made every inch of my body hum with desire. My touch became more frantic.

345

Could I honestly climax just by tugging my nipples? Was I that sensitive?

"Slower," Andrei grunted.

This was ridiculous. Anyone could stroll into the showers after sweating it off in the gym. They could find me fondling my breasts for a man. And the image only made me wetter.

I trailed a hand down my belly, traced my navel. I reached lower, and circled my clitoris with my thumb, wanting to prolong the torture. Instead, I went for a home run and cupped my mound.

I shuddered as I stuck my forefinger inside the wet heat and pressed down on my clit.

"Ah," I sighed, dipping another finger inside me. My eyes squeezed tighter as my inner muscles clamped around my fingers. "Oh, Andrei."

"Yes," he groaned. "Fuck yourself for me."

The knot in my belly grew tighter as I came closer and closer to tipping over the edge. The squelching sound my fingers made as they thrust into my pussy seemed to echo in the empty shower room. I was panting, gasping for air that seemed pungent with the scent of my wet, inflamed sex.

"Come for me, baby."

Maybe it was the way Andrei's voice grew soft, reverent, as if he was in awe of what I was doing. Maybe it was the final rub of my swollen clit. Maybe it was the way he rasped the endearment I found so sexy on his tongue. Or maybe it was the combination of all three. Because before I knew it, I came with a scream, eyes still closed as I surrendered to the intense sensation I was creating.

I leaned against the wall, catching my breath and opening my eyes.

346

"Disgusting," someone rebuked. "I'll shower at home."

Through heavy-lidded eyes, I realized that that someone was Mrs. Simon. She was turning to leave, silver grey head bowed as she quickly scuttled out the otherwise empty room.

I was absolutely mortified that my fourth-grade teacher just caught me masturbating.

So that was my cruel and unusual punishment.

This was not my dream.

"Andrei!" I called out, picking my way around the various treadmills and elliptical trainers in my way. "Where are you, you heartless bastard?"

"Shower," he called back.

I had never been in Witness Fitness when it was empty. The gym equipment seemed ethereal without people using them. I quickly skirted past them all and headed through the locker room and into the shower.

"Hilarious prank this afternoon," I said dryly, finding him with a towel wrapped snugly around his waist. "The seventy-year-old woman that discovered me with my fingers up my cunt could have had a heart attack." Despite my annoyance, I exploded with laughter when the horror wore off. After all, my satisfaction was great.

"Prank?" Andrei arched a brow. "I don't do pranks, Rainelle. You forget who I am. Now let's take a shower."

"I'm sleeping. I don't need one."

"Suit yourself," he said as he let his towel fall.

At the sight, my mouth immediately dried up.

"I'm in Moscow right now. It's understandably cold."
He stepped into a stall and the water came on.

I couldn't resist the pull to follow him inside. Didn't want to resist it.

It was cramped with the both of us inside but that didn't matter. Andrei pulled me flush against him, kissing me fiercely. His hand gripped the back of my neck and my arms were slung around his.

"What are you doing to me?" Andrei's voice was pained.

I broke away from him, searching his eyes for something. I shook my head and went down on my knees before him, sliding my hands down the sinews of muscle that made up his powerful thighs. Hot water beat down on me but my vision was clear. Andrei's shaft was an angry red, the tip pointing to the high heavens. I am always fascinated by the uncut head, the thrumming web of veins, and the sheer size of it. It always seemed that I would never be able to take all of him.

"Rae," he said thickly, clutching a clump of my hair in his hand. "You are the most beautiful creature I have ever seen."

"Considering the fact that you're old as fuck and have been to different dimensions, I am humbled by the compliment," I murmured, taking him in my hand.

He chuckled, the laughter dying on his lips when I took him into my mouth. I held him at the base, using my other hand to guide him inside my mouth. Its realness hit me when I tasted his hot flesh. It was only a dream, wasn't it? But it was real, for the both of us.

Andrei began to thicken in my mouth, his hold on my hair becoming unbearably painful. He pushed forward, hitting the back of my throat. He wasn't even all the way in but I was greedy for more of him. Wanted him to be rough, to take.

"Yes," he breathed, releasing my hair and sliding his hand down the back of my head and to my neck. "Shit, yes."

He pumped into my mouth, his thrusts short and quick. I cupped his balls, rubbing the swaying nodules with the pads of my fingers.

"So." Thrust. "Fucking." Thrust. "Amazing."

I couldn't look away from his face. There was something carnal about looking into his eyes as his cock drove past my lips and into my mouth… something incredible about making him lose his control so greatly, so intensely.

Andrei's sapphire eyes were hazy with overwhelming hunger as his hips moved faster, forcing him to plunge even deeper.

"Coming," he groaned, my lower lip pressed against the base of his shaft, tipping him over the precipice.

The hot gush of his semen filled my mouth and I swallowed every drop, savoring the salty taste. His breathing became erratic. Then he pulled me to my feet and crushed his mouth against mine, tasting himself on my tongue.

"Your turn," he whispered against my lips.

I began to protest, wanting him to know that, much as I adored his talented tongue, it was his dick I wanted inside me just then. The shower fizzled into nothingness and then we were in my bedroom in Paris.

The bedspread was gone. A large expanse of white sheets beckoned in its place. Andrei gently deposited me atop them and I breathed a sigh of contentment. When he was sweet like this, I could almost believe in romance. But then, more often than not, I quickly recover myself and beg for his roughness, his darkness.

"Andrei," I gasped, heat bubbling low in my belly.

He was kissing his way up the inside of my thighs, hot, open-mouthed kisses that made every hair on my body stand at attention.

Tension knotted in my groin when he kissed his way to my clitoris. Hands grasping my hips, he blew cool air on the folds of my labia. I was drenched, bucking against him, aching for his tongue.

He inhaled deeply. "This is the most erotic smell in the world, Rae," he declared, his voice raspy. "Do you know what the scent of your arousal does to me? It drives me fucking mad. You want me to eat you out?"

"Yes," I hissed, grabbing a handful of the cotton sheets. "Please, please, please."

"Tell me what I want to know." He massaged the outer lips of my opening. Slowly, teasingly.

I huffed out a sharp breath. "You know you're the only one," I whispered. "I only want you. Need you."

"Look at me."

With great effort, I propped myself up on my elbows and stared at his face between my legs.

"I belong to you. I am yours," he said softly, placing a reverent kiss on my hipbone. "And you, Rae, are mine. Now, watch me tongue-fuck your beautiful pink pussy."

Dear God!

The second Andrei latched himself onto my center, I lost all sense of being. I was liquid. I was a cloud of smoke. I was nothing. He licked up my slit, exerting the perfect amount of pressure that made me lock my thighs around him.

"Good," I moaned, feeling him thumb the lips of my sex apart.

He plunged his tongue into me, his nose thumping against my distended little nub. I writhed, screamed, fought against the pleasure. His tongue came out, flattening against my clit. Pressing against it. Then he drew it into his mouth and my back arched.

"Can't," I murmured. I gasped when one of his fingers breached my moistened folds and slipped into me. "Ah. Don't stop!"

Andrei knew what made me tick, what drove me half demented. He wielded that power like a sword and I let him. There was no other way.

I love you.

"You taste so damn good," he groaned, sliding his probing digits in and out, in and out—until finally, tremors of sensual bliss inside me shattered, and I came long and hard in Andrei's mouth.

Everything inside me was liquid and I was vaguely aware of Andrei placing a soft kiss on my clit as he held me through the aftershocks.

My eyes fluttered closed.

When I opened them, it was morning and I needed to pee. I barely made it to the bathroom. And once I saw the dry discharge coating the inside of my thighs, I decided to slip into the shower.

Sex with Andrei put me in a great mood and I even felt less antagonistic toward Selene. I wasn't going to question her comings and goings, wasn't even going to probe her about sex as a guy. In fact, I was thinking of introducing her to *Game of Thrones*. She would probably appreciate the elaborate sets and costumes used in the show, since she was billions of years old and George R.R. Martin did mention that he based some of the story's setting on the Middle Ages.

So after throwing an old pair of sweats on, I bounded downstairs.

"Selene?" I yelled.

The house was eerily quiet. Instantly, I put my guard up. After yesterday's sexercise, I was a little sore, but it was nothing I couldn't tolerate.

"Selene?"

I stood by the entrance of the living room... and froze.

Blood, thick and burgundy, was congealing on the cream carpeting. There was so much of it that I doubt it would be possible for the donor to still be alive and kicking.

Someone was killed in my house, I thought, my mind swirling. *Selene killed someone in my fucking house!*

I was going to kill her.

"Selene!"

"Rainelle," said a familiar voice.

I spun around and bit down on my bottom lip, instantly tasting copper.

"Teddy," I whispered, eyes widening. "What the hell are you doing here?"

He had shaved the ridiculous moustache he'd been sporting the last time I'd seen him but his head was still a gleaming egg. This time, he wore a dark suit. Unease settled in my belly. He resembled a staid mortician.

"Your father would be disappointed, Rainelle," he said quietly, a shadow crossing his face. "He would be ashamed to call you his daughter."

Anger bubbled inside me. "Bastard," I spat. "How dare you break into my house and say that?"

"How dare I?" he snapped, moving toward me.

I instinctively stepped back.

"Raymond was one of my closest friends. I made promises to him, promises I had intended to keep. Until I found out that his daughter—a girl who called me her uncle—is willingly having relations with demons!"

All the breath rushed from my chest. I stepped in something warm and slimy. It took me a few seconds to register that it was the blood. I jumped a mile.

"Get out of my house!" Each word forced through gritted teeth.

Teddy's wheat-colored eyes were menacing. "You share your bed with a demon," he went on, completely ignoring me. "And not just any demon." He pulled out a gun. "The king of all the incubi. Rainelle, you sicken me."

Teddy pointed the gun at me. It was easily recognizable—a Beretta. Lovely model. And that was probably a silencer extending from it, wasn't it?

"Then I guess you know about Selene," I speculated, resigned to my fate. "Where is she?"

Teddy laughed, a cold, empty sound that sent shivers down my spine. "The succubus?" he sneered. "That's her blood you're standing in."

Chapter 22

Blood and I had never really been great friends. But after the Damien Ivanov incident, my tolerance for the crimson liquid became nil. My tolerance for the man standing before me was at the exact same level and that was what propelled me right to him.

Teddy's hesitation to shoot me was obvious, which was why he didn't react with a bullet to my head in the split second that I decided to become a human cannonball. We fell to the floor in a messy heap and since he had at least twenty pounds on me, my only advantage was the element of surprise.

And with all the strength I possessed, my elbow connected with his throat, momentarily stunning him, and then I took that opportunity to scramble to my feet and sprint to the front door. All kinds of frantic thoughts were running through my mind: that Teddy was indeed a sociopath, that he just couldn't have killed a billion-year-old demon without breaking a sweat, and that there was no fucking way I was going to let him kill me.

The front door was wide open and I all but launched myself through it… and came up against a wall—a wall that was not there.

Panic skated through me. My brain took a while to register that I couldn't get through the door because something invisible was stopping me, keeping me inside.

"I had hoped I would not have to resort to violence, Rainelle," Teddy croaked from behind me.

I spun around to face him, anger sizzling in my veins. "What have you done?"

"A simple spell to keep you from doing something… stupid."

"Hunters aren't that powerful. Only witches could do something like this." I craned my neck to look over his shoulder, anticipating his secret sidekick of the occult loitering in the background. But I suddenly got the sinking feeling that I was alone with Teddy.

"Ah, but I am both," Teddy stated matter-of-factly, rubbing the column of his neck. "You're making it difficult for me not to want to hurt you."

"What," I snarled through clenched teeth, "do you want from me?"

He smiled this time, a sly, wolfish grin that looked more like a grimace than anything else. "Your cooperation."

"Well, would you cooperate with a big fuck like you if you were me?"

The smile left his face. "You don't seem to grasp the seriousness of the situation, Rainelle. You don't know what I am."

And with that declaration, invisible hands began to choke the life out of me. They brought me to my knees, tightening around my neck. They were making it hard to

355

swallow, hard to breathe. Everything inside me begged for oxygen, for the gift of respiration.

The unseen hands released me and I turned to one side and emptied my stomach.

"Apology accepted," Teddy said quietly.

I ached. I seethed. I yearned to end his life slowly, painfully, and creatively.

"I hope my father can see you now for what you are," I choked out, hating the sour taste in my mouth.

"Same to you," he snarled, the venom in his voice so tangible it could've been lethal. "You will come with me and you will do as you're told, when you're told. Do I make myself clear, Rainelle?"

Go to hell, bastard.

I wasn't going to make this easy for him. He was going to have to drag me away kicking and screaming, and if that just pissed him off, he was more than welcome to kill me. Whatever it was that he wanted from me, he was delusional if he thought I'd roll over and just give it to him.

"You will do this, my girl," he said gently, "because if I can successfully take on a demon as old as your succubus friend, rest assured that a demon king will be just as easy."

I went still. *Andrei.* Tears pricked my eyes and I furiously swiped them away, glancing down at the ring shimmering on my finger. It was selfish of me to keep it on, to convey all my fears and desperation into it and, consequently, to Andrei. The selfless thing to do would be to take it off, to make sure he didn't find me. But that would have been futile. He would always find me, regardless of whether or not I wore his ring.

"Okay," I whispered. "I'll cooperate."

"Good girl. Now close your eyes, Rainelle. Everything, and I do mean everything, will be fine."

Drowsiness besieged me. Each of my eyelids felt like it was carrying an anvil that was weighing them down. My final thought before blackness swirled around me was of Andrei. He had the most beautiful eyes... like the sea... only they were mine to look at.

I was in Culebra, standing on the beach and watching the waves roll to the shoreline. Wind whipped my hair but the Puerto Rican sun heated my skin and warmed my blood. He was coming, wasn't he? I wanted him to come and he was somewhere near—so close, I could feel him.

On the horizon? I thought, shielding my eyes and staring out into the wide expanse of shimmering azure.

"Baby." His voice came from behind me and I immediately felt at ease. The weight on my shoulders, whatever it had been, was lifted.

I turned to look at him, to be reassured by his icy blue eyes. But they were stormy, threatening.

He gripped my shoulders, his fingers painfully firm. "Where are you hurt? What the fuck is going on? Who has you?"

"This is my dream?" I sighed heavily, inhaling the sea breeze. "Yes. This is my dream."

Andrei cupped my chin, narrowing his eyes as he looked into mine. "Dilated. You've been drugged. Fuck, fuck, fucking hell."

Why was he so worried? We were in a virtual paradise together. The sky was blue; the sea was even bluer. Didn't he like us being together like this? There were no sadistic fallen angels, no idiotic demons planning a coup d'état, no flirtatious succubi, no pushy hunters... Nothing and no one awful to contend with. No one but us.

"Oh, you smell great," I murmured, burying my face in his solid chest. His natural musk was familiar and comforting. It wasn't even arousing... just nice. Pleasant. Lovely.

"Rae, listen to me." His voice was softer. He forced my head up. "You are in a warehouse in Sallow Bay. The one near the abandoned industrial site. Do you remember how you got there?"

"I remember how good you are. So, so good. How can you be so good? It's bad to be so good."

Andrei cursed under his breath. "I'm trying not to be mad at you."

I laughed... hysterically. "You're almost always mad at me."

"Not this time, *mea domina*. Please. Make yourself remember. Who is in there with you?"

"Come to me," I said breathlessly, putting my hand over his, which was on my cheek. He always came, even when I didn't want him to.

He looked pained. "I can't breach the ward. You have to wake up. You have to come to me."

I pulled his hand back and kissed the inside, skimming my lips over the calluses there. "This is one of the reasons I love you, Lord Andrei Anghelescu. You make me believe I can do anything." I switched to an open-mouthed kiss, savoring the taste of his skin. "I... love... you. You're my king."

He stepped back as if I'd stung him but his hand was still in mine. "You are not yourself, Rainelle. You don't know what you're saying."

"Oh, but I do love you," I beamed, and I briefly wondered if that had been the weight on my shoulders. The words sounded amazing out loud, and to the right person. "And I love this island! Catch me, Andrei. If you love me back, you'd better catch me!"

Before he could blink, I pulled away from him and ran, *Pulling up the hem of my wedding dress?* No matter. It was blue lace, the strangest thing I had ever seen. Laughter escaped my lips, and still I ran.

But Andrei wasn't chasing me and a dull ache in my head grew to a sharp and painful throbbing, freezing me to the spot. The island fizzled away and I desperately wanted to hold on to it, freeze it in time, to stay there forever.

Unfortunately, I blinked myself awake, groggily taking in my surroundings.

Every inch of my body hurt... even my fucking hair follicles. Memories sharpened and faded, memories that made my head hurt some more. Red... there was a lot of red in my recollection. Had I cut myself? I was clumsy sometimes. Teddy was at my house. *But why?* And where did Selene disappear to? She was obligated to tell me when she left me alone, wasn't she?

Where am I?

I wasn't in my bed. Heck, I wasn't in a room. Not really.

Propped up against a wall with concrete floor, I was in what could only be described as a cell. Directly in front of me was the exit: a steel door that was stainless and looked impenetrable. A rusty wrought iron bed was pushed against the far wall, a chipped toilet bowl was beside it, and adjacent to that was a tiny sink. The steady drip, drip of the leaking faucet was already beginning to grate on my nerves.

I craned my neck and found that the minute window above me was the source of the single ray of light in the room. Breathing in deeply, I tried to get to my feet. Pain instantly bit through my wrists and panic seeped into my blood.

Chained.

I was chained to the wall like a dog!

Breathe, Rae, the voice in my head gently instructed. *Do not panic.*

Easier said than done.

Impulse took over and I tugged at the restraints, despite the knowledge that it was useless, that I was only going to end up hurting myself. My brain calculated this fact but my heart was too frantic, too stubborn to listen. Instead, it pumped blood faster and adrenaline spiked in my veins.

I tasted bile… and forced myself not to gag. *Epic fail.*

Tipping to one side, I heaved loudly. Nothing came out. The rumbling in my stomach told me why.

Don't cry. Do not cry, you pussy. You'll figure this out. You will. Just… don't… cry.

I squeezed my eyes shut and breathed. I tried to block out everything but the sound of my heavy breathing, and slowly, my memories flooded back to me. The blood on my carpet… Teddy and his insulting behavior… his magic… and Andrei invading my dream.

My eyes flew open as a renewed strength coursed through me. There was no time for weakness. Teddy was deranged and knew too much about my life. The thought that he knew who Andrei was all along, and had faked ignorance when he dropped by my penthouse in Paris, crossed my mind.

Oh, he deserved an Oscar for his performance as a concerned family friend. If he was some fanatic puritan who felt personally slighted by my relations with demons, there was no knowing what he was capable of.

"Theodore fucking Bunting!" I screeched at the top of my lungs, ignoring the idea of self-preserving docility. My voice was hoarse and it hurt so much to even breathe out a syllable. "I will fucking kill you, you psycho bastard!" The heavy iron chains dug into my wrists, eating at my skin. "I don't care what voodoo shit you've got going on. I will crush you! I will. I will!"

Minutes of silence passed. Tears made a salty path down my cheeks. Everything ached. And I was half-deranged with hunger.

Finally, the door was pushed open.

I steeled myself to face Teddy once again, the rage I felt bubbling inside me. My hatred for this man was indescribable.

"I swear, Rainelle, I didn't know."

Daniel closed the door behind him, leaning against it for support. We stared at each other in silence after that, until he finally got the balls to elaborate.

"This isn't the way things were supposed to go," he muttered, approaching me. "Teddy said he'd just put you to sleep and wait for the demon king to walk into the trap. But now… Oh God, he hurt you." He crouched beside me, reaching out to touch my neck.

"Don't," I choked out, leaning away from him. After screaming myself ragged, it surprisingly hurt less and less to speak. "What trap?"

"Why would you do this, Rae? Willingly succumb to an incubus?" he wanted to know, ignoring my question.

"Hunters are immune to incubi so don't even pretend to be a poor, beguiled victim. You have hunter blood in you, much as you want to pretend otherwise."

"What I do with my life is none of your business!"

"It isn't?" he snarled, putting his face in mine. I couldn't believe I had ever been attracted to him, even for a second. "This entire time, you've bleated on about how you wanted nothing to do with the supernatural, yet your sex life was just that! You've spat on your father's grave a thousand times and you seem incredibly chuffed with yourself!"

I spat at him, although the spit that came out was embarrassingly pitiful. Anger sparked in his hazel eyes and he grabbed my chin, forcing me to look at him.

"My mum was tormented by one," he declared, reaching out to swipe a handful of my hair out of my face with his free hand. "Oh yes, Rainelle, we are more alike than you know. Only difference is, while your mother was a whore who ended up wanting seconds and thirds, my mum was... taken against her will... every single fucking night." He stared into my eyes. "No one believed her, and it was just her and me. I saw it once, the monster. But I was weak and couldn't do shit to protect her. All I could do was throw up whenever it was in the house." He paused. "Mum killed herself the day after my eighteenth birthday. Finally, she was free of the demon then, so I couldn't hate her for that. Your father believed me. He let me know what I was. Who I am."

"Daniel, I'm sorry about your mother but the demon king I know isn't..."

"Evil?" Daniel sighed heavily. "All demons are evil incarnate, Rae. But incubi? They're an especially perverted kind," he said slowly, as if he were talking to a child. "They violate humans, kill them with the most primal of acts. They

362

barter souls for a one-off sexual experience. They spill their seed into women and increase their warped population." He gave me a sad look. "And you're fucking one—their king, no less."

"What trap?" I repeated, my voice shaky.

Daniel regarded me for a long time before saying almost gleefully, "Your demon is outside. Once Teddy and Paisley have completed their spell, the ward will drop and *voilà!* He's ours."

"You're an idiot," I snarled, pulling at my restraints. "Andrei will kill all three of you in one breath." I changed tactic. "If you let me go, I can make him let you go, Daniel. What do you say?"

His eyes narrowed. "As long as we have you, it will be perfectly harmless. I'm still trying to understand how you've gotten a fucking demon so pussy-whipped." He shook his head ruefully. "You've practically domesticated the creature."

"He's not an 'it', you cocksucker," I fumed. "He's more of a man than you could ever hope to be and when he's decapitating you, he'll be the last man you'll see."

Daniel laughed in my face. "Be good or you won't get your early supper."

My stomach growled, clearly excited to hear his annoyingly English terminology for something it so desperately wanted. Daniel laughed again, holding up a Tupperware container I didn't notice he brought inside with him.

"It's probably a bit rank for someone of your rich palate," he confessed, removing the lid, "but I guarantee it's better than anything old Ted wanted to feed you." He picked up a plastic spork and dug it into the mushy-looking gunk swimming in a little soup. "Ramen noodles," he clarified,

363

catching my look of disgust. "I hope you like chicken?" He loaded the spork with noodles and brought it to my mouth.

Defiance and hunger fought for dominance; hunger won. I parted my lips and allowed him to feed me, all the while seething inside. Everyone from my father's past was worthy of my wrath—Teddy, Lauren, and now, Daniel. Nothing was as it seemed with them. And when I really thought about it, I hadn't pushed hard enough to cut them all out of my life.

It was ironic that half of the few people I trusted were demons I was taught to fear and despise. Hunters protected people from demons... but who protected people from them?

"That's good, Rae," Daniel was saying, and I looked down to find the lunchbox empty. Daniel picked up a bottle of Gatorade, uncapping it and putting it to my lips. "I probably should've given this to you first. Ted said you were vomiting."

When I chugged the drink down, Daniel rose, smoothing the front of his jeans. He gathered the empty container and turned on his heel to leave.

"Wait!" I called out.

He paused, not bothering to turn around and look at me.

"I... This won't work, Daniel," I said in a rush. "The king doesn't like me as much as you think he does. I'm just a toy. Disposable. He won't care what happens to me and you'll all end up dead."

"Then why has he been trying to get in here for the past eight hours?" Then he left the room, slamming the heavy door behind him.

For a few seconds, I stared at the wall and then took in a deep breath. I had to do the one thing I could to help Andrei.

I had to sleep.

Chapter 23

It was scary how easy it was for me to fall asleep, especially under such circumstances. The dream was hazy, and I figured it was because I wasn't in a deep sleep yet. Grey mist drifted around me, its ghost hands caressing my skin. There was no fixed setting and I began to panic, wondering if that meant that Andrei wouldn't come. He didn't need to be asleep to slip into my head, I knew. But if he was busy, there was no way he could multitask and just drop by.

I called out his name, the sound of my voice echoing back to me. Then silence.

That damn silence drove me half insane with anxiety.

At any moment, Daniel, or Teddy, or the blonde witch named after a flowery girly pattern, would come in and wake me up and then everything would be screwed. Of course, I was screwed either way, because there was no light at the end of this fucked-up tunnel.

Andrei, please, please, please show up.

"Rae."

His voice came from above me, behind me, inside me... around me. It was the strangest thing and yet, the most reassuring. His voice made me feel like nothing could ever harm me, like world peace could be achieved if he just kept talking.

And I was in danger of sounding like a character out of a Nicholas Sparks book.

"That fucker Teddy broke into my house and claims he actually killed a billion-year-old succubus, but how is that even possible?" I said to the fog. "Then there's the little fact that he has magic, which is impossible because he's a hunter, not a warlock, right? You were so right about Daniel. I am going to enjoy fucking him up."

I sucked in a huge gulp of air after my spiel, squinting in the grey to see the one person in my life I could trust implicitly, wholeheartedly.

"Have they hurt you?" Andrei's voice was no more than a harsh growl.

"It doesn't matter, Andrei. If Teddy really killed Selene..."

"He didn't. But I am going to kill him. How many hunters do I have to get through?"

"There's Teddy and Daniel, plus their witch sidekick, Paisley." And before he could cut me off, I told him everything I knew so far. It was obvious that they drugged me, so most of what I remembered was still frustratingly fuzzy. But what Teddy and his posse were planning for Andrei was what mattered.

Daniel's confidence that they would trap a demon king that had been around for-fucking-ever worried me. But there was no possible way to do that, was there? They were either suicidal or delusional—or both. Right?

"I want to see you," I breathed, mentally telling the mist to go away.

"You can't. You're not ready."

366

"Not ready?"

"Do you remember what you said to me earlier? In your dream?"

This made me pause. Everything that had happened before I stirred from my drug-induced sleep came to me in bits and pieces. Pissed off, I vowed that today would be the day I killed for the first time. But I always thought it would be a demon I'd end up killing. I guess life was funny that way.

"What did I say?" I asked, after racking my brain for a few minutes and coming up empty.

"Rae, when I come in, I want you to stay the fuck out of my way. Can you promise that?"

"What did I say?" I mindlessly repeated the question.

Silence stretched into eternity, but time pass differently when you're asleep.

Until, at last, Andrei's faraway voice said, "I want you to be awake when you see my true form. Then you can decide if you meant those words or not."

A shiver tickled my skin. I didn't know what to be more apprehensive about: the fact that I was going to finally see him for what he was, or that roofies apparently made me chatty.

"Someone is waking you up now, Rainelle, and the ward is being lifted," Andrei intoned.

Sure enough, my dream was dying away, and I found myself clinging to it with fervor. Because once I woke up, everything would change.

Blonde, blue-eyed, and elfin, Paisley could've passed off as an angel. Unfortunately, she could also pass off as Damien Ivanov's little sister.

She was hunched up beside me, tongue sticking out in concentration as she began to unshackle my wrists, picking the locks with tiny bobby pins.

"Why can't you use your precious magic?" I muttered, wincing as the metal only became tighter before it got loose.

"Because it's exactly that, precious," she replied in a lilting voice. Of course, she had to be a dainty English flower. "You have two minutes to use the loo and then we should leave. Just because I won't waste my magic setting you free, doesn't mean I'll hesitate to set you alight."

I glanced at the toilet. "The loo. Right. Obviously a euphemism for shit bucket." But I wasn't going to look a gift horse in the mouth. My bladder was full and it was making things dangerously uncomfortable for me.

"Get up." Paisley stepped back, a safe distance away from me, watching me unsteadily get to my feet and limp to the toilet. I wondered if Teddy had warned her that I was feral.

"You know," I told her when I was done, "back in the day, you would've been the one worrying about me barbecuing your skinny little ass."

She huffed, combing her fingers through her perfect flaxen mane before wordlessly grabbing me and tugging me through the door. Invisible bonds had snaked around my wrists, making any attempt at throttling the bitch impossible. It didn't make any difference; I was still feeling lethargic. I could barely shuffle forward, let alone go Chuck Norris on her ass and give her a roundhouse kick.

I froze once we were outside the door, instantly recognizing the expansive building we were in. Everyone in the

Bay knew the old, abandoned climate-controlled Winkler Warehouse. It was huge, isolated, and rumored to have been the personal icebox of a serial killer during the seventies. Solely made up of brick and steel, no one really remembered what exactly the storage space had been there for, save for the fact that it was owned by the Winklers.

So yeah, now I was being kept in this veritable haunted house.

Paisley moved to stand in front of me. "I have to ask you something," she said, making me look at her.

It was on the tip of my tongue to tell her where she could shove her questions but her look of genuine curiosity stopped me.

"What is it?"

She was wringing her hands now, looking over her shoulder at the bleak, empty space behind her before turning back to me. "The demon," she whispered. "Are you its sex slave?"

I stared at her, grinding my molars. "No, I'm not his slave."

"Then... you're with him of your own volition? Why?"

I couldn't believe we were having this conversation. I couldn't believe we were having it now.

"Because being in love with someone means you can overlook a whole lot of crap," I murmured, humoring her. "Even if that crap just happens to be the fact that he's a demon lord. There's a reason they say love is blind."

Paisley's blue gaze scorched me. "Does he love you?"

Good question.

I didn't know if demons were capable of love. Lust, yes. Anger, definitely. Jealousy, hell, yeah! But love? That was a different story. I knew that Andrei cared about me, cared about what happened to me. I knew that he didn't want to be without me, that he wanted only me.

But that didn't equate to love, and that was why, I suspected, being in love with him was going to destroy me.

"You don't have to tell me. I can't judge you," Paisley said softly. She glanced over her shoulder once more, then gave me a meaningful look. "Teddy doesn't want to kill him, Rainelle. Daniel doesn't know this but..."

"Paisley."

At the sound of her name leaving Teddy's mouth, Paisley visibly stiffened, her eyes pleading with me to be quiet. I didn't understand her... at all. She had been about to tell me what Teddy really wanted, and I had no idea why.

"Thank you for bringing her out. Daniel needs help in the office upstairs." Teddy jerked his head upward, bringing my attention to the high ceiling and strip of walk space above us. "Be ready, my dear. We've come too far for you to... make new friends." He fixed me with a pointed stare.

The witch sprinted away without giving me a second glance. Then I was alone with a psychopath. A psychopath who was wearing a ridiculous black robe, which was probably supposed to make him look like he regularly practiced the dark arts before dinner, but only made him look ridiculous.

"You do know I didn't mean to hurt you, right? Rainelle," Teddy confessed, hands behind his back as he approached me. He flashed me a fake smile. "Raymond was a good friend. You were like a daughter to me, and to Josephine."

I looked away, seething. I had never been so bloodthirsty but it was impossible not to imagine the many ways I would like to kill Theodore Bunting... and make him my first kill.

"Look at me when I'm talking to you."

Without touching me, he jerked my head in his direction. Magic. He practically sparkled with the stuff. I realized that the oddity of his power was what scared me. He couldn't possibly be both a hunter and a warlock. Witches were born with their power, passing it down to the next generation by blood, and to my knowledge, hunters never had any in their bloodlines.

"If everything goes according to plan, you will walk out of this building." Teddy's voice broke into my thoughts. "If not, well… that's what you get for sleeping with the enemy."

"Fuck you."

"Sorry, what was that?"

"Fuck you!"

He smiled devilishly. "I thought so." With a casual flick of his wrist, he brought me to my knees again, choking the life out of me.

This time, I felt something compress my lungs, sucking all the air out of me. I couldn't scream. But I wouldn't have wanted to, even if I could. I wasn't going to give him the satisfaction. And when black spots peppered the back of my eyelids, I vowed that if I didn't kill him in this life, I would in the next one. Or the one after that.

God, please make it quick.

Air rushed back into my lungs just as Daniel and Paisley appeared. Daniel pulled me to my feet, dragging me to the center of the space, facing the wide steel door. I leaned against him, catching my breath, grateful for the gulps of life-sustaining oxygen.

To Andrei, the scene would probably shock him because it looked like Daniel was embracing me, if one could ignore the fact that my wrists were awkwardly restrained. We were the ones caught off guard, however, by the explosion in the far wall.

Brick and metal flew everywhere, throwing us to the ground, dust billowing in its wake. Someone screamed. Paisley. I tried to crawl away from Daniel but he grabbed my ankle, dragging me back toward him. Protection, of course. He needed to be around me. Andrei wouldn't hurt him if there was the slightest probability that he could hurt me in the process.

So I kicked him with all my might, catching him in the face and scrambling to my feet. For some reason, the invisible rope around my wrists was gone. And so, on shaky feet, I stood up and scanned the room, my heart racing a mile a minute.

Teddy was nowhere to be found, but Paisley…

I cupped my palm over my mouth, swallowing a scream.

I want you to see my true form…

I tasted bile and gulped it back down, refusing to empty my stomach for the second time that day. And it had everything to do with the beast looming over a cowering Paisley. She was going to die and there was nothing I could do. I was rooted to the spot, my vocal cords useless.

He took up a hell of a lot of space. As a human, he was big. As a demon, he was immeasurable. Hovering high above us, talon-tipped black wings that spanned the width of the room jutted out of his massive back. Wild, jet-black hair flowed from his scalp down the middle of his back—his only feature that I was familiar with. From behind, his body rippled with huge bulky muscles, ones that looked as though they were made for destruction, under his reddish leathery skin.

And that tail…

Prehensile, my biology teacher's voice said in my head.

Yes, it was flexible… and could probably pick me up. Right then, it was twisting about, actually whipping about like a lion's tail. Wrath radiated from his every pore… wrath that was unequivocally directed at the scared-shitless woman in front of him.

And behind him.

Because I was scared… out of my fucking mind!

Andrei released an unholy sound that echoed throughout the room, and then reached for Paisley, picking her up as if she were as insignificant as a piece of lint. In fact, she was a dot compared to his massive size. And when he began to squeeze, began to crush her bones in one hand, all she managed to do was let out a strangled cry... before she bled out and became but a bloody crumpled chunk of skin and bones.

I squeezed my eyes shut, willing myself to fight the nausea. But there was so much blood. So much red. So much…

He whipped his entire body around, his wings ripping through the walls during the sudden movement. I stumbled backward, tripping over debris and landing on my backside. Icy fear relentlessly gripped me and it seemed that there was no way I could free myself from it.

Dear God.

Bright red eyes burned into mine, searched my soul, and seemingly found some foothold there. I tried to focus on them, focus on their familiarity. But my eyes wandered to the tall, pointed horns that were protruding from his forehead. They were visually striking. They looked menacing.

Andrei stared at me, the features of his raw, red face impassive. His claw-like hands hung at his sides, glistening with Paisley's blood. His extensive chest was heaving with every breath he took. He stood still, his ominous stare never wavering.

I'm not afraid of you. Craning my neck to look up at him, I sent Andrei that single thought as I took one step in his direction.

But you are, Rainelle. I can feel it. His voice came back, clear in my head.

Surprised, I faltered. And that was when the entire room suddenly lit up. I spun around, squinting through the dust that still had not completely settled, and focusing on the lit candles that ran along the remaining walls of the warehouse.

Behind me, Andrei growled, the low sound bouncing off the walls and piercing my eardrums. Teddy was chanting loudly, the smell of burning herbs suddenly filling the air. My eyes were instantly drawn to the ground, to the pentagram that held Andrei captive. It was written in chalk into the concrete and I wondered then how I missed it. But that didn't really matter. What mattered was that I did... and now...

An arm came around my waist, hoisting me up into the air. Andrei grimly towered over us all, yet in that moment, he could do nothing. I fought against Daniel, screamed the filthiest words at him, and when he finally dropped me, I did the one thing I had been aching to do: punch him in his smug little face.

The satisfying crunch of my fist connecting with cartilage and bone was worth the dread that he would hit me back. He stepped backward, simultaneously cupping his bleeding nose and cursing me out.

I didn't stick around to listen. Instead, I threw myself at Teddy, who was murmuring praises to Lilith. Daniel was on me before I made contact. We rolled to the floor. I was trying to hit Daniel, and Daniel was trying to restrain me.

"Say goodbye to your demon," he hissed into my ear, sitting astride me and holding my arms above my head. "Once

374

Teddy banishes it to a faraway dimension, you can bet on the fact that you will never see it again, Rae."

It was immature of me to spit at him but I did, and a childish joy bubbled inside me when my saliva landed smack-dab in the middle of his face. His features turned murderous and his grip became painfully tight.

"Two-faced little fuck," I screamed, pain radiating through my arms. "When I kill you…"

"When? Keep dreaming, sweetheart," he snarled.

With more strength than I thought I possessed, I twisted out of his clutches and flung him off me, panting from the effort. Daniel was still on the ground when I got up and kicked him. My foot met his gut, which brought out a pained groan from his mouth. Only when I was sure that he was immobile did I turn my attention to Teddy.

He was sitting on the ground now, eyes firmly shut. Andrei loomed above him, his eyes filled with bloodlust and unadulterated rage. The only thing keeping him from crushing the hunter was some fucking drawing of a star in a circle written in chalk!

I grabbed a brick and flung it at Teddy's head with all my might… and cried out in frustration when it didn't even touch him. Fucking magic. Fucking hunters.

"You little bitch," Daniel growled from behind me, slinking his arms around my waist.

Andrei's eyes flickered from Teddy to me, and in that second, I knew that even in his beastly form, he did care about me. But was that love?

"I thought I knew you, Rainelle," he spat, spinning me around to face him. "You're willing to die for a demon?"

The fight went out of me. How many hours had I been here? The sky was dark now, speckled with tiny golden stars. So pretty…

"I love him."

Daniel's top lip curled in disgust and he twisted me around in his arms, forcing me to stare at Andrei. "That monster? You love it?"

I love you, I thought, and the voice in my head was more confident than it had ever been. *I love you as you are. I don't care what you are. No matter what happens, you will always be mine, my Andrei.*

Teddy jumped to his feet, staring up at the man I loved. "The spell is done, demon," he declared on a loud sigh. "You are mine to control, to command. O Lilith, I thank you."

"What?" Daniel's incredulous voice rang in my ear, making me wince.

Teddy turned to look at him. "Don't use that tone with me, boy. I'm not Raymond."

"I'll talk to you however the fuck I want to when I've been deceived!" Daniel threw me to the ground. I fell to my knees, the throbbing in my body increasing. "What the bloody hell do you mean it's yours to command?" Daniel continued. "Did you make it your fucking slave when the plan was to send it away?"

"Demon, revert to your human self," said Teddy, snapping his fingers for emphasis. "And you, Danny, this is your final warning. I don't answer to you. Remember that."

"Paisley's dead, and for what? For you to suddenly want to be some big, bad powerful warlock with a demon lord for a slave?"

"I can assure you that this wasn't sudden. Sit." He motioned for Daniel to do just that, against his will, and the

376

young hunter fell to the ground beside me. "You have no idea how much power I have with Lord Andrei under my command."

I zoned out, meeting Andrei's blue-eyed stare. He was getting blurrier and blurrier. It took me a while to realize that I was crying. I hated that. I hated this whole damn situation.

"Rainelle!" Teddy snapped at me.

I fixed him with a mutinous glare. His answering glare was equally hostile.

"I would like to thank you for your part in this," he bellowed, reaching out to push a hank of my hair out my face. I shuddered. "Without you as bait, this would never have been possible. It will go down in history, how one man was able to compel a demon lord to be his slave. And you, my dear, are lucky not to be one of the casualties."

From beside me, Daniel cursed.

"Unlike Josephine, right?" I snarled. "Unlike Paisley?" This was what she had wanted to tell me.

Anger flashed in Teddy's eyes.

"Don't even think about it," Andrei growled from behind him.

"You are the one who shouldn't be thinking," Teddy warned, briefly glancing at him. He scowled at me. "Josephine died for the cause."

A light bulb went on in my head. "She gave you her powers, didn't she? Before she died. She passed them on to you."

"A worthy sacrifice."

"You're sick."

"That's subjective." Then he clapped his hands together. "Thank you both for your help."

I scrambled to my feet, pushing past him and sprinting for Andrei. If Teddy was going to end up killing me, I could die happy if I heard the words. Just once. I only had this one chance.

"You're wearing my ring," Andrei murmured, allowing me space to step into the pentagram with him. I kicked at the circle. The chalk didn't smudge. The movies had lied. Andrei took my hand in his, admiring my middle finger.

"Of course," I whispered, savoring the feel of his calloused hand in mine. "Andrei, what will he do with you? To you?"

"Don't worry about that, baby," he growled, cupping my face in his hands. "This is only for a decade. When my service is over, I will slit his throat and watch him die."

Only a decade? Only?

"How could he do this to you? You're a king. You're supposed to be…"

"You are my Achilles' heel, Rae." He looked away. "Please, do not cry."

"This is my fault. Temp warned me that people would use me to get to you," I choked out, despising the weakness in my voice, despising the feel of Teddy's leery eyes on my back. "If I had stayed away from…"

"This isn't your fault," he said sharply, his brow furrowing. "I wanted you." He paused. "No one, mortal or otherwise, has ever loved me, Rae. Genuinely. But you… you're my fucking everything. I love…"

"I hope I'm not interrupting anything," Teddy's singsong voice interjected, "but we really do have to get going, Lord Andrei. And if you don't mind, I would be so grateful to experience the joys of teleportation."

378

Andrei's glare could have melted diamonds. His eyes, swimming with emotion, swiveled back to me. "I love you, *mea domina*." He placed my palm over his beating heart. "Yours."

"Mine," I whispered, tilting my head back as his mouth descended over mine. He gripped the back of my neck, pouring out his anger, his hunger, his love into the melding of our mouths.

He pulled back just as Teddy pulled me away from him.

"I am going to enjoy fucking your empty eye sockets after I've killed you," Andrei barked, eyes flashing a deep red. "Or perhaps I should keep you alive for that part."

Teddy laughed, stepping beside him. "Let's get out of here, demon."

I met Andrei's eyes, mouthing the words again. He closed his eyes, just as Teddy glanced over my shoulder at Daniel.

"As soon as we leave, Danny boy, you know exactly what to do."

Andrei's eyes flew open, but a second later, he and Teddy vanished into thin air.

Weak from the immediate loss, I wanted to crumple into a dejected heap and cry my eyes out. But Daniel was there and I had to get as far away from him as possible.

I turned to go and bumped right into the brick wall that was Daniel.

He gave me a strange look. "I'm sorry, Rainelle," he muttered. "I would never want to physically harm you despite everything but... he put a spell on me. I'm sorry," he repeated.

379

The first blow took me completely by surprise. His fist rammed into my gut so fast, I didn't have time to react. Winded from the force of it, I doubled over.

I was too weak for this. My stomach was already in knots, with pain and hunger, and the rest of me ached as well.

Maybe I should let this happen, I thought, receiving the next blow to my skull this time. Daniel grabbed my hair and hurled me to the ground. *Yes, this is the coward's way out.*

You're no coward, Rae. You weren't afraid of me at the end, were you?

Andrei's voice was in my head, as clear as day. I savored the memory of it... and went numb.

Chapter 24

"Just because you're a girl, doesn't mean you have to be weak," said Jared, picking up his water bottle from the grass and dousing himself with the cold liquid. "Stand over there." He jerked his head toward the apple tree his father had threatened to chop down..

"I'm an Erickson. We're not born to be weak," I grumbled, refusing to admit to myself that the thought of spending the day ogling a sweaty, shirtless Jared was way more productive than his misguided attempt at playing a game of wax on, wax off.

My father had taught me how to throw a punch the day I started walking. Faking inexperience with Jared was like being an AP student forced to dumb it down to fit in. My hormones didn't mind though. It was totally worth it pretending not to know how to kick someone if I got to stare at Jared's tanned, tattooed body...

"Focus, Rae. You want to end up like that woman they found the other day? Mugged and beaten half to death?" He sent me a level stare. "The fact is, a guy will underestimate a woman two seconds after looking at her. I would never forgive myself if something happened to you that I could've helped prevent."

I rolled my eyes at him and socked him right in the face.

After the black-eye incident, Jared never underestimated me again...

I felt a smile tilt the corners of my lips at the vivid memory. There was another man who would never miscalculate me: Andrei. The man I loved, undeniably. Monsters could be loved as well. Whatever happened, I knew he would hold on to that. And he would come back to me.

But in the meantime, I had some ass to kick.

As soon as I returned to the present, I became aware of the blood trickling into my eyes... and my mouth. The taste of copper reminded me that I was still there, still conscious. I was a ball of cuts and bruises, yet none of them hurt. Beneath me, the ground was icy and it chilled my skin. I scrambled blindly for something behind me and found a brick. It weighed heavily in my hand, and bracing myself for the impact of a kick to my ribs, I launched it at him.

A blinding pain instantly reverberated through my chest from the twisting motion but that was nothing compared to the crack in my shoulder. I rolled onto my knees, wheezing from the effort. Beside me, Daniel gasped for air, clutching his chest where the brick had struck him.

Relying on the adrenaline spiking in my veins and the urge to kill, I grasped the brick again and cracked it against the side of his head, tearing a guttural cry from his throat.

The liquid-gold eyes I had once thought beautiful became unfocused. He garbled out a string of words, the head wound obviously fucking with him. In that moment, I knew what true vengeance was. I fed on the sound of the brick bashing his head inside… fed on the sound of a once daunting man being reduced to a screaming, mangled mess… fed on the sound of him dying.

Blood, his and mine, started to dry on my face and on my hands… on my entire body. This time, I didn't shy away from it, didn't cower. The blood was evidence of my strength, of my fight. And as Daniel's writhing ceased, it was a testament to my survival.

"I told you I'd kill you," I whispered, my anger seeping out of me with the words. I was exhausted, could barely see through the rain of crimson, and could barely move from the pain in my every bone.

But my hands moved of my own accord, continuing to break his skull, even after the life had left his body. Everything hurt. It hurt to breathe, to blink, to even move. But I kept at it, sobbing when even my adrenaline-induced bashing became too painful to do.

And that was how Officer Paul Marino found me, sobbing over the bloody body of a man who lived in the house next to mine… in the quiet English countryside of Parishville.

It was very easy to spin the story of Daniel Lawless as a deranged stalker whose plan to abduct me had sent him to the Bay. Paul bought it. The other officers bought it. Ren and Lorenzo bought it.

The only thing I couldn't explain was the damage to the building. One side of it was completely gone. Only the roof held up by steel columns had survived Andrei's entrance. It was nearing sunrise and the sky was so beautiful, tinted with vivid amber and muted scarlet.

The town was so small that by the time the ambulance came, my best friend and her husband were already there. I didn't realize the full extent of what Daniel had done to me until I saw the looks of horror on everybody's faces. I went to high school with one of the EMTs who attended to me, Jocelyn Something. I didn't remember, but she obviously remembered me. Her eyes widened unprofessionally as they led me to the ambulance. I refused the indignity of a stretcher because, irrationally, I felt as though Daniel was still winning if he rendered me unable to move on my own.

Even though every step I took felt like reliving the assault all over again.

"Oh God," Renée wailed, following me into the ambulance. They let her in because she was family. Once I lay inside, she gripped my hand, painfully. "How could he do this to you? What kind of sick motherfucker would hurt you like this?"

I looked away. Daniel was dead. I killed him. I killed a man. And not the conventional way, oh no. I bashed his brains in, and fractured his skull multiple times... and tasted his blood on my lips when it spattered against me.

The reality of what I just did hit me like a hurricane, and I rolled onto my side and dry heaved.

"He's gone, Rae," said Ren, smoothing my hair down as I tried to force something out of my empty stomach. Her voice was choked up with unshed tears. "He's gone."

Yes, he was. But so was Andrei.

I knew that this was a dream because, well, let's face it, I didn't feel like Daniel had beaten the shit out of me—and I knew he did.

I was in Vegas, in the main casino at the Hotel Kamenev.

"Over here, Rae," a familiar voice said from behind me.

I spun around, coming face to face with Temp. Relief like nothing I'd ever felt before flooded through me and I accepted his open arms, burying my face in his chest. The casino was empty, but even if Temp had filled it with people, I wouldn't have cared. I sobbed openly into his chest, unashamed of the wave of emotions that were threatening to drown me.

"It's going to be okay, Rae," he murmured, stroking my hair and patting my back. "You're going to be okay."

"He's gone, Temp. How could he be gone?" I sobbed, blowing my nose into the soft cashmere of his sweater. The emptiness I was beginning to associate with this train of thought was too much. "How could Teddy be that... that strong?"

Temp pulled back from me, holding me at arm's length so he could look into my eyes. "I'm gonna level with you, Baby Phat. Your boy Teddy is playing with fire. You don't deal with black magic and come out unscathed." He ran a hand down my cheeks, wiping my tears away. "He appeased Lilith, and a whole other bunch of higher demons, somehow, and so he got Andrei. I know that sucks but…"

"Sucks? This isn't a joke!" I snarled, wrenching myself away from him. "I love him and he finally said the same to me. And now what?! He has to become a puppet because of it?"

385

Temp's face remained composed. "He wouldn't be the first. Every few centuries, a witch channels enough power to be able to do it. When the demon's decade of service is over, he usually goes on a rampage, killing any mortal that had anything to do with his humiliation."

"Then... why do it in the first place? If Andrei will only kill Teddy in the end, why would he risk it?"

"For some people, power is worth the risk, I guess," Temp replied. "Besides, there are witches who have managed to trap demons in dark dimensions when the demon's service is over. Maybe Teddy figures that's just what he'll do."

I swallowed, balling my hands into fists. "Then I'll find him and kill him before that happens. I'll search every corner of the earth until I have his bald fucking head in my hands."

Temp shook his head. "And die in the process? I won't let you do that. Andrei wouldn't want you to do that."

"You can forget about telling me what I can and can't do, Temp," I said through clenched teeth. "I'm not just going to sit back and let Andrei suffer because of me." I took a deep breath. "Because I'm his Achilles' heel."

Temp's face softened. He pulled me to him again, resting his chin on the top of my head. "Oh, Baby Phat. You do love him," he said gently. "It's time for you to wake up now, though."

I raised my head. "How are you in my head again? I never knew cambions could do that."

He gave me a smile. "Well, we can. Now wake up. I'm just outside your room."

"My room? At the house?"

But it was too late. I was already blinking awake, expecting to find the familiar features of my bedroom... but seeing a brightly lit sterile hospital room instead. A private one, at least, and a large one at that. I winced, the blinding sunlight from the windows punishing my eyeballs. Huge flower arrangements surrounded me, their colors radiant in the sunlight. Calla lilies were practically shoved up my nostrils. I wrinkled my nose, finally noticing the array of tubes running from my body to a beeping machine beside the bed.

I tilted my head to the other side, the dull ache thrumming throughout my body serving as a reminder of the events that had brought me here, and found Renée snoozing in a chair. She was propped up in an awkward position, a People magazine balanced precariously on her lap. Her usually immaculate hair looked like a rat's nest and the sweats she wore had seen better days.

"Ren," I croaked.

She bolted upright, her jade green eyes instantly wide and alert. "Rae? Oh, thank God! You're awake!"

I cringed. "Loud."

"Shit, hon. I'm sorry," she hissed, reaching out for my hand. It was warm to the touch. "Can I get you something? Water? Food?"

"Water."

Ren helped me get into a sitting position and held out a paper cup of water, directing the straw to my mouth. I slurped up the lukewarm liquid, grateful for the respite. Then, Ren propped up the mound of pillows behind me before I could lean back.

"Could you draw the curtains, please?" My voice was still raspy. I cleared my throat as I watched Ren bolt around my bed to close the curtains before she returned to me. "How long was I out for?"

"Five days. Nearly lost you in the ambulance," she replied, her voice soft. "They had to induce you into a coma to

387

make sure you'd start to heal nicely. You lost a lot of blood, had to get a blood transfusion, and had a couple of broken ribs, too. Plus that shit really walloped your head…" She trailed off before breaking into a grin and squeezing my hand. "They say it's a miracle the babies are okay. Lorenzo and I have been praying for you every——"

"The what?"

"The blood transfusion? I knew you'd probably think it was risky, but Rae, you needed it," she said in a rush. "Lawless beat you bloody. For the babies' sakes, I had to let them do it."

"Stop it," I protested weakly, squeezing my eyes shut. "I'm not pregnant."

"You mean… you didn't know?" Even with my eyes closed, I knew Ren was gaping at me. "You're six weeks along. Twins, they said. It's a miracle that twisted fuck didn't hurt them," she snarled. "The police found the room with the chains and your doctor made sure to check for signs of rape, even though you didn't say anything about that in your statement. They just thought it was best to make sure, you know?"

Ren was babbling, a sure sign that she was nervous. I felt like I didn't know how to breathe anymore. Her words were playing on a loop in my head like a broken CD.

Six weeks… Twins… Six weeks… Twins… Six weeks…

My mind was still fuzzy but conscious enough to do quick mental calculations. If that was the truth, the babies were conceived the night Andrei came back after leaving me hanging following his torturous foreplay, the night before I went to look for JP without Temp—the night before Damien let me know just what was going on in the basement of his club.

"But I had my period after," I said monotonously.

388

Ren was so in sync with me that she knew exactly what I was referring to. She scoffed. "Remember in high school, how we said that sperm can live in our bodies longer than we can last in the wild? That's three days of potential fertilization," she stated matter-of-factly. "You were probably just spotting." Her face softened at my horrified expression. "Blood tests don't lie, babe. And I know you've been through hell but do you... do you know who the father is?"

"Ah, Ms. Erickson, welcome back to the land of the living." The doctor breezed into the suddenly-claustrophobic room, saving me from answering Ren, but I barely registered his face. Shell-shocked, I think that was it. "Mrs. Marino, if you'd step out of the room for a little while..."

"Mrs. Marino? Don't even," Renée scolded him. "We went to school together, Zach. You wet your pants in third grade when Mindy Turner asked you for a Crayola." She received a dirty look from, now that she mentioned it, Dr. Sheppard. "All right, all right. I'm going." She paused at the doorway. "By the way, there's an Adonis outside waiting to see you, babe."

My head cleared. Barely. "You met my brother, huh?" I mumbled.

"Your what?"

I winced. So this was the one time Temp hadn't pulled the brother card. I shuddered to think about the interrogation he was about to get from my best friend. She bolted out the door to presumably do just that.

Dr. Sheppard and I were alone now. I didn't want to hear anything he had to say. I couldn't. It was one thing hearing it from Renée, but there was no way I could pretend it was a mistake if it came out of a doctor's mouth.

"Hey, Rainelle," he said gently, scooping up my chart at the foot of the bed as he made his way to my side. "Despite urinating on myself when I was eight, I am more than capable to be your doctor."

The smile on my face was forced and it hurt.

He flashed me a real one. "I'm sure Renée filled you in but…"

I listened to his detailed description of my injuries with half an ear while he removed my catheter lines. I didn't care about the broken ribs, or the concussion, or the almost-dislocated shoulder, or the various bumps and bruises I would have to tolerate for a couple more days. Only when he got to the part about "the healthy fetuses" did I pay attention.

"…and everything looks good. There was a bit of trauma to your abdomen and truthfully, we are all in awe of these babies. They shouldn't have survived, but they did. They have a very resilient mother."

"And I'm six weeks along?" I asked dazedly.

"You had no idea." It wasn't a question.

"But… I had my period," I murmured stupidly. And again, I sounded like a broken record.

"It's not unusual to experience vaginal bleeding during pregnancy," Zach said gently, glancing down at the clipboard in his hand, "but since you're in the early stages, it's safe to say that it was what we call implantation bleeding. The twins are perfectly fine, despite the trauma you all sustained. I'd like to monitor you here for a day or two though, just to be safe. I'm glad you woke up when you did, Rainelle."

The rest of his monologue went over my head, and then he was gone, with promises of sending a nurse in with lunch.

Pregnant.

Me.

With Andrei's babies.

With a demon king's babies.

The past few weeks made sense now. The weight gain I'd attributed to too much good food. The constant nausea even when I wasn't around demons. My hormones in overdrive. Bacon turning my stomach…

The door was pushed open and Temp strode inside, closing it behind him. The clicking sound it made snapped me out of my panicked rumination.

"So yeah, your friend just tried to molest me and I wasn't even putting on the charm," he complained, looking like he'd just strolled out of a GQ magazine in a polo shirt and slacks. "Hope you don't mind but I had to charm her away when she started asking about us." His eyes widened when he managed a good look at me. "Ho-lee-fucking-shit!"

"That bad, huh?"

"Worse." He crumpled into the chair Renée had vacated only moments before, his eyes scanning me with heavy concern. "They said you turned the guy's brain into scrambled eggs. If he were still alive, I would've done it for you and laughed while doing it."

The image of Daniel's body on that concrete floor flashed behind my eyelids. I shook it away. But I knew it would be back.

"No?" said Temp, mistaking my headshake for a negative. "He hurt you, Rae. Could've killed you. Nearly did. I would've…"

"I'm pregnant."

Temp's jaw dropped, hanging there like a drawbridge. The sight would have been funny but there was really nothing to laugh about. I didn't think there would be ever again.

Temp was finally able to close his mouth and offered an uncertain "That's… great?"

I let out a bitter laugh, breaking down on the pillows. "Yes. Great. Every single one of Andrei's sperm cells probably wore an 'S' on their tiny little chests because I know I took the pill every day." I paused, deliberating. "Okay, maybe not every day. I might have missed one or two days but… God, Temp, this can't be happening. It can't be. Two babies? I… can't."

He cleared his throat. "Rae… you do know that contraceptives do jack shit when it comes to killing a demon's sperm, right?" he mumbled, suddenly very interested in the floor. "The only sure-fire way is charmed birth control, which you can get from a witch, or a condom."

"Excuse me?"

He looked up at me. "If an incubus doesn't want to impregnate someone, which, by the way, is very rare since we're all arrogant little shits, he'll make a conscious effort to shoot blanks. Unbelievable… but true." Temp paused. "Andrei might just have… forgotten one time," he finished lamely.

I stared at him for a moment, feeling yet another wave of panic threatening to overwhelm me. "So you're telling me the whole time I was swallowing that goddamned pill, I might as well have been swallowing a jellybean for all the good it did me?"

"I thought you knew this stuff. I mean, didn't you understand what you were getting yourself into by going steady with an incubus?"

"No one told me this!" I snapped. My head beginning to pound. The dull ache in my chest was building up to a sharp pain. I was going to make myself fall apart.

"Rae, calm down," Temp chided. "You don't want to give yourself high blood pressure, do you? It's not good for the…"

"The babies?" The word was an acquired taste on my tongue. Mixed emotions swirled inside my chest. What am I supposed to be feeling right now? Joy? Apprehension? Anger? My eyes strayed down my body.

Beneath my hospital gown, beneath the bruises that I was sure peppered my belly, there were—not one, but two—babies. Each one half of me, and half of Andrei.

Half-human. Half-demon.

I gingerly splayed my fingers over my stomach and let out the breath I hadn't realized I was holding. Then the psychotic laughter started up, which was a veritable torture to my ribs. They still hurt like hell but that didn't stop me. No, this laughter was an unstoppable force.

My demon boyfriend had forgotten to shoot blanks. How ridiculous was that? When he came inside me, the birth control I had been taking religiously (Oh, the irony!) was useless in the face of his bionic sperm, and now I was having his twins. I knew squat about kids and now I would have the pleasure of having two (two cambions, no less!) at the same time? What else could I do but laugh?

"Rae, stop laughing. You're hurting yourself."

Tears flooded my eyes, both from the pain and from the reality of the situation. I couldn't stop laughing, despite how much it hurt. "Oh, God, Temp. Don't you see how hilarious this is?" I sputtered, clutching my painful sides. "Forgot to shoot blanks? Forgot? In this world, being sterile is embarrassing. Many guys leave the doctor's room in tears because of it. And incubi can turn it on and off like a tap?

393

Sperm faucets!" I choked on my laughter, and the choking morphed into sobbing.

Temp was at my side in seconds, holding a new cup of water to my mouth. I could barely latch on to the straw to drink through my uncontrollable sobs. So Temp set the cup down and tentatively wrapped his arms around me. I let myself break apart in his embrace, dribbling and sniveling into his shirt.

"I'm here for you, Baby Phat." Temp's voice rumbled in his chest, the vibrations tickling my cheek. "You'll be fine. I'm Nanny McPhee with kids. But with great highlights and a dick."

I snorted with laughter. He slowly released me, looking at me with intense chocolate eyes. "I'm serious. I'm here for you. We're... family." His fingers intertwined with mine and squeezed my hand.

"I know," I whispered, squeezing back.

His eyes became more sober. "There's something I have to tell you."

I shut my eyes. "I can't take any more bombshells, Temp. Please. Not now." But every time I closed my eyes, I saw Andrei's face and my heart clenched. Then I saw Daniel's—the mangled, raw flesh that was left of him. Those images made me sick.

"I know. And I'm sorry. But you need to know this." He took a deep breath. "Andrei destroyed Nicolette and Damien is likely coming after you."

My eyes flew open. "Destroyed the club?"

"For you. He saved those girls," Temp relayed slowly. "Of course, Damien took it personally. They were his toys. And what happens when you take away a kid's toys? He gets mad. And then he finds something new to play with."

"Me," I said numbly.

"You," he confirmed.

An elderly nurse chose that exact moment to barge into the room, pushing in a trolley of food. She gave Temp a severe look. "I'm sorry, sir, but visiting hours are over. It's time for the patient to eat."

I held fast to Temp, refusing to release his hand. I didn't want to be alone just then. He looked down at me, smiling in understanding. Then he fixed the woman with a different kind of smile, the kind that wouldn't fail to disintegrate her panties.

"Yeah, but you can make an exception for me, can't you, sweetheart?"

The nurse practically swooned. "O-of course. Take your time."

"Thank you, darling. You can go now."

So Temp stayed through lunch, tapping away at his iPhone.

During lunch, I forced myself to eat. Yes, hospital food was the worst, and under normal circumstances, I wouldn't have done so much as sniff it. But I was eating for three now.

With Temp fully occupied, I was forced to be in my own head. I had no idea what I was going to do. The only thing I was absolutely sure of was that I was going to go through with the pregnancy. Abortion had only crossed my mind for a millisecond and then I'd squashed the idea immediately. Despite how scared out of my fucking mind I was, killing innocent babies was too horrific to even really consider.

But how long will they be innocent? They're half-demon. Half-evil. Half-unnatural.

My eyes strayed to Temp, whose blond head was bent over his phone. He was a cambion, a halfling. He was my brother. He was normal. And he had what most demons couldn't even begin to fake: humanity.

But there was so much I couldn't even begin to grasp about cambions. Would they grow up like normal kids? Would they be screwing around by the time they hit kindergarten? Would they kill?

My appetite fled. I pushed the tray aside, and with great effort, kicked the covers off.

Temp's head shot up. "Where d'you think you're going?"

"The bathroom," I muttered, bracing a hand on either side as I heaved myself off the bed.

Temp was before me in a flash, helping me to my feet.

"Thanks," I said.

He walked me to the bathroom—a nice, big space with a nice, big tub and shower—and hovered for a while before I kicked him out. Bracing myself, I faced the mirror.

Daniel Lawless had really done a number on me. It was funny how I wasn't able to register where he hit me exactly when he was doing it, but now, looking at the purple bruises scattered all over my skin, it was impossible to believe that I didn't feel it.

I gingerly fingered a particularly ugly mark just below my eye—correction, my black eye. Looking at it, it seemed as if I had a black eye patch that took up half my face. A few of the bruises were already beginning to yellow and could probably be covered up with make-up—the rest, not so much. I was glad that I wasn't awake to see the swelling. Still, I wouldn't be winning any beauty pageants anytime soon.

"Because your looks are so important right now, Rae," I mumbled to myself, struggling to remove the gown. My "nearly-dislocated" right shoulder hurt like a bitch.

Naked, I stood in front of the mirror, holding myself up against the sink. A myriad of colorful bruises decorated my skin, along with a few tiny stitches here and there. They had to be excruciating when they were still fresh. My eyes zeroed in on the marks on my belly and the one thought that resounded in my head was that the tiny beings forming inside me could have died.

Daniel could have killed me, but more importantly, he could have killed my babies. Now that I knew about them, knew that they were growing inside me for over a month... I knew that I would do anything and everything to protect them. If it meant being haunted by the images of Daniel's battered face for the rest of my life, so be it. I would kill him again in a heartbeat.

This was me, a woman who, just last week, had no maternal bone in her body.

"Hey, guys," I murmured, placing a hand on my stomach. It would never be the flattest but it still looked the same. "Aren't we a trio of survivors?" I rubbed circles on it for a bit, feeling foolish for talking to my tummy. "I'm sorry about what I said about your dad. Bionic sperm is an exaggeration."

"Hey, Baby Phat! You okay?"

I glanced at the closed door, offering Temp a quick "I'm fine!" before returning my gaze back to my belly. "I miss your dad like crazy. And the thought of not knowing when I'm going to see him again scares the shit out of me. And now I have you little guys to think about." I let out a sigh. "I'm not mad that you're here. I know it may feel that way but I'm not. I'm just... stunned. And scared. Mostly scared. I..."

I stopped, dropping my hand. What was that? That couldn't have been a kick, could it? I was six weeks along, not six months. Clearly, I was still concussed.

Head shaking, I fixed the gown up, used the facilities, and shuffled back into the room.

Chapter 25

"That dude's still standing out there," Temp growled, finally letting the curtains close again. After sporadically peeking through my living room window like a guard dog for the past twenty minutes, he was finally taking a break. "You know, the nasty-looking thug with all the scars? Prowling about every day like a loser. I swear, Rae…"

"Ignore him, Temp," I muttered vaguely, balancing my laptop on my knees as I reached for my fourth waffle that morning. I was making a half-hearted attempt to check my mail and an even feebler attempt to resist Temp's incredible waffles. "Like everyone else, he probably heard about the beating yours truly received and wants to see if it's true that half my face was knifed clean off."

"Small town, small people."

I couldn't deny that. The Bay might be one of the most beautiful places I ever saw—and even had one legitimate celebrity living in it, but I still tried to escape it. And of the main reasons for that was its microscopic size. The fact that news here traveled at the speed of light was testament to this. It had been a week since I returned from the hospital and people were still bringing food and flowers to my door. They could pretend that they were concerned about my well-being, but truthfully, they just wanted some juicy gossip to dissect for bingo night.

"I heard the psycho raped her and now she's having his kid."

"Zachary, bless his soul, had to stitch her face back together. It was so grisly."

"She led her abductor on. You remember the Ericksons, don't you? Strange Swedish fellow raising a sexed-up daughter alone? Rest his soul but no wonder this happened to her."

They didn't get the chance to say those to my face, of course. Temp, my mediator, just relayed their awful gossip to me… while they thought I was shacked up with a lover. Temp didn't bother to dispel this rumor. I didn't particularly care. They could speculate all they wanted, as long as they left me the hell alone. Thankfully, Temp got one of his warlock buddies who owed him a favor to put up a special kind of ward around my house. One that could keep out anyone who wanted to do me harm.

Too bad that didn't include gossipmongers bearing chicken pot pies and fake smiles.

"Hey, you all right?" Temp sat at my feet, fixing worried eyes on me. "If you think this guy's more than just a creep, I'll go take care of him."

I smiled wryly. "He's twice your size. I don't want to watch you die senselessly. I already have enough sickening images in my head."

He flashed me a wide grin. "Don't get sappy on me now, Baby Phat."

But all I did was get sappy these days. Just last night, I cried like a baby when Morgan Freeman died and Temp had to scramble to turn off *The Bucket List*. It didn't matter that I already watched it a hundred times before. I still bawled my eyes out and scared the crap out of my brother.

Then there were the nightmares, the stifling blanket of guilt settling over me whenever I so much as shut my eyes for a nanosecond. Daniel's face constantly invaded my subconscious. He was practically living behind my eyelids.

I didn't want to feel guilty but I did. I wanted to hate him for the way he behaved at the end. I wanted to pretend that he did have a choice before he attacked me. But then I remembered the Daniel I'd imagined in my head before I knew who he was. The Daniel who used to undress by his bedroom window. The Daniel who dragged me out the bar when I drank too much. The Daniel who wasn't a backstabbing demon hunter.

"Rae."

Temp gently shook me, dragging me back to earth. I focused on my laptop screen, finally registering how full my inbox was. Things had not changed. Men were still dogs and women were still trying to keep them on a leash. I wasn't in the right frame of mind to deal with their problems right now though. Not when I had a whole lot of them myself.

The primary one, no surprise there, was Andrei. Andrei Anghelescu wasn't the type of guy to forget to do something. He didn't forget how I couldn't stand pickles and made sure to remove them from my Big Mac before handing it over, which always surprised me. He didn't forget that I loved his hair, loved to grab and yank it. So he never trimmed it. And he

401

didn't forget that I loved his foot massages. So how could he forget to inform me about something as major as the fact that he could make me pregnant?

My eyes traveled down my stomach, to where my palm was unconsciously stroking it through my sweatshirt. Since I left the hospital, the action was quickly becoming a habit. The knowledge of the tiny lives growing inside me scared me to death, but at the same time, it made me want them more.

I paused mid-rub, biting my lower lip at the thought of that week in the white room: the hospital. If I never saw it again, it would be too soon. I never wanted to see Dr. Sheppard again, not after seeing my chart, in which he'd penned "eight weeks"... then "seven"... before crossing that out and settling on "six". The evidence hit me smack-dab in the face. Even a medical professional wasn't sure how old my babies were.

"Okay, Baby Phat. Whatever you're thinking, just stop it," Temp was saying, seizing my computer and setting it on the coffee table. He forced me to look at him. "Talk to me."

I didn't have the courage to say the words aloud, which was stupid, to be honest.

"Did... did Lauren gestate for nine months? Thirty-six weeks? Thereabout?" I blurted out, feeling heat bloom in my cheeks.

Temp raised a brow. "Is that what's worrying you? Jeez, Baby Phat. You look scared shitless!"

"Please," I said, my voice high-pitched. "I need to know that two winged creatures aren't going to be flying out my girly parts next week."

He let out a short bark of laughter. "Okay. One, who even says 'gestate' anymore? This isn't Animal Planet. Two, you're carrying hybrids, not Daenerys' fucking dragons. And three, you're going to have a normal pregnancy." He sucked in

402

a deep breath before exhaling. "So try to relax. Look at how motherfucking awesome I turned out to be."

I heaved out a shaky breath. "A normal pregnancy?"

"Part of my charm is that I can easily integrate with full-blooded humans," he said with a wink. "How else are we cambions supposed to pretend to be normal if we're out of our moms after ten weeks?" Then, when he saw that I wasn't fully placated, he said more solemnly, "Why didn't you ask me this stuff at the hospital? I've been trying to find out what the hell was up with you for the past week."

"Well, I'm asking now."

He sighed. "I get that you're scared. You have every right to be," he said gently. "But don't get trapped in your head. You killed a guy, woke up from a coma, and discovered you're having a demon king's kids—all in the space of one week. No one could walk away from all that and not be changed. You can ask me anything. I'm gonna take care of you." He scrunched up his face. "Fuck, Rae. Don't cry."

"I can't help it," I blubbered. "It's like onions are permanently stuck under my eyes."

"Yeah, well, if you're gonna keep me from getting laid, at least make it worth my while and be great company."

I slapped his shoulder. He cringed as if I'd really hurt him. I had to smile.

"Can I ask you something?" I said after a while.

Temp leaned back, folding his arms behind his head. "Go ahead."

"When did you lose your virginity?" It was an invasive question, and truthfully, I didn't want to know. But I had to. So I braced myself for something ridiculous, like *In the sandpit, when I was five. It was recess.*

403

"My sixteenth birthday." He laughed at the incredulous look that was probably painted on my face. "Contrary to popular belief, we don't pop out our mothers and fuck. For all intents and purposes, Rae, we're normal when we're younger, just smarter, cuter, and way more intuitive than the average kid. Did I mention cute?"

"What about the evil part?"

Temp's eyes flickered with something. Anger? "There's no such thing as a good demon, Rae. But there are choices. My father wanted... Well, let's just say I'm a big disappointment to him. It was my choice to be like this, just like your kids will choose what they want to be."

For a moment, neither of us spoke, lost in our own thoughts. I felt stupid for scaring myself with my own wild assumptions. Temp was my personal *What to Expect When You're Expecting Demon Hybrids* book, yet I was too afraid to come to him... probably because I was afraid of his response.

"Do you think Andrei would be happy?" I didn't mean for the words to slip out but once they did, they hung in the air beside *Do you think he'll ever come back? Will I make a good mother? What the hell are we going to do about Damien Ivanov?*

"I think," Temp began, "Andrei will be happy to be with you."

It was a vague response and didn't really answer my question, but it was what I needed to hear.

Temp wordlessly reached for the bottle of folic acid on the table and handed it to me. Not for the first time I regretted not growing up with him. He was the only thing keeping me sane right now.

I was going stir-crazy. No, scratch that. I was stir-crazy.

There were only so many YouTube videos of skateboarding animals a girl could watch in one week. Sitting around and doing nothing just wasn't my M.O. but Temp was a bully when it came to my leaving the house.

"No fucking way," was what he explosively said to me when I told him I was going to the beach.

"I wasn't asking you, Temp. I was just telling you where you could find me."

"Don't test me, Baby Phat."

"Fine. Renée was going to come over anyway," I told him through clenched teeth.

"No. No visitors right now. You want to put your bestie in danger?"

And that was the end of that. I understood him completely, and because I knew that he did love me, I couldn't even hate him. I prided myself on my independence but there was a warm, fuzzy feeling in my chest whenever he pretended he was older than me and got all protective.

That didn't change the fact that I was bored out of my damn mind though. And now that Temp went out to feed, I was scared that I would do something impulsive… like sneak out to meet Ren… or go out for a burger.

I was pacing the living room when the knock at the door came.

Even with the ward up, I couldn't be too careful. I hadn't fired a gun in years. But now, one of my father's handguns was permanently near me. I snatched it up from the coffee table and held it behind my back as I padded to the front door, peeking through the peephole. I instantly recoiled, heart hammering in my chest.

Fuck.

Scarface was standing on my doorstep. Temp had warned me about him just the other day. Loitering around my property was suspicious enough but coupled with his grisly appearance, who knew what the hell he wanted? I wasn't exaggerating when I reminded Temp that this man was practically twice his size. Cloaked in a navy trench coat in this heat, he had the rugged, brutish appearance of a gladiator who'd been in one too many fights and had barely survived.

"Yes?" I called to him, pressing my ear to the door. "What is it?"

"Rae. Please. Open up."

A flicker of something familiar scurried up my spine. I placed my palm against the door, inhaling sharply.

"I will not hurt you."

That much was obvious, otherwise he wouldn't have been able to come through the gate, let alone right up to my porch.

I unlocked the door, wrenching it open and revealing myself to him. I stifled a gasp at his appearance. From afar, he was creepy. Up close, his face was positively in tatters. Pink, jagged lines crisscrossed his face, one of them extending to his scalp, hidden by a thick mop of golden curls. Some scars looked to be stitched up, while others were already healing on their own. Deep-set cobalt eyes were watching me watch him.

Really familiar blue eyes.

I staggered backward, suddenly dizzy. Panic skittered through me, panic for my babies. *Have I eaten? Is something wrong?* The dread evaporated almost immediately, however, and I was able to take a deep breathe.

"Andrei?" My voice was hesitant, barely a whisper. It was a voice full of hope, hope that would never recover if it was dashed.

The man stepped over the threshold, ducking slightly, until he was in the foyer. He kicked the door closed behind him with a booted foot. I was stunned into silence. Even with him looking like this, I knew. I knew it was him.

"Rainelle," he said quietly, my name sounding strange on this stranger's lips. Except he wasn't a stranger. He was mine. He was here.

The gun fell to the ground, the clang of metal against linoleum doing little to drag our eyes from each other. Those eyes, they were the same. Penetrating. Stormy. Beautiful.

Tears pooled in my eyes. Furious, I chased them away with the back of my hand. There were so many things I wanted to say but they could wait. Just knowing that he managed to get away from Teddy was enough. I made my way to him, ready to throw my arms around him and welcome him back.

But his next words stopped me.

"I just need you to fuck this better," he flatly stated as he pointed at his disfigured face, "And then I'll be on my way."

~to be continued~

Can't get enough of Andrei and Rainelle?
Make sure you sign up for the author's blog
to find out more about them!

Get these two bonus chapters and
more freebies when you sign up at
kimber-lee.awesomeauthors.org!

Here is a sample from another story you may enjoy:

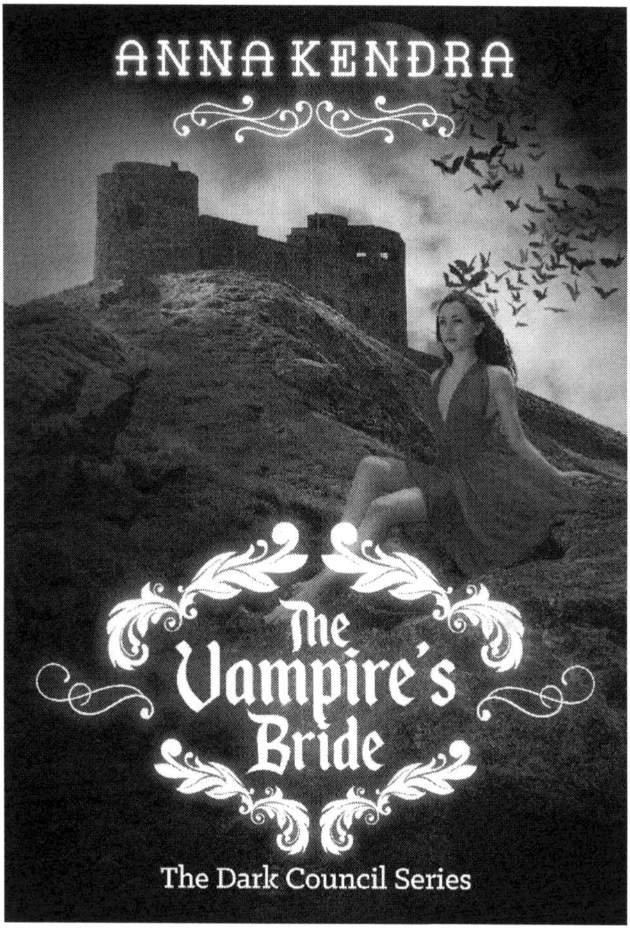
ANNA KENDRA
The Vampire's Bride
The Dark Council Series

Chapter 1

Alina

"I'm sorry, love. I really am, but it was her last wish. I hope that you'd at least give it a try," my father said to me. Worry was evident in his voice.

"Please, Papa! There has to be another way." I pleaded as I sat on a chair beside his hospital bed. His hands trembled in mine, but it wasn't due to old age. My father was dying.

"There would have been if Sheena was..." His eyes watered as he spoke her name, and my heart broke all over again. He loved her even now. I knew that part of the reason his condition kept getting worse, even after the best treatment in the world, was because he had given up on life the day my mother's heart stopped beating. The only thing that held him here, right now, was me.

"B-but I don't want to get married, Papa! Not yet! I'm only twenty-two." I tried to keep my voice pleading, but even I could hear the panic seeping in.

"I'm so sorry, my darling. I don't want to see you get married so early either, but I don't have much time left. I have to know that you'll be well taken care of," my dad said sadly, "that you'll be safe."

"But, Papa, they're va—"

"Ms.Deluca, visiting hours are over." The nurse cut me off as she strode into the room, saline bottle and more medicines in hand. "He's been better this past week, so try to visit as much as possible, but he does need to rest now," she said with a smile.

"Yes, of course. I'll see you tomorrow. Goodnight, Papa." I gave him my best smile even as tears pooled in my eyes and planted a kiss on his forehead before I turned to leave.

"Goodnight, love. Be safe."

I walked out of his cabin and said goodbye to people I knew. Occasionally, I also waved at little children who skipped and pranced around me as they made their way to the playroom in the children's ward. I already knew some of them since my father's room was right next to the nursery. Today, though, I couldn't even manage a smile. The instant I walked out into the parking lot, the heavy rain hit me like a bullet, drenching me from head to toe.

Good, I thought. At least, it would hide my tears. It would keep people from knowing the demons that haunt me and of the secrets I could never tell even if it killed me.

I stood alone in the parking lot next to my car with the rain mercilessly tattooing against my skin. The only thing I wished with all my heart was to erase a night four years ago that had changed my life forever.

Chapter 2

Alina

Science states that the evolution of mankind wasn't a straight line. Several species had to become extinct for the ultimate survivor to reign on this Earth: humans or *Homo sapiens*. Human beings came from the prehistoricapes and have evolved over a span of millions of years. Exactly how many, even scientists have their doubts. Their best bets are from the hominid fossils that they'd discovered from various parts of the globe. They use all sorts of criteria, from quadruped to biped locomotion, an increase in cranial capacity,changes in food habits, etc. But one thing they agree on is that it took millennia to ultimately result in the perfect modern man who has made Earth the supreme habitat.

If you believed the same, you couldn't be more wrong.

Human beings weren't the only creatures who survived the eons of trial that Mother Nature inflicted upon us. No, there were others, beings who were stronger, faster, deadlier, and higher on the food chain. They never lost the habit of devouring raw flesh and blood, surviving purely on animalistic instincts, speed, and agility that were a part of their genetic makeup. For centuries, they'd been in hiding, never letting any human be aware of their existence until it was the last thing they knew. They preyed on us and stayed out of our sight just like a predator because they were the most impeccable of them all. They were the vampires.

How did I know all of this? How did I even know that vampires were real? How did I know about their history? No, it was not because they've been discovered by scientists or they've made themselves known to the world. It was because my father worked for them.

I ought to know because I was engaged to a vampire. I was to be Erick Stayton's bride.

He was the heir to Stayton Incorporated, a company that specialised in marketing blood from donors and had blood banks in several parts of the U.S. It was a charitable organization looking for the betterment of the world and interested in helping people in need. No one really knew that it was just a facade, for only ten percent of the blood they collected went to charity. The rest was supplied to vampires all over Canada. They also ran a security service for VIPs and business tycoons, those who were in need of protection. All in all, he and his family were super rich, super arrogant, and very, *very* powerful.

Erick Stayton, my fiancé, was one of the most eligible bachelors in Canada. A lot of girls would die to catch his attention. However, he was too conceited to stay with one person for more than a week, that is according to Men's Fashion and GQ. He was a ruthless and savage predator. For me, vampires have never been a part fairy tales. They have always been the people I'd known to fear, and Erick was always at the top of that list.

My family were some of the few who knew about their secret. My father was the branch manager of the Main Canadian Blood Bank. Our families have been close even before I was born. Erick was the youngest child of his family, so we had an age difference of about three years. My mother and his were the ones who had arranged this wedding right after I was born. I didn't have any idea why, though. Why did they choose a human girl who has no interest in vampires whatsoever? Why didn't they choose someone more fitting like someone of the same race? It was no secret that I never liked vampires to begin with. Blood banks were a relatively modern creation. Who knew how many lives they took before the invention?

Everyone expected us to be great friends, Erick and I. They thought that we would grow up loving each other, but it was the exact opposite. I hated him with a passion. It was not just because he was a vampire, though. Oh no, it ran way deeper. You see, I had always avoided Erick ever since I was a child. He was always with the popular crowd, the bullies. Being naturally attractive, as was with every other predator on the planet, he always got away with it. So it was natural to avoid him and stay away from his line of sight. It was not that he didn't know about me, but we just kept our distance right from the start. However, as I began to grow, I started attending parties with my parents, and he finally started to notice me. By then, it was still going okay. I could handle a few snide comments here and there, but it was when he and his mother came to visit my parents one day when everything went wrong.

We were all at the dinner table that night. I went to the kitchen to fetch an extra dish when I stumbled on the doorjamb and fell to the floor, but not before hitting my head on the counter and wounding myself. The wound wasn't deep, but the hit caused the skin of my forehead to slit open and gush out blood. The next thing I knew, Erick was there, feeding from me until I was too weak to open my eyes.

When I regained consciousness, he warned me not to tell our parents or he would kill me. I, being the wimpy little child that I was, kept it a secret. I was eleven then. From that day onwards, he came to feed from me occasionally.

"You're my fiancée. It's your duty to feed me," he used to say to me. I believed him for a long time until I grew old enough to understand the folly.

I would have still forgiven him, considering that he was a young vampire who had no control over his hunger if it wasn't for what happened next.

I had just turned eighteen. It was Erick's twenty-first birthday, and there was a party at their house. My parents wanted me to go, but I declined, making an excuse that I had a test the next day. In reality, I only wanted to stay away from Erick and his gang of browbeaters. My parents were always away on business trips, and I was often home alone. It was around two in the morning when I heard the front door of our house being forced open. I rushed downstairs to check and knew instantly that I shouldn't have. Erick was leaning against the doorjamb with his clothes and hair in disarray. He was dead drunk.

I thought he was going to feed from me again, which had stopped for a while since he had plenty of girlfriends to drink from in his college. I was so, so wrong.

I didn't remember what exactly happened that night, probably because of PTSD, but I do remember the next morning when I woke up bruised and bloody. My clothes were torn, and there were claw marks on the carpet all around me. Erick himself was in a similar state of undress.

Erick's expression was unreadable. He only stayed to put on a few bandages on me so he wouldn't get caught and left immediately with the same warning of killing me if I told our parents. However, I'd had enough. I never wanted to keep it a secret in the first place. I wanted so badly to tell my parents about all of this. I promised myself that I would the second they came back even if it meant dying at the hands of a ruthless vampire... but that never happened.

The next day, I had to rush over to the hospital instead. Papa had several serious injuries, and Mom was gone. They got into an accident on their way back home. An eighteen wheeler truck smashed into their car on a narrow road. After that, my life had never been the same. I completely closed off. I kept to myself and avoided company as much as I could. I no longer trusted people. What happened to me didn't even compare to what happened to Mom, the person who never in a million years deserved this. Papa was so heartbroken, it was painful to watch.

He recovered after staying in the hospital for six months. However, he was diagnosed with stage two leukaemia. Now, he didn't have much time left. It had been four years since the accident and my mom's death. My father was already on his death bed, and Erick had never once visited even though his mother had so many times.

That was another reason why I was to be married to Erick as soon as the end of this month. Since my mom was dead and my Papa was nearing his, I would need protection from vampires who would gladly make main course out of me. After all, they couldn't have me screaming to the world that *they* exist.

It felt like the walls that I have built after all these years were breaking apart. My life was crashing down on me, and I had no way of stopping it.

I woke up with a start. It took me a while to realise that someone was ringing the doorbell of my apartment and that I was no longer at the hospital trying to convince my father to call off the wedding.

I rubbed the sleep from my eyes and looked at the bedside clock. It was nine twenty-seven in the morning, and since I took a few days off from work, I wasn't expecting anyone.

I hurriedly got out of bed and put on my robe. The lime green satin night dress that I was wearing reached my knees, and the robe went a little longer. My long dark-brown hair was in wild curls around my face and reached my lower back. Running my hands through it a few times to look presentable, I went for the door.

"Yes?" I asked as I opened the door without checking first. I instantly wished I hadn't.

Standing on the other side of the door was none other than Erick Stayton, the man I hated and feared. He still looked the same, except he no longer had the boyish charm he had when he was younger. In its place were all hard angles and a chiselled appearance. He had a devilishly handsome face, broad shoulders, and long legs clad in grey dress pants. The muscles on his arms strained the rolled up sleeves of his navy blue shirt. His sandy blond hair was short and perfectly styled while his ocean-blue eyes sparkled with an unknown emotion, a smirk playing on his lips.

"Hey there. Remember me?" he said as I visibly paled.

"W-why are you here?" I asked, internally cursing myself for the stutter. How could I ever forget him? What he did to me aside, he had a face no one could easily forget.

"Just came over to check on my wife-to-be." He crossed his arms over his chest.

"Well, now that you have, you should probably get going." I went to slam the door shut on his face, but a sudden gust of wind blew past me. When I turned around, Erick was there in my living room, looking around my apartment.

My apartment was small, but I loved living here. I decorated everything myself, from the colour of the walls to the furnishing. The dining room was a combination of light green and blue with a blue carpet and white couches. The kitchen was just next to the living room with two chairs before the counter and an open kitchen behind it. The walls were a light cream colour, and the boxes were made of wood. There was a twenty-eight inch LCD TV on the wall next to the counter and the entrance to the kitchen. A floor to ceiling glass wall stood facing the couches that gave a splendid view of the compound backyard and the fountain. My room was medium sized with white walls and had various false plants and flowers, as well as a green grass carpet. All the decorations made it look like it was in the midst of nature. The guest room was painted in red and gold with only a bed and small wardrobe. That was all, but the apartment was my safe heaven. I bought it with the money I received upon selling my parents' house right after my father was hospitalised a year ago.

"I like the decor. You did this yourself?" Erick asked.

"Yes," I said in a hard voice. "How long are you planning to stay here?"

"You know, there is no need for us to be so tense, right? We are getting married in a few weeks," he said, coming to stand in front of me so that we were chest to chest.

"You're right. We *are* getting married in a few weeks, but we're not married *yet*. So it'd be better if I didn't have to see you unless it's absolutely necessary." I didn't step back even though every cell in my body kept telling me to run as far and as fast as I could.

Erick raised an eyebrow, and his lips tilted up to one side. "You've changed. I like that, but you seem to have forgotten that you're not marrying a commoner, Alina. You're marrying the prince of all vampires, so look alive and get me some coffee."

The nerve of him! Yes, apart from being one of the most influential families in Canada, Erick's parents were the king and queen of all vampires, making him the Vampire Prince, but that did not give him the right to order me around. I gritted my teeth together so hard, I was afraid they would crack. How dare he say such a thing as if he hadn't done anything four years ago?

I will not lose my temper, I had to remind myself. *No, I will not lose to this monster.*

"Get out of my house, and get your own damn coffee!" With that, I strode to my bedroom and slammed the door on his face.

If you enjoyed this sample then look for **The Vampire's Bride on Amazon!**

Introducing the Characters Magazine App

Download the app to get the free issues of interviews from famous fiction characters and find your next favorite book!

iTunes: bit.ly/CharactersApple
Google Play: bit.ly/CharactersAndroid

Acknowledgements

Firstly, a big thank-you to my parents for encouraging me to read and write (even though I occasionally wrote in my reading books). Without your support, I wouldn't be so passionate about what I do today. Thanks for loaning me your laptops, by the way!

A big thank-you goes to my English teachers over the years, who would have heart palpitations if they ever read my work. You women were incredible to me, and one day, I will tell you this in person.

I think it's fair to say that every one of my followers on Wattpad deserves a shout-out. There are too many of you lovely ladies with filthy minds to name but I hope you know how much you mean to me. Every message/comment/vote/anecdote meant a great deal to me, and I know Andrei and Rainelle's story wouldn't be shared with the world if it weren't for you special bunch of people. I love you so much, Kimberlions. Thank you.

A huge thank you to everyone at BLVNP for seeing something in my book. Le-an Lai Lacaba deserves a special mention because she is epic and I am so privileged to be able to work with her. Her enthusiasm is contagious!

Lastly, thank you to you, the reader, for giving my story a chance. I hope you enjoy reading it as much as I enjoyed writing it. A lot of the places in here are fictional. Sometimes you can find love in imaginary places.

Special Thanks to:

Nadia Sabah
Joann Zarate
Shyann Truett
Samantha Mitchem
Kimberly
Miracle Martinez
Yap ZhiXiu
Katerina Beguhl
Maria Eduarda Oliveira
Kashia Hue
Karen Chaparro
Kelly Ann Beaudin
Victoria Hernandez
Emerlyn Santos
Stephenie Diep
sarah jane
Victoria Martinez
Destanie Collins
Alisha
LaShelle
Melia deriarta
Lilliana
Sara D'Antonio

And all of you amazing people!

Author's Note

Hey there!

Thank you so much for reading How to Kill an Incubus! I can't express how grateful I am for reading something that was once just a thought inside my head.

I'd love to hear from you! Please feel free to email me at kimber_lee@awesomeauthors.org and sign up at kimber-lee.awesomeauthors.org for freebies!

One last thing: I'd love to hear your thoughts on the book. Please leave a review on Amazon or Goodreads because I just love reading your comments and getting to know YOU!

Whether that review is good or bad, I'd still love to hear it!

Can't wait to hear from you!

Kimber Lee

About the Author

Kimber Lee comes from South Africa and commutes to class on an elephant named Bill (not really). She started writing horror stories as a child and now, she writes erotica as an adult. Her favorite kind of hero is exotic and probably has a heavy accent. He's weak when it comes to the heroine and a total badass outside the bedroom.

If Kimber Lee could find a surgical way to be permanently joined to her laptop, she would. But until then, she'll continue to be a night owl and write until dawn. When forced into daylight, she enjoys reading scary stories, Indian food and EDM. She dreams of going to Greece or Sweden because... accents. Oh, and the scenery.

Like her on Facebook: facebook.com/kimberleeauthor
Sign up for her blog: kimber-lee.awesomeauthors.org

Printed in Great Britain
by Amazon

62048804R00258